DEMON DRINK

KRIS ASHTON

Published by Crystal Lake Publishing
Where Stories Come Alive!

Crystal Lake Publishing
www.CrystalLakePub.com

**Follow us on
Amazon:**

WELCOME
TO ANOTHER

CRYSTAL LAKE PUBLISHING
CREATION

This is for Wade Mellor.

Cousin, brother, friend, purveyor of the demon drink,
first reader.

Believer.

CHAPTER ONE

ACLICKING DOOR LATCH startled Truman Smythe from something resembling slumber, although his twittering heart, dry tongue, and thumping temples suggested the resemblance had been vague at best. In the now-open doorway stood Truman's lover, Maurice, which didn't jibe, because Truman's thighs were spooning the back of another man's. He wondered if he might be floating in the narrow void between sleeping and waking, when the two states were almost indistinguishable, but decided no dream could posit such convincing, creeping nausea. Also, he could feel the fine tickle of leg hairs, a detail too insignificant for a dream. Besides, Maurice was a competitive cyclist. He waxed his legs.

Truman couldn't say, "This isn't what it looks like," because he didn't know what "this" was. On available evidence, he appeared to be in bed with a stiff patch of fitted sheet between him and a man whose identity had been sucked into a memory hole. Dark hair and slender shoulders, the only clues above the sheet, did nothing to solve the mystery. Even though plenty of early spring sunshine filtered around the plantation shutters, Maurice tilted his head and narrowed his eyes, as though trying to make out something in low light.

That single moment froze solid in Truman's recollection, a mammoth captured in ice, and he would study it over and over in the days to come. But such idle contemplations were at present a luxury. He tried to make his scattered-pinball thoughts come together and form a coherent line. The one fact he could ascertain emerged from his mouth.

"You're home early."

Maurice's brows knitted. Then he turned on his heel and closed the bedroom door behind him—so gently that Truman heard the latch click again. This decorous gesture added to the sense reality had slipped its gears. Truman sat up, unable to decide whether he should leap from his bed and pursue Maurice or let him go; but then the townhouse's front door slammed shut, rendering the question irrelevant unless he planned to scurry buck-naked along one of Paddington's more desirable residential streets.

Instead, he swung his feet onto the carpet and blinked at the objects strewing his bedside table. A bottle of red wine he didn't recall opening, from the expensive end of the rack. Two tannin-stained glasses. A dusting of powder, as if it had snowed in miniature while he slept. While *they* slept, he corrected himself. Beside the empty coke baggie was an upturned driver's license. Truman flipped it over. It put a face and a name to the form currently occupying Maurice's side of the bed.

"Amir," he said.

No response. Truman's nail-bombed brain bypassed logical explanations and went straight to the possibility he now shared his bed with a corpse. He extended a shaky hand to the man's neck and let out a whistling breath of relief when his fingers touched warm flesh. Amir's shoulders lifted and fell with each slow respiration. So slow. Probably more unconsciousness than sleep. What if he couldn't rouse him? The thought of pottering around the house and trying to pretend everything was normal while waiting for Amir to wake brought on a fresh wave of anxiety. Christ, how much cocaine had he snorted? He didn't even remember buying it. He cast his mind back to retrieve the nearest memory from the previous night. With Maurice away on a work trip, he had decided to spend a quiet Saturday evening at the local wine bar. A glass of Grenache, tapas for one, and a book he had been trying to read for weeks. Like more and more of his 'quiet' nights in the past two years, however, it had gotten loud. One of his more agreeable neighbors, Danielle, had shown up at the bar and cast aside his bookish intentions. He dimly recalled her introducing him to someone—perhaps Amir?—and then nothing. Blur and black.

"Amir," he said again, shaking the man's shoulder. Amir stirred, the sheet falling away and revealing a hairy back. God, he had gone the full bear. Why? Hairy men were not Truman's thing. Never had been. All at once he felt he was at the wheel of a car aquaplaning across a busy intersection, responsible but not in control.

II

"Amir, wake up, please."

More misplaced cordiality, like Maurice's first civilized *exeunt*. But this time, Amir rolled onto his back and his eyes fluttered open. He stared at the ceiling, perhaps trying to make sense of the unfamiliar light fixture, then his eyes rolled sideways to regard Truman's naked form.

"You look like The Thinker," Amir said. His accent, something Middle Eastern, was faint but detectable.

"I look like what?"

"You know, the statue," Amir said. He smiled, and Truman got some inkling of how his coke-and-booze-impaired self had looked beyond the heavy brow and the five o'clock shadow. That only made the remorse worse. He got up, feeling sordid and exposed, and scrabbled through a drawer for some underpants.

"I don't mean to be rude," he said, his back to Amir, "but I just wish you'd go now. I didn't even know your name until I found your license on the side table."

"I still don't know your name."

Truman, now clad in underpants, turned to face him. "Look, I'm sorry if I gave you the wrong impression. I don't remember a word we said or anything we did. But Maurice and I are happy. We've been together a long time."

"My wife and I have been together a long time, too," Amir said. "That doesn't always make us content."

Truman was having trouble following his own words, let alone trying to decode someone else's philosophical aphorisms. He could feel something boiling up inside, like hot mud. "Please just leave. I need. . .I need to be alone."

Amir smiled again and for a horrible moment Truman thought he would say something dumb and breederish, like, "Why don't you try and make me?" But then he tossed aside the sheet and stood up, leaving the Maurice-side of the bed empty. Truman hadn't realized how much he hated seeing someone else in that spot until the intruder was gone.

Last night's one-night stand pulled on a pair of tight black pants and a button-down shirt. The fabric concealed the body hair and tightened in all the right places, and—fucking hell! Why was his mind drifting down this unfaithful canal again when the self-loathing was so fresh and hurtful?

Cocaine was why. He could still feel it circulating through his thoughts, directing them, a residual electric charge. In his right mind, he wouldn't touch coke. A few drinks in, however, his judgement would slide and then someone would suggest doing a few lines and his willpower would falter altogether and. . .

And then he'd end up doing something he regretted. Leading to awkward next-day glances, dressing-downs from Maurice, relentless low-level anxiety as he tried to recall what he'd said or done to someone who could influence his career. He had lost a good friend and a great agent when—

God, he just wanted to squeeze all this negative shit out of his head. Amir was pulling on his socks. Sitting on Maurice's side of the bed and pulling on his stupid socks. Now loafers, *desperately* passé Italian leather yet somehow just right when seen with Amir's light-caramel skin, and—why couldn't he just go away and leave Truman alone?

Amir stood up and faced him. He looked almost divine with the window backlighting him.

"Please just go," Truman said.

"I need something first."

Truman put a hand to his forehead. "For God's sake, what? I told you, Maurice and I are committed to each other, although now I don't know if—"

"My license," Amir said. That same beatific smile again, as if the toxic remnants of light night's excesses weren't tincturing his blood and poisoning every thought. Truman bent to pick up the license, blew some cocaine off it, handed it to him.

Amir slotted the card into his wallet. "You and the cocaine and drinks, you are my escape. You are some fun. This morning, I return to the life my parents arranged for me. It is a good life. I hope I have not cost you yours."

Truman stared at him, wondering how an inspirational meme had manifested as a person. Amir's final words had opened up a reservoir of dread which now spilled into him, turning his insides to a frothing cesspool.

"Wait," he said, extending an arm as Amir shaped to leave the room. "What happened last night? Do you remember?"

Amir nodded, but offered nothing further.

"Did we. . ."

"Perhaps you should spare yourself the details. You already appear to be carrying quite a burden on your conscience."

Truman's desperation reached febrile heights. "You aren't?"

Amir shrugged. "I am not you."

Another smile filled with incomprehensible solace. Then he left Truman's bedroom, his loafers almost soundless as he descended the stairs. The front door clacked shut a few moments later, leaving Truman and the townhouse cloaked in Sunday morning silence. The cocaine buzzed through his head, scuttling straight thoughts. On some primal instinct or subliminal car-crash urge to look, he went to the bed and lifted the sheet. A discolored patch, slightly darker than the powder blue around it, stood out like an island in an ocean. Hating himself, Truman bent down and sniffed it, hoping against hope it could be grog or sweat or even urine. But the pungent chlorine smell was unmistakable.

He began to scratch at his pubic region, even though he kept it trim and tidy the way Maurice liked it. Where were last night's clothes? He couldn't remember that, either. He strode towards the bathroom. When he got there, he stripped off his fresh underpants and stepped into the shower. Never had Truman been more thankful for the strong flow as it needled his skin. He stepped back and let the jet hit his groin. Soon after he and Maurice had moved in together, Truman had complained about the shower's dismal water pressure. Maurice had unscrewed the shower head and taken out the little plastic ring that restricted its flow, a piece of handyman magic that cemented Truman's love for him in some mundane way other romantic gestures hadn't reached. Now, even that memory had been sullied.

No, it hadn't been sullied. He had sullied it.

The coke made him crazy. He still felt crazed, even beneath a warm morning shower. He needed to counteract it so he could devise a way out of the quagmire he had blundered into while doing the coke-head version of sleepwalking. He distrusted prescription downers, which fuzzed his mind and hampered his creativity; and anyway, the likelihood of finding a GP open on a Sunday (let alone willing to write him a script) was too remote to contemplate.

He brushed his teeth, dressed in fresh clothes, and went downstairs. Last night's red wine leached up through his tongue, pushing back against the toothpaste, and swirled in his stomach like burgundy acid. Just thinking about raiding the wine rack nauseated him. He opened the fridge instead, following a hunch that someone had left behind a six-pack of craft beer after a dinner party a few weeks ago. When he found nothing but weekly staples, panic set in.

Desperate, he squatted and winced as something given rough treatment last night got stretched again. The cocaine comedown whispered doubts, amphetamine spirits haunting his head. But when he opened his eyes, there was the beer at the back of the shelf above the vegetable crisper. He dragged out the six-pack and almost cuddled it as he put it on the island bench.

Some sort of golden ale made in a micro-brewery a few suburbs away. "Headache in a bottle," Maurice called it, or sometimes, "Breast milk for rednecks." Right now, with the cocaine marching jackboots through his head, Truman didn't care. He fumbled around in the second drawer for a bottle opener but, apparently, blacked-out Truman had failed to return it to its proper spot.

"Fuck *meeee*," wide-awake Truman wailed. He paced back and forth through the townhouse, eyes darting in sync with his thoughts. His brain seemed to have a yellow scum over it, which did not permit the light of reason. On the verge of tears, he tried a Hail Mary and pulled back the sliding door to the downstairs toilet. There it was, resting on the cistern lid like some sort of pauper's treasure. Truman snatched it up and hurried back to the kitchen.

He popped the top off the first bottle, took a long swallow (as much as his coke-clenched throat would allow, anyway), and then carried it and the other five into the lounge room. He put the beers on the coffee table, sat on the sofa and switched on the television. He needed to find Maurice, *would* find Maurice, but first he needed to silence the senseless yammering that filled his head. Rather than opt for a streaming service, he put on regular free-to-air TV and selected one of the banal renovation shows he sometimes watched to lull him to sleep if he had insomnia. The beer tasted pretty good, for which he was thankful. The first bottle disappeared in a few minutes, despite his shriveled stomach, and once he'd depleted the second the spent-cocaine anxiety began to fade into the background. Little by little, the sense of black doom and opprobrium dissipated. Enthusiastic American voices waxed lyrical about "granite countertops" and "tiled backsplashes." Truman could imagine Maurice getting upset as he explained why "backsplash" was wrong and "splashback" was right and going into furious grammatical detail to justify his position. Yes, he and Maurice would be okay. He would fix things somehow. He just needed to clear his mind.

Keys jingled in the front door. Truman sat up as if electrocuted, blinking away blear and trying to recall where he was. A sharp pain in his neck suggested he had been sleeping with his head at an acute angle. Before he could properly gather his wits, he saw Maurice standing in the townhouse's small foyer. Maurice's eyes noted the beer bottles littering the coffee table, tallied them, squinted in disgust.

"Jesus, Truman. Are you serious?"

"You came back," Truman said, standing up, wobbling forward, over-correcting and falling onto his bottom again. "I need to talk to you. I—"

"I came back because this is my house too and I'm exhausted and I have to go to work tomorrow. I'm not interested in hearing what you have to say."

"Please, Maurice, don't shut me out. I know I fucked up, but—"

"I'm not ready to talk about this," Maurice said through tense lips. "If you can't respect that, find somewhere else to stay for the night."

With that, he left Truman to the sofa and disappeared upstairs. The TV droned on. Sounds of showering carried down. Enough alcohol remained in Truman's system to fire up into an indignant flame, in spite of everything that had happened. What gave Maurice the right to be so high and mighty? All he wanted was to apologize, yet the supposed love of his life had brushed him off as if he were a door-to-door insurance salesman. Truman poked his phone awake and was astonished to see it was almost six o'clock. Maurice didn't want him around? Fine. There were other places he could be.

He set out for a row of nightclubs nearby, but a few paces beyond next door's cast-iron gate he quailed. Nightclubs meant exposure to drugs. While the beer still warmed his blood, it could not blot out the morning's raw shame. Instead, he crossed the road and walked half a dozen blocks to a new whisky bar he'd heard about. It occupied a small warehouse that had once served the rag trade and then stood empty for years. The new owners had ripped away all the plasterboard to expose the beams and copper piping and polished the concrete floor to an ice-like sheen. The bar and the stools attending it were all fashioned from reclaimed timber, giving the place a rail yard atmosphere. The lone patron was a man in a suit flicking through his phone. Probably a businessman returned from an overseas conference and treating himself to a nightcap before heading home. That thought set off a fresh flare of guilt. Truman tried to quell it and recoup his earlier grievance without much success. In the end, he shuffled forward and perched himself on a stool.

"Evening," said the barman. His long-sleeved checked shirt and bushy red beard added to the rail yard ambience. "What can I get you?"

"Something to dull the pain."

One cheek raised into half a smile. "I don't think this is the bar you're looking for. If that's really what you want, Jack Daniels can do it for half the price."

"I'm an artist, okay? It's what we're supposed to say."

"An artist. I see. An artist as in a painter? Or an artist as in piss in a glass box and say it's art?"

"The first one. Although there's nothing wrong with the second."

"We'll have to agree to disagree on that. Would I know any of your stuff?"

"Probably. Maybe. Look, can I have a drink or not?"

"I'm a barman. I'm supposed to chat. But if you're not in chatting mood, why don't you run your finger down that menu and see if anything takes your fancy?"

Truman gave it a perfunctory glance, felt overwhelmed, slid it away. "I'll trust your judgement."

"This one's new," the barman said, plucking a stout little bottle off the top shelf. "Out of Melbourne, believe it or not. Used to be you wouldn't touch an Australian whisky, but some of the boutique distilleries are killing it. This one's light, like a single malt out of Ireland. How do you have it?"

"Neat."

"That was a test. If you'd said, 'with Coke' I would have thrown you out."

The barman poured it into a cut-glass tumbler. Truman sniffed it, tipped some onto his tongue, drew air over it. Smooth on the way in, pleasantly hot on the way down. He could feel its fumes anesthetizing his sprained mind. While the barman made some chit-chat with the businessman, Truman tossed the remainder down his throat. It didn't taste anywhere near as good that way, but then savoring it had never been his intention. When the barman returned, he nudged the glass towards him.

"I do like Melbourne," Truman said, dragging the menu back in front of him, "but all of a sudden I've got the travel bug. This one's from New Zealand?"

He made it to Japan, Ireland, several locations in Scotland and back down to Tasmania before the rail yard barman cut him off. He tried to protest, but his cheeks and lips were too senseless to form words.

"How do you want to pay your tab?" the barman asked. His jovial manner had vanished, like the sun disappearing behind storm clouds.

With the final bill too high for tap-and-go, and uncertain he could operate an EFTPOS terminal, Truman just kept handing over legal tender until the barman nodded and bid him good evening. The cooling night air added oxygen to the rocket fuel coursing through his veins.

Along the footpath, he weaved port and starboard while unleashing a rambling monologue that even he couldn't follow.

When he arrived home he spent a good while trying to insert the key in the lock. Each tiny tap sounded like a brass band in his ears. Waking Maurice would be tantamount to waking a vengeful spirit. Once inside he staggered, almost on autopilot, towards the wine rack and cracked the lid off a bottle of merlot he had picked up on a weekend trip to the Hunter Valley.

"Fond memories," he slurred.

He collected a glass from the cupboard and then, for reasons that would be lost to him later, went back outside and sat on the porch to drink it.

Just as it had twenty-four hours earlier, the sound of an opening door woke him. Only this time, he was on the outside. He forced his eyelids apart and found himself lying on his side face-to-face with a purple vomit puddle. It had filled the grout between the porch tiles; polluted water in a complicated aqueduct system. His limbs vibrated with winter's leftover chill.

"Really, Truman?"

He looked up and found Maurice standing in the doorway, the morning sun polishing his dark forehead to a sheen. His eyes broadcast an emotional variety show: anger, disappointment, disgust. It felt unfair somehow that Maurice would judge him so harshly for something he didn't mean to do and couldn't even recall doing. Without another word, Maurice stepped over him, off the porch, and towards the street.

"Please, Maurice, don't walk away from me."

Maurice stopped dead, paused, then spun around fast enough to fling out the work satchel slung over his shoulder. "When I asked you to marry me, Truman, you said why bother, that it was for breeders. But now I know the real reason, don't I?"

"That's not true. It's just that I've. . .you know, I've been struggling lately."

"Struggling *lately*? When was the last time you made a substantial sale?"

"It wasn't that long ago. . ."

"Five years, Truman. I've been supporting you for the past five years." He checked his watch. "I have to get to work. Try to be sober when I get home. We'll discuss. . .where we go from here."

Truman sat on the porch, heart thumping, and watched Maurice climb into his car. Five years. It couldn't be five years. Maurice had exaggerated to hurt him. Incensed, he got to his feet and beat a groggy path through the house, up to the study. He logged into his email account and was confronted with so many unread emails it made his heart race faster still. Ignoring them, he tapped the search field and typed in *Greg Richards*. He had not contacted his business manager in months and it had been close to a year since they spoke in person. Twelve unread emails popped up, all of them with the same subject line: *Monthly statement*. He opened one after another, finding only minuscule sales. "Rats and mice" Greg had called them, back when small sales were infrequent and therefore subject to flip remarks. Truman went even further back, seeking the last respectable price. Maurice was wrong; it hadn't been five years. It had been four years and nine months. A net profit of $1900 after auction fees and Greg's percentage.

He picked up an old auction catalogue, from a time when his

artworks had been sought after enough to appear in an auction catalogue. Up near the *front* of the catalogue, if you didn't mind. *Truman Smythe, 'Crocodile Tears', oils on canvas. Guide price $10,000.* He remembered that auction well, because he had been in attendance. A small bidding war broke out and when the hammer went down an old lady with purple lips and a severe hair bun had agreed to part with just a shade under twenty grand. For a picture that had taken him a Saturday afternoon and a Sunday morning to complete. Life had been easy, then. Paintings poured out of him, money poured into his bank account.

How had "Australia's artistic wunderkind", as a *Guardian* art critic once described him, ended up here? *Cocaine*, his mind offered, and it was just glib enough to be credible. He and Amir had been coked up when they did whatever they did. But when Truman climbed high enough in his mind to mull it over in one long panorama, he saw cocaine use was a symptom. Booze was the disease. The city scene, the art scene, the gay scene. . .he had too many scenes, too many excuses to socialize, to expose himself to drink. Even dinner with friends involved a bottle of wine. Usually two.

Seeing his old paintings in the catalogue gave him a yearning to view more. Once upon a time, not so long ago, they had hung on the walls or been carefully archived in the storeroom of his little studio in Surry Hills. But the monthly rent had become more than he and Maurice could justify, especially after the big sales dried up. Most of his unsold and unfinished works were now in storage in his parents' garage. Those he couldn't bear to part with were in the tiny shed out in the courtyard, bundled up in bubble wrap. He went out there now and ripped the tape off one, unwound the yards of protective plastic. He propped the canvas against the shed wall so the morning light could fall on it in full. Christ, had he thought this was good? His style had always been cartoonish but serious, the visual equivalent of truths spoken in jest. But this was just a fucking cartoon, a drunken argument depicted in oils.

That got him thinking about his artistic heroes, the men and women who inspired him. John Murray, who took simple outback subjects and rendered them with color and vibrancy. The obscure Hawkesbury artist Margaret Mackisack, whose line drawings uncovered human features and emotions in the rusting hulks of abandoned logging trucks. The late Pro Hart, whose talents had so impressed seven-year-old Truman, he had been inspired to ask for paint supplies and an easel for Christmas. The common denominator between the three struck him like an iceberg: isolation. Hart lived and died in Broken Hill. Mackisack found her inspiration in forgotten places. And Murray, once a city dweller like Truman, had forsaken its comforts to pursue his artistic passions and open a gallery in one of the state's remotest towns.

What did his future hold, should he remain in Paddington? More temptation. More self-loathing. Abase and supplicate himself for months trying to win Maurice's forgiveness. And even if he did, it would not absolve him of a transgression he couldn't even remember. The damage to their relationship was permanent. Like scraping the side of a brand-new car on a brick fence. It would still go somewhere, but it would be scarred, a rolling reminder that he had fucked up and, in so doing, disfigured something beautiful. And would Amir keep his mouth shut about their tryst? Probably, since it sounded like he had a lot to lose as well, but no doubt Danielle had borne witness to their initial prurient interest in one another and likely seen them leave the wine bar together. And she couldn't keep her mouth shut even if she used dental wire and a tube of superglue.

No, he needed to get away from it all. Go somewhere he could be anonymous, where no one would call him over for a drink. Whittle his life down until it was sharp enough to cut something again. He remembered a town he and Maurice had passed through a few years back on another of their winery tours. Set out along the spine of a hill that overlooked a pastoral valley.

Within his mind, a plan took shape.

Tongue parched and head throbbing, he packed a suitcase with everything he would need and nothing he wouldn't, then collected his art supplies from the shed and put them all in a garbage bag. Then he reversed his old hatchback out of the narrow garage and popped the tailgate. Once he'd flattened the rear seats, his easel fit with an inch or so to spare. He loaded up everything else and closed the tailgate again.

Before he set off, he leaned against the rear fender and typed out a message on his phone. The first draft was quite long, but what he finally sent to Maurice simply read: *The townhouse is yours for $100k. Email me a contract and I'll sign it over.*

Still intoxicated enough to be confident, Truman drove away from his life, stopping only at a service station to pick up a chocolate bar and a bottle of Powerade.

CHAPTER TWO

EVEN PATRONS. Six o'clock on a flawless early-spring Friday night and the pub had mustered seven patrons.

Shirley Goodsall stood behind the bar and tried to occupy herself polishing glasses, checking fridge stock, adjusting spirit bottles, but she was fooling no one. Black Wattle's sole physician, Dr Sneddon, nursed a glass of Sauvignon Blanc and traced his finger through the daily paper, peering at something now and again through his wire-framed spectacles. A few slack-mouthed farmers gazed at the televisions, sipping their drinks or making a laconic remark. Two tradesmen carried a quiet conversation over dinner and a beer apiece. They were in town to complete a small corporate landscaping job and would be on their way back to Sydney come Tuesday morning. In the far corner, a girl sat scowling at her phone. She couldn't be relied upon for patronage, either, because she was only fifteen and also Shirley's daughter. The lemonade she was ignoring had taken money out of the pub's till, not contributed. Tomorrow Elle would be off to stay with her father on the Gold Coast—a prospect she dreaded much less than Shirley. And who could blame a teenager for preferring the glitzy Gold Coast to a half-empty town which dozed above fells yellowed with drought?

These thoughts clouded Shirley's face and she forced them to clear as patron number seven approached the bar. Eric Quinn, who ran the post office up the road. He and Dr Sneddon seemed to be in an enthusiastic race towards old age, each man a living patchwork of snowy hair, age-spotted hands and wattled skin. If they passed away this evening, she ruminated morbidly, by Tuesday the pub's patronage would be more than halved.

"Quiet night, eh, Shirl?"

"Every night's a quiet night, lately. What can I get you?"

"One for the road, thanks."

She pulled him a glass of beer. Not so long ago she would have filled the pouring time with a clever in-joke or enquired after Eric's family or at least asked how things were at the post office. But her conversation no longer sparkled. At best it flickered, a flashlight with a failing battery. Eric looked pained to see her that way.

"Bet this'll be the best beer I've ever had," he said, lifting the glass to his lips. "Yep."

"What would your wife say if she knew you were chatting up the barmaid?" Shirley managed. The lame quip appeared to relieve Eric's concern.

"She'd say I was kidding myself." He laughed at his own joke and then his expression became sympathetic. "Might have a few games of Keno before I head home. If I win big, maybe I can retire. Can you get us an auto-pick, love?"

Jesus, the financial equivalent of a pity-fuck from the local postmaster. She handed over the tickets and tried not to cry as Eric returned to his seat and stared at the numbers flashing up on the Keno screen. How had it come to this?

The Ironstone Hotel had been hers a little over two years. Shirley knew marketing, she knew social media, she knew how to get magazines and newspapers talking. She had taken a ramshackle pub with its rotten deck and piss-smelling toilets and made it into a Black Wattle sensation. But endless reports about droughts and bushfires frightened away the city tourists, a knife in the back for a shire that had already suffered a thousand tiny cuts. The pub had been the lone licensed venue on a long stretch between two larger towns and that, along with its designer décor and friendly atmosphere, had seen its reputation grow.

Now. . .it traded on loyalty and habit.

By seven o'clock, even the die-hard locals had made their farewells. Shirley totted up the day's takings. After overheads and taxes, her net profit amounted to just over one hundred dollars. Shirley stared at that figure, wishing she could believe she had made an arithmetical error. One hundred. If Elle got herself a job at McDonald's down in Goulburn, she would stand to make that much in a single shift.

"Maybe tomorrow night will be better," Shirley said, not because she believed it, but to ease the pain in her heart. She looked up at Elle, whose eyes were still glued to her smartphone. A thought tried to enter Shirley's mind, one so awful she repelled it before it was fully formed, but she knew well enough what it had been: *At least there's one extra expense I won't have to worry about after tomorrow.*

"Home time, kiddo," she said.

"Oh, *finally*," Elle said, jumping to her feet.

She was slender and tall, like Richard, but had not become gangly in the way so many teenagers did. Pretty in an understated way.

"If you were bored, you could have helped me tidy up," Shirley said.

"It's illegal for anyone under eighteen to work in a licensed venue."

"I don't see any police here, do you?"

Elle lowered her voice and her eyes became watchful. "They might be staking out the place."

Shirley laughed. "Come on crazy lady, let's go home. You've got a big day tomorrow."

She couldn't understand why parents clashed with their teenage children. Perhaps separating from Richard had given her a surfeit of love. Whatever the case, nearly all the overflow spilled out towards her daughter. She put an arm around her—and nothing in the world would ever be as comforting as Elle's arm slipping around her waist in unconsidered and unconditional reciprocation.

They switched off the lights, locked up, and walked home together in the cooling night, which smelled of cows and cut grass.

Loneliness stole over Shirley the moment she opened her eyes the next morning. She went to the second bedroom and leaned against the doorjamb. Blonde locks spread out across the pillow like curly tentacles. Another physical gift from Richard (although his hair had begun to collect in the shower drain during his mid-twenties). In the growing light, Elle's face looked angelic.

Loneliness scythed through Shirley as she thought of that visage a thousand kilometers away for a fortnight of school holidays.

"Rise and shine, Ellie-Bellie," she said.

Elle stirred, rolled over to face her. "Don't call me Ellie-Bellie."

"Sorry, you'll always be my Ellie-Bellie."

"Okay, Shirley-Whirly."

They ate breakfast and drank a cup of tea on the porch. The weatherboard cottage, situated at the western end of Black Wattle, offered no curb appeal, not even by relaxed bucolic standards, and in the first few weeks Shirley had regretted her parsimonious choice. But once the ephemeral craving for metropolitan comforts wore off, she came to love its scruffy charm.

It also commanded only modest monthly rent from mum-and-dad property investors who were pleased to have the long-term lease. A more extravagant option would have already exerted untenable pressure on her finances.

Shirley finished her tea and pulled up the sleeve of her dressing gown.

"Time we get dressed or you'll miss your train."

Half an hour later they walked out to Shirley's dust-caked SUV, Elle trailing a wheeled suitcase along the gravel driveway. A cow lowed a deep-throated opinion about something.

The Wainwright farm ran behind the southern end of Shirley's property and in the distance, she could see Oscar Wainwright forking hay bales off the back of a truck. Troubles were relative, she mused, although watching poor old Oscar essentially rolling money out of the tray to keep his cattle alive didn't make what was coming any easier.

Goldfields Road cut through the center of town in a long curve, like the sharp edge of a scimitar. Black Wattle was already abuzz (or as buzzy as it ever got now) with Saturday morning errands. Locals milled back and forth between the post office, the bank, Ray Worrell's general store (which also served as a petrol station), and a farm supplies depot. Many clustered in and around the one and only café. In most small towns the pub was its beating heart, but in Black Wattle, that distinction belonged to the Old Rose Coffee Shop. Founded back in the 1950s, it served tongue-scalding, flavorless coffee that seemed to predate multiculturalism. The proprietor, Marla Smith, wouldn't have known an espresso machine if she tripped over one, but she was a serving member of the Country Women's Association and the Old Rose had been the place to network and gossip for four generations. In the country old habits didn't just die hard, they were close to immortal.

Ten minutes out of town, Goldfields Road connected to the highway which brought Elle and Shirley down to Goulburn and the train station. They found a parking spot and then Shirley walked Elle up to the platform that would take her to Sydney—and, courtesy of a discount flight, the Gold Coast.

"Now, your flight's at—"

"Two p.m., make sure I check the gate number, etcetera, etcetera," Elle said. She grinned. "I have done this before, you know."

Shirley tried not to make a scene whenever Elle left because it wasn't fair on her, but this was Elle's fifth time making the journey to stay with Richard, and seeing her depart wasn't any easier. When the train's metal face appeared in the distance, Shirley's feelings gushed over and she pulled her daughter into a fierce embrace that startled a couple of nosy parkers watching on from the seats.

"I love you, sweetheart," she said into the warm sweetness of Elle's blonde curls.

"Love you too, Mum. I'll call you once I'm through security."

The train pulled up, opened its doors, swallowed her daughter whole, and lurched off again. Shirley waved to Elle through the window, feeling like an old telemovie cliché. When Elle returned the wave Shirley felt better, but only fleetingly. Once the train was around the bend and out of sight, the weight of it all collapsed on her. She mashed away a couple of tears as she walked and, when she was in the SUV again, she flipped open the sun visor's vanity mirror so she could clean away trails of black mascara.

Feeling ugly and bereft, she backed out the SUV and commenced the return trip to Black Wattle. Stress fluttered her heart as she drew nearer to the Ironstone. Yet another thing she loved slipping through her fingers. She tried to direct her mind towards something positive, strategies to improve patronage, low-cost promotion, but the marketing branch of her brain refused to go live.

Shirley opened the pub at a quarter past ten, technically fifteen minutes late, but it mattered not a jot since no one was pacing back and forth outside or hammering on the doors to be let in. She switched on as few lights as she could and left the air conditioner inert—a saving she could only bank on for another month. Her business acumen, once directed to such bright purpose, now only served to find novel cost-cutting measures.

The Ironstone remained stone-empty until just before midday. An older couple, tourists braving the region in spite of the media's doomsaying, ambled inside and peered around as if they had never set foot in a hotel before. The man locked eyes with Shirley, took a step forward, faltered, appeared to regret his initial decision, then concluded it was too late and continued on towards the bar.

"Been to the caves this morning?" Shirley said.

"Yes, as a matter of fact," he said. "How did you know?"

"People who stop in have usually been to the caves or the goldfields. They're the two biggest attractions in the area. What can I do for you?"

"We were after a bite to eat. Do you have a menu?"

"We have a bar menu," Shirley said, handing over the little clipboard.

Man and wife put on their reading glasses. They made a few doubtful noises to one another, then the man put the menu back on the bar. "Thank you, we're going to have a look around."

When she was alone in the Ironstone again, Shirley fought off the day's second bout of tears. It wasn't so much the rejection as its back story; six months earlier she'd been forced to let her chef go after cutting his hours from five days to four and then four days to three. As a result, the menu now consisted of items she could remove from a pie warmer. She couldn't blame Antoine for walking out. Roles reversed, she would have done the same.

She wondered if the Old Rose had seen a similar downturn (even though it might not appear so from the outside looking in). She thought about closing up until the afternoon. If nothing else she could go down the road and pour her heart out to Marla, who spent hours in the café but never seemed to do anything except gossip while a couple of local girls buzzed around like bees in a hive.

Shirley had got as far as picking up the remote control to switch off the televisions when a man came in out of the day's rising heat. She hadn't seen anyone like him in a long time, not since moving her life to Black Wattle. He wore a tailored suit and his slicked-back hair exposed manicured eyebrows to their fullest effect. His complexion shone from a recent shave. Unlike the reluctant tourists, his eyes landed on Shirley immediately and he strode up to the bar.

"Good afternoon," he said in a clipped English accent, "my name is Damon Prince."

His hand was large and pudgy but unexpectedly cool given the day's warmth. The other hand presented a business card, which Shirley accepted and looked at but didn't really see.

"I represent a boutique brewery operating out of Cowra. May I assume you're familiar with that town?"

"Look, if you're selling something, you've accosted the wrong person," Shirley said, trying to get her head above this sudden whirlwind. "I'm about one bad month from ending up in the red and—"

"Not at all, not at all," said Damon, raising his hand in a 'stop' gesture. "We know times are tough. We live in the country, too."

Somewhat reassured, Shirley glanced at the card in her palm.

DAMON PRINCE
Business Development Manager
Red Horn Brewery

"Red Horn?" Shirley smirked. "I think you need to work on your branding."

"I know, I know," Damon said, rolling his eyes and returning her smile. "I tried to tell the boys who own the brewery but they wouldn't listen. You sound like you know your stuff, though."

"I used to work in marketing. I specialized in branding and social media. That seems like a long time ago, now."

"I think you'll appreciate why I'm here today. As I said, I'm not selling anything. I'm here to offer a quid pro quo. You help us, we help you, not a dollar changes hands. No contracts, no bulldust, just two small businesses propping each other up. Sound good?"

"Too good to be true."

Damon laughed. "Fair enough, you're right to be suspicious. You don't know me from Adam. So I'll let the proposition do the talking. Don't like it, I walk out and I never say another word. How about that?"

"I'm all ears. But I'm not sure how a backwater pub like mine can help."

"It's simple. The boys at the brewery have finished the first batch of Red Horn Lager. They think it's something pretty special and they want to get the word out there. Trouble is, the big conglomerates have the pubs in their pockets. It's almost impossible for a little brewer to get a start these days, unless he—or she—knows someone. Since Carlton United Breweries got bought out a few years ago, it's been almost a monopoly."

"So what exactly do you want the Ironstone to do?"

"We'll give you three kegs of Red Horn Lager free of charge. That's straight up, no surprises, no fine print. We'll even hook them up to the tap for you. All we ask in return is you let us leave a Red Horn sign outside your pub and do your best to up-sell the beer. You keep all the profits from those first three kegs. Think of it as a loss-leading brand exercise. Then, if it proves popular with your customers, we sell you more, you sell them more, everyone's happy. If the kegs aren't empty after a week, we come back and take them away and that's the end of it; we go our separate ways. But between you and me, I don't think that will happen."

"That's a tempting proposal," Shirley said after a while. "But you'll pardon me if I'm a little skeptical. Do you know how many patrons I get through here in a week?"

"That's no skin off our nose," said Prince. "We don't have a marketing budget as such, so we're doing it the cheap way. Word-of-mouth. If ten of your patrons have a Red Horn, and they recommend it to one person each, then that's the potential for twenty new customers. Maybe a few of them mention it to friends or on social media and it goes viral in its own little way. We're not expecting miracles, don't think that, but we're confident we have a popular product on our hands."

I don't even have ten patrons, Shirley thought.

"What the hell," she said, "sign me up."

"No need to sign anything. Let's just seal the deal with an old-fashioned handshake."

They reached across the bar again and this time, his hand was warm. Evidently, delivering his sales pitch had got his blood flowing.

"Our truck is parked out on the street," Damon said. "I'll be back in a jiffy."

He disappeared into the glare and returned a short while later lugging the signboard. It had a black metal frame and the sign hung from it on small chains. Dominating a stark white background was a horn graphic, perhaps a rhino horn. In blaring red lettering above and below it was RED HORN LAGER.

"What do you think?" Damon asked, grinning.

"They sure won't miss it."

"Getting noticed is half the battle. But I don't need to tell you that, do I?"

"No. No, you certainly don't," Shirley said.

By the time two young men in high-vis orange vests were hauling kegs into the cool room to connect them up to the lines, Shirley already had the bones of a marketing campaign rattling around in her head.

"See you in a week," Damon said.

Then he and his men were gone and Shirley stood alone in her empty pub, feeling optimistic for the first time in months.

CHAPTER THREE

GLACIERS MOVED WITH greater vigor than Don Winslow's life. Each morning he rose at six, went for a forty-minute walk around Black Wattle's goat tracks, then wondered how to fill the remainder of his day. His only son, Blair, had moved to Canada and now came home once or twice a year and called maybe once a week. Sometimes Don went to the Old Rose and tried to conjure interest in the various conversations, but most consisted of idle gossip or farm talk. In the early days after the head-on crash—which had stolen Nettie and forced him to retire from the coppers twenty years before he had any intention of doing so—he had frequented the Ironstone most afternoons. But he had begun to enjoy the company of a beer glass too much, so gave it away. Disappointing, since the licensee, Shirley, numbered among the few in Black Wattle who could hold a conversation worth holding.

For the greater part of any day, Don could now be found in the town's old police station. Established in 1852 in response to the gold rush, it ceased operations on the same day as Don's right arm, which now spent its days beside him, atrophied and useless. The higher-ups had seen Don's crippling as a fine, if regrettable, opportunity to close down Black Wattle Police Station, considered the appendix of regional stations for more than a decade. They offered him a desk job in Goulburn as recompense, but moving away from his hometown had been unthinkable. The lone constable under his command, a nice if somewhat dim kid called Aaron Partridge, got transferred up to Sydney. So now it was Don and his police station, as defunct as one another.

A day after deciding he should keep his distance from the Ironstone Hotel, Don had made a second decision: he would rent the old cop shop, where three generations of Winslows had served as police officers, and turn it into a museum. It would focus on old police memorabilia and related stories, but also serve as a repository for general Black Wattle history. He had plenty of the former stowed away in his garage and attic space. The latter he compiled from local donations and, to a surprising magnitude, his morning walks; abandoned farming and mining tools, old bottles and tin plates, even a steel helmet that research had determined dated from World War One. After pausing to chat with a sheep farmer one morning, he had been invited to investigate an outbuilding where he discovered every piece of furniture from a school room that had closed its doors in the early 1900s, almost perfectly preserved.

With the help of two local teenagers looking for some after-school work, he had convened it all, restored every piece, and set it out with information boards. On the first day of spring two years ago, he had opened the doors to the Old Police Museum. Stories in a couple of local newspapers and tourism magazines had generated a short flare of interest. But then it fizzled and Don had burned through too much of his insurance payout to buy display advertising, let alone an advertorial on a website or magazine that mattered. Not even Shirley's pub going gangbusters could revive the museum's fortunes.

So now he came in each day and tinkered. On the better days, he might add a tin mug to the mining collection, or a plaque from a long-demolished monument some anonymous person had sent him in the mail. But most days he shifted things around or polished already gleaming buttons or fiddled with the wording on the information boards. Once in a while Shirley might wander down, ostensibly for a social call. But even though she never came right out and said it, he intuited that things weren't going so well at the Ironstone, either. He often felt glum after she left.

He was in the poky back room (once a holding cell where drunk miners slept off their spent earnings) pecking one-handed at some historical copy on his laptop, when the little bell on the museum's front door tinkled. Only a thousand souls called Black Wattle home, give or take, and few arrived or departed without Don's notice. His heart rose as he wondered if the museum might have its first bona fide customer of the spring season, but as he drew closer he saw it was a younger man, probably late thirties. Beneath his nondescript jacket he wore a uniform of some kind. With no wife or kids in tow, the likelihood he was a tourist thinned down to a sliver.

"Good morning," Don said anyway, "care to have a look around the museum?"

"In a sense, yes," the man said. He reached into his breast pocket, brought out a wallet and flipped it open. "My name is Chris Brooks, Australian Federal Police. I need to speak to Donald Winslow. Is that you?"

"Depends. What's this all about?"

"Either you're Donald Winslow or you're not, sir. Please don't be uncooperative."

"Uncooperative? Who do you think you are, barging in like this?"

"As I said, I'm Chris Brooks with the Australian Federal Police. I need to—"

"I don't care if you're King Shit of Muck Hill, unless you state your business you can get the hell out of my museum."

"So you are Donald Winslow, then?"

"Don to my friends. You can keep calling me Donald."

"Excellent, good to know, Donald. I'm here this morning on behalf of the Australian Government to serve a compulsory requisition order. For the next fortnight, the Federal Police will assume control of this property and its grounds for the purposes of special operations training."

"Special operations? Why would you want this place for special operations?"

"I'm afraid I can't go into specifics. I have the signed requisition order here." He put a document on the counter and pivoted it so it faced Don, then placed a ballpoint pen beside it. "I need you to read it through and sign here to show you understand its contents."

"Listen, mate, I'll jam it where the sun don't shine in a minute. What gives you the right to come in here all high-handed and try to tell me what to do with my museum?"

"It's not your museum, sir. The building and its grounds are Crown land, currently under lease to you on a three-year contract. The government is well within its rights to requisition the property for other purposes if deemed necessary. It wishes to use it as a temporary base of operations during the specified dates."

"An old building and a small yard? Why in God's name would the Federal—"

"Everything is spelled out in the requisition order if you'd care to read it, Donald. Including the terms of your compensation."

All at once Don became calm, as if he had entered the eye of a storm. "Compensation?"

"Three hundred dollars per day for the duration of our stay to offset any inconvenience and financial losses incurred."

"Does that include weekends? The museum gets busy on weekends."

"Of course. All you have to do is sign the order and the money will be deposited into the bank account linked to the museum's business number."

Don did some quick sums in his head. Over four thousand tax-free dollars for sitting on his freckle. That sort of cash could buy an advertorial in the regional tourism guide, maybe even a double-page spread. If that didn't put wind in the museum's sails, nothing would. There might even be some money left over for a new exhibit. Or he could get some pamphlets professionally designed and printed and ask the information centers to put them on display.

"What are you planning to do to the place? I don't want anything lost or broken."

"As I said I can't discuss it, but the museum will be returned to you in the same condition in which we found it."

"And if something does get damaged?"

"Then I imagine you will be compensated for that, too."

Don lowered his head and began scribbling his signature. Using his left hand still felt cacky and probably always would. A copper had to sign a lot of documents and Don had cultivated a simple but lavish signature over the years. His dumb-hand signature looked like it belonged to a fourth grader just getting to grips with running-writing. "Why didn't anyone get in touch with me beforehand?"

"Governments work in mysterious ways," Brooks said. "I got the call last night and drove up here this morning."

"When do you need me out of here?"

"Midday at the latest. Now, if possible."

"Jesus, you're not mucking around. Anti-terrorist exercises?"

"I'm afraid I can't—"

"—disclose anything, yeah, yeah," Don said. "If you wanted to keep everything a secret, you've come to the worst town in New South Wales. Marla at the Old Rose will be onto you in a flash. Rumors swirling by teatime."

"Thank you for your assistance, Donald. In the event we complete our operations prior to the designated end date, I will be in touch."

"Do I still get—"

"You will be paid for the full two weeks regardless, yes. Please vacate the premises at your earliest convenience and hand the museum keys to me. I have a marked vehicle parked outside. Good day to you."

Brooks took the requisition document and put the pen in his jacket pocket, then stalked out as if he had somewhere important to be. *Good day to you.* Jesus, what a flog. The federal police of Don's acquaintance had been good blokes, mostly. A little full of themselves, a step closer to politicians than the state police, perhaps, but nothing like Brooks. Maybe he wasn't a federal copper, *per se*, but a pencil pusher in some bureaucratic offshoot. It would explain a lot. Don considered pottering around the museum until 11:59 a.m.—just to watch the officious little turd's face turn red—but in the end he closed his laptop, switched off all the lights and left.

Outside he found a van with AFP markings parked across the museum's driveway. No reason for the obstruction; no other cars occupied the street for the length of the museum's frontage. Brooks had blocked the driveway just to show he could. Don approached the driver's side window and found him fingering a mobile phone. The van's engine was running and, below it, Don could hear the burr of an air conditioner. Beautiful country spring morning and Brooks had sealed himself in a rolling bell jar. Don tapped on the glass.

"A parking inspector does the rounds in Black Wattle sometimes," he said when Brooks had rolled down the window. "Real bitch. She'd book her own mother and be proud of it. Be a shame if she decided to swoop through today for some reason."

Brooks looked at him a while, expressionless, then said, "I assume you have some keys for me?"

"Yeah, here you go," Don said, dropping them into his waiting palm.

"This is the only set?"

"Yep. As far as you know."

Now Brooks studied him more intently, a jeweler identifying some inappropriate facet on a cut diamond. "Your service to the

New South Wales Police was one of the reasons we selected this site for our operations training. My superiors believed you would be understanding and cooperative, but so far that's not a phrase I would use. I hope we won't have any trouble from you, Donald. It would be a shame if the offer of compensation we discussed had to be revoked."

Choice rejoinders piled up at the back of Don's tongue. If he were in uniform, if his right arm weren't shriveled up into a five-fingered T-Rex claw, Brooks wouldn't have had the audacity (or the courage) to speak to him in such a condescending fashion. But Don wasn't in uniform and he didn't possess two able arms and the financial carrot dangling before his nose looked too tasty to ignore.

"Take good care of my museum," he said.

He returned to the footpath and walked at pace down the gentle grade towards the Old Rose Coffee Shop. Marla would know all about this little development, never mind that. As he passed the post office he heard an approaching semi-trailer's diesel grumble. Black Wattle got its share of trucks passing through to the towns further north and, in his time as sergeant, Don could name all the trucking companies that operated along Goldfields Road. As this one buffeted him, he glanced up and saw a demountable building secured to its flatbed trailer. Emblazoned across the side was a checkered strip with a fluoro-orange outline and three letters in the center.

AFP.

CHAPTER FOUR

EARLY AFTERNOON SUN added a blazing halo to the crest as Truman piloted his hatchback along the final run into Black Wattle. The road flattened out, revealing a motel on his right, its faux-shingled roof and cement-rendered walls expressing the tasteless design so popular in its heyday. Even the name on the fading plastic sign threw back to a period when cheese and chic were almost interchangeable: The Goldmine Motel. It looked like an oversized kiosk in a theme park or the gaudy entrance to a pub's gaming room. The town had struck him as cute and quaint on his only drive through Black Wattle, more Victorian high country than New South Wales tablelands. He wondered how the idyllic picture in his memory had omitted this vulgar eyesore.

Had he been drunk at the time? Probably. The end of a long day's wine tasting. And alcohol, in memory as in painting, scrubbed away blemishes.

Any misgivings had to be set aside, though, because it was the Goldmine Motel or sleep in his car. He indicated and turned in. The carpark's concrete was cracked and lifted in places and turning to rubble where it met the road. A single car occupied a single space outside an archway marked OFFICE. Truman parked beside it, then mentally pulled on a pair of disposable latex gloves and went inside.

No one greeted him at reception. In lieu was an ancient MANAGER ON DUTY sign and below it the name *Sean Garratty*. Taped to the desk was a doorbell, the sort of thing available in Bunnings for twenty dollars. Below it, a note handwritten in pen on a slip of paper (also taped down) advised him to RING BELL FOR SERVICE. He did so, trying to ignore how the button's grey rubber had become brown with the touch of a thousand fingers. A tinny chime sounded in a back room somewhere. A chair dragged its legs across timber floorboards and then footsteps drew nearer. A man emerged, salad roll in hand, rheumy eyes expressing mild irritation at the interruption. A piece of shredded carrot stood out loud and proud amongst the grizzled push-broom of his moustache.

"You'll be wanting a room, I expect?"

Truman cleared his throat daintily, fighting the urge to flee. "Yes, please."

"Hundred a night," Sean said, putting down his roll. It shed some carrot hairs onto the counter. "Barely worth the bother, but what's a man to do? Can't get the pension. The government says I have too many assets," he scoffed. "Too many assets. Like to see the politicians make do without their perks. How many nights?"

The rant became a question so seamlessly it caught Truman off guard and his mind scrambled to find an answer. The drive had given him ample time to think, yet he had devoted almost no brain power to the finer details, preferring to daydream about the bigger picture. "Um. . .let's start with three nights."

"Fill this out for me," Sean said.

Truman scribbled his details into a form that looked like a photocopy of an original that had been printed using a mimeograph.

"Three hundred, thank you," Sean said.

Truman thumbed a debit card out of his wallet. Sean looked at it as though it were Monopoly money.

"We don't have EFTPOS," he said. "Cash only."

"How can you not have EFTPOS?" Truman asked, flabbergasted.

"Don't believe in it," Sean said.

Truman stared at him, waiting for him to break into a smile or start laughing or something, but he only returned the stare with vacant eyes. Truman shook his head a little to dismiss this surreal turn of events, then put his debit card back and opened the note section. On a whim he'd used an ATM while stopped at the roadhouse—four crisp fifties, supposed to be emergency funds. This was an emergency of sorts, although not what he had imagined.

"I guess I'll make it two nights, then."

Sean licked his finger and thumbed through the notes before opening an old timber drawer and popping them in. "Room one," he said, handing Truman a key. "No room service here, in case you were wondering. Best place for breakfast is the Old Rose in the center of town."

"Thank you," Truman said. Adding in his mind, *I think.*

Musty air greeted him as he opened the door to his motel room. Every fixture and piece of furniture confirmed the room's age; beyond that, it appeared tidy and clean. Truman brought in his suitcase and stood it against the unused patch of wall between the door and a pine cabinet which housed a cathode-ray television. Then he locked up again and walked towards town, his hand raised as a visor against the westering sun.

The Goldmine Motel was in an isolated spot and he covered the better part of a kilometer before he reached the town proper. The first building he passed was an historic pub that someone with a tasteful and sympathetic eye had recently renovated. He wondered if he could get his money back from Sean and change his lodgings, but then decided being a staircase away from a row of beer taps would defeat his mad plan's purpose. The sweet smell of fermentation caressed his nose as he passed the doorway and he quickened his pace to put it behind him.

An old freestanding home had been divided up and converted into three shops at some point and the real estate agency occupied one of the trio (another sold 'boutique fashion' and trinkets, the third had a FOR LEASE sign stuck to its glass door). Truman climbed the central staircase and went to the real estate agency's front window. On display were twenty or so homes. As he scanned them, his heart began to sink. Most were situated on hectares of farming land and/or located in areas surrounding Black Wattle rather than the township itself. Ropes of panic began to constrict around his chest. What the hell had he been thinking? He was like a child running away from home because his parents had yelled at him. His callow daydream—formulated while still half-sozzled and influenced more by Hollywood than rational thought—had run headlong into reality. Had he really—

Then his eye landed on the final listing at the window's bottom right and his crazy sense of serendipity returned. A small home overlooking the valley, country-style décor, leased fully furnished. Modest and manageable backyard. Three hundred a week. It was as though someone had reached into his mind, plucked an idealized image from his imagination and popped it on a real estate listing. The ropes slackened and his heart began to pulse at double time as he pushed through the doorway.

A couple of easy chairs attended a circular coffee table in the waiting area, and no one attended the long reception desk. Truman leaned over it, hunting for a bell like the one at the Goldmine Motel, but found nothing aside from neatly arranged pens and highlighters, a stapler, a printer and a pile of letterheads with Black Wattle Realtors in the top corner. A talkback radio announcer muttered somnolent words through a small speaker in the ceiling. Truman jammed his hands on his hips. Had he intruded on some town-wide siesta?

He cleared his throat noisily. When that elicited no response, he said, "Is anybody here?"

The tuneless tinkle of cutlery on crockery replied and a few moments later a late-fifties lady appeared, still wiping her mouth with a serviette. She wore faded jeans and an old mauve cardigan, an ensemble that took Truman's mind back to interminable Christmas lunches at his great-grandmother's house before she became too infirm to host the family.

"I do apologize," she said, "you caught me having a bite to eat. How can I help you today?"

You can dress professionally and give me some reassurance that what I'm about to do is not utterly insane, Truman thought. *Maurice would take one look at you and walk straight back out again.* But it was not enough to slow his rocketing enthusiasm, so he put on a smile and said, "I'm interested in a property you have for lease."

"The two-bedroom place on Panorama Avenue?"

"That's the one."

"You have a good eye. It's an investment property, recently renovated to a high standard. The owner's a wonderful lady, too. Her name's Pamela."

The realtor's eyes twinkled and this time Truman's smile came naturally. He offered her his hand and said, "Pamela, I presume?"

"Pamela Daley, Pam for short."

"Truman."

"That's a nice name, you don't hear it very often."

"Thank you."

"We can go and inspect the house now, if it suits you. I'll close up and put the phone on voicemail."

"If it's not too much trouble."

"No trouble. We've had a lot of listings in Black Wattle lately but not many sales. No one predicted the bottom would fall out of the market the way it did, or I certainly didn't anyway. If not for a couple of overseas investors I'd be living hand to mouth."

She seemed a sweet lady, like a kindergarten teacher who had wound up in the wrong job. Truman couldn't help wondering how an obvious ingenue had lasted so long in the cut-throat real estate market. Working in the country probably afforded a certain leeway.

Pam handed him a leaflet with the property's details and then showed him to the door. Truman took the stairs down to the footpath and as he stepped out someone crashed into him. His teeth clicked together and he saw starbursts, stumbling backwards until he sat upon the stairs.

When the shock had passed he looked up and found himself staring at a man in full religious garb, probably Catholic, although Truman didn't know much about the various species of God-botherers. The hem of his cream-colored dress (or whatever it was called) had stained dirt-brown and between the man's nose and Adam's apple coarse salt-and-pepper whiskers sprayed in all directions. Truman could smell the whisky coming off him like fumes from a petrochemical factory.

"Sodomite!" the priest bawled, pointing down as if he were standing on a pulpit. "Sodomites shall burn in hell for eternity! Read your bible, heathens. It's right there in Leviticus 20:13!"

"Oh, go away, Patrick," Pam said, waving a hand at him. "No one wants to hear your brand of hellfire, especially when you're rambling drunk. Go on, get lost. Go home and sleep it off. If Don was still running the police station you'd be in the drunk tank already."

He peered at her for a long while, perhaps trying to make two images resolve into one, then lifted his sleeve to reveal an old Seiko watch. "Sun's over the yardarm," he slurred, before stumbling past her and proceeding uphill towards the pub.

"I'm so sorry about that," Pam said, assisting Truman to his feet. "He thinks everyone's a homosexual when he's had a skinful. Which is nearly all the time these days."

"No offence taken, I assure you," Truman said.

"I—Oh!" Pam laughed. "Oh, I see. No business of mine, I'm sure. Well, I hope Patrick hasn't put you off the idea of living in Black Wattle."

"No, of course not."

The entire town couldn't be populated with parochial, insular cretins, could it?

"This is my car," Pam said, pointing to an aged four-wheel drive parked on the street. "Did you want to follow me there?"

"I'm afraid I left my car up at the motel. I could walk back up and—"

"Not at all, don't be silly. Hop in and I'll drive you there. It's only a short way."

Upon opening the passenger's side door Truman discovered a whole new biosphere composed from the scents of horses and sheep and wet dogs and hay and a few other things he couldn't pinpoint. Perhaps her husband was a farmer. Dog remnants remained, in fact— hair embedded in the upholstery's weave like little white spears. Truman was overdue for another drink of water and his escalating hangover intensified his aversion. He actually had to steel his mind before sliding onto the seat.

"I apologize again about Patrick. Black Wattle was a bit slow to move into the twenty-first century. Like a lot of country towns, I suppose. Once the police station closed and Don Winslow retired, things changed pretty quickly. Especially after Shirley took over the pub. I won't say Don ruled the town with an iron fist, but he was well respected and he exerted a great deal of influence over its character. Not many things happened here without his input. But that's enough tales out of school. What brings you to Black Wattle? Tree change?"

Her question dug fingers into his wounded psyche. He had to bite back on a spurt of emotion and put a hand to his mouth as if in thought. Once under control, he said, "Something like that."

"What do you do for a job?"

"I'm an artist."

"Oh, how exciting! An artist in residence. That would give Black Wattle some cachet."

Truman shifted around in his seat. An unnerving dampness was transferring from the car seat to the seat of his pants. He hoped Pam had just left the window open on a rainy day, but judging by the yellow lawns drifting past, that was thin hope indeed.

"It's been a while since my name lent cachet to anything."

"Every little bit makes a difference. There's not much work since the fires came through. The roads in and out were cut off for a day or two, but that was as bad as it got. Despite the name, Black Wattle doesn't have many trees and the fire never came up this far. It just sort of made a ring around us and moved on. But we saw a downturn along with the rest of the region. A few farmers are hanging in there. We need tourism to come back. When Shirley's pub became a foodie destination, you could barely get a parking spot at lunchtime."

They had taken a road perpendicular to the main street and now appeared to be approaching a dead end, but as they drew closer Truman saw it hooked around in a crescent and ventured east. A barbed-wire fence created a metal-toothed barrier between the road and a vast slope that cruised gradually to the valley below. Here and there grey rocks poked up through the earth-toned tablelands and, at the lowest point, Truman could just make out the shining gold ribbon of a river. This panorama made something twitch inside him and in the immediate instant, he feared it was a cocaine craving. But as it opened up and blossomed, he realized it was a different urge. His hands wanted to move, interpret the input from his eyes and create something.

"This is us," Pam said, guiding the four-wheel drive one-handed onto an apron of blonde-brick gravel that might have only been spread and levelled a few days earlier. The drought-dry grass had been mown and edged and it delineated the property's frontage like a straw-colored sea. Garden beds filled with gazanias offered a jubilee welcome either side of timber steps that led up to a whitewashed porch.

"Welcome to 66 Panorama Place," Pam said, opening the front door. She gave him the tour: central kitchen and living area, separate bathroom and laundry, two bedrooms on the south side (a godsend in summer), fully furnished in a budget-conscious but tasteful fashion. But Truman barely saw any of it. His mind languished back in the sunroom, which ran in a big rectangle along the eastern side of the house. To any other potential lessee, its generosity probably looked like overkill, wasted footprint that would have better served to make the kitchen more spacious or the bedrooms less cramped. But to Truman, it was already a gallery, the best paintings from his past and all the masterpieces from the coming renaissance period exhibited to grand effect in the natural light. It called up a delicious wildness inside him.

"The kitchen has gas burners, and in the living room—"

"Take me back to town," Truman said. "I'm ready to sign the lease."

Pam beamed. "I'm so glad you like it," she said. "This house belonged to my aunt. She passed away last year. She'd be thrilled to know it was becoming an art studio. She used to dabble a little herself. Purely amateur, but she enjoyed it. Sold a few pictures here and there, mostly at markets."

"Well, that's nice," Truman said. Hearing about hobby painters' exploits made him uncomfortable. He never knew what to say. His present eagerness to sign his name on the dotted line redoubled the discomfort. It must have written itself across his face because Pam clapped her hands together gently.

"Right, let's head back to the office and make it official."

The wet-dog seat in the four-wheel drive became more tolerable on the return trip. It only took Pam a few minutes to prepare the lease documents. He scanned and initialed each page, then signed and dated beneath the words TREVOR KEVIN SMYTHE. Pam, bless her, had made no comment about his birth name. One day he vowed to change it by deed poll, make it official. He might even get rid of the second while he was at it, although it would have to be another K-name—ever since his late teens he had signed his paintings T. K. Smythe and his career was too far along for a rebrand.

He walked back up the hill to the motel (the spring in his step belying the hangover in his head) and put his suitcase back in the car. He went up to the office and managed to garner Sean's attention again. He handed over the room key. "As it turns out, I don't need to stay anymore."

"No refunds," Sean said quickly, snatching the key with a magician's deftness. "It's right there in the policy document you signed."

"I didn't think there would be," Truman replied dryly. "Good luck with your motel."

He had a fabulous time during his first afternoon as a Black Wattle resident. He set up his easel and other materials at one end of the sunroom, then set out his canvases in the approximate places they'd go when he bought fixings to hang them. Just before five o'clock his stomach rumbled and brought him out of his waking daydream. He drove up to the general store and purchased some staples: bread, milk, condiments, a pack of fiber cereal. Simpler fare than he was used to, but then he wasn't in Paddington anymore. Simple seemed in keeping with his life's reinvention.

The day ended on a low, though. As he pulled into the driveway, his gaze went further along Panorama Avenue than it had earlier. In the distance, maybe a three or four-minute walk, he could discern the pitched roof and gables of a nineteenth-century church. On the highest steeple, calling silently to the faithful across the valley, stood a cross as tall as a grown man. Truman stared at it a while, then shut the car door and wandered inside, digesting this new information.

It appeared Patrick the Homophobic Priest lived maybe three hundred meters down the road. By a country measure, they were practically neighbors.

CHAPTER FIVE

"**W**HAT IS GOD?" Patrick Burnham thundered across the pews. "God is love. But God is also judgment. One day, He will judge us all, saints and sinners alike, as we seek to pass into the grace of His everlasting kingdom in heaven. His judgment is infallible because He is God. On earth we are also judged, but these are the petty judgments of men. Without a scintilla of the Almighty's omniscience. And some are judged more than others."

The final word echoed through the empty church and faded into nothingness. Patrick unscrewed the cap on his flask, slurped back a mouthful, wiped his lips on his sleeve. The dirty-sweet smell of a hundred other wipes lingered in the fabric. He screwed the cap back on, as if he wouldn't be undoing it again in a minute or two. His ten a.m. Sunday congregation had once filled pews, the faithful sometimes driving half an hour and forsaking their local churches to hear him preach. Now the church alone spectated and bore witness to the Word of the Lord.

St Luke's Anglican Church dated back to the mid-19th century, when Protestants still built their houses of worship with the same eye for grandeur and ornamentation as the Catholics. An imposing sandstone edifice with arched stained glass windows, it had been a refuge for sinners. Goldfields were often sinful places. Sometimes Patrick fancied he could hear the anguished echoes of shamed men who had sought absolution and forgiveness within its walls.

Or perhaps that was just the scotch amplifying his own thoughts.

An Irish Protestant was unusual, although he was only Irish by bloodline; six generations of Burnhams had been born in Australia and on his mother's side it was five, traced back to a socially unpopular Anglo-Irish marriage that had instigated emigration by ship in the late 1860s. Red hair and fair skin had almost been bred out by the time Patrick assumed his place in the lineage. A fine thing, too, otherwise he would be like old Sean who ran the motel—a virtual recluse during the summer months for fear the sun would blister his milky skin.

Now and then he tried to blame the drinking on his Irish heritage but, in his honest moments, he knew better. It had begun as medication, something to dull the pain. Nothing more sinister, really, than taking paracetamol to alleviate a headache. In the evening a few scotches to quell the insomnia and make his bedroom seem less empty. But the nightcap started earlier and earlier until it merged with a tipple before dinner time and then, because dinner started happening in daylight hours during the summer, the taboo of drinking before sundown fell away. Once that rule lifted, starting time crept further back until it became one and the same with lunch. Before he knew it, Patrick was downing a hair of the dog prior to standing at the pulpit to deliver his Sunday sermon. Then. . .

Then it all became rather hazy. Somewhere along the way he had graduated from functioning alcoholic to barely functioning at all. But he remembered the turning point.

He had been returning from a Rotary lunch in Cowra, where he had been the fundraiser's guest speaker. His drinking hadn't progressed past the self-medicating stage back then, but this was no ordinary preachment from the comfort of his pulpit at St Luke's. A lot of well-off business people were attending the luncheon and his speech would go a long way to prizing open their wallets. So to stave off nerves, he knocked back a couple of scotches at a nearby hotel before turning up at the club's function room.

The speech went well—the audience laughed where they were supposed to and offered generous applause at the conclusion—and Patrick wondered later if his success contributed to his downfall. The luncheon was served, as was wine. Everyone wanted to talk to him and a hovering waiter ensured his glass never got below a quarter full. The dark sorrow that had shadowed his every move for weeks began to recede in the wine's ersatz brightness. It was mid-afternoon before his companions decided they should return to their various offices.

Patrick only understood how drunk he was once he climbed into his car and peered through the windscreen. The sensible thing to do, he knew, would be to check into a motel and drive home the next day. But his libation not only disarmed his common sense, it made him hostile to it. An hour's drive home or ten hours and at least one hundred and twenty bucks wasted? In his wine-addled mind, drunk-driving became the sensible option.

Events almost vindicated his decision, too. He and his little sedan were only five minutes from Black Wattle when a cow stepped out onto the road. Not there one second, filling the entire lane the next, or so it appeared in Patrick's recollection. The car broadsided the cow at the best part of one hundred kilometers an hour. The bonnet caved in and the airbag deployed, sparing Patrick injury save some light bruising to his legs and chest. The ploughed cow landed ten meters up the road, its barrel-sided body now a wonky concave shape. Patrick got out gingerly and pushed his banged-up sedan onto the shoulder. Traffic in and out of Black Wattle was light at the busiest times, but with business hours over and dusk approaching, Goldfields Road was deserted.

Patrick inspected the cow. A long trail of blood oozed from its mouth and, although it remained warm to the touch, he could detect no respiration. Just to be certain, he touched its big bovine eye with a finger. No corneal reflex. The cow was, to use his father's favored phrase, dead as a doornail.

"Thank God for that," Patrick whispered.

Adjudging himself only a mile and a half shy of town, Patrick determined he would walk the remainder of the way home and worry about cow and car tomorrow. He went to his disabled vehicle to collect a few belongings.

He was closing the passenger's side door when a siren whooped, just the once. A highway patrol vehicle approached, red and blue lights flashing, and pulled onto the verge behind Patrick's sedan.

Only a short time ago it would have been Don Winslow or his constable in the car and Patrick could have anticipated a friendly chat about his hard luck. But the big black letters on the cop car's bonnet indicated this vehicle operated out of Cowra and, when the officer stepped out, his face was a stranger's. Patrick's heart beat faster, adrenaline-tinctured blood rushing into his veins.

"You okay, sir?" the constable said.

"Yes, I'm fine. Just a little sore. Better than my car, anyway."

"Looks like quite an impact. Didn't see the cow blocking the road?"

"No, it ran straight out in front of me." Patrick articulated each word carefully. It was much trickier than it had been a few hours earlier behind the microphone. Trying not to expel any breath in the policeman's direction compounded the problem.

"Need to watch out for stock and wildlife on these roads. It pays to stay alert. Where are you headed?"

"Just up to Black Wattle. I live there."

"Where were you travelling from?"

"Cowra. I was out there on business."

"It must have been a busy day. You look tired."

"It was, actually."

"Got your license on you?"

Patrick surrendered it. The cop—Constable Moore according to his name tag—studied it and handed it back. "We can't leave this cow here. I'll call someone in to remove it." He stared at the dead beast for a second or two, scratching his chin, and for the duration of that pause, Patrick believed Constable Moore had exercised some Sergeant-Winslow-style discretion. But then he turned to Patrick and said, "Sit tight for a minute."

Tight was an apt word. Anxiety squeezed Patrick's chest until he thought it would burst. Constable Moore called in something on his radio, then sauntered back over. . .breathalyzer in hand. He held it up to Patrick's face.

"Given the circumstances of your collision, I'm conducting a breath test. Can you count up to five for me, please?"

The car proved fixable but Patrick's driver's license was a write-off; he tested in the medium range and was disqualified from driving for six months. While his conviction didn't include jail time, he was in effect imprisoned at Black Wattle, with a single daily bus his only way in or out. The farmer sued him for the death of his cow, too, even though the nearest STOCK CROSSING sign was five kilometers distant. Two thousand bucks on top of his six-hundred dollar fine for drunk driving. The day he paid out on the cow was the day the whisky went from medicine to problem. Initially, he would toss down a couple of fingers before his Sunday service, but soon he kissed the bottle good morning. His preaching became more vehement and less coherent. Word got around about his conviction and his behavior and within weeks his congregation dwindled to a few hardy souls who would sit half a dozen pews back and try not to look mortified as their beloved Father raved, spittle flying from his lips and raining booze-scented drizzle on the first row.

Staring blur-eyed and blur-minded at his deserted church, Patrick now unscrewed the flask and lifted it to his lips. An action that had become as automated as breathing. But when he tipped it up, less than a sip dribbled onto his tongue. He closed the cap in disgust and stumbled towards the rectory attached to the church on its southern side. It had served Patrick and Becky well enough, in spite of its compactness. These days, Patrick had all the room he needed. He fumbled open the door and shuffle-stepped to the kitchenette, where once Becky had cooked delicious meals and now no one cooked anything. He opened the cupboard above the stove, where he stashed his scotch bottles, and found it bare.

"Some bastard drank all the scotch," he said, topping off his witticism with something between a growl and a laugh. He walked back outside and gazed at the dimming sky. The general store would be closed, but Shirley up at the Ironstone would sell him a bottle or two on the sly. She seemed to be the last compassionate person in the whole damned town. He started to walk up the hill, then took umbrage at the inconvenience, at his whole situation. A perfectly good car stood outside the rectory. Why the hell should he take Shank's mare just because poor old Don Winslow had been in an accident and some snot-nosed copper had seen fit to purloin Patrick's license?

"Fuck it all," he said, storming back into the rectory and snatching the car keys off the hook where they'd hung untouched for nearly three months. He strode towards his car, tripped over a loop of Kikuyu grass, fell onto his knees, swore, got up, and continued on. His car had remote central locking, but no push-button start, and as he tried to insert the key into the ignition he found his aim was off. It took him several attempts before it slotted in and he could crank the engine to life. He reversed straight back and the car made an unholy thump as he missed the driveway and went off the gutter.

"Oh, shut up," he said, wrenching it into drive.

He concentrated on keeping the wheel straight as he moved along Panorama Avenue. He glanced down at the speedo, and when it came into focus he saw he was travelling at only thirty kilometers an hour. Might as well have a flashing sign on the car that read DRUNK MAN DRIVING. He pressed the accelerator a little harder and watched the needle creep up to sixty. When his eyes returned to the road he had already arrived at his turnoff. He hit the brakes and turned sharply, tires wailing as he rounded the corner.

"Not far now," he said, urging the car up the hill. "Straight line and then one turn and you're at the pub."

He stopped dead at Goldfields Road and peered in either direction with slow-blinking eyes. No traffic. He didn't quite trust his sight, though, so he checked twice again before creeping his car into the intersection. The pub wasn't far along and he pulled up outside, thankful the road here didn't have high gutters like those outside the shops in town.

Patrick remained in the car a moment, gathering himself, trying to find the sober person drowning inside all the booze. He mused—as well as he could muse in such a state—that his relative newcomer status as an alcoholic was acting against him. A seasoned drinker would have been more capable after consuming the same quantity. Shirley was nice, but she was also bound by responsible drinking laws like any other publican and wouldn't risk her license selling grog to a bloke who was already intoxicated.

When he thought he had remastered his faculties, Patrick got out and shut the door. The warm afternoon sun beat down on his exposed neck and broiled his already parched brain. He should have rehydrated first. Too late to worry about that now. One foot in front of the other, straight line, don't sway, don't trip up the step.

Once he was inside, the artificial light made the charade of sobriety (or semi-sobriety, anyway, no sense swinging for the boundary) easier to maintain. Shirley stood behind the bar, a pensive look compressing her face.

"Afternoon, Shirl," Patrick drawled.

She glanced up, as if startled to see someone there. "Oh, hello, Patrick. Never mind me, I was off with the pixies. What can I do for you?"

"A glass of ice water please." He waited until she had filled a glass with ice cubes before adding, "And if it's not too much trouble, a few bottles of single malt."

Shirley paused to look at him, post-mix hose in hand, then applied it to the glass and pressed the button for soda water. "Couldn't get any at the general store?"

"I didn't know I'd run out," Patrick said, punctuating it with an aw-shucks grin.

"Again?"

"Besides, Ray's range is terrible. Nothing but Johnnie Walker Red and it's been sitting there for months. You stock the top-shelf stuff."

She put the soda water on the counter with a thump, studied him, then sighed. She disappeared out the back and returned with three bottles of Glenfiddich and stuffed them into a paper shopping bag. "You know this isn't a bottle shop," she said. "Anything I sell you is supposed to be drunk on the premises."

"I know, I know," Patrick said, pulling out his wallet. "I tell you what, I'll go over there and drink my water. You busy yourself out in the cellar for a while and when you return I'll be gone, along with the scotch. No court in the land would convict you."

He put a pile of notes on the counter, then took a single swig from the soda water. "See. Responsible service of alcohol."

"Or RSA for short," she said, a reluctant smile lighting up her face. "Just get out of here you silly bastard, before I get fined."

"Thanks, Shirley."

He toddled out to the car, sweating with the exertion of exhibiting sobriety or a simulacrum thereof. Once he was behind the wheel he cracked open a bottle and tipped it up to his lips. Irish fire invaded his mouth and he burned with a mingled sense of relief and shame. He twisted the cap back on, returned the bottle to the bag on the passenger's seat, and began the return journey to the rectory. He was thankful Goldfields Road was so wide and obstacle-free, because now that he had relaxed again his impairment returned with a vengeance. He turned right, oversteered, and corrected his position with a jerk of the wheel. As the car rolled down the gentle slope his mind faded in and out; one moment he seemed to be there manipulating his existence, the next he was little more than a passenger watching on. During the transition between these two states, something dashed across the road in front of him. It collided with his car's bonnet and folded in two before disappearing from view. A sick sense of déjà vu overwhelmed his senses, but the booze provided enough emotional cushioning for him to pull on the handbrake and get out.

He moved forward, steadying himself on the car's front fender, and stopped to look at what he had hit.

The body stared up at him with dead eyes. Its gaze cut through the whisky smog and, all at once, some primal instinct hibernating in his brain snapped awake and Patrick's senses came alive. Backing away, he crossed himself twice then fell into the car and slammed the door. He cursed his inebriation as he tried to recall the central locking's whereabouts. When he located it he slammed his hand on the button, then threw the car in reverse and peeled away in a fresh screech of tires. The back of his car jumped the gutter and crashed into a fence post. Drive again. He tromped the accelerator and the engine revved until it screamed, the wheels hopping and scuffing as they strove for purchase on the bitumen. Patrick's full-moon eyes groped through the encroaching shadows to verify the thing on the road had not moved, that it was not now bearing down to smash through the window.

At last, the tires dug in and propelled the car down the hill. Patrick allowed himself a single peek at the rear-view mirror, but could not tell one way or another whether the body remained on the road. He cut the corner into Panorama Avenue so acutely that he almost mounted the gutter again. Once St Luke's was in sight his hands wrung the steering wheel and his lips bunched up tight.

He drove right to the church doors, got out, tripped over his own feet and crawled up the flight of three steps. He lurched upright, fell against the timber doors and ground the old-fashioned key into the keyhole. The tumblers gave with agonizing slowness and he was overcome with a biblical sense of doom as his mind proffered high-fidelity images depicting the thing on the road. But then the door hinges creaked and he fell into the church's vestibule. His elbow hit the unforgiving flagstones and the keys went flying from his grasp. He reached for them, as a drowning man would reach for a life preserver, and clawed them back. Then he slammed the church doors shut, locked them from the inside and put his back against them, chest heaving. He crossed himself twice more, slumped to the floor and began to pray.

Listening to his own whispered words from the Good Book soothed him and gradually stilled his nerves. Even though he wished it gone now, the whisky took hold again, draping its stultifying tentacles around his brain and lulling him closer and closer to the inky blackness within. His lips slowed, turned God's words to sibilants. Then they stopped altogether and Patrick's head nodded forward until his chin came to rest on his clavicles.

He woke to full darkness, the church nothing but geometric shadows and faint outlines where starlight passed through the stained-glass windows. When he lifted his head pain needled deep in his neck. It shocked him to full consciousness and he remembered the thing on the road. His limbs stiffened and his ears strained. He heard nothing but crickets and the warble of a night bird.

Patrick got to his feet and rubbed a hand absently across his neck. His tongue was a tacky sponge filling his mouth; his palms were made of parchment. He needed water or he would end up vomiting from dehydration. Sleep had somewhat counteracted his impairment but the whisky still fogged his thoughts. It was like driving on a winter's morning without first demisting the windshield. He put his ear against the door and listened. Only the crickets, the faraway whoosh of a truck passing through town, the chitter of a flying fox eating nectar from the early spring blossoms.

What exactly *had* he seen? Those eyes. . . A trick of the light? Patrick began to wonder if the whole thing had been a hallucination, a precursor to full-on *delirium tremens*. It was certainly the more plausible explanation.

Perhaps, but nothing bad ever came from precautions.

He unlocked the church door, ear cocked to detect the slightest sound, and eased it open. He wished he'd oiled the hinges. But notwithstanding the gothic soundtrack, all that awaited him outside was his car, the church grounds, and a night sky subdued with light cloud. He scanned Panorama Avenue and the slope beyond, like a hunter-gatherer hoping to spy a deer or a rabbit. Nothing appeared out of the ordinary; it was the same scape that greeted him after services for more years than he cared to count.

He shrugged, went to the car, popped open the door. The scotch bottles clinked against one other as he lifted out the bag. Cheers. The sound made him thirsty for more than water. He closed the door and moved towards the rectory, then paused mid-step.

It didn't hurt to take precautions.

He went back through the church doors instead and started to prepare.

CHAPTER SIX

EVERYTHING WAS PERFECT.

The morning dawned bright and clear with just enough cloud to lend the sky texture and emphasize its azure complexion. Through his studio window, Truman had an uninterrupted panorama of the valley to the north, a barbed-wire fence offering a coarse foreground contrast to the pastoral pulchritude beyond. The footstool he had pilfered from the kitchen boasted a padded seat and was the ideal height for his easel. On the windowsill to his left steam rose from a fresh cup of English breakfast tea. All his artist's tools were in easy reach, yet not crowding him as they had in the townhouse's spare room. His favorite works surrounded him, an appreciative audience in an intimate theatre.

Yes, everything was perfect. Everything except the picture appearing beneath his paintbrush.

It put him in mind of a scene from the 1980s remake of *The Fly*, a movie that had so traumatized him as a boy he wondered if it had left a permanent ding in his psyche. His father had rented it on videotape, a weekly. Because Truman lived around the corner from school he had begun walking home at an early age—quite the convenience for his parents—and each afternoon he had an hour or so to occupy himself before his mother arrived home from work.

He spotted the cassette case on the entertainment unit one Monday afternoon. When he picked it up to study the cover he found the case unexpectedly light. His father had fallen asleep while watching the movie late on Sunday, stopped it when he awoke, and taken himself off to bed without ejecting the tape. Had it been in the box, Truman wouldn't have watched it—grown-up movies were still verboten, especially horror flicks—but he figured he could plausibly say he believed there to be a different tape in the machine when he pressed play.

It bored him at first and he had been on the verge of switching over to television when a new scene began. A woman in a hospital gown lying on a bed with her legs akimbo, surrounded by doctors in green scrubs. Truman had seen enough TV to know she was having a baby, although this scene was far more graphic than the boring dramas his mother watched. He and the woman knew something about this birth was wrong. Truman stood there open-mouthed and shaking inside as the woman brought into the world not a squalling baby but a segmented worm thing that squirmed in the obstetrician's hands. (It would be a few years before Truman saw his first maggot.) As he lunged for the stop button the movie revealed this was only a nightmare, but the damage was done.

A tad melodramatic on his part, perhaps, although he could understand why that particular anecdote had come to mind. He was trying to bring something beautiful into the world and instead birthing a deformed monster—in artistic terms, at least. He tossed down his brush and abandoned the tea to its windowsill. What the hell was wrong with him? This was supposed to be the dream, the apotheosis: unfettered, uninterrupted, inspired creativity. But he couldn't even manage the simple transitions between yellows and browns he saw in the grass.

Maybe because he was contriving interest. All the famous Australian bush painters had an affinity for their subject. Albert Namatjira, the indigenous artist, came to mind. He didn't need to call up the bush in his mind; it existed in his blood and poured onto the canvas. What did Truman know about Black Wattle? He'd driven through it once and been a resident for less than a day. Hell, he barely knew the bush at all, save for what he had seen on the road between wineries. He needed to immerse himself. Become a Black Wattler, or whatever the locals called themselves.

He checked his watch. Nine in the morning. The coffee shop would be open, that was as good a place to start as any. And suddenly tea seemed too delicate a drink, he needed a caffeine jolt. He put on his sunglasses, grabbed his car keys and hustled into the morning, the heavenward sun dispelling the early chill. Its warm kiss on his right cheek stopped him with his hand on the car's door handle. It couldn't be more than a kilometer to the café. What better way to get his footing in Black Wattle than on foot?

His new home was almost dead center in Panorama Avenue, which bent around at either end to become different streets.

Heading east would take him past the church. Some part of him wanted to go that way, to visibly spite the hateful priest, but Truman's new existence felt too embryonic to introduce confrontation into the mix. So he ventured west instead, loving the feel of sun on his back.

Most homes he passed heading up the gentle hill of Tower Street (the connecting road between Panorama Avenue and Goldfields Road at that end) were modest and unrenovated.

The drought-parched lawns and simple steel fences gave them an austere and somnolent look, as though they were all taking *siesta* while waiting for the rains to come. Maybe there was something in that. Truman tucked it into his jumbled mental file and continued along.

Turning left into the town center, he passed by the real estate agency and glanced through the glass doors. No one appeared to be inside, so he pressed on past the post office and general store to the Old Rose Coffee Shop. The sweet scent of fresh-cooked pastries wafted out in a country-style greeting and the hiss of an espresso machine mixed with general chatter to create white noise. A youngish girl with a harried face stood at an espresso machine, long list of orders on the bench beside her. Just inside the doorway was another woman, this one in her late sixties or early seventies. Although she wore an apron, she did not appear to be involved in café operations, instead holding forth among a cluster of customers seated at the tables or standing by for takeaway coffees.

As Truman entered she paused in her monologue and gave him the quick once-over. "Morning love. You after a coffee?"

"You read my mind."

"Just passing through?"

"No, actually, I moved here yesterday. I'm leasing Pam's place down on Panorama Avenue."

"Oh, yes? Well, Sadie there can look after you."

Truman nodded but the old lady had continued her monologue, something about a farmer allegedly being overcharged for a vet bill. Truman went to the register and asked Sadie for a flat white, then assumed a two-seat booth on the opposite side of the doorway.

So this was country hospitality. He stared out the window which gave onto the main road. A few souls drifted by, the odd car. A FOR LEASE sign made its blaring announcement in the empty shopfront across the street. He couldn't understand why Black Wattle had left such an imprint on him when he and Maurice drove through that day. Just another rural town in a countless succession of them dotting the thousands of roads crisscrossing New South Wales.

Oh, don't be such a drama queen. What did you expect? An invitation to sit with them? Some sort of Black Wattle smoking ceremony to welcome you to town? Pam was warm and courteous because she was looking for a tenant. Desperate to find one, if the weekly rent is any guide. This isn't a movie. They're country people, probably living a hardscrabble life, and you're an imposter from the city trying to pretend you're one of them. Give them time. Give yourself time. It's been a day, for heaven's sake.

The girl on the counter, Sadie, brought over his coffee. Truman sensed something amiss when he saw the cup and saucer: fine china with an ornate floral pattern and gilded edges. Another psychic throwback to those long afternoons bored out of his skull at his great-grandmother's house. One look inside the cup assured him his morning wasn't about to get any better. Sadie the barista had apparently taken the flat in flat white literally and when Truman picked up the cup intense heat conducted through its thin china side and onto his fingers. He put it down to let it cool a while. When it did reach a temperature that wouldn't raise nests of blisters on his tongue he sipped it and tasted only milk. His longed-for coffee jolt had eventuated as brown milk, not far off the Horlicks his mother had sometimes drunk to get a good night's sleep. Truman considered complaining and then decided he didn't need the attention. What sort of impression would that make on the Black Wattle locals?

He pinched the bridge of his nose and closed his eyes. When he opened them again someone new had stepped into the café. Pretty, in a motherly sort of way, eyes bright. In her hand, she held a sheaf of flyers.

"Morning, Marla," she said.

The café's loquacious matriarch paused in delivering the local news. "Hello, Shirley love. What brings you in so early?"

"I'm having a trivia night up at the Ironstone. I'm doing the Australiana and Don's putting together some local questions." She began passing out the flyers. "Kicking off at six. Two-dollar schooners as well."

"Now you're talking," said one of the men.

"I've got a brand-new beer that's supposed to be something special. It's a promotional thing from a brewery out of Cowra."

"Craft beer?" said the man, wrinkling his nose. "What about Reschs?"

"Sorry, Ted, Reschs is full price."

The banter continued for a minute or two but Truman heard none of it. The tasteless coffee had only intensified his caffeine urge and the word "schooners" had transfigured that urge into an urge for alcohol. He clasped his hands together and squeezed.

Christ, you've barely been sober twenty-four hours and at the first mention of beer, you're ready to get sozzled again. You're supposed to be here to get away from booze and coke, remember?

Yes, he remembered. All too well. His brain had begun to yammer about it, in the affirmative rather than the negative.

Once Shirley had put a flyer in every hand, she turned to leave. On the way out, her eyes fell on Truman in his little corner booth. He expected her eyes to alight again as soon as she determined he wasn't a local. Instead, they softened and she smiled. "Would you like one?"

"I. . . Uh, thank you," Truman said. "I only moved here yesterday, so I don't think I'll do too well with the local trivia."

"Welcome to Black Wattle! You should definitely come. It'll be a great way to get to know everyone. The pub is the heart of any country town. Well, during the day it's probably the Old Rose, but when Marla closes up, the Ironstone takes over. That right, Marla?"

"Wouldn't have a clue," Marla said. "I'm usually asleep by eight." Her barrel chest heaved as she laughed and her audience laughed along with her.

"Come tonight," Shirley said to Truman confidentially. She tilted her head towards Marla and her audience. "They can be a little standoffish at first, but they're a great bunch of people once you get to know them."

"Thank you," Truman said. It was the only non-committal thing he could think of.

Shirley left the café with a bunch of flyers still between her fingertips and crossed the road. To start distributing them on the other side, he presumed. He wanted to take Shirley up on her offer. Get drunk, get loose enough to get to know the locals, learn a bit about their history. That might open the gummed-up creative taps inside his head. But the tickle of Amir's hairy legs against his, the shame of waking on the front porch to find Maurice staring down at him, were still fierce enough to dissuade him. One or two beers with trivia would lead to three or four, then five or six. Another night lost. Only he would lose more, because he would smudge his clean slate—the entire justification for his wanton abandonment of life as he knew it. No, he needed to stay as far from temptation as possible.

Out of politeness, he choked down all the dirty milk he could, then prepared a farewell for the townsfolk. No one was looking in his direction. Not a jot disappointed, Truman cut a direct line to the door and commenced a fast-footed walk down to Panorama Avenue.

Did the town have a cocaine dealer? Some rural towns suffered ice epidemics, or according to the media they did, so a coke dealer didn't seem far-fetched.

These thoughts scooted through his head and he walked on faster, shoes slapping the bitumen. He would go back to his new home, get some painting done, *grind* a fucking artwork into existence if that was what it took.

He went straight into the studio, sneered at his room-temperature tea and picked up a brush. Self-doubt nipped at his heels and he ignored it, pushing the bristles across the canvas, come what may. The terrible coffee seemed to help, somewhat, and he felt his creative aperture opening. After ten minutes or so he fell into a rhythm.

He stopped to make a sandwich at some point (lunchtime, he assumed), but his subconscious mind never really downed tools. He continued on, food in one hand and brush in the other, determined to ride this creative wave into shore.

Around two p.m. he got off his stool, back aching, coccyx screaming, a blunt knife blade just below his scapula. . .but now regarding his first completed painting in almost eighteen months. It needed a second pass for detail and even with some finishing touches it was nothing he would expose to the public—but it was a start. As a young man, he had watched Ian Thorpe compete in the four-hundred-meter freestyle at the Olympics (Thorpe had not come out of the closet at that point, but even straights with a half-sensitive gaydar suspected) and been anxious at his torpid first fifty. But Thorpe had only been holding his energy in reserve and two laps later he streaked away from his opponents with a champion's ruthless efficiency. Truman doubted this painting was his first fifty, more like taking his place on the starting blocks, but it was nice to be competing again.

As he gazed out the sunroom windows and stretched the muscles in his back, two cockatoos alighted from a nearby tree, zipped across his field of view, then wheeled around and screeched at one another before disappearing over the roof of his house. Something he could add to the painting when it came time to fill in the details, perhaps. A burring sound from the kitchen interrupted his agreeable contemplation. His phone, on silent, which he had left on the table. With acrylic cockatoos still circling in his head, Truman didn't apportion any thought to what the text message might be. When he picked it up and saw Maurice's name, however, it dispersed the cockatoos like a gunshot.

He dropped the phone. Picked it up, put it down. Thought about removing the SIM card and ending all communication. But after a while, gnawing curiosity got the better of him and he unlocked the phone to read Maurice's message.

I'm not buying you out. You don't get to run away from your mistakes.

That was all. No outrage, no admonishment, not even elaboration on how he felt. Just a salutary line of the tritest variety, like something Truman would expect from his father. Fuck, had Maurice ever really loved him? How could he be so cold?

All at once, Truman wanted company. Needed it. Involuntary solitude had a noise, as deafening as any lawn mower. His mind went to Shirley from the pub, the confidential way she had smiled at him. Not just business-friendly, the way Pam had been, but a genuine attempt to connect. In that environment, where he would join a trivia team and they would automatically have something in common, he could get to know a few Black Wattle residents properly. If he answered some of the Australiana questions, won their trust, perhaps they would warm to him.

This is just a bunch of self-serving bullshit. You're a queer in Hicksville, how friendly do you think they'll be once they find out there's no Mrs. Smythe to help out at the Country Women's Association and no little Smythes waiting to join you once you're settled in? No, you're planning to attend the trivia night for one reason, and it has nothing to do with general knowledge.

He needed to distract himself, push his mind in some other direction. His new home might be "fully furnished" but a television did not number among the available appliances. He picked up his phone, flicked away from Maurice's message as though it were counting down to self-destruct, and tried to bury himself in the first social media app that arrived. But the little progress wheel went around and around and after a while an alert popped up telling him his phone couldn't connect to the internet and asking if he'd like to retry.

"What the hell is this?" Truman said, hating the whine that had entered his voice. "Impossibly faggy," David Sedaris would have called it. He pressed retry and achieved the same result. Only then did he check his service and find it down to a single bar—and that fading in and out.

"What is this, the fucking Dark Ages?"

He moved around the house, hoping the kitchen happened to be an anomalous dead patch. Other rooms garnered no more coverage. He almost threw the phone in frustration, only hanging onto it at the end of the pitch. He drew in a few calming breaths, tried to slow his thoughts. He didn't need an internet connection, he could go old school and call someone. Maybe that would steady his nerves.

His coke dealer's number jostled to the fore and sat there blinking with gaudy neon brilliance.

Truman shut his eyes, pressed his palms against his head, and squeezed. For some reason—probably one a psychologist rather than a neurosurgeon could explain—it helped.

He could ring his parents. His mother was a long way from doddery and always complained he never called enough. Some idle and unconditional conversation might be a salve. He had punched in the first four numbers before he had second thoughts.

What if word of his blacked-out indiscretion had got back to them somehow? His mother wouldn't utter a critical word, but his father—although never openly judgmental—was old enough to harbor quiet beliefs about homosexuals and their promiscuity. That was a conversation Truman didn't need to have. Not even tacitly over the phone.

He cancelled the call. Perhaps friends? No, most of them would have got wind of what happened thanks to Danielle. An older brother or sister seemed the right person to confide in.

Sure. A sibling he didn't have. If wishes were fishes, the world would be an ocean.

But perhaps a bartender with a sympathetic ear could serve the same purpose.

Throughout the afternoon he dithered around the house in an agony of hedonistic urges, indecision, and self-reproach. In the end, his ambivalence did him in as much as anything else. He wanted an escape from the pathological procrastination, the emotional and intellectual no-man's land. For the second time that day, he snatched up his car keys and gusted out of the house, a sideways glance at his finished painting his only concession to better judgment.

Long shadow-fingers clawed at the road as he drove along Panorama Avenue, his eyes shooting right to the church rather than the street's namesake on his left. With the towering elm in the front yard still denuded and skeletal from the winter chill, the church looked ancient and abandoned. Forsaken, to apply a biblical word. Not an ounce of sympathy flowed through Truman's heart. If the priest wanted to propagate hatred from the pulpit, let the churchyard become his graveyard, too.

Truman licked his lips as he drew to the top of the hill. Now that he had let his thirst slip its leash it sprinted like a greyhound. A reckless feeling, both exhilarating and terrifying. He turned left onto Goldfields Road and then hit the brakes, stopping the car dead.

Ahead, lurching across the footpath towards the pub, was none other than Patrick the Homophobe. Truman's uprush of abandon died off in a second. He left the car idling half on and half off the road, his eyes fixed on the priest as he disappeared through the dark rectangle of the pub doorway. A few minutes later he stumbled out again cuddling a paper bag. Truman didn't need X-ray vision to know what was inside; he had smelled it on Patrick's breath the previous day. Seeing him carrying an armful of booze infused Truman with fiery rage. How could Shirley serve that hateful, prejudiced piece of shit? Fuck her and her stupid pub. He heeled the steering wheel around and made a blind U-turn, almost colliding with a passing truck. The driver gave him a reproving look and shook his head as he went by.

That broke the madness and it was like waking from a fever dream. If he lost his sobriety, whatever the justification, Black Wattle would have two town drunks instead of one. The thought that he could have anything in common with Patrick the Homophobe so horrified Truman, he planted his foot and his little hatchback roared down the hill.

When he got home he shut the door and locked it, as though that could somehow confine him. Perhaps, on a psychological level, it would. He went into the studio and found his picture dry to the touch. When his hands were no longer jittering, he picked up his paintbrush and started filling in the finer details.

CHAPTER SEVEN

THE *RED HORN* beer sign stood outside the half-concertinaed pub door. Beside it, Shirley had added an old sandwich board painted black. Calligraphed on the board in white chalk was TODAY ONLY RED HORN LAGER $2 A GLASS.

Earlier that morning, she had worn away some shoe leather getting word of the trivia night around town. Now, she stood at the bar with a laptop researching and putting together the Australiana questions. Don had promised he would email his Black Wattle trivia to her by three p.m. so she could combine the two.

"How many questions do you need?" he had asked.

"Ten will do."

Disappointment crossed his face, so she said, "Okay, how about you give me twenty and I pick my ten favorites?"

He smiled. "Do you have a pen and paper?"

"Actually, it would be easier if you could email them to me."

"Oh." The light had gone out of his day again. "I have an email address but I don't really use it. I think I remember my password."

Shirley handed him the pub's business card. "Can you send it to the address on the bottom there?"

He squinted at the card, held it further away. "I'll need my reading glasses."

"Thanks, Don."

"No trouble. I've got plenty of time on my hands. A bunch of Federal Police have commandeered my museum."

"Federal Police?"

"Something about training exercises. I know the place technically belongs to the government, but you should have seen the way this smug A-hole came in and told me to pack my things and get out. I felt like that family in *The Castle*. You remember that movie?"

"Of course."

"Thought you might be too young."

"No, you didn't. But I'll take the compliment."

Don laughed. "Okay, Shirl, you'll have the questions by two o'clock. Maybe two-thirty. I was a hunt-and-peck typist even before this." He waggled his atrophied arm.

"I really appreciate your help."

"No worries. I'll see you tonight, eh?"

"First schooner's on the house."

"Nah, I'm still on the wagon. Won't knock back a Coke, though."

"I'll even put a slice of lemon in it."

"Blegh. No thanks. Ice'll do."

With that, he tipped her a wink and sauntered out into the sunshine. He would have been a charismatic man in his prime, Shirley thought, every bit the self-possessed country copper. She hadn't known Don before the accident, only the withered and retiring man who'd haunted the corner of the pub like a restive spirit while everyone else caroused and traded raucous stories with each other and the friendlier tourists. Numbers thinned after the fires and, rather than a ghost, he had become more like a tiger caught in a trap, one gradually exposed as loggers cleared its habitat. When Don stopped taking money from his pocket and putting it in hers, it gladdened her heart—notwithstanding she could ill-afford it amid the precipitous drop in custom.

Name the last female Australian tennis player to win Wimbledon. For a bonus point, name the year.

An easy one to start, get everyone in the mood. Inspired by her conversation with Don she put in one about *The Castle*, then consulted a search engine for a geography question that might challenge the audience. She was double-checking which year Cyclone Tracy had hit Darwin, when a couple in their early twenties came into the pub. He wore a moustache which, given November was still a couple of months away, couldn't be ironic or a fundraising effort. No matter how many times stand-alone moustaches tried to make a comeback they always reminded Shirley of childhood, her dad's friends standing around the backyard with beers in their hands or splashing through shore breakers wearing a pair of Speedos. The young man's girlfriend wore the regrettable female equivalent which also refused to die:

high-waisted jeans. But whatever her old-lady opinion of their fashion sense, they were all smiles and brightened the pub. Shirley remembered the feeling well—the first road trip with a significant other. Playing adult while laboring under few real adult responsibilities.

"We saw the sign for two-dollar schooners and we had to stop," the young man said.

"*You* had to stop," the girl said, smiling at him. "I hate beer."

"Ladies first," Shirley said. "What can I get you?"

"I'll just have ice water, thanks. We've still got a bit of a drive ahead of us."

"Where are you headed?"

"We're on our way to see my friend out in Griffith. She's going to uni there."

"After that. . ." The boy grinned and shrugged. "Who knows? Actually, I've always wanted to see the Deniliquin Ute Muster. When's that on?"

Shirley smiled across the top of the beer tap. "I'm afraid you're eight months late. Or four months early."

The young couple took their drinks to a table by the door—the fresh breeze softened the warm day to pleasant—and hunched over a smartphone map while discussing in animated tones where they would proceed after their stay in Griffith. When they'd finished their drinks, they got up and waved to Shirley on the way out.

"How was the Red Horn?" she asked.

"For two bucks it could have tasted like dishwater and I'd still be happy," the boy said. "But it was actually really good. I'll have to hunt up a case at Dan Murphy's."

"The brewery's just up the road in Cowra."

The young man grinned. "We might have to make a detour."

"Don't even think about it." His girlfriend pushed him in the back playfully. "Come on let's go. We've still got a big drive ahead of us."

"Have a safe trip," Shirley said.

They got in their car and continued west along Goldfields Road. Seeing them go made Shirley a little sad, as though watching her own youth depart a second time. She and Richard had been that couple once, drunk on one another, sharing existence in a constant happy delirium. Some never seemed to lose that bonding high, not even after fifty years of marriage, but for so many couples middle age's mounting troubles and responsibilities acted like a solvent, wearing down seemingly unbreakable bonds until everything fell apart. In her and Richard's case, neither one had noticed the deterioration. The hook holding up their marriage had been rusting away and then one day it just dropped its burden. None of the animus that poisoned so many divorces afflicted theirs. Their separation was more like a funeral.

Emerging from her reverie, Shirley got back to the business of compiling trivia. She had barely woken the laptop from its nap, however, when she heard the far-off squeal of tires and a metallic *thunk*. She went out onto the pavement and peered down the street, shading her eyes against the afternoon sun. In the center of town, about five hundred meters away, the kids' car had veered onto the median strip and collided with the small war memorial obelisk that grew up from a bed of brightly colored geraniums. The obelisk now stood at an angle, inclining its head in a gentlemanly greeting. Federal police were on the scene already; she could see a marked vehicle and several men in uniform swarming around the kids' car, which sat with its front wheels in the flower bed and its nose bent out of shape. She hoped the kids were all right. If the boy was driving, she suspected a breath test would be imminent. Shirley glanced at the beer tap that had RED HORN written on it in wax pencil. Lagers weren't usually strong, not even those from craft breweries. A schooner wasn't even two standard drinks, he would have been under the legal limit. Nowhere near enough to explain him veering into the middle of the road and striking the obelisk.

In any case, police were on the scene and would administer first aid until paramedics or Dr Sneddon arrived. Shirley put the couple out of her mind and returned to her laptop. Once she had compiled a good list of questions she checked her email and found Don's contribution waiting as promised. Over the next hour or so she learned an awful lot about Black Wattle. Much of it the lifelong residents would know, she assumed, but a few facts were so obscure she decided to reconfigure them into multiple choice questions.

When the two lists were combined she added some images to illustrate the trivia sheets and give them color, then printed out two dozen on the ink-jet printer in her office. Assuming four people per team, that meant close to a hundred participants. Probably a pipe dream, but then it had been a pipe dream couple of days. She left the sheets in a pile beneath the bar, then opened the storeroom and poked around on its dark shelves until she found the old microphone and speaker. Another presumption the pub would be filled to its farthest corners, but what the hell.

Her belly was beginning to flutter when Patrick Burnham ambled into the pub. Shirley could see from his bloodshot eyes and careful gait he'd already had a skinful and was attempting to put forth a veneer of sobriety. He could be an obnoxious drunk and she had seen him go full gobshite at local and tourist alike when the mood took him, but he had never directed so much as a stern word at her. Perhaps for that reason, she viewed him with a sympathetic eye, considered him more stray dog than wild animal. Given the hour she suspected the reason for his visit, but he was calm and cordial and she sold him what he wanted, even though it was in violation of her license. One glass of beer and a few bottles of scotch weren't about to lift the Ironstone out of its pecuniary straits, but they felt like a warm-up for the sales sprint ahead.

A local girl, Karen, arrived just after five o'clock. In another life she had tended bar in Sydney, but gave it away when she got married. Now, on busy nights, she helped out at the Ironstone. It had been a long time between shifts and her reinstatement soon began to look premature. Half an hour from the trivia night's scheduled starting time a couple of Sunday regulars were the only ones in the pub. Panic wormed through Shirley's heart. If two-dollar beers and a concerted face-to-face and social media campaign couldn't entice customers to the Ironstone, she figured she might as well deadlock the doors and walk away for good.

But at five-thirty Don rolled in to order his complimentary Coke and others soon followed. Only the reliables at first—Dr Sneddon, Oscar Wainwright and a few other farmers—but then less familiar faces. Talk was all about the crashed car in the middle of town and Shirley wondered if that had pushed up numbers. When the Old Rose closed at three o'clock, the Ironstone subbed in as gossip central.

"One of the occupants fled the scene," said Don, who appeared to be leading the speculative chatter. "I saw her go. Not sure what happened after that because the federal coppers made us disperse. This joint's become a bloody police state all of a sudden."

"You ruled the roost pretty well yourself, Don," said Oscar Wainwright.

"Not like those bastards. Whole lot of no good, if you ask me. Chucking a bloke out of his own museum and all this Secret Squirrel stuff. Something's up."

But a moment later a few federal police turned up, seated themselves at an unoccupied table, and began studying the trivia sheets. One among them visited the bar and ordered a round of lemon, lime and sodas.

"Maybe you can ask them yourself, Don," Oscar said, chuckling.

Before long a snake of customers had formed at the bar, something Shirley hadn't seen in months, and Karen was earning her keep. A smile blossomed onto Shirley's face and she sauntered over to the trestle table she had set up with the microphone and little speaker on it. She settled in, tidied her question sheets, and allowed herself one more look at a full Ironstone. Then she picked up the microphone and her thumb was set to flick the switch to ON when her phone vibrated.

She almost ignored it—came within a filament of doing so, in fact—but then put down the microphone and stood up to fish the phone out of her jeans. Any other name on the screen she might have rejected it, but it was Elle's. Later she would wonder how things might have turned out had she followed her first instinct. She swiped the call to life.

"Hello, Ellie-Bellie. Everything okay?"

Indistinct words tickled her ear, disintegrated into sobs and crackles, became words again. The connection or Elle's voice breaking up. Shirley could barely hear anything over the pub's white roar. She strode into her office and closed the door.

". . .doesn't give a fuck about me!"

"Slow down, sweetheart, slow down," Shirley said. "What's going on? Start from the beginning."

Elle drew in a long watery breath and sniffed. "He was supposed to pick me up from the airport at four o'clock, he said he'd meet me at the gate. I got off the plane and there was no one there. I waited and waited and then at four-fifteen I decided to ring him. I thought maybe he'd got stuck in traffic or had an accident or something. A woman answered the phone."

Tar-pit dread filled Shirley's stomach.

"I said, 'Who's this?' And she said, 'It's Sally.' And I said, 'Is Richard there?' And she said, 'He's in the shower.' He forgot about me, Mum!"

The final sentence broke up into fragments and became a howl. Shirley stood in her office, mind burning, heart blipping, hand squeezing the phone in a rictus grip. The euphoria from sixty seconds ago seemed like a weird childhood dream. She wanted to scream, preferably into Richard's face, until this new sensation exuded from her body. But she was a mother, and mothers didn't get to fall to pieces. Fathers, apparently, could do whatever the hell they wanted, abdicate or neglect responsibility if the opportunity to get laid presented itself, but not mothers. She covered her eyes for a moment to free herself from all other input and try to get her thoughts straight.

"Where are you now, Elle?"

"Sydney Airport."

"Sydney Airport! How?"

"I used the emergency credit card you gave me and flew straight back down here. I was going to catch the train to Goulburn but I missed the last service and now I'm stuck here. I hate him! I don't want anything to do with Dad ever again."

It took Shirley some time to process this information, because the human mind is resistant to change and on some fundamental level and hers still envisioned Elle as five and not fifteen. A little girl too shy to talk to the cashier at Woolworths, let alone locate the ticketing desk in a sprawling airport and buy a return flight to Sydney.

"Why on earth didn't you ring me earlier?"

"Because I knew you would tell me not to come. But I couldn't go to his apartment, Mum. I couldn't even bear to look at him."

"Does he know where you are?"

"I texted him and then I turned off my phone."

And of course Richard hadn't called Shirley to tell her what was going on. Richard and his stupid male pride. He never accepted responsibility for his mistakes, that was one reason she had divorced him. Rage welled up inside her and threatened to spill out, but she stoppered it. Emotion, self-pity, were indulgences she could ill-afford.

"Jesus, Elle. Where are you now?"

"I'm in the food court, near the security gates."

"Okay, stay put. Don't move until I get there."

"Okay, Mum." She began to weep again. "I didn't mean to make you upset. It's just. . ."

"It's all right, sweetheart. Just sit tight, I'll be there as soon as I can."

Shirley ended the call, slipped the phone in her back pocket and returned to the pub's jovial din. The bar line had grown longer still. Perverse, desiccated joy sprinkled across her heart and then blew away in the prevailing winds of dismay. She located Don, took him by the wrist. "Can I borrow you for a second?"

She towed him away from his conversation until proximity and background noise gave them privacy. "Something's come up and I need to get away and deal with it. Can you take over hosting trivia for me?"

"Of course," Don said, putting his good hand on her shoulder. "Nothing too serious, I hope?"

"No, just family dramas. I'll fill you in later. I need to go."

"Sure, go do whatever you need to do. I'll hold the fort. Actually, I'll probably do a better job than you, anyway." He gave her a wink.

"Thanks, Don. You're a lifesaver."

She grabbed her handbag from behind the bar and leaned in so Karen could hear her. "I have to duck out and I probably won't be back before closing time. Are you okay to lock up?"

"Take your time," Karen said, "I could use the money."

Shirley departed in rapid steps with her eyes cast downwards so no one would try to talk or ask where she was off to. Sundown had snap-frozen the air and she wished for a jacket in the short trip between the pub and her car. How long was the drive to Sydney Airport? With good traffic, probably two and a half hours. As she backed out onto Goldfields Road and put the car in drive, she pondered last-minute alternatives. No form of public transport could be guaranteed free of drug addicts or pedophiles or gang rapists. Hell, what was to say a few individuals among the airport staff didn't have a thing for underage girls, especially an attractive one like Elle?

She pressed her foot down, allowing the speedo to creep up over one hundred, even around bends where speed advisory signs suggested seventy-five or eighty. She turned on the radio to kill the silence but didn't listen to a single word or note. Goddamn Richard. They had been divorced nearly eighteen months, and he had every right to see someone else, but not at the expense of Elle's well-being. The thought of her alone and tearful at the ticket desk buying passage back to Sydney because he'd been too busy getting his rocks off to remember his responsibilities, made Shirley's hands constrict around the steering wheel. If Richard had been in the passenger's seat at that moment she would have grabbed his scrotum and twisted it a full three-sixty degrees.

Lightless and almost bereft of cars, Goldfields Road exacerbated Shirley's creeping fatigue and she was glad to hit the highway's harsh glare and weekender traffic. She stopped only once, at a service station, to pick up a can of energy drink. At eight-thirty she rolled into the airport's short-term carpark and came to such an abrupt stop she triggered her car's anti-lock brakes.

The late hour meant lines through the security gates were mercifully short and no one bothered to stop her and run a wand over her or check for explosives residue, so she was through in under a minute and tripping down the stairs to the food court. Elle spotted her and jumped up, dashing forward. They met at the foot of the stairs, Shirley enfolding her daughter in a hug that felt like relief, love, and hanging on for dear life.

"I'm sorry, Mum," Elle muffled into her shoulder.

"No, it's your father who should be sorry. He really fucked up."

Elle pulled back to regard her mother, a smile pushing through the tear-streaked mess. "Did you just drop an F-bomb?"

"If you can get yourself from the Gold Coast to Sydney on your own, I think you can handle an F-bomb from your mother."

They moved back up the stairs together, arms around one another's waists. To have her daughter back, warm and real and unhurt beneath her wing, left Shirley narcotic with happiness. She couldn't remember a day with such extreme highs and lows, not her wedding day, not Elle's birth, not the long morning when she and Richard had discussed whether they should get divorced and what the ins and outs of that might entail. Their separated life would have a whole new dimension now, but she didn't want to think about that. Her daughter was safe, her pub was full, and her ridiculous neglectful ex-husband was a thousand kilometers away.

During the drive back to the Ironstone they talked around what had happened, but neither was in the mood to dive deep on the subject. Instead, Shirley shared the odd serendipity of the Red Horn Brewery leading to her pub buzzing for the first time in months and Elle shared her friends' various dramas and what she was expecting when school went back the following week. They ate dinner in a roadhouse just outside Sydney, which was an adventure in itself. By the time the car's headlights washed across the town sign's fading illustration of a wattle sprig, Shirley had begun to wonder if Richard's fuck-up and Elle's subsequent pilgrimage back to Sydney constituted a blessing in disguise. She and Elle were cocooned in the car, bonding as never before; bonding as adults. Shirley was so ensconced in the feeling she scarcely registered the federal police car haring along Goldfields Road in the opposite direction and gave the Ironstone only a cursory sidelong glance. All its lights were off, the windows shining black pools in its hand-hewn brick face. Good old Karen. If business stayed buoyant, she would look at hiring her back full-time.

Fatigue crashed into Shirley as she pulled up at the cottage and stepped into the night air. Warmth ebbed off the car's bonnet as she passed it, making her feel even sleepier. Elle let out an enormous yawn while Shirley unlocked the front door. The day had taken as much of a toll on her daughter as it had on her—probably more. Shirley remembered fifteen. Teenage life burned with a magnesium-flare intensity that an adult plunging into middle age could barely remember, let alone comprehend. She let Elle take first shower and then stood at the doorway to her bedroom, hand resting on the jamb, which was as far as she indulged the urge to tuck her in and kiss her goodnight. Elle might be an angel as fifteen-year-olds went, but even she had her limits. Biology made parents embarrassing and kiddie things such as goodnight kisses anathema.

"Sleep tight, Ellie-Bellie."

"Sleep tight, Shirley-Whirley."

Shirley-Whirley went to bed, but could not honor her daughter's request for a long time. Thoughts trotted through her head, around and around, horses on a wooden track. What refused to allow her heart rate to slow above all else, though, was the mobile phone on her bedside table. She seethed at it, willing it to flash into life with at least a text, but it remained blank until after midnight, when her exhaustion reached critical mass and she nodded off with a scowl etched across her face.

CHAPTER EIGHT

DON WATCHED SHIRLEY go behind the bar to fetch her handbag, twitter something in Karen's ear, then make a surreptitious exit. Nobody else appeared to notice; they were scribbling team names on their trivia answer sheets, chatting to one another, lining up for drinks, scuttling out to the smoking areas for a quick cigarette before the questions got underway. Questions that were now his responsibility.

He had only made an appearance at the Ironstone for Shirley's sake. A stupid, school-boyish reason to do something, but when combined with the opportunity to showboat his historical knowledge he had found it irresistible. Now he stood there, alone at the microphone table, not just jonesing for a beer but trembling within at the prospect. Under the influence of a few beers (and at two bucks a schooner, it could easily be a few fews) his withered arm no longer seemed so withered, his authority in town no longer diminished down to a fleck, his every shouting inadequacy muffled to a whisper.

When tempted in the past he had sought respite in his museum, even in the dead of night, but the federal police had stolen that solace. His home was dry, he could hole up there until the pub closed, but then he would be leaving Shirley in the lurch and he would rather lose himself on a three-day bender than do that. His eyes darted around the room, desperate, searching. So many familiar faces. The redeeming quality of living in a country town where economic life could sometimes be an unbroken series of hardships. Now, however, that same quality had a cutting edge. Confessing his predicament, admitting that foolish pride had entangled him in it, would be hard enough with a stranger's ear. To ask for help from those who had once looked up to him, respected him. . .it made him quail, and Don was not a man who quailed often.

But he had no option. He had suspended himself above the horns of a dilemma and now he had to choose which horn to sit on.

His eye fell upon Dr Sneddon, seated towards the back with his wife and another older couple from town. Just sipping the head off a beer. Charles Sneddon (always Charles, never Charlie or, God forbid, Chas), had been Don's physician since he was a kid. Dr Sneddon had seen him cry during an immunization needle, seen him naked, felt his testicles (during a short but terrifying examination that had identified a fatty lump rather than a cancerous tumor), recommended a nursing home for his mother when dementia set in and Don The One-Armed Bandit couldn't care for her. He'd checked his pride and dignity at Dr Sneddon's office door long ago. Also, if he asked the doctor for assistance he could frame it as a medical issue and at least be assured confidentiality.

That got his feet moving and weaving through the tables. Three sets of female eyes made soundless enquiries when Don leaned down so he could be mouth-to-ear with the doctor.

"Charles, I wonder if I could borrow you for a moment?"

"Of course, Don. Excuse me ladies, secret men's business."

The women tittered and Don could feel their curious gazes trailing him. Don guided the doctor into the pub's office, just as Shirley had guided him a minute or two earlier.

"What can I do for you, Don?"

"I've got myself in a bit of a pickle," he said. "Shirley's been called out to a family emergency and she asked me to take over trivia. I told her I'd be happy to do it but I'm having a bit of trouble with. . .well, it's been a difficult couple of days and I'm struggling with my sobriety."

"Say no more," Dr Sneddon said, raising a hand. "I understand. How can I help?"

"I was kinda hoping you'd MC the trivia for me. You know, just read out the questions and mark off answer sheets after each round." He gave Dr Sneddon a weak smile. "Make sure no one is googling the answer."

The doctor returned his smile. "Mobile phones have all but ruined pub trivia. Leave it with me, Don, I'll sort something out."

"Are you sure it's okay, Doc? I know it's a lot to ask when you were supposed to be having a relaxing Sunday evening—"

"No trouble at all," Dr Sneddon said, raising his hand again. "In fact, you're doing me the favor." His eyes darted furtively towards the door. "My wife's an interesting and intelligent woman, but her choice of companions leaves a lot to be desired. Now I'll have a valid reason to excuse myself and I won't have to drink to numb the tedium."

The doctor's dry humor surprised a laugh out of him. "Thanks, Charles. I really owe you one."

"Don't beat yourself up, Don. Romantic feelings are a lot like alcohol, really. They impair judgment."

Don blushed. "Is it that obvious?"

"Fifteen or fifty, it doesn't make much difference. We're all slaves to our biochemistry, your humble physician included. Go home, Don. I'll try to do you both proud."

Don followed doctor's orders, only giving his museum one (maybe two) miffed glances as he drove past. Driving, at least, was one thing not denied the single-handed. Police tape now lined the door frame and in the glass, a sign read AUTHORISED ENTRY ONLY. Dim interior illumination gave the station an otherworldly glow, perhaps a lamp or the safety lights, the self-same ones Don Winslow had installed out of his own pocket. Exercises complete for the day, whatever they entailed. Top secret exercises so goddamned important to national security that all hands were now out for a pub meal or in the museum's back room playing cards or asleep on portable cots. Don decided he would make it his mission to find out what was going on in there, one way or another. He knew people who knew people who could find out things. But that would be tomorrow's tussle, or more likely next week's—he wasn't so delusional as to believe an ex-country copper could get the lowdown on a federal operation while it was still in progress. Tonight he just wanted to get settled back in his booze-free home and avoid all sources of embarrassment and aggro.

Inside, the front door locked, he microwaved himself a cup of warm milk—a home remedy he hadn't bothered with since the sleepless nights after Nettie passed on, then slid between the sheets and tried to let the day's humiliations drain away. He inventoried the museum in his head, piece by piece, section by section, something he had taken to doing if sleep proved elusive. He hadn't even got through the early gold panning equipment before slumber crept up and mugged him with large and cushiony hands.

Don woke to the lonesome sound of a currawong singing its woes to the morning. Cold light filled the gaps around the bedroom blinds. Don first thought someone must be shining low-wattage lamps at his house, perhaps the federal coppers on one of their infernal training exercises. But then the sleep haze lifted and his sense of disorientation evaporated. Home alone without his wife (bad), but also without the sour taste and mental horrors indicating a hangover (good). All his faculties intact and functioning, he decided to get up and charge at the day as only a sober man could. He dressed in jeans, a T-shirt and a fleecy jacket (a daily operation at which he had become faster and more skilled to the point where it almost pleased him), drank a glass of water at the kitchen sink, and headed out for his morning walk. If he couldn't be in his museum, he could at least find it some additional inventory.

The southern fence line along Wainwright's farm had yielded a couple of good finds and the area around the Goldmine Motel had once been the grounds of a second hotel, so it was another hot spot. But both sites would necessitate Don walking past his museum and he wasn't in the mood to clap eyes on it. It was too early to feel dispossessed. So instead he set out for the town's western end, which was sparsely populated and allowed a man to ramble back and forth without interruption or diversion. Occasionally, Don brought along a small metal detector but, on some sub-level of his mind, he suspected that morning's walk was more about the walk itself than historical treasure. So, he left the detector in the garage and set out.

A flock of corellas joined the morning chorus, their high-pitched shrieks cutting the quiet morning to ribbons. Don watched them loop around in the early grey sky, pursuing one another in an erratic spiral before coming to land as one in a field on the far side of Goldfields Road.

Don walked on the thin strip of dirt and crumbled bitumen between the road and the culvert, running his hand along the paspalum's drought-crisp seed buds. The council apparently considered a footpath beyond the town center an unjustifiable expense. Don supposed they had a point—not much foot traffic made it out that far. Come to think of it, he had seen little vehicular traffic, either. Had a single car or truck rushed past and whiffled his hair? Don didn't believe so. Even at such an early hour, a trucker would usually be finishing an overnight run from somewhere to Sydney.

A sliver of sun broke the horizon and bled truer colors into the world. Ten minutes earlier, Don mused, his eye might not have picked out the different browns, but with the light over his shoulder, he spotted something small and circle-shaped on the ground ahead. He trotted forward and dropped to one knee, swiping away dust and stone chips.

Pressed and impacted over an untold period, the coin was almost one with the earth. Don tried to get his fingernail underneath it, but he might as well have tried to prize up a floor tile.

He cast about for a stick or some other makeshift digging tool and eventually came upon discarded trim from an old car window. He went back to the coin and scraped out the dirt around its circumference until he could wiggle the window trim in underneath and pop it out.

He spat on the coin and rubbed it with his thumb to properly make out the stamping. A kangaroo and an emu either side of a coat of arms identified it as a threepence. Dated 1925. Not worth much, maybe ten or fifteen bucks to a collector needing that specific year to complete a set, but for Don it possessed a different value. It conjured up stories in his mind: a man trudging back from the mines and the coin slipping from a hole in his pocket, or a schoolboy (back when Black Wattle still had a school) losing it on his way to the general store to buy gumdrops, a rare treat.

Don was postulating more pleasing histories when he topped a long rise and found the road out of town blocked with black and yellow barricades. Federal officers armed with semi-automatic rifles guarded each end. Nearby was one of the demountable buildings Don had seen trucked into Black Wattle the previous day. It explained it all—the absence of morning traffic, the prominence of bird chatter, the uncommon quiet.

One of the feds lifted his rifle and pointed it at Don.

"Are you injured, sir?"

Don raised his hands—or hand—in a placatory gesture. "I'm just out for my morning walk. What—"

"Sir," the officer said, the syllable rising, "are you injured?"

"No. Why the hell would I be injured?"

"That's far enough. Come any closer and I will open fire."

Don halted. "I'm not even armed, you lunatic! What's this all about?"

"Your arm. What happened to it?"

"I injured it in a car crash, not that it's any of your business."

The officer's eyes narrowed as he continued to study Don's arm. "This is an emergency situation. No residents in or out of Black Wattle without authorization."

"No one in or out? Why the hell weren't we notified? Residents are supposed to be given at least—"

"Sir, return to your home immediately and await further instructions from police. That's an order."

"An order? I don't know who the hell you think you are, mate, but I'm a retired police sergeant and I—"

The officer discharged his firearm, its flat bark obscene in the country quiet. Bitumen exploded before Don's feet and pelters stung his shins. He hopped back reflexively.

"Black Wattle is now a restricted area and under quarantine. You are in immediate danger, sergeant. Return to your home. Don't make me ask you again."

"You sound like a bad Hollywood movie," Don spat, but he backed away. Once the fed lowered his weapon Don turned around and began to walk apace, fingering the coin in his pocket at he went. Yes, he would return to his home as instructed, but someone's ass was going up in a sling for this. Firing a warning shot at his feet. Don shook his head in disgust. Had he been wearing shorts, as he often did on a summer morning, the exploding road grit would have drawn blood on his shins, maybe even seriously injured him. Whoever was responsible for this abuse of power would have their leash yanked, *hard*. Don would see to that.

Lost in his thoughts, Don didn't notice Marla Smith until she was halfway down the path that connected her front door and front gate. He turned to bid her good morning and only then registered that she wasn't ambling along her ornamental garden path but running in a slightly bow-legged arthritic gait, her dressing gown billowing out behind like a sail, exposed arms pumping up and down. Her mouth hung wide open, as if in permanent surprise. Her eyes stared straight ahead in mechanical fashion, a dummy's eyes, seeing all and seeing nothing. Don stopped dead for the second time that morning, his nerves suddenly singing in a strange baritone. As Marla drew closer he saw scratches down one side of her face, temple to chin, deep enough to leave ragged flaps of skin hanging and expose the raw-steak flesh below.

Before Don could find his voice, one of Marla's slippers skidded off her foot and she stumbled. This released some sort of cerebral hammerlock and she screamed, a rending noise that sounded like it should be emerging from a power tool, not the mouth of a sixty-something lady. She completed the remaining distance at a hobble and crashed into Don. She was heavier than he expected and he almost toppled over backwards—likely would have if his legs and back weren't already limber from his morning walk. Her fingers dug into his shoulders and she pulled herself close until they were almost nose-to-nose. Her eyes seemed to be swelling with fluid.

"OH CHRIST, IT BURNS!"

Her whole body shuddered, as if it were a blender puréeing a carrot. Then she pushed him away violently and fell to her hands and knees. She arched her back and lowered it, again and again, creating shapes no human spine should naturally create, before she unleashed a burp so savage it reverberated the air around Don's legs. A rotten-egg smell fouled his nostrils and Don clapped a hand over his mouth, backing up a step. Marla's fingernails clawed at the footpath and one broke off with an audible snap, blood oozing from the quick. Then her whole being heaved and her bodily contents ejected onto the concrete in a projectile splash.

Don had seen plenty in his time as a copper, including a few fatal crashes, but this was so far beyond even his worst imaginings that he cried out and shrank away. Amid bubbling fluid the color of dried menses, he could make out semi-digested bran flakes and what appeared to be decomposed bodily organs—the translucent sack of Marla's stomach, twists of small intestine—plus logs of shit that had come out of her the wrong way. Don wanted to step forward, come to her aid in some way, but the sight (and smell) of her viscera splattered all over the pavement clenched up his own, while some primal self-preservation instinct froze his limbs.

All at once Marla sat back on her haunches, tilted her head to the sky, and uttered another scream that needled Don's eardrums before dropping in register and becoming a grizzly bear's guttural growl. All the teeth fell out of her mouth at once and rattled on the path; they reminded Don of the knucklebones he and his friends played with as kids. A new set, decay-yellow and sharp as the points on a bamboo fence, sprouted from her gums. Blood drizzled from her mouth and formed a dark-brown puddle in her lap. Her limbs began to swell and her skin flushed a blotchy red. Thick black nails speared from her fingertips.

She lowered her chin slowly, as if some divine orchestra only she could hear had finished its overture, and opened her eyes. Shot through with red and yellow, mucous-and-blood marbles, they looked at once hungry and furious.

Wet lips slithered back. Teeth dripped with viscous saliva.

Don broke into the first full sprint of his middle-aged life. Something in his knee popped—he felt it go, like a corn kernel on a hotplate—and unleashed a thunder-strike of agony, but rather than stop he used the pain to push on harder. His shoes barely touched the footpath with each stride, his widowed arm working like a piston and the dead one flopping around beside him. Breath whistled in and out and burned his airway. He strained his ears for sounds of pursuit, not daring to look over his shoulder when he was in a footrace with...

With what?

Lactic acid coursed caustic channels through his thighs as he summited the hill. Rather than coast along the flat, he tried to find another gear, drive forward harder, but when a man was in his fifties, Don discovered, gears were in short supply. With every step he expected to feel those nails dig into his shoulders, for the thing to bring him down the way a lion brings down an antelope. When he took the corner into his street he allowed himself a minnow of hope. He vocalized every breath, *huh-huh-huh*, as though reciting a chant. Drawing up to his driveway, he reached in his pocket and yanked out his keys. A big bunch, and he wished in that frenetic moment he separated them into house, car and museum keys. He leapt onto the porch and crashed back-first into the front door, ready to lash out with a kick or use the keys as a makeshift mace, but he could see nothing lurching up Petunia Parade.

His fingers found the right key and slipped it into the deadlock. Never had a metallic click sounded so good. He pushed inside, slammed the door and engaged both locks, then raced to every window and the back door to ensure they were secure before pulling down the blinds.

He collapsed onto the sofa still sucking in the big ones, his whole chest cavity scorched and loose, his limbs quaking.

When he had calmed enough to permit rational thought, he drew himself a fresh glass of water from the kitchen tap and leaned against the sink to drink it. His mind replayed flashes of Marla down on all fours, spraying innards and teeth all over the footpath. What had happened to her, he couldn't begin to guess. Like nothing he'd ever seen on the job. But Don felt certain those federal fuckers knew. He scoffed out loud. Tactical exercises. Something wasn't right, he had sensed it from the first. Don knew police. Federal police were a different breed of cat, true enough, but at the basement level they were still police.

He shook his head, finished off the water, and went to his bedroom. In the back of the built-in wardrobe was a small safe. He punched in the electronic code (since Nettie's passing it had been her birth date) and opened the little blue door. Inside lay a service revolver. Not a Glock, but the old Smith & Wesson they'd had when he first joined the force, back in the days of dinosaurs. Beside it was a single box of ammunition. Don had purchased the firearm from the NSW Government and registered it, more a commemorative act than anything, a nostalgic link to a professional life that misfortune had stolen away. But he had never quite let go of his self-image as Black Wattle's protector, either—however delusional that image might be.

Whatever his motivations, he was glad to have the revolver now. It took some time to remove the .38 caliber bullets from their box and slot them one-handed into the chambers, but once he had, the gun's loaded weight reassured him.

Don leaned back against the foot of his bed and tried to decide what to do next.

CHAPTER NINE

A FRENZIED EVENING of painting and coffee left Truman wired and exhausted. He collapsed into bed a short while after midnight, spent, yet unsure what all his creative output had wrought.

Sleep arrived quickly despite the caffeine in his system, but it was a thin sleep. He woke late the next morning, around nine, feeling unrested and, ironically, kind of hungover. Dry unfocused eyes, scratchy brain, general sense of malaise. He decided he needed a hair of the coffee dog and made a cup along with some buttered toast. Eating it in the kitchen, he let his mind wander over the previous day, the weird ups and downs, his close shave with the booze.

Once he'd demolished the toast to crumbs and drunk half the coffee, he did feel a little better. He got up and drifted into the studio, wincing at what a new day's harsh light might reveal about last night's efforts.

But looking upon his pictures after ten hours' separation, he realized his pessimism had been groundless. The valley landscape would never win an award, but his second painting—a brooding abstract of blues and blacks and greys—was aggressively out of character for Truman and he loved it. All his darker emotions spilled out onto a canvas, fighting with one another, creating a cold and black maelstrom. Perhaps 'Maelstrom' would be a good title.

He regarded the other paintings arranged around the studio and decided it was time to officially declare his art studio an art gallery as well, and open it to the public. Fine art critics were, he assumed, quite the minority in Black Wattle and the only thing most punters knew about art was what they liked. With nothing for sale, though, he would be guaranteed no sales.

Truman paced around the studio—gallery—evaluating each

artwork and arriving at a list price for it. Low enough not to scare off customers, not so low as to appear desperate. Shirley's work ethic had inspired him, even if it had almost pushed him off the wagon. Once he had settled on numbers, he would drive into town and ask Marla if he could post an advert in her window, tell her he was happy to reciprocate with a stack of flyers for the coffee shop. (Recommending the Old Rose's coffee would ping his conscience, but when had altruism ever made a mark in the business world?)

He pulled some clothes from his suitcase, silently promising to unpack properly as soon as time permitted, and got dressed. The morning sky held a deep winter azure; once spring really got going it would boil down to a washing powder blue at midday. As he climbed into his hatchback, it occurred to Truman he had stopped noticing such things; the booze and coke had apparently scoured it from his psyche. No wonder that, on the rare occasion he had tried to paint, everything had come out flat and lifeless, dead at the end of his brush. What was art without color perception?

Continuing to ponder this (and appalled to find the mere academic consideration of cocaine caused a subtle itch for more) he parked right outside the Old Rose, thinking nothing of it until he pushed through the café doors and into untrammeled silence. He glanced left and right, taking in all the empty seats and booths, the unattended espresso machine, the cash register's blank grey LCD screen. The whole scenario threw him for such a loop he turned around to check the opening-hours sign hanging from a suction cup on the door. MONDAY 6AM TO 3PM.

Of course the café is open, you idiot, otherwise it would be locked.

"Hello?"

He moved further inside, wondering if Marla and the café regulars had moved to a rear courtyard so they could bask in the morning sun. Garrulous mobs were not synonymous with quiet, however, and inclining his head towards the kitchen area, he detected only funeral-parlor silence. Not so much as the *chop-chop-chop* of a knife reducing chives to garnish or a whisk frothing eggs for a hot pan. His ears ached for input.

Then, at last, something: the low hiss of steam escaping from a small valve. He turned his head, bird-like, trying to ascertain the sound's origin. The hiss faded out, replaced a second later with a slow bubbling, as though someone were sucking air through a bong.

Behind him. The sound was behind him.

He turned slowly, a high-pitched whine filling his ears. Something had arisen from behind the counter and now observed him with fervent blood-egg eyes. Either side of its sprained-ankle face were the ratty remnants of curly hair which, along with the situation, permitted Truman to identify the young girl who had made his cup of brown milk the previous morning. Sadie. His mind tried to find a rational explanation, riffled desperately through a series of them, everything from an elaborate Halloween costume to a practical joke employing high-end Hollywood special effects. But his nerve-endings would brook no reason. His eyes darted towards the doors, optic muscles so tense it hurt. The thing's lips fluttered and pulled away to expose rows of pointed cannibal teeth, its pinkened skin flushing almost crimson where it bunched.

Truman started for the door and the thing leapt onto the counter with an acrobat's agility, its hooked black nails clicking on the polished timber surface. Truman backpedaled, almost tumbled over, then reclaimed his balance and retreated until his thighs bumped into one of the café chairs. He dragged it around and lifted it just before the thing sprang at him. It crashed into the chair legs and knocked him onto his back, thumping the air from his lungs. Groaning, he tried to push away with his legs, his shoes slipping and scuffing on the polished floor. The thing reached for him, nails seeking to rend the flesh from his face, but the chair's wide frame kept it at bay. It hissed, droplets of sulfur-smelling fluid spattering across Truman's nose and chin. It had heat to it, like water left in the sun on a hot day, and every instinct demanded he wipe it off. But he dared not release his grip on the chair or relax his arms, so he squeezed his lips shut against the fluid and snorted out.

It lunged again, razor claws scoring the chair. Had it been an open-backed chair, Truman thought, his guts would probably be spilling onto the floor beside him. How could something so agile be so damned heavy? So strong? If he lay prone much longer his luck would run out, chair shield or no. He drew his feet up to his backside and thrust his legs out, like a frog attempting backstroke. The motion wrenched the chair out from under the creature and put a little distance between him and it, enough so he could scramble to his feet and get the chair upright. When it sprang at him again he went on the offensive, charging forward to meet it in mid-air. The impact jolted his arms and the chair dug into his ribs, but it also knocked the thing onto its back. Its limbs tangled in the frame long enough to let Truman scoot across the café and through the kitchen's swinging door. He dragged a trolley table over and then peered through the door's strip window. The thing cast off the chair with such force it shattered to kindling. Then it hopped to its feet and took two gazelle-like strides before crashing through the kitchen door. The concussion knocked the trolley table onto its side but also stopped the creature dead. It dropped to the floor, its relentless gaze broken for a moment.

Truman stole this half-second's grace to take stock of his surroundings. Kitchen implements hung from a row of hooks above a large island bench—cast-iron pots and pans, spatulas, spoons, knives, meat cleavers. He reached for the largest knife and wiggled it off the hook as the swinging door squeaked open again. The creature entered, nails clicking on the tiled floor, single-minded resolve back in its eyes. Another serpentine hiss escalated into a screech so scathing it fluttered his eardrums. He danced sideways and put the island bench between him and the creature. It pursued him, but in such tight quarters, could gain no advantage. They circled back and forth, like clock-hands gone haywire, then the thing stopped and locked eyes with Truman. Never had he imagined two eyes could be so dispassionate yet burn with such hatred. He could almost feel its rage spewing forth, like superheated air blasting from a crematorium oven. It mewled in frustration, then dropped into a crouch and leapt onto the bench, its balding dome clanging against the overhead light's steel hood. It made a wild lion's paw swipe at his throat and Truman swayed back and away, colliding with some open shelving that dug into his back. Glass jars and bags of flour rained down on his head, one catching him across the bridge of the nose. Blood spilled and tears filled his eyes, turning everything into a blurred kaleidoscope. He heard the scratch of nails on the bench and knew the thing had launched itself at him. Truman jabbed out the kitchen knife in a fencing foil thrust. He felt it pierce something and make a rotten-fruit squelch, then hot blood—hotter than bath water—spilled down his forearm. The thing's dead weight pressed against him and he shoved it away with a moan that was as much revulsion as fear. Its body slapped against the floor tiles and Truman blinked his eyes furiously to try to clear them, backing away as he did.

The creature now lay supine on the kitchen floor, knife handle between its teeth, blood the color of treacle spouting from its mouth and splashing the tiles, flooding the grout. Its billiard-ball eyes gazed at the ceiling. But as Truman leaned forward for a closer look, the eyes rolled sideways in their sockets and locked onto his face. Then the thing sat up, making a choked burbling that was presumably supposed to be a screech. Its fingers closed around the knife and yanked. Gouts of blood jetted out and splashed into its waxen lap. The noise alone triggered Truman's gag reflex and, as the creature's hand closed around the knife again, he turned away, not needing or wanting to see what happened when it wrenched the blade all the way out. Instead, he turned to the row of kitchen implements and groped for the meat cleaver. Once he had it, he turned back, brandishing the cleaver above his head. The creature, now upright, tossed away the knife. The blade hit the wall, leaving a brown streak, and jangled onto the floor.

"How are you still alive?" Truman whispered, wanting to hear the rational sound of his own voice. "Just fucking die."

The thing's eyes studied the cleaver (which Truman now waggled nervously), then dropped to fix on his neck. The pupils dilated into black marbles, as though the thing could already taste Truman's blood on its serpentine tongue. When it dropped into a crouch again Truman held fast, defying the hysterical flight response surging through his limbs. He'd suffered weekly tennis lessons for three months before a screaming match with his father put an end to them and, for some absurd reason, his coach's inexorable mantra returned to him now: *Eye on the ball, eye on the ball, eye on the ball.*

The thing made its spider-monkey leap and time seemed to both slow down and speed up, as if the very qualities of existence had become rubbery. Truman could see its nails, ebony piano keys honed to a cut-throat point, its bloated and glistening skin, the tyrannosaur savagery of its talons curled and ready to dig into his thighs. Its eyes were narrowed to a murderous precision. A wasp about to descend on its blundering victim.

Eye on the ball, Truman.

The cleaver, a huge meat axe designed for separating beef carcasses, came down in a diagonal arc and chopped into the creature's neck. Its arms wrapped around Truman's shoulder and back in a loathsome hug, but they were limp, crash-test-dummy arms. Its weight knocked Truman sprawling, however, and a bucketful of that spa-hot blood gushed onto his neck and chest. He uttered scream after vacuous scream, pushing at it, kicking it off, certain those claws would dig into his side or lash out and scratch his face. At last, he was out from under the creature and he hopped to his feet, moaning at the sopping and sticky feel of his blood-soaked shirt.

The meat axe had severed through gristle and tendons and vertebrae and nearly come out the other side. The creature and its head were now almost separate entities, only a single flap of gory pink skin connecting the two. Seeing this, Truman went to grab the cleaver, then thought better of getting into the creature's reach again. He spun around to the implement rack and snatched up the meat axe's smaller brother. With cleaver in hand, he made a lap of the island bench so he could approach the creature's spasming body from the head-end and evade the hands, which were still somehow grasping and clenching at the air. So much blood had spilled from its nigh-headless body that Truman's shoes sploshed as he came within range. The thing's eyes rolled up into its skull until they showed nothing but a nauseous yellow. Truman brought down the cleaver, its blade ringing out against the tiles. His aim was a little off this time, but enough of the sharp edge caught its intended target. The head rolled away such that the creature could only stare at the wall. Decapitated or not, the body's arms reached up to grab Truman's ankle and he hopped back with a yelp, the nails swiping across the bottom of his shoe.

He continued to back away, breath coming and going in little strips, the rotten-egg stench of the creature's blood permeating his nostrils and clogging his skin. He wished he could find a zipper and peel off the entire sullied layer of himself. His knees wanted to give way and dump him in a loose pile beneath the shelves.

It might have happened, too, if the thing's body hadn't rolled over and got onto its hands and knees.

"No," Truman said. The word had a solemn, prayerful cadence, like *shalom* or *amen*. "No, this can't be happening. I cut your head off you *fucking thing!*"

The body cared nothing for what could or could not be. It rose up to a kneeling position, hands groping alternately in what appeared to be a perverse substitute for sight. The thing that had once been Sadie the barista got itself upright, its neck's tattered remains sagging like an unspeakable hibiscus blossom wilted after an early autumn rain.

Overcome with a surge of caveman rage, Truman roared and dashed forward, plucking up the large cleaver as he went and throwing his entire weight behind a sidearm swipe at the creature's knee. The blade sliced through cleanly and came out the other side, Truman's momentum throwing him forward and his shoe skidding out on some of the spilled blood. He fell onto his backside, jarring his tailbone and sending a sizzle of agony through his pelvis.

Groaning, he rolled onto his side so he could at least get the creature back in his field of view. It stood there, one-legged, wobbling back and forth, arms extended in plane wings for balance. Truman could just make out the profile of the thing's severed head and its jaw appeared to be working, as though uttering silent curses. Then the body over-corrected and tipped backwards, collapsing full-length onto the tiles. Any blood that had not already escaped now came out in spillway gush. Truman's stomach finally relented and gave up its breakfast, the resulting pool touching the creature's blood in vile confluence.

The body's arms began to wave like cockroach antennae and this time Truman got on the front foot. He splashed through the blood and hacked at the thing's arms and legs until his shoulder ached and his wrist throbbed and strands of sweat-slick hair hung in his eyes. Once he had reduced the body to a torso and an assortment of appendages, he stumbled backwards and collapsed against the island bench. The thing's legs still kicked but could only go around in circles, while the hands clenched open and closed in impotent rage. Even if they figured out how to sit up on their fingers and scuttle across the floor, they were trailing an entire limb and Truman felt certain he could outrun them. He let the meat cleaver fall from his clawed hand. It clanged on the tiles.

Just what had he hacked to pieces? Such academic questions had been lost in the red blizzard of survival. But as he watched the thing squirm around on itself, like a worm cut in half by a garden spade, he found he had an urgent need to know. Behind this was an uncomfortable notion he had imagined the whole thing, that his cold-turkey withdrawal from snake venom and the devil's dandruff had brought on acute hallucinations. But the more he allowed that idea the less probable it seemed. The previous day, his mind had been waking up rather than turning on itself and going septic. Why, if he were on the cusp of such a severe psychological collapse, would he have been in such a positive frame of mind ten seconds earlier? That just wasn't how withdrawal symptoms and mental illness worked. While his breathing and heartbeat remained a fraction quicker than usual, he felt clear-eyed and in control.

Operating on that assumption, then, he could further assume his experience had been real and would also be evident to a passerby. That meant something extraordinary, something outside even his imagination's fervid and generous boundaries, had entered humdrum reality. But what? What the hell could it be?

Perhaps someone wiser, with a full fount of local knowledge, might posit an explanation. Whatever the case, Truman felt an overbearing need to *share*—to offload at least some of the burden of knowing and not knowing. Although Marla had been aloof toward him she made the obvious choice, since it was her employee now writhing around on the floor in half a dozen pieces.

With a nod to himself, Truman set off across the kitchen but then paused as the swinging door gave way before his hand. The thing he had killed—well, disabled—might not be the only one lurking about in Black Wattle. Hell, it might not be the only one in the Gold Rose.

He went back to collect the carving knife and meat cleaver from their resting places, blanching at the feel of their sticky-blood coating. Not only sticky—it remained warm, too, and Truman realized the blood soaked into his shirt had not cooled or dried, either. He put the implements on the bench, gave the break-dancing legs and silently-ranting head a quick glance, then peeled off his maddening shirt and cast it away like a fisherman's net. It landed on the tiles with a wet slap.

Collecting the knife and cleaver again, he moved through the swinging door. Cool air passed across his bare chest and, in the café proper, the tacky blood on the bottom of his shoes stuck to the floorboards. His eyes roved for signs of another one, another *thing* crouched behind the counter or curled up and biding its time in the shadowed corner booth, but nothing stirred. The only sound was the infernal clicking of nails on the far side of the swinging door as the dead-alive hands refused to accept defeat.

For a while Truman stood at the café's front window, eyes darting first one way and then the other. His immediate path looked clear. . .but perhaps too clear. Where were the country folk running errands? The cars beetling back and forth along the street, the courier vans angled in or double-parked to make deliveries?

Just after ten on a Monday morning and not even one truck passing through?

Truman watched a little longer, then opened the café door and stepped onto the footpath. With a weapon dangling from each hand, he looked like a military robot from a bush mechanic's workshop. Nothing accosted or assailed him. A crow sitting on the lip of a rubbish bin cawed its disapproval at his emergence and took flight.

Marla. If Marla wasn't at her coffee shop, where would she be? He had no idea where she lived. Maybe someone else in town would know. His only two other acquaintances were Pam and Shirley. The pub wouldn't be open yet, and besides, he didn't feel comfortable setting foot near it after nearly falling off the wagon. So Pam it would have to be.

Knowing he looked like a serial killer but unwilling to return home first to get clean, Truman set off up the street, eyes squinted against the low-hanging morning sun and ears twitching for input in the unnatural quiet.

CHAPTER TEN

THE CARTILAGE IN Shirley's ear hurt and she lifted the mobile phone away to permit blood flow again. Richard's voice became the tinny murmuring of a talking toy. That didn't make it any less infuriating. Her phone cover creaked and she made a concerted effort to relax her hand, permit her knuckles to return to their regular color.

"She had no idea where you were, Richard!" Shirley said. "She's fifteen for fuh—For crying out loud."

"She did know where I was!" he retorted. "I sent her a text message to say I'd be running late. I would have called her, but she was still in the air and—"

"How does that make it okay?" Shirley said, although the needle on her righteous-rage-o-meter had slipped from ten to seven or eight.

"I'm not saying it does, I admit it wasn't the best decision I've ever made—"

"You think?"

"—but she was alone on the train and in Sydney airport anyway. What the hell difference would a few minutes in Gold Coast Airport have made?"

Shirley sighed, glanced at her watch. "Richard, I have to go and open the pub. This conversation isn't over. I'll call you tonight."

He tried to say something else but she jabbed the red dot to kill the call. She leaned against the kitchen counter and closed her eyes, trying to clean her emotional and mental slate for the next conversation. She ventured into the cottage's small sitting room, where Elle reposed with her legs extended and earphones plugged into her ears. Animated images played across the smartphone screen and Shirley wished from the center of her heart that it was an innocent cartoon, something like *Little Charley Bear* or *Paw*

Patrol, two of Elle's favorites as a child. But no self-respecting fifteen-year-old would sit through either one, unless they were in the company of a little cousin. Shirley waved to get her attention. Elle paused whatever she was watching, unplugged her ears, and looked up at her.

"I just got off the phone with your father. Elle, I need the truth. Did he send you a text message telling you he would be late?"

Guilt flashed across her face. "Well. . .yeah, but then when I called—"

"Oh, Christ, Elle," Shirley said, smacking her own forehead hard enough to sting. "That would have been useful information before I spent ten minutes tearing strips off him."

"What difference does it make? He still—"

"Okay, just give me the damned phone. Let me see what he wrote."

Before surrendering it, Elle swiped to her messages app and tapped on the conversations with her father. Why she would want to prevent her mother from seeing any other messages was one worry too many to deal with. Worries were already spilling over the sides of Shirley's barrow and a good deal of bumpy ground lay ahead. Elle scrolled down to the last message and handed her the phone.

Running a bit late, sweetheart. Should be there around six-thirty. Just wait in the café near the baggage claim.

"When did you get the message?" Shirley said, trying to fend off a siege of conflicting emotions.

"When I was on the plane, after we landed. I called him when I got inside the terminal and his little hussy answered instead."

"Elle, that's enough of that," Shirley snapped, although who she was actually snapping at was open for debate.

"Why? That's what she is."

"Elle. . ."

She had been about to say, *Elle, you'll understand when you're older*, but what exactly was hampering her understanding now? Maybe her daughter had a better grasp of the situation than she did. Purer, free from the shades of grey adults cultivated to cope with life's travails. Such as divorce, say, or fighting to keep afloat a business that someone else had insisted on starting and then dumped. An adolescent view might lack nuance, but that didn't make it entirely wrong.

85

"Elle, he has a right to see other people now. That doesn't mean what he did to you was okay, not at all, but what he does in his own time is his business. Hating him for that won't make things better, it'll make them worse."

Elle's lips puckered, as if she were deep in thought, and then her face crumpled and she began to sob. Shirley swooped in and pulled her close, fighting back tears of her own. How had it come to this, she wondered for the umpteenth time, how had her marriage and her predictable life dissolved in a matter of months and left such a mess? Why did the person she cherished more than anyone on the planet now have a shattered heart?

"Elle, I'm sorry, baby. We can talk more about this later, but the pub is supposed to be open in ten minutes and I haven't even tidied up from last night."

Elle wiped her streaming eyes on her shirt sleeves and ironed the hitches out of her voice. God, she was strong. Most girls Shirley remembered from her teenage years would go to pieces over the smallest slight or spend the day in a huff when they didn't get their way.

"Wouldn't what's-her-name have tidied up?"

"Yes, Karen closed up for me, but. . .well, you know I'm fastidious. Plus, I want to go through last night's takings and see how much we made. We could do with some happy news."

Pristine mornings and clean air were two reasons Shirley had chosen to stay in Black Wattle and try to make the Ironstone pull its weight. This morning was a beauty, too good to be a Monday, she thought. More like a Friday in disguise. Warm sunshine had peeled away the night-time chill and the faintest grass-scented breeze added a dash of briskness. Shirley turned her face up to it as she unlocked the car, wishing she could lie on the porch and soak it up like a house cat. Life's rotten moments helped a girl appreciate its simple pleasures.

Before long, though, her argument with Richard permeated her head again, bushfire smoke drifting into a valley, and clouded out everything else. She didn't begrudge him moving on, it had been the best part of a year after all, but why did he have to complicate an already complex situation with asshat behavior?

"Where is everyone?" Elle said, gazing out the window.

"Not sure, sweetheart," she answered absently.

Asshat behavior toward her, instead of Elle, she could have tolerated (if not condoned), but thanks to Richard's actions a second rift had appeared in their fragile family unit. If she was honest, it hurt her pride, too. Not only because her ex-husband had moved on before she had, but because he had rocked their cordial post-marriage equilibrium. Shirley had assumed stand-up rows were the preserve of divorcees who should never have tied the knot in the first place, that she and Richard had been victims of circumstance. *Their* marriage had been run off the road rather than defective from the outset.

"It's pretty deserted, even for Black Wattle."

"Mm-hm."

It had seemed like the truth, too, at least until twenty-four hours ago. What did it mean for the future? Shirley needed to get face-to-face with Richard, talk it over, have it out, whatever was required to try and find a new stasis. Elle deserved stability. She was only a spectator at this shitshow. When she called Richard back she would be calmer, more constructive. One of them had to be. If this new woman could make him forget about his own goddamned daughter—

She wrenched the steering wheel hard to port and the car jounced over the lip of the driveway into the pub carpark.

"Shit, Mum, I nearly bit my tongue."

"Sorry. I'm a bit preoccupied."

"I noticed."

"Come on. Let's go inside and see if two-dollar schooners made us rich."

She tried to turn the key in the lock. It wouldn't budge. She pulled the key out and double-checked it was the right one even though she knew it had to be. The only similar key belonged to the cottage's new back door. She slotted the key in again and turned it for the same result.

Shirley wondered if some imbecile had perpetrated a practical joke in her absence, squeezed superglue into the workings or something, but then the real problem dawned on her. She was attempting to unlock an already unlocked door.

She cranked the handle and sure enough, the door popped open.

"Bloody hell, Karen," she muttered.

Elle patted her shoulder. "No one locks their doors in the country, right, Mum?"

Shirley stared at her for a beat. A smile twitched her daughter's mouth. Her own lips worked in response, then she gave in and let the smile form.

"We'll be lucky if the place isn't looted," she said, walking in. "It's not like Karen to be so sloppy."

Any facetious inclinations dried up as they stepped inside. No one had bothered to pack away the MC's table. The microphone lay underneath it, dropped and forgotten, perhaps kicked there. Chairs stood in disarray, a couple overturned. Schooner glasses smashed to crooked diamonds littered the floor and tabletops.

"It looks like there was a bar fight," Elle said.

"Or a robbery."

Shirley hurried to the cash register and found it secure. She punched in her staff code and when the drawer popped open it revealed blooms of blue and orange and yellow notes—the float and revenue, untouched. She slammed the drawer shut again and stalked through to the wall safe in her office. She entered the combination and there was a metallic clunk as the door unlocked. Within she found takings from the bar, TAB and Keno…but she recognized the arrangement of bags and coin pouches. They hadn't been disturbed since she counted up on Saturday night.

Her first thought was to call the police. But what would she report? Disturbed furniture? Damaged glassware? It couldn't be called a robbery and she had no idea what had transpired while she was in transit to and from Sydney. Well, whatever the case, it couldn't hurt to report the incident. For all she knew, there was more serious damage elsewhere in the hotel and she might need to file an insurance claim.

She searched for Goulburn Police Station's non-emergency number and went back to the bar to make the call in case the officer logging the report wanted specific details. Elle had flopped into one of the pub chairs, thumbs hard at work writing a message to someone. Not Richard, Shirley hoped.

She tapped in the number for Goulburn Police and was about to hit call when she looked up from her phone. It took Shirley a moment to resolve the other forms in the room because they were silent and motionless, apparitions suddenly made solid. Her mind tallied them: one at the foot of the stairs which led up to the hotel accommodation, another washed in the television screens' flickering glow, a third at the far end of the bar. Shirley's eyes seemed to creak in her head as they rolled sideways and identified a fourth figure in the passage between the bar and the disused kitchen. Stretched across its bloated pink face was a pair of wire-framed spectacles, arms dug into the thing's glossy skin, thin metal bridge bent into a V-shape, lenses cracked.

Shirley knew those glasses well, had seen them most days before the thing's swollen rosé-colored head had deformed them.

"Dr Sneddon?" she whispered.

Behind those crazed lenses, two vein-streaked eyes narrowed to slits. The thing's chapped and broken lips drew back to expose two full rows of canine teeth. Saliva dribbled onto its chin and an enormous tongue, resembling a bruised and blackened penis, lolled out and mopped up the expelled fluid before disappearing again. Shirley's gaze fell to the phone in her hand. Even if she pressed call and relayed the situation to a constable or fed him a fake story so a car responded at top speed, it would still take fifteen minutes to arrive.

"Elle," she said.

The thing hissed, as though she had said something insulting, and a spray of drool splattered the floor at its raptor feet. Elle looked up from her phone, stood up with a start, eyes wide. "Mum? What the hell is that?"

"Run to the car, Elle. Now."

"But you're—"

"They're behind you, too. Run!"

Elle glanced over her shoulder, no more than a quick flick of her head, then bounded away. The creatures, whatever the hell they were, screeched in unison and surged forward to attack. Shirley made a break for the gap in the bar and as she went she raked her arm across the liquor shelves, sending a dozen or more bottles tumbling to the floor. The creature from the back room lunged for her, but its foot rolled on an unbroken bottle. Swiping claws whickered past Shirley's right ear before the bottle skidded out and dumped the thing on its back. As Shirley rounded the bar and took off she estimated the other creatures would be on her in seconds. Elle pushed open the door, stepped outside and swung around, eyes hectic.

"Go, Mum! Go!"

"Get in the car!" Shirley screamed.

Elle set off in athletic strides. Shirley could hear feet scratching and scrabbling across the floorboards, close, so close. Without breaking stride she swung her arm in a wide arc and caught the door's edge, slamming it in her wake. Timber crunched as something collided with the door frame, plate glass raining down on the entryway pavers. Shirley ignored an urge to turn and check the damage, instead pressing the central locking button on her car's key fob, which with luck she had put in her jeans pocket rather than her handbag. Hazard lights flashed.

Elle wrenched open the passenger's side, literally jumped in, and pulled the door closed.

Behind the windscreen, her flushed face formed soundless words as Shirley rushed past the bonnet and performed a sidestep so sudden she almost twisted her ankle. The thing that had crashed into the hotel door had regained its feet. As Shirley pulled open the driver's side door, admitting Elle's hysterical voice, the creature dropped to its haunches and sprang at the car.

Its feet caved two divots into the bonnet and shook the car on its springs. Shirley grabbed for the internal door handle, but her sweat-slimy fingers slipped off and she almost fell out of the car. The creature dropped to its knees and slashed at her. Had she been upright its bladed fingers would have ripped her neck to shreds. Instead, they sliced only air, and as it regathered itself for a second strike Shirley hooked her fingers around the handle and yanked the door shut.

The creature hacked at the windscreen, its nails scoring three lines across the glass in a chalky squeak. Shirley hit the starter button. Shrieking in fury, the creature leapt to its feet as a second one launched itself from the pavement and crashed down on the roof. Shirley and Elle screamed together. The first creature lifted one leg, its sick-yellow eyes focused on Shirley's face as she engaged reverse.

It brought down its foot and Shirley planted hers. Instead of piledriving through the windscreen, the creature's foot kicked out harmlessly. It fell backwards and straight onto its head while the second creature tumbled off the roof and faceplanted into the bonnet. Shirley kept the hammer down, missing the driveway by a long shot and launching the car backward off the gutter. There came an alarming crunch as the rear end hit the tarmac, but the thing on the bonnet flipped forward and hit the road in a rolling tangle of limbs.

Shirley slapped the gear shifter into drive and hit the gas. The front wheels chirped for purchase and then rubber bit down, throwing Elle and Shirley back in their seats. The engine rose to a scream, the rev limiter keeping it just below redline, and the steering wheel vibrated under Shirley's hands. Ironbarks on either side of the road flashed past faster and faster until they melded into a botanic blur. Shirley didn't know what insane contagion had infiltrated her pub and the town, but she intended to get her daughter as far from it as she could. She fumbled over her shoulder for her seat belt, pulled it down, fastened it. Elle had already done the same.

Shirley flung the car around a sweeping bend, the tires protesting and the traction control kicking in to keep everything on course. She feathered the brake and, as she exited the corner, lifted her foot ready to stamp the accelerator again, before crying out and tramping the brake instead. Inertia threw her and Elle into their seat belts and the anti-lock braking system activated to keep them from going into an uncontrollable skid. Shirley felt like her foot was through the floor and touching the road. The digital speedo began to decline, but slowly, too slowly. From the corner of her eye, she saw Elle throw up her hands and cover her face.

The car ran out of momentum no more than six inches from the back of another vehicle. Panting, pupils dilated, Shirley tried to prize her fingers from the wheel and found them locked like vice-grips. It hurt to unstick them. She emitted a few shaky breaths, then put the car in park and pulled on the handbrake. They had come to a stop so close to the car in front she couldn't see the number plate. Beside her, Elle whimpered.

"Are you okay, sweetheart? Are you hurt?"

Elle nodded, shook her head, continued to whimper. Shirley could see the heads of two men above the car in front. Normal humans, not whatever the fuck had infested the pub. She put the car in reverse, gave herself enough room to get by the car in front, then maneuvered onto the shoulder. "Wait here," she said.

She popped open the door, planning to give the two men a mouthful about stopping on the far side of a blind corner, but when she stood up she was speechless.

The car she had almost rear-ended belonged to Don Winslow. The man arguing with him was a federal police officer. And behind them, a roadblock of armed men had isolated Black Wattle from everything to the east.

CHAPTER ELEVEN

ROLLING THROUGH Black Wattle's streets with his .38 on the passenger's seat, Don almost felt like a new recruit patrolling Bankstown again. That had been his first station after graduating from the academy, and he had joined at a time when robberies and gang violence had spiked in the area. Don and boredom were seldom companions during those two years, but few also were the weeks when he didn't agitate for a transfer to a country station. Bankstown had been a baptism of fire, given him a hard shell that would serve him well in later years, but Sydneysiders could keep their traffic and their pollution and their gang rapists.

Don had decided to do some reconnaissance, find out precisely what happened to Marla. Images of her on her knees like a dog and in what appeared to be mortal agony kept flashing up in his head like the old advertising slides they played at the cinema when Don was a kid.

His gut told him Chris Brooks and his men were somehow to blame, the coincidence of their arrival and supernatural shit going down was too great to ignore, although he couldn't fathom a link.

What he hadn't reckoned on were the deserted streets, even accounting for the roadblock. He and his battered old station wagon rolled alone, passing only vehicles in driveways or parked empty on the street. Drifting through the town center at no more than jogging pace, he noticed the general store, farm supplies depot and the post office all locked up, even though business hours were underway. The Gold Rose's doors stood open, but when Don pulled up and peered in he could see no staff, no customers, no signs of movement. Marla wouldn't be holding court that day, of course, but then she always left the opening chores to her younger staff.

Don arrived at a reluctant conclusion: whatever happened to Marla that morning had not been an isolated incident. He needed to collar Brooks, interrogate the officious little turd—at gunpoint if it came to that. He crept the Holden forward another hundred meters or so until it lined up with the museum's front door, which was ajar a crack. It appeared dark inside and he could make out nothing, especially not from his car's cockpit. He palmed the steering wheel around and parked nose-in to the gutter. When he looked up at the museum door again he thought he caught a flash of movement. He stared, unblinking, into the gloom long enough to make his eyes water, but saw nothing else.

This was supposed to be the AFP's base of operations, yet not a single car or uniform was in evidence. It didn't add up. Don put his car in park and picked up his firearm, bouncing it gently to feel its weight. Men could be standing guard inside the doorway while Brooks was out back formulating a plan to contain the unholy mess spreading through the town. It made logical sense to eliminate the museum first, at any rate. Either Brooks would be there, Don could demand to know Brooks's whereabouts, or the place would be empty. Satisfied, he put the gun in his lap so he could open the door, then picked it up again and stepped out.

Something cannoned out of the museum, its theropod legs propelling it towards Don's car with horrifying swiftness and its ravenous maw opening to expel a screech that trembled his eardrums. With no time to aim, Don lifted the .38 and fired off a blind shot. The bullet caught the thing in its right eye, black jelly exploding across its face. Its head rocked back and its legs collapsed under it. Don edged forward and fired two more shots, one blasting a hole in the underside of its chin, the second leaving a crater where its nose had been. It lay on the footpath jittering, as though tasered, and Don crept a step closer to study it better.

This one appeared a fraction different to whatever Marla had become. Its translucent rose-colored skin had blackened crusts and some areas were blistered and sloughing off, as though burning up from the inside. Don shuffled his foot forward once more. The trembling ceased and the thing sat up, rotten goo spilling from its nose and eye socket.

"What the. . .?" Don said, then capped off another round, hoping to hit it in the heart. His aim looked true but the thing didn't even flinch, continuing to get to its feet as dark honey-colored blood spilled from the chest wound.

Don opted to save his last three bullets. He backed up, tossed the gun onto the passenger's seat, got behind the wheel and started the engine. The thing raced at him, its remaining eye blazing pure hatred, on a clear kamikaze mission to smash through the windscreen and chomp out Don's throat. Acting on cop's instinct, Don slammed the station wagon into drive and mounted the gutter, the car's bumper cutting the thing down at the knees. It belly-flopped onto the bonnet and its head took the brunt of the collision, splattering blood in a wide halo, some of it speckling the windscreen. Don pressed the car forward to trap the thing between the bonnet and the museum wall, then accelerated hard. The tires spun until they smoked and the rear end stepped out. The thing raged at him through the windscreen, salivating through its serried fangs and raking its nails down the bonnet hard enough to strip the paint to bare metal.

Don dropped his car into reverse and the thing fell onto its face, its midsection now a gelatinous and gruesome pancake. The thing tried to struggle to its feet but its torso folded over backwards and it hit the deck again. Don kept his eyes on the rear-view mirror as he spun the steering wheel so the car faced east on Goldfields Road. Then he slammed it into drive and gave it the beans.

Black Wattle had been compromised, that much was clear. Evacuation was essential. If he had avoided the infection or whatever it was, others likely had, too. As he streaked down the road Don kept his eyes busy searching for survivors, but he reached the Goldmine Motel without seeing a single soul, normal or mutated. A few moments later he rounded a bend and came upon a second roadblock, even wider and more elaborate than the one at the town's western end. Plastic barriers had been erected from tree line to tree line and, just beyond them, a pair of vans were parked crossways, nose to tail. On the roof stood two men armed with automatic rifles. Don stopped and got out of his station wagon. Two of the four men trained their rifles on him, the two others paid him no heed, their eyes scanning the wooded area.

Standing outside the car, Don could see more armed operatives scattered through the farmland beyond the dense stands of ironbark trees.

Not only was something happening, something *big* was happening.

"I'm not one of them," Don called to the police atop the vans. He slapped at his dangling left arm. "This is due to plain old nerve damage."

This information did not move the men either way. The small black eyes of two rifle barrels continued to stare at his chest. "I'm looking for Chris Brooks. I need to speak to him."

The sentries, or whatever they were, remained unresponsive as he took slow and cautious steps towards the roadblock. He was about to say something else when the door to one of the vans slid open, revealing none other than Brooks himself. His hair, gelled back at some point, had broken its bonds and now hung across his forehead in hanks. Deep lines crossed his forehead and bracketed his mouth. Darkened skin around his eyes gave him a skull-like appearance. Don knew that look well: an emergency services worker who had already pulled a double shift and conceived no end in sight.

"What do you want, Mr. Winslow?"

"What do I want? Maybe you could start with the truth."

"The truth about what?"

"The truth about what you've done to my town."

"I told you before, the federal police are simply conducting—"

"Don't feed me that line of shit again, Brooks! You think I'm a fucking idiot? This is no police training exercise. You've got men carrying automatic weapons spread for half a kilometer in every direction. Your mates up there look like they'd shoot me if I so much as farted."

"The federal police are simply conducting a training exercise," Brooks deadpanned. "I apologize for any inconvenience, but you should know that interfering with—"

"I've seen two of those things, you know," Don said. "The lady who runs the café in town, Marla, she turned into one of them. I watched it happen."

Even though Brooks' expression didn't change, the color remaining in his cheeks drained away. He looked like a man suffering sudden-onset stomach flu. "Interfering with federal police operations is an offence and is punishable with—"

This time it wasn't Don who cut him off but a bellowing engine. Brooks glanced up, eyes wide, and Don spun around to look as well.

An SUV came around the bend flat-chat, swinging wide enough for its tires to cross the double white lines. Don thought he recognized the vehicle and a second later a visual of the driver confirmed it. Shirley Goodsall's mouth pouted into an O-shape as she clocked the brand new dead-end that had sprung up on a previously unimpeded highway. She threw out the anchors and her SUV's nose dipped towards the road. The tires chuffed and left behind small puffs of smoke as the car's brain calculated the best way to stop two tons travelling at a hundred clicks. Don backed off instinctively and lifted a protective arm, Shirley's daughter doing the same in the passenger's seat. Don and Brooks became spectators to a morbidly compelling race between the SUV's momentum and the onboard computer retarding it. Don cringed as the distance between his car and Shirley's got used up at a fearful rate. But the automated braking system really clamped down in the final twenty meters, wiping off a chunk of speed and bringing the SUV to a dead stop inches before impact. The vehicle wobbled on its suspension for a second or two, mechanical jelly, then fell still.

"This roadblock is as dangerous as those fucking things in town!" Don said, rounding on Brooks. "The next person who tries to evacuate might not be so lucky."

"Don?" Shirley said. She left her car door open and approached. "Don, what's going on?"

"That's what I'm trying to find out, but our friend Mr. Brooks here doesn't want to share."

"There were these things at the pub. They tried to attack us but we got away. Why is the road blocked off?"

"Another good question, Shirl. I suspect they've isolated the town, put up a perimeter. Brooks won't tell me why, but maybe he'll tell you. How about it, Brooks? Wouldn't want to disappoint a nice lady like Shirley here."

Brooks' face slackened. He looked like someone who'd received a stage-four cancer diagnosis. Then he appeared to rally, pushing his shoulders back and presenting an official's polite but impassive expression. "Return to your homes and lock all doors and windows. You'll be safe there. The federal police have the situation in hand and we will notify you when—"

"Safe in our homes?" Don spluttered. "You mean like Marla Smith?"

"I'm afraid I don't know who that is," Brooks continued in his aggravating bureaucratic tone. "If you don't move on as instructed, I will be forced to. . ."

The just-business front faltered as his eyes fell on something further down the road. Don and Shirley both looked back. A man approached; a man wearing blood-soaked chino pants and no shirt, with a carving knife in one hand and a meat cleaver in the other. The whites of his eyes stared from his blood-slathered face. Don tried to peer past the sanguinary disguise but still could not identify the man, an uncommon and unsettling scenario for him. Maybe an unfortunate tourist that had been caught up in whatever madness had befallen Black Wattle.

"You can't kill them," the man said, his pale, hairless chest heaving and glistening with sweat. "You have to chop them up so they can't move anymore."

The staring eyes and vehement words suggested he might be loosely tethered to his sanity. Don hoped at least one of the automatic rifles was now trained on this new arrival. Sometimes a small threat could go unobserved amid the mayhem that a bigger one generated. But the man stopped at a prudent distance from Don and Shirley, looked at them both, then looked at Brooks and the armed men standing guard atop the vans.

"What's going on?" he said.

"That's the million-dollar question," Don said dryly. He cocked his thumb at Brooks. "Eddie here has the answer but he's not telling anyone."

"Sadie is one of those things," the man said. "You know, the girl from the café. She wouldn't die, so I had to chop her into pieces." He lifted the meat cleaver, as if showing a courtroom Exhibit A. "The pieces kept moving, but. . ." He trailed off, shrugged his shoulders.

"Dr Sneddon is one, too," Shirley said. "The thing was still wearing his glasses."

"Well, Brooks," Don said, "looks like the cat's out of the bag. We're all in on it now, whatever the hell 'it' is. Maybe you'd care to share what you know. Caring is sharing, after all, and you're in the country now. We share everything. Especially when we're in trouble."

Brooks' lips shaped the outlines of some possible words but rejected each in turn. He swallowed. He appeared ready to try again when gunfire peppered the air. His head snapped to the right, eyes filled with vacuous terror.

Flames licked from gun muzzles as men in the northern field opened fire at something only they could see. Before long, however, the targets came into view—a swarm of creatures rushing at them in great antelope strides. Those leading the charge slowed a touch as bullets ripped into their chests, expelling little puffs of blood, but the rest flowed around them and bore down on the gunmen, sandpaper screeches filling the air. At a quick count, Don estimated the horde numbered twenty-five or thirty.

Cupping his hands around his mouth, Brooks cried, "Aim for their heads! Cut them down at the knees!"

One of the soldiers—for that's what they were, Don now believed—ejected a magazine from his weapon and slapped in a fresh one. Before he could lift it, though, one of the things hit him full force and the gun spun off like a helicopter blade, coming to rest amid the tussocks of yellow grass. Talons dug into the soldier's thighs, knife-like nails penetrated his ribcage, and the thing tore out his throat before he hit the ground. Blood geysered from the vessels in his neck and soaked into the parched earth like red rain. The creature tossed away the chunk of flesh between its teeth, an act that was somehow more obscene than the bite itself, then sprang off the body and re-joined its bloodthirsty brethren which had changed direction and were now coming towards the roadblock in a herd. Some of the field soldiers had retreated and reconfigured their positions to form a rear-guard force, their weapons chattering. A few head-shot creatures dropped into the turf, but most surged onward, a barbed-wire fence and a stand of trees the only things standing between them and the roadblock.

"Run!" Brooks screamed. "They're demons, run!"

He tried to flee into his van, but Don collared him and pulled him back. "Oh, no you don't," he said, dragging him towards his car. "You're coming with me."

"What the hell are you doing?" Brooks said, stumbling backwards. He tried to swat at Don's face but he was off-balance and it was all he could do to stay on his feet. When they got to the station wagon Don dumped him onto his backside and opened the passenger's side door.

Brooks jumped to his feet, ready to take a swing, but found himself nose-to-nose with Don's revolver.

"You and I are partners, now," Don said. "Get in."

Brooks' haunted eyes darted between the vans and the field, where a firearm's sudden silence and a gurgling scream suggested things weren't going well for the home team. Giving him a haughty glare, Brooks dropped into the seat. Don kicked the door closed and trotted around to the driver's side.

Shirley, as sharp-witted as they came, had already jumped behind the wheel of her SUV and backed it up so Don was no longer boxed in. The shirtless man now sat in the back seat. Don put the .38 in the door pocket, fired up the Holden, and reversed out at reckless speed, executing a J-turn so he faced town again. He dropped it into drive and planted his foot, nothing in his mind except escaping the present situation. Shirley fell in behind and their convoy of two surged along the highway.

"Oh, fuck," Brooks gibbered, clutching his arms around his knees and rocking back and forth. "They're going to break containment. Oh fuck, oh fuck, oh fuck. . ."

With some distance between him and the hot zone, and clear road ahead, Don's mind came back online. He gave Brooks a sidelong glance and shook his head. "You're a goddamned pencil-pusher. Aren't you? All that cloak and dagger bullshit, getting all high and mighty with me, and you haven't seen a minute's active service in your life."

Brooks moaned, like a child with a belly ache. "You don't understand."

"How can I? You won't tell me anything. What is it, some sort of contagion?"

Brooks appeared indisposed to disclose anything more, choosing instead to harrow his fingers through his hair again and again. They passed the Goldmine Motel and the Ironstone and were cruising into the eastern end of town when Don spotted what appeared to be a protest in the middle of the street. But no one marched or chanted or held aloft placards. Outside Don's museum bodies milled to and fro. When the Holden's growly old engine reached their ears (or the molten gobs of flesh that now passed for them) every head in that commotion of bodies turned in unison. Eyes—so many eyes, almost innumerable, like a clutch of fish eggs—fell upon the car. Don's heart went into freefall as he began to understand just how outnumbered they were. The mass of malformed bodies surged towards them. The pistol in the car's door pocket might have been a cap gun for all the use it would be against them, even if he reloaded the chambers.

Pure panic flowed into his veins. He yanked down on the steering wheel, the car's rear end sliding out and then correcting as he gave it some gas. Checking his rear-view mirror to make sure Shirley remained on his tail, Don raced down Tower Street and power-slid around the bend onto Panorama Avenue.

"Did you say they were demons?"

Brooks nodded his head, face downcast, as if ashamed to admit it.

An idea filtered into Don's mind. Two hours earlier he would have dismissed it as superstitious crackpot nonsense, but now it had a comforting logic. The valley's sun-bathed splendor scrolled past unseen, Don focused on the old building at the end of the road.

The Holden jounced up the driveway, Don and Brooks flopping around in their seats, and came to a skidding stop outside Patrick Burnham's church. A murder of crows took flight at the disturbance and sought quieter perches. Don opened the door, reached into the pocket for his pistol, and stepped out.

"What are you doing?" Brooks said, staring at the church as if it were a circus big top.

A fine question. Now that Don was here and confronted with the truth of his comforting idea it looked like lunacy. But what recourse did he have? Common reason had been trampled beneath the feet of a thousand demons. Fight fire with fire, went the old saying, so perhaps he could combat superstition with superstition. And if nothing else, the church's sturdy sandstone walls, hardwood doors and high windows meant it would serve as the best type of refuge—one that was also a fortress.

Besides, they were out of time and out of options. Shirley's SUV pulled up behind the Holden and all three occupants piled out.

Don wagged the gun barrel between Brooks and the church. "Let's go," he said.

CHAPTER TWELVE

"**W**HAT THE HELL** are we doing, Don?" Shirley muttered as she pulled in behind his banged-up station wagon.

The knife and meat cleaver lay crossed in Truman's lap like some odd form of heraldry and they clinked as he picked them up and got out. Don's race-driving antics had put perhaps a kilometer between them and the horde up on Goldfields Road. The agency man or whatever he was emerged reluctantly, as though Don planned to walk him to jail or the gallows. If they were headed where they appeared to be, Truman considered the actual destination only a smidgen pleasanter.

"What's going on?" Shirley said, walking up the drive with her arm around what Truman assumed was her daughter. "Why did you bring us here?"

"Even if we could find a way around that wall of demons, Brooks and his men have the other end of town blocked off, too," Don said.

"Demons?"

"Brooks' word, not mine."

"If you're hoping for sanctuary or salvation," Truman said, "I think you've come to the wrong place."

Don sighed, rolled his eyes, dropped his good arm in exasperation. "Anyone got any better ideas?"

Truman, Shirley and her daughter looked at each other. Brooks ignored them all, gazing up the hill apprehensively. No better ideas came forth.

"Come on, then, we need to get inside."

They started up the path to the church doors, Brooks in the lead and Don behind him, perhaps nervous he would try to vamoose. Judging by his stooped shoulders and erratic eyes,

Truman thought it unlikely. Brooks looked more like a man who had resigned himself to death because he could do nothing to thwart it. Even the manner in which he opened the church door suggested its futility. He stepped inside, anyway. As Don's foot crossed the threshold a demon dropped off the church roof.

The high eaves donated a half-second to react and everyone scattered. The demon sliced only air and its nails clicked as it landed on the concrete path. It lunged left, catching Elle's ankle and tripping her up. She screamed and fell full-length into the dirt, sending up a billow of dust. She dug her fingers into the stony soil, trying to pull herself away while at the same time kicking the demon with her free leg.

"Elle!" Shirley shrieked. She had recanted from her evasive move and Truman could see she was about to throw herself on the demon's back, pure mother-bear instinct. He bolted forward and shoulder charged her, knocking her off-course so she stumbled towards the church door. Then Truman assumed her role, leaping onto the demon's back and plunging the carving knife deep into its skull.

The thing spasmed under him, as if throwing a fit, and its hand clamped harder around Elle's leg until she screamed in agony. Truman ripped out the knife, a bloodthirsty Excalibur, and unplugged a fountain of blood that splashed down on the demon's shoulders. The hand not clenching Elle's ankle groped around, nails flicking around in a blind attempt to scratch. Using his left hand, Truman brought down the cleaver on the shoulder joint. It failed to dismember the arm altogether but chopped through enough muscle and sinew to make the limb a separate entity. It wriggled and thrashed around in a puddle of blood, like a worm dug up in a vegetable garden. Then Truman stabbed the knife blade sideways into the demon's temple. The demon's hand released the pressure on Elle's ankle and she rotated her foot and yanked on it until it came free and she could commando crawl away.

Finding his feet and dropping the knife, Truman wielded the meat cleaver like an axe, chopping away at the demon's neck until the blade cleft through its vertebrae and the gore-splattered head rolled off down the grade, gathering dust as it went.

"They're coming!" Shirley cried as she helped a weeping Elle to her feet.

"Get inside," Don said, putting himself between them and the oncoming demon horde.

Truman collected the knife and ushered the girls through the archway. The flat blast of gunfire rattled Truman's ears as he stepped in behind them and spun around, grabbing the door handle. Don hopped through and Truman slammed the door shut hard enough to rattle it in its frame before shooting the bolt. He put his back against it and slid to a sitting position on the paved floor. The old timber stuck little splinters into his flesh as he went and he wondered if he now looked like some half-assed human-echidna hybrid. He began to cackle at his own thought and clapped a hand over his mouth. Don sat beside him, index finger still hooked through his pistol's trigger guard, and added his body weight to the door.

Elle continued to wail (*wail song*, Truman's mind offered, leading him to wonder if the preceding hour or so had knocked its bolts loose) and Shirley escorted her to one of the pews, where they sat arm in arm. With some shushing and coaxing Elle quieted to sniffles. Between the two sections of pews Brooks stood alone, eyes at once blank and hectic, an electric charge with no circuit. Everyone slowed their breathing to listen.

Truman's city-attuned ears picked up nothing save for the *cheek-cheek-cheek* of a corella flock disputing where they would stop for brunch. His eyes roved from face to face, trying to interpret each expression. He leaned over to Don and said in a hush, "Where are they?"

"No idea. I thought they'd storm the place."

The voice rose from somewhere amongst the pews. "Oh, they'll be out there. Waiting."

Brooks's hands twitched, as if to slap away a punch. "Who's there?" he said.

A head emerged from the second-row pew and it belonged to none other than Patrick the Homophobe. He rested his elbows on the pew's backrest, as though it were the bar-top at the Ironstone, a half-empty scotch bottle dangling from one hand. His eyes had trouble focusing on any one thing, so he let them flutter up into his skull for a while. That appeared to reset them.

"Patrick Burnham's the name. Father Patrick Burnham. Man of the cloth, lately town drunk. Quite the combination, eh? I don't think they can come into the church. They haven't tried, anyway. I could be wrong."

Don glanced at Truman as if to ask, "You got this?", then propped himself on his good hand and rose to his feet. The stained-glass windows threw multi-colored murals on the flagstones, sidewalk-chalk art in the medium of light, and they printed themselves across Don as he moved towards the altar. "Do you know what these things are, Patrick?"

"They're a little dumb, like all things evil."

"You're not exactly Mother Theresa yourself," Truman said, getting to his feet.

"Different denomination," Patrick said, "but thanks for playing."

Shirley had taken off her jacket and folded it into a crude pillow, upon which Elle now rested her head. She moved out into the aisle. "Are you saying they're really demons?"

Patrick nodded at Brooks. "Why don't you ask your new friend there? I suspect he knows more about this than I do."

"But you know about them?" Don said.

"Know about them? I suppose. The Anglican Church let go of its superstitions and rigmarole long before most other denominations did. The new suburban churches are more like community centers, or a house with a sign stuck on the front wall. But I'm forty-eight. I came up under the last of the old guard, so I've seen things. Paintings, texts, quaint paraphernalia that would mortify my younger peers. I ran over one of those things in my car yesterday evening. Got out, took one look at it, and drove down here and holed up for the night. My faith has been tested in recent months, but seeing that thing on the road helped me reclaim it in a hurry. Is that what you were after, Don?"

"Not really."

Patrick laughed. "Well, I'm afraid that's all I have to offer. Moral and spiritual guidance. Here's the spirit." He tipped the bottle to his lips, grimaced, swallowed. "As for the morals. . .well, I'm afraid I'm in short supply."

Truman scoffed. "You can say that again."

Patrick stared, nearly going cross-eyed. "I seem to have upset you somehow, friend. I do that a lot these days, but I don't have a good memory, so you'll have to fill me in."

"I was with Pam Daley. The real estate agent. Ring any bells?"

"Sorry, no."

"You called me a sodomite and told me I'd burn in hell."

"Did I? Well, when I black out I say all sorts of things. I wouldn't take it personally."

"Why wouldn't I take it personally?"

Patrick peered at him a while longer, the inner workings of his mind apparently gummed up with whisky. "You *are* a sodomite? Oh, I see. That certainly explains why you're so touchy."

Truman gasped. "Touchy?"

"Yes, you know, sensitive. It must have come as quite a shock."

"What are you on about? What must have come as a shock?"

"That demons exist. If demons are real, then it stands to reason all the other rot in the Bible is probably real as well. Leviticus 20:13. 'If a man lies with a male as with a woman, both of them have committed an abomination; they shall surely be put to death; their blood is upon them.' There's lots of stuff about homosexuality if you care to look. It usually results in 'punishment by eternal fire' or some such."

Shirley bristled. "Patrick, why are you being so awful?"

His stupid business-as-usual leer vanished under the heat of her admonishment. "Me? I didn't write the damned book. Don't shoot the messenger, Shirl."

"Mum?"

They all turned. Elle had arisen from her pew and now stood in the aisle, face ghost-white and crumpled, dry-crying. "Mum, I don't feel very good. I—"

Her eyes fluttered up into their lids and her legs gave out, as if the bones inside had turned to powder. She fell sidelong onto the floor, arms tangled beneath her ribs. Shirley and Don both rushed to her aid.

"Roll her onto her back," Don said. "Feel for a pulse."

Shirley pressed her fingers to Elle's wrist while Don got down and put his ear to her chest and then above her mouth. "She's not breathing," he said.

"No pulse," Shirley said. Once those words were out, they uncorked a rising terror and Shirley's next sentence came out in a half-scream. "What's wrong with her, Don?"

"Not sure. Do you know CPR? I do, but. . ." He sneered at his arm.

"I know CPR," Truman said, kneeling beside them. "My. . .well, I had a friend who insisted I stay up to date."

They moved back to give him space. He ran the acrostic through his head. Don and Shirley had completed the first couple of steps, so he tilted Elle's head to ensure her airway was clear.

Tongue where it was supposed to be, no foreign object. He inhaled and covered her lips with his.

Her body bucked, mashing their teeth together, and as Truman gasped in pain a foul brown jet of muck sprayed out of her mouth and into his. He sucked some into his lungs and exploded into a coughing fit that felt like a cross between drowning and inhaling mustard gas. He crawled away and dropped on his side, gagging, wheezing, needing to throw up, desperate to breathe, every function demanding attention and obstructing the other. Tears spilled from his eyes as, at last, his outraged lungs expelled the vile substance. It sat on the floor in a brown gobbet, a sight that pulled the drawstring on his stomach and only failed to bring forth vomit because his gullet was empty already.

As Truman's eyes cleared he saw Elle's spasming muscles flip her from a supine position and she landed on her face, flattening her nose into the flagstones. If it hurt she showed no sign, instead retracting her arms into her sides and pushing up onto her knees.

"Look!" Brooks squealed, stabbing his finger at Elle's leg.

On the soft triangle of flesh between her Achilles' tendon and nub of ankle bone was a small scratch. No more than a centimeter across, but deep enough to draw a trickle of blood.

"What the hell's got into you?" Don said, but as he looked at the scratch something seemed to cross his mind and his face became pensive.

Elle crawled forward, a fifteen-year-old baby wearing sandal-thongs and a dress that had ridden up to expose her underwear, then stopped and lifted her head as though she were about to play wolf and howl at an imaginary moon. Her mother, crying and shaking her head in pitiful negation, moved towards her in small steps.

"Ellie?" Shirley said. "Ellie-Bellie, are you—"

Elle's head dropped and a flatulent sound reverberated through the church. Her pink underpants turned red in an instant and brown sludge escaped the elastic and spilled down her thighs. Shirley uttered an anguished cry and reached out to her daughter, although terror had also riveted her feet to the floor.

"Somebody help her! Somebody help her, please!"

No one moved. . .aside from Brooks, who had been backing away step by step until he now stood by the church doors. Elle lifted her head again, a dog listening to its master's whistle, then rocked forward and ejected a foamy shower of half-digested food and black blood. Chunks followed; white fibrous tissue, something that resembled a plastic bag, a rotten tomato thing that left behind red splat-marks as it bounced twice and rolled to a stop. The aisle became a slaughterhouse floor without a drain. The fresh olfactory affront overpowered the rotten stink already inside Truman's nose, triggering another gagging fit.

Once Elle's body had emptied itself she fell still, although her muscles flexed and twitched. The skin on her arms and legs inflated and stretched thin until it could have been the material on a lampshade. Her swelling feet snapped the straps on her shoes and curved claws pushed out through her toes, the existing nails falling away like scales off a dead fish. Clumps of Elle's hair dropped out and lay in bundles around her fingers, which now sported dagger-like nails. Agony twisted her pretty face into a godless grimace; manifested in a scream that remained all too human.

"She's changing!" Don exclaimed, as if that weren't already evident. "This is what happened to Marla!"

He lifted his pistol and pointed it at the back of Elle's head. Shirley saw this from the corner of her eye and swung around, knocking his arm down. "No, Don! That's my Elle. Please! Please don't. . ."

Don looked at Shirley doubtfully but kept the gun pointed at the floor.

"Don't be idiotic!" Brooks said, storming up the aisle. "It's too late, I'm sorry. We need to get her outside. Get her out or we're all dead!"

"You're not in charge anymore," Don said. "Why don't you disappear back down there and keep hiding, you yellow streak of shit?"

"Don, look," Shirley said.

The Elle demon unfolded its body and stood on its hind legs. With Don, Brooks and Shirley behind it, the first thing its infected eyes fell upon was Patrick, who had not moved from his barfly pose on the pew. The demon lowered its head and emitted a sibilant hiss through its bristling maw. Patrick watched it with half-interested and half-focused eyes, then tipped the scotch bottle to his lips. The demon's hiss escalated into a screech of rage and it went for him, black sabers poised and ready to slash open his throat.

Patrick spat a mouthful of scotch in its face.

The effect was immediate. The demon fell onto its back as if it had been coat-hangered, howling and clutching its face. Yellow smoke issued through its elongated fingers and drifted up to the ceiling in powdery curls. Patrick took another sip of scotch and sent it through his teeth in a small stream that bisected the demon's elbows and splashed against its neck. Its agonized screech sawed through the air and seemed to shatter Truman's brain inside its skull. Another pall of smoke climbed to form a yellow cloud in the church's rafters. Shirley dropped to her knees and outstretched her arms, a Muslim woman worshipping inside the wrong holy building. "Stop hurting my Elle!"

"You'll want to grab her feet," Patrick said. He might have been chewing gum for all the situation appeared to perturb him. "Watch out for the claws."

Don placed his gun on the floor and lumbered forward. Brooks showed no signs of volunteering and Patrick the Homophobe evidently considered his role advisory, so Truman spat and staggered to his feet. So many revolting smells filled his nasal cavity that his eyes ached and his stomach quaked. Don had one leg and Truman grabbed the other, the nerve endings in his fingers sending up touch-signals his forebrain was too advanced to compute. Something deeper and more primordial lit up instead, yammering at him to let go and run for the nearest cave or conceal himself in the thick canopy. But he reasserted his conscious will and he and Don began to drag Elle's body (if it could still be called that) along the floor, her head bumping on each space between the flagstones.

"Get the door!" Don bellowed. "Open the door you useless sack of shit!"

Brooks scuttled ahead, reduced to a man-mouse under Don's commanding voice, and wrestled the bolt from its iron slot. The demon removed its hands from its scorched face, exposing a waxwork horror visage. One of its eyes had melted onto its cheek and formed something akin to yellow chewing gum. Across the rest of its face were pockmarks and craters, some still smoldering, volcanoes suppurating on an ancient moon. It reached for its porters, arms flailing and swiping, but Truman and Don had elevated its feet to shoulder height and it didn't have the reach to overcome this deficit. It let fly another screech that percussed through Truman's brain. Don squinted and gritted his teeth against the noise. "Brooks! Get ready!"

Perchance demons still lurked on the far side, Brooks stoppered the toe of his shoe against the base of the door before pushing down the handle. He watched avidly as Truman and Don grew closer, then threw the door wide open and scuttled backwards. They used their momentum as a pendulum to toss the body forward and into the air. The demon threw out its arms in a wild crucifix to try to scratch something, anything, but Truman and Don were already out of range and it fell onto the path in an undignified heap. It wound itself around gymnastically and was on its feet in a flash, but Brooks slammed the door and Truman and Don pressed their shoulders against it while he shot the bolt home.

"ELLIE!"

Shirley tried to get to her feet but her legs went to rubber and she collapsed, falling against the side of a pew. Seeing this stirred Patrick from his seat and he made a dignified if somewhat meandering B-line for Shirley, sitting on the pew and placing his hand on the back of her neck. She shook beneath his gentle sympathy, her grief now past vocal expression.

While Truman absorbed this with vulgar fascination, he became aware Don appeared to be growing, inflating from within. Truman glanced at him askance, wondering if he had succumbed to the demon infection or whatever the fuck it was, but in the next second Don clamped his hand around Brooks' neck and shoved him forward, an old-time principal marching a recalcitrant student to his office.

"Take a seat, Brooks," he said, compressing him into the nearest pew. "You're going to spill your guts, right now, or I swear to God I'll get my gun and end all your worries."

"It's. . .it's classified."

"I'm declassifying it. Start talking and keep going until I'm satisfied."

A woebegone Brooks put a hand to his forehead, like one of the dames in the black and white movies that were Maurice's guilty pleasure. Then his hands fell in his lap, a gesture of defeat. "It wasn't supposed to be this way. They double-crossed us."

"Who double-crossed you?"

Brooks, like his namesake, began to babble.

CHAPTER THIRTEEN

"**REMEMBER THE COVID-19 PANDEMIC?** The virus escaped from a biotech lab in Wuhan, just like all the 'crazy' conspiracy theorists said. Seeing China brought to its knees made America nervous about its own biological warfare program. With China decimated, Russia began rattling its saber. Behind all his bluster, the president decided he needed to get on the front foot, come up with a weapon that would put the States back on top of the superpower dung heap without the potential blowback that brought China to a standstill."

"The Chinese death toll was only in the thousands, though," Truman said. "Horrible to say 'only', but it was a minuscule fraction of China's total population. Doesn't seem like a very effective bioweapon."

"Most victims were elderly, too, weren't they?" Don said.

"The mainstream media regurgitated what it was fed, like it always does," Brooks said. "Snippets of the truth made it onto social media. Those pictures you saw of authorities spraying disinfectant through the streets, welding people up in buildings, digging mass graves with industrial excavators? Just the tip of the iceberg. The actual toll, according to classified reports, was nearer to forty million."

"Holy shit," Truman said.

"So, as you can imagine, germ warfare fell out of favor for the first time in a few decades. America called a special meeting of its most trusted and long-standing allies and arranged funding for research projects exploring possible military alternatives. The Australian Government was put in charge of a feasibility study on supernatural warfare."

"Supernatural warfare?" Don said. The words didn't sound any less insane the second time around. His thoughts returned to his earlier hunch about the federal police in Black Wattle. "You and your men aren't feds at all, are you?"

"Well, we are in a sense. They're soldiers, an Australian Army special unit. I'm a historian by profession. I'm consulting with the Department of Defense on this project. They brought me in as an agent and a negotiator. A go-between, if you like."

"A go-between?" Don said. "Between the government and who?"

"Well, I did my PhD on the Occult. Wrote two or three books on the subject. Pretty dry stuff, only of interest to other academics. But I also published one mass market book on the subject, *Satanists in Our Midst*, and that's what caught the Americans' attention. You don't write about a weird subculture without making contacts."

"Contacts," Dons said flatly.

"The occult is very much alive and kicking today. If you don't believe me, stick your head out the door and see for yourself."

"Okay, let's assume you're telling the truth and this has something to do with witches and demons rather than lab-coat dickery gone wrong. Why are you stuck in here with the rest of us?"

"Like I said. They double-crossed us."

"Who double-crossed you?"

"Damon Prince and his merry band of Satanists."

Upon hearing this, Shirley, who had been sitting cross-legged with her face in her hands, snapped her head upward so fast her neck clicked. She stared at Brooks open-mouthed.

Don said, "Who the fuck is Damon Prince?"

"The High Priest of the Satanic Church in Australia. He staged a coup a few years ago and assumed control of the cabal that runs the church. Most modern-day Satanists are atheists who consider Satanism a personal and political philosophy rather than a religion, but Prince wanted to return the movement to its theistic roots. Black magic, ritual sacrifice, the whole bit. The government didn't want to get its hands dirty dealing with a controversial figure directly, so they called me in. Initially as an advisor, but then they made me head of the project.

"I interviewed Prince's predecessor while researching *Satanists In Our Midst* and even then I got a sense that Prince was breathing down his neck, plotting his demise. I heard about the coup through the community grapevine, too, so I was well aware of Prince and who he was before the Department of Defense called me at the university and asked to meet."

Listening to this, Don could feel his mind trying to slip its straps. It sounded like testimony from someone headed for the nearest loony bin, yet it was no less believable than the things lying in wait outside the church. As he contemplated the whole mess, a slow anger simmered in the center of his brain. Brooks had warmed to his own story, his face becoming bright and animated as he told it. Don's good hand folded itself into a fist.

"He's a charismatic man, no question about it," Brooks continued. "He and I met with one of the generals to decide what the project would look like. It took about a week of meetings to determine the framework and then another six months to iron out the logistics, but fundamentally it was a simple plan. Prince would put the essence of the Dark Lord, as he always refers to Satan, into a batch of beer. Then we would give the beer to a small, isolated pub with an incentive to sell it, stand back, and see what happened. Decide if it could be weaponized on a grander scale."

Don had to prize his teeth apart and relax his jaw before he could speak. "So why the federal police cover story, then?"

"Control was paramount to the operation's success. People see the army, it makes them nervous. People see police, they're reassured. We knew the Black Wattle residents would be more amenable to a police operation in their town. More co-operative. And that was important. We didn't want them alarmed or scared off. We also needed the test contained and Black Wattle's population and geography made it the perfect candidate for a real-world test. Small and isolated, one road in and out. Then, once we had the data we needed, Prince would lift the spell and Black Wattle would go back to normal."

"Jesus Christ," Truman said. "Couldn't you see that was a disaster waiting to happen?"

"Well, it might seem so in hindsight," Brooks said, riling, "but you have to remember this was uncharted territory. There was no template to follow, no precedent. No one even knew for sure that Prince could imbue the beer with satanic properties. All we had was his word. God knows, I was skeptical. I've been studying the occult for nearly two decades and most of it is myth and hocus-pocus. But Prince must have found the kernel of truth, the practical core at the center of it all. The first real-world test went like clockwork. That young couple that crashed into the war memorial? The driver was patient zero. My men were onto him and had him isolated before the transformation was complete."

"So how did you fuck it up so badly?" Don asked.

"Prince deceived us. Only imbibing the hexed brew was supposed to open the soul to demonic possession, but on Saturday night we found out the hard way he had made it transmissible through scratching and biting. He was meant to be there to reverse the possession as well, but after he and his men delivered the beer to the Ironstone Hotel, he absconded and left us to deal with the fallout. You know the rest."

With his tale told, Brooks' anxious expression returned. Don had seen that look more than once in his career—the freefalling terror of a man promoted past his competence trying to turn around a project headed for catastrophic failure. Academics seemed especially prone to it. Put in charge for their theoretical expertise, which counted for nothing in the field. How many coppers and servicemen had labored under ridiculous policies concocted by clueless academics and politicians who had never seen a minute's action? He doubted a single one wouldn't have a story to tell.

As if to confirm this, Brooks turned to Patrick with hopeful eyes. "Perhaps the Father can help us out of this mess."

Patrick regarded Brooks for a long time and then broke into peals of laughter. "Help you? What would you have me do?"

"You repelled that demon. You burnt it with. . .well, with your. . ."

"Not much more than a parlor trick. Backyard magic. You said it yourself, most of this stuff is myth I had no idea if it would even work. Frankly, I'm surprised it did." Patrick studied the bottle in his hand and clucked his tongue. "Blessed whisky. What a fucking pisser."

Brooks quailed visibly, like a man who had tried a lever that said PULL IN CASE OF EMERGENCY and found it unresponsive. "We have to destroy the demons now or they'll instigate a pandemic that makes COVID-19 look like the common cold." He plucked his walkie-talkie off his belt. "I'm calling in reinforcements."

"Hang on a minute," Don said, grabbing Brooks' wrist, "these are Black Wattle residents, not ducks in a fucking shooting gallery!

Shirley's daughter is out there. You need to come up with a better plan than kill or be killed."

"A few thousand deaths is preferable to the alternative," Brooks said. "You have to start thinking about this as an infection. Quarantine and destroy. If it's left to run rampant, it will spread exponentially."

"You keep saying that," Don said, releasing his wrist slowly, "but something doesn't add up. There must have been, what, sixty people at Shirley's pub on Sunday night? Let's assume a few didn't drink the beer or get scratched and managed to escape. So that's fifty, then. They disperse into the town and attack another fifty people. That's a hundred. Then two hundred, four hundred, eight hundred. Black Wattle is only tiny as towns go, but it's probably still got a circumference of fifteen or twenty kilometers. Can you honestly tell me your bullshit little company had enough manpower to patrol the whole perimeter? The demons should have spread into the countryside and been invading a neighboring town before dawn."

"We don't know that they haven't," Brooks said.

"Stop panicking and think logically," Don said. "There were twenty or thirty of them in that pack that went through your men near the eastern roadblock. Why didn't they all escape then, if that was their plan? They turned as a herd and came up towards the road."

"They wanted to make sure they'd finished us off."

"No, Don's got a point," Patrick said. He left Shirley and moved across to join the conversation. "Prince could have made his nasty little lager anytime he wanted and sold it to an unknowing public. But he didn't, he orchestrated an elaborate partnership with the government instead. Now why would that be?"

They ruminated on this. No solutions emerged from their think-tank of three. After a while Don said, "Well, Damon Prince started this, I bet he can stop it. He's your mate, Brooks. Instead of calling in the army and wiping out innocent civilians, get on the blower and tell Prince to fix this shit."

"Even if he'd listen to me, which he won't, I don't know where he is."

"Wouldn't he be at his brewery?"

"That was all a front. We had a regular brewer in Cowra distill it to his specifications and then Prince. . .did whatever he did to it.

He wouldn't let anyone else attend the ritual, not me, not even the general. He's probably gone to ground now. He knew we'd do all his dirty work for him."

"And you did, didn't you?" Don said. "The classic sucker. Useful idiot. You're not very useful now, though, are you? Dump us all in this mess, the entire fucking town, and you don't even know where your partner in crime is."

"Hey, I was just following orders," Brooks snapped back. "You used to be a copper, of sorts, I thought you'd understand—"

"Of sorts? Who do you think you are, you disrespectful little—"

"Hey—"

"—fuck, I've still got one good—"

"HEY!" Truman screamed. His voice ricocheted off the church walls and the arguing men winced.

"What?" Don said.

"Shirley's trying to tell us something."

She looked up at them, her face drawn and haggard, as if the mere effort of lifting her head again had sapped her final reserves of strength.

"I might have an idea," she said.

CHAPTER FOURTEEN

SHE HAD SOLD the beer. She was the gullible Typhoid Mary who had spread this pestilence to the town and for that, she had paid the highest price possible: her daughter.

Upon hearing Damon Prince's name she snapped out of her grieving stupor. Until that moment she had believed her capacity for personal horror topped out. But learning her blind desperation to make the Ironstone succeed had led to Elle becoming one of those things. . .that opened a whole new season of self-loathing, sorrow and guilt. Curtains of greasy hair obscured her vision as her head dipped again. She tried to cry and found she couldn't. Somehow she had moved past that, the way desiccated earth will repel water. How was it possible to feel so awful and remain alive? Perhaps she had transformed into a demon without knowing it and this was how it felt. Cursed to forever relive the moment her gorgeous girl burst at either end and became an obscenity.

But then Don's words cut through the blackness like a small shaft of light. ". . .get on the blower and tell Prince to fix this shit."

Get on the blower. Fix this shit.

A mote of hope, no more than a firefly in a cavern, started to glow within her heart.

Once Don and Brooks had stopped yelling at one another and were paying attention to her she said, "I might have an idea."

"That's one more than we have now," Don said. "Let's hear it."

"I have Damon Prince's business card."

Silence reigned in the church as everyone stared at her, digesting this. In the end it was Don, ever the pragmatist, who cast the first comment.

"I don't think that helps us, Shirl. Why would the number on the card be real if the rest of the 'business' was made up? Anyway, Brooks already has his phone number and I gather he's not answering."

"No, Shirley might be onto something," Brooks said. He paced as he pondered, and it was easy to imagine him doing the same in a lecture theatre with an audience of history students. "Once his plan was in motion Prince was finished with me, but he would have wanted a way for Shirley to contact him in case something went wrong. That's probably why he gave her the business card. He and I never discussed printing one, I can tell you that."

"What can it hurt?" Truman offered. "Pretty soon either Brooks' men will be demons or the town's residents will be shot to pieces. Anything's worth a try, even if it's a stab in the dark."

"Or a Hail Mary," Patrick said.

Don turned to him. "I imagine you have a phone here, Patrick?"

"There's one in the rectory. It would mean going outside, but it's only half a dozen steps from the church's rear door."

"You game, Shirl?"

"I'm game," she said. "But there's another problem."

"What's that?"

"I don't have the business card on me. It's up at the pub."

Many deep breaths were drawn and exhaled, the polite alternative to groans. Don massaged the back of his neck. "You can't remember the number?"

"I only looked at it once and it was a mobile number. I have a good memory, but not good enough to remember ten digits at a glance."

"Okay, fair enough. Consider me slapped down." He fetched his gun, tucked it into his left armpit and pulled out the chamber. "I knew it was empty, but I couldn't resist checking. Human nature, eh? All right, looks like we're taking a road trip. As it stands, we have an unloaded gun, a meat cleaver and a hell of a big knife. Truman, you happy to offload one of those to someone else?"

He nodded and passed the knife to Shirley, handle first. "You're the most important person in the group, you should have the biggest weapon."

Shirley accepted it without meeting Truman's eyes. She could barely stand to look at him full stop. Dried blood had caked in his eyebrows, around the shell-curves of his ears and nose, on his hands, along the waistband of his pants. She couldn't help but see the symbolism in him passing the blade to her, a baton of butchery. Shirley didn't even like killing spiders; the notion she might need to chop up some Black Wattle residents revulsed her. But among those residents numbered her Ellie-Bellie, and for her, Shirley would do anything. So she found a comfortable grip on the knife and let it rest at her side.

"You're forgetting something," Brooks said, wearing a teacher's-pet smile. "Patrick's bottle of holy scotch!"

Patrick regarded Brooks with a lizard-like tilt of the head, then went back to the pew where he had been consoling Shirley and picked up the whisky bottle. He turned it upside down and two drips came out; Shirley counted them as they made dark circles on the flagstones.

"All out, Brussels sprout," Patrick said.

Brooks was still formulating a response to this when Patrick smashed the bottle against the pew. Most of it went to shards, but the neck remained in his hand, a glass flower. He walked up to Brooks and smiled.

"Here you go," he said. "Irishman's knife."

A deflated Brooks tried to find a way to take it without lacerating his hand, ultimately holding it gingerly between two fingers.

Patrick raised his arms above his head and said in theatrical strains, "Suddenly I feel the need to deliver a sermon."

While everyone watched on bemused, he strode up the aisle and put himself behind the pulpit.

"What are you doing, Patrick?" Don said. "We don't—"

"Yes," Patrick boomed, "I need to preach to Don Winslow about the importance of carrying extra ammunition." He lifted his arms again and smiled. In each hand, he held a full whisky bottle.

Don and Brooks laughed out loud and Truman snorted as he stifled his. A smile crawled onto Shirley's face against her will but died as fast as it had come. Smiling felt immoral after everything that had transpired that morning. Christ, how could it still be morning? Inside her mind, a grandfather clock chimed perpetual midnight. She almost wished she could take one of Patrick's bottles, hole up somewhere, and drink the darkness away. But it didn't work that way, did it? If it did, Patrick would have sunbeams coming out of his face instead of two weeks' worth of salt-and-pepper whiskers.

"Are we going to do this or not?" she said.

Patrick left the pulpit to join them again, cracking the lid off a bottle. "Let's drink to our health," he said. "Spit don't swallow." He nudged Truman in the ribs. "Something you'd be familiar with I imagine."

"Just give me the bottle," Truman said, snatching it and putting it to his lips. He poured a good dose into his mouth and held it in his cheeks, like a squirrel storing nuts to take to its hollow, then passed the bottle to Shirley. Puffed out that way, his face became whiter than ever and she thought he looked unwell. She could understand that—she didn't feel too chipper herself— but as she received the bottle she noticed a similar pallor to his hand. Thoughts about Elle quickly crowded out other concerns, however, and she sloshed some scotch into her mouth. As the fumes filled her nose and throat she almost choked and spat out the liquor prematurely, but she kept her lips clamped tight and, after a while, the burning died down to a hot, gassy feeling in her sinuses.

The bottle made its way around the circle, finishing up in Patrick's hands again. Once they were all loaded, Don nodded to confirm readiness. Receiving four nods in reply, he disengaged the bolt and opened the door wide enough to permit his eye. Shirley half-expected a black claw to pierce it and jut out the back of his head, but that didn't happen; nor did anything crash through the door and trample him. Don extended his head out, tortoise-like, to check for another ambush from above. When nothing tried to decapitate him he stepped outside and made a quick three-sixty- degree sweep of his surroundings, before motioning for the others to come out.

They scarpered towards their cars. No more than ten meters, but it felt like the span of the Sydney Harbor Bridge. Shirley kept expecting the patter of demon feet across the scraggly lawn, a thump as one landed behind her and sank its fangs into her neck. Such tenebrous fancies came about under a bright morning sun; she couldn't begin to imagine what Black Wattle's less fortunate residents had gone through the night before, with those things stalking them through deep-sea darkness under a moonless sky.

Her SUV remained unlocked, a welcome convenience—until it occurred to her that one of the demons could be lying in wait on the back seat or huddled down in the cargo area. Her brain did a little *do-si-do* as it tried to decide whether remaining out in the open or jumping straight in the car posed the biggest danger. In the end, Patrick—encumbered by no such analytical musings—decided for her, ripping open the passenger's side door and tumbling in.

When nothing set upon him and rent the flesh from his face with black hand razors, Shirley followed suit and hauled the door shut. She hit the central locking button, handed her knife to Patrick and fired up the engine. Once it was running she ran down the electric window and spat a nauseating cocktail of scotch and saliva out onto the powdered earth.

"Sacrilege," Patrick said, smiling.

In no mood for another quip, Shirley put the window back up and threw the SUV in reverse. The others had piled into Don's wagon and she could see from the illuminated brake lights that they too were ready to roll.

"I wonder where they all went," Shirley said, once they were off the church grounds and tracking along Panorama Avenue.

"Maybe they got bored waiting for us to come out," Patrick said. "I imagine there are still easier pickings."

Yes, easier pickings. Such as the occupants in their little two-car convoy. Shirley wondered what in God's name they would do if they arrived at the Ironstone and found its roof and walkways acrawl with demons. Or what if they lay siege to the cars while they were in motion? Patrick's car had stunned one, or so he claimed, but if enough stampeded into a vehicle at once they would probably stop it and damage the engine. She didn't know whether to drive faster or slower, and for Shirley Goodsall indecision was an unwelcome intruder.

She allowed her gaze to dart to the rear-view mirror. Don's station wagon stared back at her with twinkling headlight eyes. How did a one-armed man stay so cool and in control? His police training, she supposed, although she doubted anything a country sergeant experienced could have prepared him for a town overrun with supernatural nasties. As they glided up the street, she also wondered where Elle might be, what was going through her head as she cavorted among others who had become what she had become. Would it be fun in some perverted way, or just plain torture?

Focus on what's at hand. Speculation won't help Elle a single scrap.

Nothing charged at the car, not even a stray kangaroo hopping across the road in search of grass. Something about that unsettled Shirley, almost as much as the horde that had chased them into the church. Where had the demons gone and why? She turned to Patrick, wanting to share her anxieties or at least know they weren't hers alone, but his whisky intake had apparently rendered him incapable of concern. Yet, though he slouched in the seat, his eyes had an improbable acuity. What kept them sharp amidst such long-term inebriation? Relentless emotion perhaps, grinding against his mind like a whetstone. Creating a cutting edge that sometimes harmed others, whether he meant it to or not.

"Handsome devil, aren't I?" he said. "Metaphorically speaking, of course. It seems important to make that distinction now."

Had her eyes lingered on him so long? She fixed them back on the road, blushing furiously. "Just trying to unpack the enigma that is Patrick Burnham."

All jocularity left his face. "You're a kind woman, Shirl. I only wish I had a deep and mysterious story to tell. But I'm afraid my situation is about as mundane as it gets. I lost my wife, I lost my faith, and I lost my mind. Because of that, I lost my flock. Now I drink, because I'm too cowardly to face the existential truth sober." He turned the scotch until the label faced upwards. "My courage comes in a bottle. Where do you get yours?"

Shirley left the question rhetorical. "Courage in a bottle might come in handy. When I left the pub, it was infested with those things."

She turned onto Goldfields Road and made the short run down to the Ironstone, slowing to school-zone speed as they drew nearer. Shirley could see no movement, nothing perched gargoyle-like on the gutters or chimney stacks. She pulled up outside and stared at the front door in silence. A few jagged glass teeth remained in the timber frame.

"Looks like it might be time for another mouthful of courage," Patrick said.

The station wagon parked alongside them. Don rolled down his window and Patrick did the same, passing him one of the scotch bottles. They looked like a bunch of seventeen-year-olds parked in an out-of-the-way location so they could get drunk for the first time.

"The exterior seems clear," Don said, passing the bottle to Brooks in the passenger's seat, "but you said there were demons inside, Shirl?"

She nodded. "They were waiting for us, or that's how it seemed, anyway."

"We need to clear the building first then, secure it."

"Clear the building?" Brooks said, voice rising. "That's mental. Just get in, get the business card and get back to the church."

"We can't," Shirley said.

"Why not?"

"Because Damon Prince is no idiot."

"What does that mean?"

"You're a smart man, Brooks," Don said. "Figure it out for yourself. Now come on, we need to get moving. Shirl, you know the basement layout better than anyone, so you and Patrick head down there. Brooks and I will check the upstairs rooms. Truman, you stand guard by the front door and yell out if you see anything. We don't want them to trap us inside. Don't engage them unless you absolutely have to. If the pub is compromised, we grab the business card, get the hell out, and try to come up with plan B. Everyone clear on that?"

A general murmur of assent.

"All right, let's do this. Quick and careful."

Everyone took a mouthful of whisky and got out. The sun was approaching its morning apogee and its intensifying light hit Shirley's skin with a feverish heat. In a nearby tree a bellbird tinkled, unconcerned about the events unfolding below. Shirley wished she could swap places with it. She stopped at the pub's damaged door, put her face through one of its timber squares, and waited for her pupils to dilate.

The pub remained as she had left it—upended chairs, microphone on the floor, a slew of smashed glass in a puddle of grog at the bar's entryway. When she was sure nothing lurked in the shadows or behind the furniture, she pushed open the door. Some loose glass shards fell from the frame and hit the ground in a vitreous rain. Shirley blanched and gave the others an apologetic look before stepping over the debris and moving inside.

Truman turned and waited by the doorway, meat cleaver at the ready. Patrick fell in behind Shirley as she walked past the bar and turned right into the corridor which led to the office and downstairs to the taproom. The office door was ajar a fraction and she used the tip of the knife blade to nudge it open. It revealed her desk, the wall safe, nothing unexpected. She heard the stairs creak behind her as Don and Brooks climbed them cautiously. Her limbs thrummed and scotch fumes swirled around in her head as she edged inside, knife raised to shoulder height. She craned her neck to see behind the door.

Finding nothing but hinges and drywall she let out a shaky breath, filling her nose with alcoholic fire. Eyes watering, she turned to nod at Patrick. He nodded back and they both returned their attention to the corridor. It ran a short distance and dead-ended at two doors; one gave out onto a disused loading dock and the other led to the cellar and taproom. Little light filtered into the corridor and, even though there was nowhere for a demon to hide, Shirley found herself taking hesitant steps toward the cellar door. In a city pub, she thought sardonically, checking the cellar would be unnecessary because only the foolhardiest publican would leave it unlocked. But this was a small country town and Shirley had become naturalized to their ways. Which meant she now had to search her own goddamned cellar for demons.

She placed a hand on the steel knob, then took a step back and mimed opening it and poking her head forward. Patrick appeared to comprehend her charade, nodding and adding some fluid to the holy flamethrower his face had become.

Shirley raised the knife, steadied herself, turned the knob.

The stairwell was almost perfect black; she could make out only the first three steps before they disappeared into the gloom. When nothing jumped out at Patrick he raised an eyebrow and shrugged his shoulders. Shirley crept forward and assumed his place in the doorway. The light switch was on the wall of the small landing at the top of the stairs, an architectural safety hazard that no post-war building inspector would have tolerated. But the Ironstone hailed from a different era, when men minded their own business and women minded no business at all, and if you fell down the stairs without somebody pushing you, it was your own damned fault.

She cursed those old men now as she stepped into the gloom and groped around on the wall, waiting for something to grab her wrist or bite off her arm. Her heart raced, her respiration became fluttery and erratic. Her hands whispered on the wall as they went around in circles and figure eights trying to locate the switch, which had apparently become mobile and crawled around evading her hands. Fight-or-flight worked well on the plains of Africa or the

North American woods or even in the back alley of a city street, but only made things worse when the task required spatial memory and a steady hand. She swallowed the whisky, fearful she would aspirate it into her lungs, then drew a long breath to tranquilize her mind. As soon as she did, her fingers landed on the old toggle switch—a bulky thing almost as old as electric lights themselves—and she wondered how the hell she had fumbled around and missed it for so long.

It illuminated a line of incandescent bulbs strung along the ceiling, below which kegs stood in soldierly formation. Plastic lines ran up from the kegs, into wall orifices and through to the bar taps. On shelving along the opposite wall was all the other stock—wine, spirits, soft drinks in cans and bottles, various exotic mixers. It all appeared in order, although that didn't discount the possibility a demon could be crouched behind the boxes or kegs. The stairs leading down were solid stone, another throwback to the pub's origins, so at least no demons could be underneath, ready to reach through the risers and grab an ankle.

Patrick joined her on the landing, surveyed everything below, then looked at her and tilted his head.

"I swallowed mine," she whispered. "I had to."

Patrick swallowed indignantly. "I'm not going to stand here and watch you drink it, am I?"

Shirley smiled in spite of herself and then nodded towards the cellar. "What do you think?"

His eyes roamed from corner to corner, enumerating and cataloguing potential hiding places. Shirley would never forget how those things had appeared in the pub earlier that morning, as if they'd risen up through the floorboards.

"Can't see anything," Patrick said. "Best to be safe, though. You stay here and leave it to me. This is an alcoholic's dream."

He winked at her, then filled his mouth with scotch and descended the stairs. She wondered how he could walk so boldly, fearless as a robot, checking behind shelves and kegs without hesitation. Then the sour truth came to her: Patrick didn't fear for his life. Becoming a demon would simply trade one form of damnation for another.

He walked the length of cellar, peering into every nook, behind every box. While Shirley watched on he swallowed the scotch and started to whistle, swinging his feet as though he were strolling through the set of an old Hollywood musical. As he passed the spirit racks his tune became a wolf whistle and he reached out a hand, snaffling a bottle off the shelf. He brought the label up to his face, went cross-eyed looking at it.

"Aw, Karloff Vodka," he moaned. "I'd sooner siphon petrol out of Don's car." He shook his head at Shirley and smiled. "You think you know a woman. . ."

"Come on," she said. "Save the comedy for another day."

"Right, serious," he replied, placing the vodka back on the rack. He saluted her. "Cellar clear, ma'am. Awaiting further orders."

"Get up here and stop dicking around. The others could need our help."

Patrick nodded, knocking off the stand-up routine and climbing the stairs. While she waited, Shirley pressed her hand against the door to the loading dock to ensure it was locked. The last thing they needed was a multi-directional demon assault.

As she and Patrick exited the corridor into the pub proper, Don and Brooks descended the stairs on their right. Shirley stopped and looked up at them.

"Rooms are all clear," Don said.

"Sparsely furnished rooms have their advantages," Brooks added.

Don rounded on him. "Did you minor in snide at university, or is it just a natural talent?"

Brooks swallowed. "I didn't mean to be rude. I was just saying it was handy because there weren't many places the demons could conceal themselves."

"It's okay, Don," Shirley said. "I'm not that fragile. Anyway, he's right—no one ever stays in those rooms. Why would they? Even Sean Doherty's dodgy old motel rooms have a television. How are things looking there, Truman?"

"All quiet on the western front," he said. "Well, actually, I thought I heard some gunfire before, but it was a long way off. We're okay for now. The door still closes and locks, so that's something, I guess."

Shirley went behind the bar, put down the knife and began rooting around in a box of receipts and other paperwork until she turned up Prince's business card. Red Horn Brewery.

Jesus, it was like he was taunting her, cackling at her from afar. She gathered her wits as best she could and began to punch in

Prince's number. Before she had all the digits on screen, another idea struck her. She cancelled the call and picked up the landline instead. If the pub's caller ID flashed up on Prince's phone, it would add a layer of authenticity to the story she was about to try and sell him. It rang for quite some time before he answered.

"Hello," he said. Toneless.

"Oh, hi," Shirley said, bubbly as an actress auditioning for a sex comedy. "Is that you Mr. Prince? It's Shirley. Shirley Goodsall from the Ironstone Hotel in Black Wattle."

A long pause. "Yes. Hello, Shirley. What can I do for you? Is everything okay?"

"This is a bit awkward, actually. I'm calling about your beer. It's not selling very well."

"It's. . .it's not?"

"To be completely honest, it's not selling at all. After you and your men left I drew off a glass and. . .well, it smelled a bit funky, like it had gone off. So, naturally, I didn't sell any to my customers."

"None at all?"

"I hope I haven't offended you, Damon. Especially after you were so generous. But I thought I should come clean. If you'd like to come and pick up your kegs, I'll be at the pub until nine tonight. Oh, I should tell you, the federal police have been using Black Wattle as some sort of training ground and they had roadblocks up yesterday evening. They might give you some grief."

Another long pause. Don and the others were grinning and pumping their fists and raising their hands in victory.

"I wouldn't worry about that," Prince said. "I can be very persuasive. I'll be there in an hour with another keg."

The line clicked and went dead.

CHAPTER FIFTEEN

IF *NOT FOR* fear of attracting demons, the whole room would have broken out in cheers. Don lifted his hand to applaud softly, forgetting in his delight that a clap required two. He patted it against his chest instead and drew Shirley into a one-armed hug.

"Hell of a performance, Shirl. Fantastic stuff. So he took the bait?"

"Hook, line and sinker, as far as I could tell. He's on his way, said he'd be here in an hour."

"Okay, that should give us plenty of time," Don said, pinching his chin. "Brooks, I imagine you'll receive a call from Mr. Prince any second now. Reckon you can deliver a performance as convincing as Shirley's?"

"I'll try my best. What should I say?"

"Tell him your men in the pub didn't know Shirley had disconnected the Red Horn until later in the night and didn't want to make a fuss about it for fear of raising her suspicions."

"I think I can manage that."

"Once you've spoken to Prince, you need to radio through to your men and tell them to collect any body parts visible from the road and draw the demons away. If Prince sees anything untoward, we're screwed."

"Assuming I have any men left," Brooks said glumly. Almost on cue, the phone in Brooks' pocket played a tune. He fished it out and raised his eyebrows. "Wish me luck."

He trotted upstairs before answering it, forethought Don wouldn't have credited to him until that moment. With leadership pressure lifted off his shoulders maybe he wouldn't be entirely useless. Some men, even the gifted and talented, weren't cut out to lead. Responsibility afflicted them like palsy.

Shirley had begun to straighten up the furniture with soldier-ant intensity. Patrick watched on, listing back and forth in time with the swell of whisky inside his head. He moved forward as if to assist her, then turned around and plonked his backside in one of the righted chairs. Don closed his eyes, giving his anger time to burn off, then picked up the microphone and put it on the folding table.

"I can do the chairs," he said. "Why don't you get a dustpan and brush and sweep up the glass? Not my forte, I'm afraid."

Shirley offered him a wan smile. "Sounds crazy to say it, but this is therapy for me. I'm nervous, and when I get nervous I start tidying things."

"Beats drinking away your troubles," he said. If Patrick picked up on the subtextual criticism, his face didn't show it. "We need it spick-and-span, otherwise Prince is sure to get suspicious. Go on, I've got this."

"Thanks, Don."

She went behind the bar and returned with an almost-new dustpan and brush. Probably purchased from the general store when she and her ex-husband had taken over the pub. Don had never warmed to Richard as he had Shirley. Evolutionary biology played a part in that, he allowed, but long before his romantic feelings for Shirley, Don had sensed a transience about Richard. The man was personable enough, knew how to treat customers, but the city stink never washed off him, not even after six months in Black Wattle. In arboreal terms he was a palm tree, only ever putting down the shallowest roots. It had not surprised Don in the least when he decided to cut and run at the first hint of adversity.

As Shirley swept glass fragments into the pan Don longed to put a comforting hand on her shoulder, help her tip the broken fragments of her old life into the rubbish bin and begin afresh with something undamaged. Of course, mooning over her had not, thus far, been a winning strategy. At that moment, he determined that if they got out of this horror show alive he would sack-up and ask her out. Better to fly and bomb out than sit on the ground wishing for wings.

Away with his thoughts, Don started a little when Shirley dumped glass shards into a plastic bin. "Sorry," she said.

"Not your fault. I guess I'm on edge, too. My mind is running a hundred miles a minute."

She put the dustpan on the bar. "Mine, too. I can't stop thinking about all those poor people running around out there as those things. My Ellie. Even if we convince Prince to undo what he has done. . ."

Truman, who had until that moment been standing watch at the door, turned to regard Shirley with guilt-ridden eyes. Clouds were coming in from the south and in the waning light his body's slenderness had progressed to emaciation, every rib and muscle delineated under his plasterboard skin.

"Then I murdered someone," he said.

"You did what you had to do," Don said. "It's no different than a cop shooting an armed ice junkie. When it comes down to a choice between you and them, there's really no choice."

"You were a cop?"

"Thirty years on the force."

"Did you ever shoot anyone?"

"No, I never had to. I drew my weapon—"

"Then how can you possibly know what it's like?" Truman said. He held up the meat cleaver, turned it to show the blood splotches along its blade. "I hacked someone to pieces with this. The girl who made my coffee yesterday morning. I chopped her up and then I ran away. No matter what happens, that will always be on my—"

Truman turned his head and was sick all over the floor. Shirley grabbed an ice bucket from behind the bar and carried it to him. Truman dropped the cleaver and put his face in the bucket, which amplified metallic disgorging sounds through the pub. Even though Don wasn't usually squeamish, his stomach quivered at the sight of the puke pond beside Truman's shoes. What bothered him about it he couldn't have said—the vomit was almost invisible against the dark-stained timber floor—but trepidation passed through him like a fever chill. When Truman removed his head from the ice bucket he had become cadaverous, color leached from every part of his face, even his ear lobes.

"I think I need to lie down," he said.

"Of course," Shirley said. "Let's get you upstairs."

To Don's surprise, Patrick vacated his seat and said to Shirley, "You got a mop and bucket somewhere, Shirl?"

"In the storeroom under the stairs. Thanks, Patrick."

"No trouble, love. Cleaned up plenty of sick in my time."

Shirley accompanied Truman to the top floor but did not

venture to touch him in any way. Perhaps she felt the same instinctual imperative to keep her distance, the same ill-defined foreboding.

Brooks passed them on the staircase. "What happened to him?"

"Unwell," Don said.

"Unwell in what way?"

"How should I know? One minute he was talking, the next minute he threw up."

"Hey, I'm just asking, okay? I'm allowed to ask. Christ, can't you cram your alpha male bullshit for one minute?"

Repelling an urge to job him one (in part because it would validate Brooks' aspersion), Don said, "He's been walking around all morning with no shirt. He's probably coming down with something."

"Maybe. And maybe he's turning into one of those things."

"If a demon got him he'd already be one by now. Elle changed, what, five minutes after she was scratched? Truman's been with us for the better part of two hours. We have enough to worry about without you freaking out. Did you get in touch with your men?"

Brooks gave him a sullen look and Don expected him to walk off in a huff, but eventually he folded his arms. "I got through to one of the unit commanders. He said most of the demons are now concentrated in several pockets in the middle of town, so keeping them away from the road shouldn't be an issue. One soldier will man each roadblock to let Prince through no matter which direction he comes from."

"How did your conversation with Prince go?"

"I barely got a word in. He spent most of the time chastising me, which is probably a good sign. If he suspected anything, he would have tried to poke holes in my story."

Don nodded. "Shirley's call must have really thrown him. He probably thought he was home and hosed."

There came a wet splat as Patrick slopped the mop onto the floorboards. Uncharacteristically for Shirley, her mop was some ancient hand-me-down that looked like a rake-thin old woman standing on her head. Her matted grey hair turned the color of gravy as it diluted and soaked up Truman's chunder. Another revulsive shudder passed through Don's belly. He glanced at Brooks, whose thin lips and large eyes insinuated a similar nausea.

"This stinks worse than a dog's ass," Patrick said, spitting at Truman's vomit as though he could somehow shun the smell. "What's that bloke been eating?"

"Car," Brooks said.

"Huh?" Don said.

Brooks pointed a finger. "There's a car coming. Look."

The blue sedan approached from the eastern end of town, moving at about thirty or forty kilometers an hour. Not a vehicle Don recognized off-hand. The sun was behind the driver, putting his face in shadow. As it went by, Don spotted a car rental company sticker on the back window.

"Did you see who was driving?"

Brooks shook his head. Patrick had been focused on his mopping. Don checked his watch. "It's only been ten minutes since Shirley got off the phone with Prince. Surely it couldn't be him already? He said within the hour."

Brooks shrugged. "Ten minutes is within an hour."

"I guess. But then why didn't he stop at the pub?"

Brooks looked at him wide-eyed. "Maybe he suspects something fishy. He could be driving through the town to see what's up, make sure he's not walking into a trap."

"Either way, we need to proceed with the plan. Patrick, get that mop and bucket out of sight. I'll dash upstairs and get Shirley. Brooks, you keep an eye out and give us a yell if he comes back."

As Don reached the upstairs landing Shirley emerged from room one and closed the door. She looked ill. "He's really bad," she said. "I wish Dr Sneddon were here."

"We've got bigger fish to fry," Don said. "A car just went past outside. We're not sure if it was Prince, but we need to assume it was. When he comes in, take him to the cellar under the pretense of collecting his kegs. Patrick and I will wait upstairs until we hear you open the cellar door, then come down so we're between him and the exit. Tell Brooks to hang back and cover the loading dock exit. We aren't very formidable, but between the four of us we should be able to stop him if he tries to make a run for it."

Shirley went down the stairs at staccato speed and availed Brooks and Patrick of the plan. Slow thumping footfalls announced Patrick's ascent, his hand clamped around the rail. In the other were his two scotch bottles. When he joined Don on the landing his breath had left him and his complexion had turned red. "Should never have given up that Pilates class," he said.

"Funny," Don said. "Slow that breathing or you'll give the game away."

"Our mystery man's back," Brooks called up the stairs. "He just parked outside. Showtime, ladies and gentlemen."

Quiet resumed. Then Shirley's voice: "It's okay, it's not him. You can come down."

"Christ," Patrick said, "I only just came up."

"Good for the heart," Don said. "Come on, let's go."

When he reached the bottom of the stairs, he saw a dark-skinned face framed in a broken door panel, hands cupped around the eyes.

"Anyone know who that is?" Don said in a low voice.

Murmurs of negation. The mystery man tried the door, found it locked, peered through the glassless frame again. "Is anyone in there?" he said.

Don stepped forward, picking up Truman's cleaver as he went, nodded at Shirley and Patrick to be at the ready. "That depends who's asking. What's your name?"

"Maurice. Maurice Monroe. I'm looking for someone. His name's Truman. I saw his car down the road and I thought. . .well, I thought he might be here."

Four pairs of eyes met. They all appeared to be wondering the same thing.

"Have you encountered anything strange in town?" Don said.

Puzzlement creased Maurice's features. "Strange? Like what?"

"Never mind. Do you have any injuries?"

"Why would I have injuries? I only just got out of my car. Do you know where Truman is or not?"

Don unlatched the deadlock. When he opened the door, Maurice retreated a step, as if he expected Don's next action to be a smack in the mouth.

"Get inside," Don said.

Maurice scuttled in and Don closed the door, setting off another tinkling avalanche of loose glass. The splintered frame wouldn't hold five seconds against a demon hell-bent on getting inside. Once Prince arrived, they would have to devise some way to shore it up.

"Show me your face," Don said, reaching out to him.

Maurice flinched away. "Don't touch me. Who do you think you are?"

"Name's Don. You don't know what you've walked in on, my friend. I need to check you over for scratches. If you don't play along, you can get back in your car and drive home again. Nothing personal, but we've been through the wringer and time is short. Now show me your face or get the hell out."

Maurice looked at the others, a wordless plea for someone to yank on this madman's chain. But finding no takers, he lifted his chin and averted his eyes in a curiously prudish way. Don examined his face and neck and found them unblemished.

"Take your shirt off," he said.

Maurice glared at him.

"Don't worry, your pants can stay on. Your shirt, Maurice, please."

With a resigned sigh Maurice pulled his T-shirt over his head, his hand bunching it into a cotton chrysanthemum.

"What on earth are you looking for?"

"I told you, scratches."

"What would have scratched me?"

"You wouldn't believe me if I told you. Hang around in Black Wattle long enough and you'll probably see one. Okay, you can put your shirt back on."

"Does this have something to do with the roadblock I passed on the way in?"

Don and Brooks shared a troubled look. "No one stopped you?"

Maurice shook his head.

"My men might not have resumed their post before Maurice arrived," Brooks said.

"Where's Truman?" Maurice asked. "Is he all right?"

"He wasn't feeling well, so he went upstairs to bed. Are you his. . .?"

"Partner, yes."

Don set down the cleaver and glanced at his watch. "Come on, I'll take you up."

The two men climbed the stairs, three pairs of eyes following them.

CHAPTER SIXTEEN

THE *ICE BUCKET* on the floor beside the bed is half-filled with treacle-brown sludge. Truman is ashamed something so vile came out of him. It's not as though regurgitation due to self-abuse is novel—in the past few years, a considerable quantity of expensive alcohol has gone out the way it came in. But this is different, something else altogether. A biblical word Patrick the Homophobe would appreciate.

Corruption.

The vomiting has abated but he feels worse. Much worse. It's as if his body has expelled retardant and the flames it quelled are free to blaze inside his bones, turning them to glowing-hot pokers. His bare chest gleams with sweat, the bedding beneath him sodden. He has become a late-autumn husk hanging from a dying tree, so dry he could crumble into dust. The ceiling's ornate cornice begins to spin—one-eighty, reset, one-eighty, reset. Someone has smeared petroleum jelly on the lens of his perception.

Through this blurred window, a face appears. Truman squeezes his eyes shut, gritting his teeth against the cornstalk of pain that sprouts into his forehead, then opens them again. It can't be. It must be a hallucination borne of the bonfire inside his skull.

But it does appear to be Maurice hovering above him, his athletic face riddled with worry lines and guilt. Why does Maurice look guilty? Perhaps Truman is misreading his expression through the shimmering heat-haze. Or perhaps Maurice is nothing more than a mirage, a comforting illusion Truman's mind has concocted to cope with whatever has befallen him.

Maurice says something. It's as if he's speaking into an old coffee tin. Truman isn't certain what he says, but it doesn't matter. Holding up his side of a conversation sounds impossible, akin to firewalking in plastic socks. His mouth feels disincorporated from the rest of his body, more like a proboscis. But he moves his lips to form what he hopes are comprehensible words.

"Got the blood in my mouth," he says. "Lots on my skin. Had to chop her up. Blood-to-blood must be slow acting, not like the scratches."

How much comes out as mush and how much Maurice understands Truman can't ascertain, but he turns away and speaks to someone else. Truman forces his head up off the pillow, sending a jolt of fiery pain from his ears to his tailbone. He sees a distorted image standing at the doorway. It might be a specter or a reflection in a funhouse mirror, but the general shape and flashes of color suggest it is Don. Truman lets his head fall back on the pillow, a wave of seasickness washing through his gullet, which clenches to expel its contents. But it is already cored out and only spasms in an ugly eunuch orgasm.

Maurice's hand enfolds his as he tries to recover from this exertion. It's a compassionate gesture, should be heart-warming, but his partner's touch (*should be husband, oh God, why isn't he my husband, why did I deny him that, why did I say no*) is cold sandpaper and he flicks it away.

"I love you, Maurice," he says. Inside his head his own words have an alien cadence and he prays his lover can understand. Words and actions are not always what they seem. Intentions are what matter, they are incapable of deceit even if they are flimsy and prone to failure. "I never meant to hurt you."

Maurice replies. It is difficult to decipher amidst the incinerator roar in Truman's ears, but he thinks it might be, "I know."

The hate seeps up, slowly at first, as if a small drill has tapped an underground well hidden in his subconscious. It is a bubbling tar pit seeking to consume everything, from the tiniest rodent to a herd of bull mammoths. An appetite for destruction as voracious and insatiable as a black hole. Maurice's face becomes an object of intense loathing, a new phobia that makes Truman's skin creep. His every fiber longs to lash out and destroy what, in the fractals of his rational mind, he loves more than anything. But those remnants are dying, burning up in the conflagration consuming him from the inside out. Time is short, soon his existence will no longer be his to command.

He sits bolt upright and screams, a thousand toothaches

throbbing all over his body, from hairline to toenails. His voice is fire in his throat. Maurice puts a hand on his shoulder and says something soothing but it only triggers the tar-pit fury again and Truman smacks his hand away as a surrogate for his true urge, which is to tear the skin off Maurice's face. Before anything else can interfere or impede his will, Truman forces himself to get up. Firecrackers ignite under the soles of his feet, blasting caps go off in his knee joints, his whole body wants to seize up, give up, submit itself to what is coming. But Truman finds an emergency reserve of willpower and lurches forward on rusty scrapyard limbs. Don is in the doorway and Truman expects he will try to stop him, placate him with some worthless platitude, but he steps back into the hallway.

Maurice yells—at him or at Don he is unsure—and then Truman is streaking down the hall towards the stairs, everything shaking and jolting and tilting as though seen through a handheld camera's viewfinder. He reaches the landing and, while trying to turn, loses his balance and almost goes headlong down the stairs. His hand strikes out and catches the rail, driving pain into every knuckle, but somehow he hangs on and stays upright and gets moving again. He can hear footsteps behind him and Maurice's voice adjuring him to stop, to wait. Negotiating the stairs is complicated, his brain and his feet now have only patchy communication, but he arrives at the bottom in a stumble, regains his footing and races on.

Shirley and the others fall back like rally-car spectators. The door, and purgation, are now in sight. The agony is unbelievable, a living thing ravaging his entire body, but through its blinding effects he spies the meat cleaver lying on a table, as though someone left it there for him. He snatches it up on the fly, unlocks the hotel door, and bursts out into a world he need no longer fear. A famous wartime quote passes through his head: *The only thing we have to fear is fear itself.*

Nobody pursues him outside, for which he gives thanks to the universe. He continues on into the bushland stretch between the Ironstone and the Goldmine Motel until pain and exhaustion crumple him to his knees. He leans back against a tree—a black wattle, in fact—then raises the meat axe and chops into his ankle. It hurts, hurts like first-time heartbreak, but it's no worse than the liquid fire filling his bones. A second and a third chop and his shoe comes off, lying sideways and spilling blood into the drought-scorched earth.

If he can't stop the transformation, then he can at least spare the others its horrors.

He manages to hack off the other foot, slicing through the last string of sinew just before every cell in his body splits in two and red flames swallow his soul.

CHAPTER SEVENTEEN

"TRUMAN, WHAT ARE you doing?"

"Keep away from him, Shirl!" Don roared down the stairs, "I think he's changing!"

"Changing?"

She shrank back as Truman stormed past, noting the red flushes spreading up his back. Maurice took the last three stairs at a bound and bolted after him. Shirley turned her palms outwards and tried to catch his eye. "Maurice, you can't—"

He crashed through her left arm and spun her around, a human turnstile. She made a grab for his shirt collar and missed. "Brooks, he's going after Truman! Stop him!"

In a single unthinking action, Brooks dived forward and tackled Maurice around the ankles. Maurice came down hard and so did Brooks, who winded himself in the process. He lay on his side gasping while one hand clung to a bunch of Maurice's trouser cuff. Shirley skirted them both, shut the door and deadlatched it again. Maurice got to his knees and crawled towards the door, trying to drag Brooks along with him.

"Let me go!" he screamed, kicking out at Brooks' face. Brooks tucked his chin into his chest and covered up with his free hand, but refused to relinquish his grip on Maurice's trousers. "I need to help him!"

"You can't help him," Shirley said, falling onto her haunches and taking his face in her hands. "If you go out there they'll get you, too."

Manic eyes bored back at her. "What will get me?"

"The demons."

This news appeared to offend him. He turned his face away and with a furious tug wrested his pants leg free from Brooks' grip. As he clambered to his feet, Shirley put herself between him and the doorway again. "You can't go out there," she said. "If you do, we're all dead."

"Get out of my way or I'll knock you down, I swear to God."

"Then you'll have to knock me down."

Maurice's hands contracted into fists, striations appearing in his forearms. If he came at her, Shirley decided, she would put her head down and charge her shoulder into his midsection. He had six inches and probably thirty kilos on her, but she figured she could slow him down if nothing else. In her peripheral vision, an out-of-focus Don was up to something near the bar. Patrick had circled around until he was in Maurice's blind spot and now crept towards him with heel-toe steps, scotch bottle poised to swing.

Maurice's shoulders bunched. His sightline darted to the street, searching for any sign of Truman, then fell back on Shirley's face with a murderous glint. Anything might have happened next, if not for the distinctive *click* of a thumb pulling back the hammer on a .38 revolver.

"Lay a finger on her and I'll put a bullet in your brain," Don said.

Maurice glared back over his shoulder. Finding himself eye-to-eye with the muzzle of a gun calmed his storm-fury a few knots. His expression became contemplative, although his fingers remained bunched into fists. "What the fuck is this place?" he said after a while. "What have you done to Truman?"

"We didn't do anything to him," Don said. He took some careful steps, closing the gap between Maurice's face and the gun barrel. "I know it's hard to believe, but Shirley's telling the truth. If you go after your boyfriend now, he'll slash your throat and rip open your belly and pretty soon you'll be a demon, too. Sound like a good way to spend your Monday?"

"Demon," Maurice said, as if testing the word's mouth feel.

"Get away from the door and we'll explain." Don jerked the gun sideways. "Move. We don't have much time."

Reluctance written across his face, Maurice moved crabwise from the door. Don's empty gun followed him like a tank turret. Once he and Brooks were obstructing a straight path between Maurice and the exit, Don lowered the weapon by degrees. The final fight flowed out of Maurice. His fists relaxed into hands again and his sturdy countenance disassembled into the whimpering face of a child who had lost his parents at a crowded country fair.

"This is my fault," he said.

Don and the others shared a puzzled glance. Maurice slouched over to a chair and sat, planting his face in his hands. Quiet sobs emerged through the chinks in his fingers. Shirley pulled up a chair beside him and caressed his shoulder.

"Shirl," Don began, "we have to—"

She gave him such a death-stare that his mouth shut with an audible *plip*.

"What's your fault, Maurice?"

"I'm the reason he came to this godforsaken town."

Don's mouth opened to protest, but he shuttered it again before words could come out.

"Why did Truman come here, if you don't mind me asking?"

Maurice sat up and swabbed his eyes with the heel of his palm. "Sorry, I'm not usually much of a crier. I must look a sight."

"Welcome to the club," Patrick said, raising a whisky bottle in friendly salute. He looked around him thoughtfully. "Or maybe it's welcome to the pub."

Maurice made a snuffling sound that might have been a laugh in disguise. "This is going to sound stupid, but Truman sort of. . .ran away."

"Ran away?" Shirley said, pushing gently for further confession.

"We've been together for about ten years. We have a townhouse in Paddington. Two mornings ago I came home early from a work trip and he was. . .in bed with another man."

"Oh, dear," Patrick said. It came out facetiously, whether he meant it to or not, and it was his turn to cop a Shirley death stare.

"That must have been a shock," Shirley said.

"It was. I didn't handle it very well."

"What did you do?"

"I just walked out and slammed the door. Like I said, I don't really do emotions. Truman's the sensitive one in the relationship. Feeling that he'd betrayed me. . .well, I was just all at sea. I ignored him, treated him like dirt."

"Sounds like you had every right to," Brooks put in.

Maurice looked up at him. "The thing is, he's not well. He hasn't been for a long time. He used to be a sought-after artist, did you know that? His paintings sold for thousands at auction.

But his life's been spiraling out of control the past few years.

Cocaine and alcohol. I thought about intervening a few times, trying to help him but. . .well, that's not how we did things in my family. So I've been standing on the sidelines watching it happen. Travelling for work a lot, too, that's always a good excuse."

His chin quivered and he put his hand over it, as though he could rub away the emotion responsible. "When I saw him in bed with another man, I just lost my mind. For the first twenty-four hours, I hated him. Pure hatred, especially when I found him in a drunken stupor on our doorstep the next morning. It was like he wasn't even contrite about his infidelity. When he took off in his car and disappeared, part of me was glad. But after a while, I realized his behavior was just another part of the sickness. The Truman I fell in love with never would have been unfaithful. One of our friends used to call us 'monotonously monogamous.' I think that's why Truman came here. He felt like he had to get away."

"How did you know you'd find him in Black Wattle?" Don said.

"Only a guess. Wine region road trips have always been our thing. We passed through Black Wattle a couple of years ago on a tour. We didn't even stop here. I thought it was just another run-of-the-mill country town, but Truman started waxing lyrical about how charming it was. Didn't shut up about it for days. He threatened to do a painting of it, but that never happened because he was already disappearing into a bottle by then. Now I guess he'll never. . ."

Maurice's voice hitched and he turned his face away. Don could appreciate his emotion. He could also feel time ticking away, and if Damon Prince rocked up, their problems would be of a much greater magnitude than one man doing the dirty on another.

"We don't know that he'll never do that painting, not for sure," Don said. "Something bad has gone down in Black Wattle, but we have a plan, or we hope we do. You've sort of walked in on it and we need to keep going, so I guess you're part of it now. That okay?"

Maurice shrugged, nodded. "Not much choice."

"Come on, we need to go upstairs. I'll fill you in." He offered Maurice his good hand and, connecting in a monkey grip, lifted him out of the chair. "You've got a lot to catch up on, so listen carefully."

They walked up the stairs side-by-side, Don launching into a narrative so absurd it made his mind ache.

CHAPTER EIGHTEEN

THE OTHERS WERE only ten feet away as the crow flew, nothing but plasterboard, ceiling joists, and timber flooring between them, but they might as well have been at the other end of the universe. Brooks radioed in to find out how Maurice had gotten through the roadblock.

"We came under attack, sir," a tinny, crackly voice explained. "He must have slipped past while we were neutralizing the threat. Sir. . .it's only Jervis and me left."

Once radio silence resumed, Brooks paced back and forth by the door like a leopard in a cage, sat down, stood up, sat again, fiddled with his phone, stood up, paced some more.

Alone with her thoughts, Shirley watched these restless antics and found herself floating on a rising tide of anger. This obsessive little man was the primary (arguably sole) reason her precious Elle was a demon and he had the gall to flit around like only *he* was under strain. Why had Brooks agreed to help the government put together its wacky little supernatural warfare project? Because he was a goddamned peacock. Look what I know, everyone! Look what I can do. Except he hadn't known what he was doing, had he? Just as the first scientists who split the atom had only a supposition that the chain reaction would stop, but what the hell, let's go for it anyway. Just as those technicians meddling with viruses in the name of pathogenic warfare had been so goddamned complacent until their containment measures failed and the whole world had ended up in isolation. Men such as Brooks, men with big brains and small minds, had given masculinity its modern-day PR problem.

The pub's interior became stuffy and oppressive and Shirley could no longer stand being in Brooks' general proximity. She got up and busied herself behind the bar. Spacing out the remaining liquor bottles so their absent brothers weren't so conspicuous. Wiping down the bar. Filling the ice tub. Televisions on. They filled the aural void and snared Brooks' skittish attention as a bonus. He stopped his caged-animal impersonation and connected to some sort of talking-heads current affairs show. Pundits and politicians wringing their hands and spouting hyperbole about matters that didn't matter. Shirley would have gladly set her hair on fire if it meant unconscious gender bias in society could number among her top twenty concerns.

She had moved on to stacking schooner glasses in different formations when Brooks' walkie-talkie crackled and a voice said, "This is Jervis. Come back, sir."

Brooks jerked like the device had zapped him. He unclipped it from his belt and turned his back to the room, as if that could afford him some privacy. "Brooks here. Go ahead."

"Target just passed through the eastern roadblock, now approaching your location. ETA one minute."

"Thank you, Jervis, understood. Brooks out."

He tried to put the walkie back on his belt, fumbled it, almost caught it, then lost it again. It clattered to the floor and he snatched it up. "Showtime," he said.

"I know what time it is. Make sure you don't fuck this up."

Brooks looked offended, just for a flash, then nodded. He scampered upstairs, where Patrick had already joined Don and Maurice. Shirley went to the door, undid the deadlock and opened it out to its fullest angle. A welcoming angle. Open for business, just look at the televisions and Keno screens.

No children or demons permitted in this area of the hotel, though.

She put herself back behind the bar, picked up a cloth, began wiping fingerprints off the cash register's LCD touchscreen. With no other movement to distract her eye, she saw the black Toyota Corolla the moment it passed the pub window. It parked nose-in at a somewhat drunken angle. The door popped open, and out stepped Damon Prince.

Then the doors on the car's other side opened and two more men got out.

Oh shit, Shirley mouthed to herself.

She almost screamed a warning to the others and then caught herself. If Prince heard it, the operation would be over before it began. She reeled in her nerves, put a woolgathering look on her face and resumed wiping down the terminal. As Prince marched up to the door, lackeys a few steps behind, he looked harried and distracted. But when he crossed the threshold his face brightened and the self-assured smile she remembered from Saturday morning completed the transformation.

Shirley turned at the sound of his footsteps. "Ah, good morning, Mr. Prince," she said, affixing a false smile of her own. Raising her voice just a fraction she added, "Brought some extra manpower, I see."

"It's Damon, please," he said, offering his hand. Shirley took hold of the repellent thing and fought to keep the disgust off her face. "And no, lugging kegs up and down stairs isn't really my thing."

"It's not mine, either, but I'm afraid it's part of the job."

"Indeed. Now, you say we've supplied you with a batch of substandard beer? I do apologize. Sometimes these things happen at boutique breweries. The product is superior but the quality control processes aren't always as stringent." He gave a down-home cluck of his tongue. "They make a hash of things and then I'm expected to come and clean up the mess. Who'd be in marketing, right?"

This appeared to be an attempt to relate, share common ground, so Shirley smiled and nodded. "It's okay," she said. "You get what you pay for."

Prince gave her a wounded grin. "True, true, but I assure you this is an anomaly for Red Horn. We're dead serious about the quality of our product and, free or not, if we've given you some bad kegs we need to rectify our mistake. You said the beer smelled a bit funky?"

"That's right."

"Would you mind drawing me off a glass?"

"Of course," Shirley said, subduing the internal voice that had begun to scream in panic. With Prince's laborers standing behind him like familiars, Shirley felt outnumbered and powerless. The plan she and Don had devised was already fraying around the edges. As she fetched a schooner glass from the ornamental stack she whipped her brain to try and make it produce an alternative plan. But it would only plod along on its original course and, when she thrashed it harder, it stopped altogether and lowered its head to crop at some clover.

She put the glass under the nozzle and pulled back on the tap, praying Karen had not emptied one of the kegs before the demonic infection broke out through the pub's patrons. Amber fluid squirted against the inside of the glass and she breathed an internal sigh of relief. She and Prince watched the level in the glass rise and form a thin foamy head. Once it was half filled, she flicked the tap off again and passed the glass to Prince.

He took it, gave her a quizzical look, then put the glass below his nose and sniffed. He swirled the beer around and sniffed again. "Smells fine to me," he said, handing it back to her. "Perhaps you were mistaken."

"I don't think so." She put her nose deep in the glass, making a show of it. "I've been doing this for a while and I know when beer has gone past its use-by date."

"I assure you, it's not."

She offered him the glass again. "Perhaps you should taste some, then?"

Prince studied it but made no move to take the glass. After a while he looked up at her and a smile touched the corners of his mouth. "You are a woman to be reckoned with, I can see that. And there's no sense arguing with a woman who has made up her mind. Very well, let's collect these 'gone over' kegs and replace them with the fresh article. Show us through, please."

Shirley left the bar and headed for the corridor. The two heavy lifters followed her but Prince tarried and for a horrible second she thought he intended to wait at the bar. But once they were all in motion he formed a caboose and they continued down to the cellar door in single file. Shirley wasn't sure how much more she could take. Tachycardia was difficult to mask at any time, let alone when the situation demanded a cool and calm appearance.

Then, as she opened the door to the cellar, another oversight hit her. If one of Prince's men picked up the keg attached to the line, he might detect its lightness. She doubted Karen had poured more than two dozen beers before the fun started, but. . .she did a few sums in her head. Two dozen schooners would add up to about ten liters, so roughly ten kilograms.

That would be noticeable.

She reached the cellar floor first and strode towards the kegs to stay ahead of the others while not making it look that way. Perpetrating this ruse was proving to be a speed-chess match, one with much higher stakes than prize money or accolades. She opened the refrigeration unit and detached the keg from the line. One of Prince's men squatted beside her and lifted the unused keg. She did the same with hers, giving a groan of effort she hoped wasn't overacted.

"Paul can take that for you," Prince said, indicating his bare-handed lackey.

"It's okay," Shirley said. "Part of the job description, remember?"

"No, I won't hear of it. Paul, please unlimber Shirley of her burden."

"It's fine, really. I can carry it."

Prince arched an eyebrow at her. "It is our keg, after all."

His voice dripped with suspicion and Shirley almost relented, before deciding to go on the offensive. "It's bloody heavy," she said. "If you don't get out of my way, I'll drop your precious keg and put a ding in it. You want me to sell your beer or not?"

Anger flashed in Prince's eyes, there and gone, biological sheet lightning. Then his salesman's smile took its place again. "Of course, you're right. How rude of me. We are partners in this, after all. Forgive me, I have some old-fashioned ideals. Mark, lead the way. Paul will be pleased to give you a breather, Shirley, but only if you need it."

They climbed the cellar stairs, Prince's heavies in front, then Shirley, then Prince behind her. His sudden accession jangled her nerves. Was he onto her? Had he hatched some plan to kill her and take his tainted beer elsewhere? Paranoia gripped her in its trembling hands. She ran pictures of Elle through her mind. Elle back to her normal self, Elle asleep and child-like in her bed, Elle's smiling face delivering a sarcastic remark as only a teenager could. This slideshow got her to the top of the stairs without falling apart. She chanced a sidelong glance at Prince as she turned into the corridor and found his gaze locked on her like a jet fighter's targeting system.

The corridor seemed darker and longer than before. Even half empty, the keg's heft had started an acid-burn in Shirley's shoulders and forearms. Ahead, Mark stepped into the pub proper, and his gait faltered, as if he had trodden in mud, but then he turned left and continued on. Likely he had forgotten which way was out. Were Don and the others still upstairs? Had they missed her signal or. . .left her to fend for herself? Shirley refused to believe that, but nevertheless, the situation had developed into a walking nightmare. Paul was only a pace or two ahead. When he stepped beyond the corridor he shied to his left, hands in a defensive posture, and Shirley's heart sang a golden song as she saw Don's gun pointed at his face.

But then the unexpected: Paul lunged forward and grabbed Don's wrist, wringing it sideways and tossing Don over his hip. Don hit the deck hard enough to vibrate the timbers and the gun skittered away. Without a thought, Shirley braced herself and swung the steel keg as though it were a cricket bat. Its blunt end hit Paul square in the face, caving in his nose and teeth. He tipped backwards like a felled tree and his head struck the floor with a fearful whack, sending up a fountain of blood. Throbbing heat engulfed Shirley's right shoulder and she dropped the keg. Before she could compute this injury, a wrecking ball wrapped in a blanket smashed into her and she went flying, her momentum skimming her across the floor until she came to rest an arm's length from the stairs. A swirling galaxy of stars filled her vision and, somewhere on the far side, a dimension of pain lay in wait.

When the stars cleared she discovered not only pain but Mark, who stood over her with his shoulders back and fists clenched. He raised his foot and she saw he meant to stomp her head. But she also saw Prince dart from the corridor. Shirley shrieked, "Brooks, stop him!" before pulling herself into a fetal position and waiting for a work boot to crush her skull or break her arm.

Instead, she heard what sounded like someone cracking a hazelnut. The floorboards rattled and when she opened her eyes again Mark lay beside her, unconscious. Don loomed over him, holding his pistol by the barrel. His breathing appeared labored and his face was twisted into a grimace.

Unable to get up, Shirley could only watch as Brooks stood gawping at Prince, who raced towards the door.

But as he made his final dash a leg shot out from the bar entrance and collected him across the shins. Prince got air, just as Shirley had, and performed the mother of all bellywhackers.

Patrick stepped out and approached Prince's inert form with a whisky bottle, ready to do further damage. But upon closer inspection, he lowered the bottle and took a step back, an oddly reverent motion.

"Looks like he hit his chin and knocked himself out cold," Patrick said.

"Is he out cold or dead?" Don asked. He tossed his gun aside, offered Shirley his hand and lifted her to her feet, then kneeled beside Prince. He touched his fingers to his neck, feeling for a pulse. His eyes developed a thousand-yard stare.

The world pulled focus around Shirley and her legs trembled. No. Not after everything she had gone through. Their one chance at redemption couldn't be—

"He's alive," Don said. "Strong pulse. He'll be back with us sooner or later."

He got to his feet and addressed everyone in the room. "We've finally had a bit of luck, let's not waste it. Brooks, you're on body duty. If that guy's dead, drag him outside and leave him there. I don't imagine zombie rules apply with demons, but there's no sense taking the chance.

When you're finished, find some way to shore up this concertina door. If the other demons come back it won't last a minute. Shirl, we're going to need rope or something similar to tie up our friends here."

"On it," she said.

"Patrick, you're with me. . ."

Don's voice diminished as Shirley ventured once more down the corridor. The cellar's cool air kissed her bare arms. It was an unusually large and modern facility, particularly for an old pub. The previous owner had expanded and updated it only a year before selling, or so the estate agent had told Shirley and Richard when they inspected the place. They had taken to storing odds and ends down there along with the beer kegs and other liquor stocks. She recalled a coil of bright green nylon rope Richard had used for some sundry purpose. It had become part of the cellar backdrop, disappearing from daily note, but handy now. She found it where she expected, just to the right of a small crate of high-end French wine no one would ever order—another Richard Payne brainwave. But when she picked it up and it unraveled, the dangling green snake barely touched the floor. It was also thicker than she remembered. If they tried to bind Prince's hands with it he would Houdini his way out of it with little effort. She tossed the worthless thing to the floor and put her hands on her hips. What else? There had to be something. If Prince and Mark regained consciousness another brawl would be sure to ensue. Christ, would this day give her one second to catch her breath?

Then, as if a guiding hand had turned her face, she spied the box of cable ties. Police often used them when they had to arrest large numbers of suspects or handcuffs were impractical.

She grabbed the box off the shelf and opened the lid. Not only was it nearly full, it contained cable ties in varying sizes. Definitely large enough to encircle a man's wrists, the bigger ones might even go around Prince's ankles. She wasn't so sure about Mark, with his brick-shithouse physique, but the ties were a fine start.

She tried to take the cellar stairs two at a time, forgetting in her excitement that only minutes earlier the brick shithouse had shoulder-charged her to the ground. Her ribs and diaphragm flared with pain and she grabbed onto the rail, wincing. When it abated, she continued on at a more sensible pace, pondering what injuries now lurked within her battered torso.

Back inside the pub, she found Prince and Mark lolling in chairs that Don and Patrick had arranged to face the bar. Only a pool of blood attested to the lackey she had kegged in the face, his body now presumably in a heap out on the footpath or in the carpark. She waited to feel the heavy press of guilt but it remained *in absentia*. Old rules of right and wrong were suspended, at least for the time being.

Mark's head rolled left and right across his chest. When he tried to lift it, he groaned.

"Just in time," Don said.

Patrick pushed Mark's hands into a mime of prayer so Shirley could slip the cable tie over and zip it closed. She didn't pull it too tight—no need to be inhumane—but made it secure enough that even if he worked up a sweat or drew blood it would not permit him to worm his hands free. The cable tie was long enough to encircle Mark's ankles. They bound Prince (who remained out cold) the same way. While Shirley was bent over zip-tying his hands she could see his chin's underside, which was the color of a squished blackberry. She wondered if he had cracked a tooth or two in the process. Hoped he had, which was not very Christian of her, but she couldn't help it. Shirley and organized religion hadn't been on speaking terms since her teenage years anyway, so she doled out turning the other cheek on a case-by-case basis. Damon Prince didn't qualify. Didn't even get to fill out the application form.

Meanwhile, Maurice and Brooks had upended a large table and chocked it in under the door handle. Around that they had arranged a clutter of upturned chairs and tables to serve as stumbling blocks. Along with the fastened deadlock, these would certainly slow any assault on the hotel. . .although if more than a few demons invaded, these defensive provisions wouldn't make a skerrick of difference.

Thus they convened—the disgraced priest, the divorced publican, the disabled policeman, the academic-cum-military-advisor, and the city man they barely knew—and stood in a semi-circle around the Satanist who had wrought hell on earth, or at least the part that mattered to them.

"Well, we've got him," Shirley said. "What do we do when he wakes up?"

"God knows," Don said.

CHAPTER NINETEEN

ACCORDING TO THE SAYING, some people drank to "still the demons"—another adage which now had a literal interpretation. But it was the old figurative version that had Patrick in trouble. For a while, as he fought alongside the others to ensure they had a future beyond the present moment, the ever-jonesing thirst receded into the background. In the present moment, with nothing to do but sit around and wait while Prince regained consciousness, it came back at him stronger than ever. Blessed or not, the whisky bottles beside his shoes sang siren songs, tempting him to drink the only effective defense against flesh-and-blood demons.

Patrick leaned back in his seat and placed an elbow on the armrest so the bottles behind the bar came into view. Schnapps, brandy, and grenadine had survived whatever onslaught claimed their brown-liquor brothers. Not a single bottle of anything worthwhile remained on the shelves. If the day continued its uneventful course and his ship sailed much closer to sobriety, however, he believed bargain-basement rum might become more than acceptable.

Downstairs. No shortage of fine scotch whisky in the cellar. The labels had stroked him under the chin as he searched for concealed demons, whispered salacious promises about peatiness and smoky notes and a refined numbness that the brain-damage brands couldn't emulate or even hope to approach. What would the others think if he excused himself to visit the gents and made a surreptitious detour to the cellar? If he were caught raiding Shirley's stocks, would liquor's warm womb be a fair trade-off for the crushing shame?

Not hypothetically, not at that moment. But he could feel his intoxication drying up like a dam in a drought, and once it reduced down to puddles. . .

"Brooks to red unit leader, come back."

Glenfiddich. Glenmorangie.

"Brooks to green unit leader, come back."

Johnnie Walker Blue Label, Highland Park.

"This is Brooks, please respond, anyone."

The static of a closing channel gave way to silence. And the sweet music inside Patrick's head: *Bowmore, Lagavulin. . . The Blessed Scotch of St Luke's.*

Maurice whistled a tune.

"'I Think We're Alone Now'," said Shirley. "Soundtrack to my teenage years."

Maurice smiled, although it was a tired-looking thing. "Truman was a big Tiffany fan, too. Terrible taste, the both of you."

"Seven million people would disagree."

"Jesus wept. Seven million people bought that single? Well, no one ever said good taste was popular."

"I'm glad you both find this amusing," Brooks said. "I don't think you've grasped the import of what this means."

Don sighed at him. "All your men have absconded or turned into demons and we're probably the only people left. That about cover it, Professor Big Brain?"

"Well. . .yes."

Mark, who had been fading in and out of consciousness for nearly an hour, now lifted his head and fluttered his eyelids. His sight appeared to come back online and he took in his surroundings via a series of sharp left and right glances. He tried to leap to his feet (apparently unaware Shirley had coaxed the cable tie closed around his ankles) and fell back into the chair. He gritted his teeth, his muscles tensed and his arms shook as he tried to snap the binding on his wrists. When the plastic wouldn't give, he slouched and stared bear traps at them all.

"Take these off," he said.

Don snorted. "Not bloody likely."

Mark turned his gaze on him. "You the soft-cock that pistol-whipped me while my back was turned?"

"That's me. Want my autograph?"

"Big man, hitting a bloke when he's not looking."

"You were about to stomp on a woman while she was down. Not sure you've got the moral high ground there."

"What's the matter, cripple? Afraid I'd beat you to a pulp in front of your lady friend?"

Don stepped forward and shaped to strike Mark across the face, but Brooks caught him by the crook of the elbow. "That won't achieve anything, Don. He's just trying to get you riled up."

"Don't let that stop you," Mark said. "Go on, hit me with your other arm."

"Shut your mouth or we'll gag you and put you in the naughty corner," Brooks said.

"Gag me with what? Your tiny dick?"

"Charming," Maurice muttered.

"I know where there's a length of rope just the right size," Shirley said, thoughtfully. "You'll be like a horse champing at the bit and we'll all get some peace and quiet."

The sheen of indignant bravado left Mark's eyes, just for a second, but then he smiled. "You're kinky," he said. "You going to whip me as well?"

Shirley ignored this question and set off down the corridor that led to the cellar. Patrick licked his lips. While no one was watching, what was to stop him taking a sip or three from the Blessed Scotch of St Luke's?

"You're all fucking dead, you know that," Mark said.

Brooks crossed his arms, seemed to study Mark anew. "You're. . .what. Prince's disciple? Is that what you call yourself?"

"Go chow your mum's vag, loser."

"Just delightful," Maurice said.

But Brooks appeared unperturbed. "Have you seen the things he unleashed on this town? What he has helped create?"

"Blah-blah-blah," Mark said, rolling his eyes. "Damon said you liked to hear yourself talk."

"Do you think he gives a damn about you? Once he's achieved his objective you'll be as expendable as the rest of us."

In lieu of another rejoinder, Mark lashed out with his tied feet and caught Brooks in the groin. Brooks let out a woof and staggered back, hands cupping the aggrieved area. He turned and leaned on the bar with his head down, sucking air through his teeth.

"What's the matter, mate? Run out of big words?"

Mark's throaty laugh resonated through the pub, several stanzas punctuated with a deep breath between each. Don's eyes sought his pistol and he probably would have retrieved it and clocked Mark again if Shirley hadn't reappeared with a hank of green rope in her hand. Mark's mirth de-escalated and then dried up altogether.

"Not before time," Don said.

Shirley sauntered around behind Mark and looped the rope around his face. "Open your mouth," she said.

Mark shook his head, turned away.

"Suddenly got nothing to say, lover boy?"

She pulled the rope taut around his chin, wiggled it up until it fell into the rut formed between his lips. Cords stood out on his neck and dimples appeared in his cheeks.

Brooks walked around (giving Mark's legs a generous berth) to stand beside Shirley. Hardness shone in his eyes. He leaned down so his lips were next to Mark's ear and said in a reasonable voice, "You're going to open your mouth for Shirley."

Mark's eyes moved sideways, showing the whites. He looked like a dog fixing to snap someone's finger off. But his lips remained pressed together.

"No dice?" Brooks said. "Okay."

He stood upright again, looked around to ensure he had the room's attention, then formed his fingers into an OK symbol and flicked the egg Don's gun had left on the back of Mark's head.

Mark screamed and the rope slipped between his teeth. Shirley pulled back hard, as though reining in a racehorse, then knotted the rope tight. Air passed in and out through Mark's nostrils and his pinched eyelids gradually relaxed to display two hateful brown jewels coruscating in Brooks' direction. Brooks smiled at him. Mark growled into the rope and tried to stand, but Shirley and Brooks pressed him into the chair again, one shoulder each. He attempted to describe their failings (Patrick surmised) and could only produce mashed-up vowels. Wrenching his shoulders from their grip, he glared at them each in turn then shook his head and stared at a spot on the floor.

"Well, now. You're a resourceful bunch, aren't you?"

Prince sat upright in his chair, eyes glass-clear, hands a neat almond in his lap. He smiled, as though pleased to see old friends. His gaze terminated on Shirley and he tossed a string of hair off his forehead. "Especially you, my dear. It's been a long time since anyone got the better of Damon Prince, but you duped me, I confess. You have my admiration." He wrinkled his nose at Brooks. "Even if the company you keep leaves something to be desired."

"You lied to me!" Brooks said, spittle flying from his lips. "This was supposed to be a controlled test, no casualties. Now innocent civilians are in pieces!"

Prince tilted his head compassionately. "Oh, what's the matter, Mr. Brooks? Playing soldier boy not working out the way you wanted?"

"You son of a—"

Don put his arm across Brooks' chest. "Prince, we just gagged your friend here because he couldn't stop running his mouth. You want to join him?"

Prince turned his attention to Don, the low-wattage smile powering up. "That's an odd threat. I don't think you want me to be quiet, do you?"

The question hung in the air, a clay pigeon sailing off into the distance. Don shuffled his feet. Brooks swallowed and glanced at Shirley and Maurice. Maurice looked back as if to say, *I only just got here, what the hell do you want me to do?* Shirley's eyes found Don and implored him to say something, anything, that would return serve.

Don cleared his throat. A preamble to an incisive rejoinder that got lost on the way to his mouth.

"No of course you don't," Prince said, filling the void, "otherwise you wouldn't have gone to the trouble of luring me here. That's what this is, isn't it?"

With everyone's attention diverted to Prince, Patrick allowed his fingers to close around the neck of a scotch bottle. He lifted it and tightened his other hand around the cap. One swig, no need for more. Just enough to right the ship, stop it capsizing into sobriety.

At last, Don unplugged the mute from his voice box. "You're going to reverse this," he said softly. "We know you know how."

"Oh? What gives you that impression?"

"Brooks told us how you. . .did something to that beer you gave Shirley."

"Did he say that? My, my, quite the insightful fellow. Do tell, Mr. Brooks, edify us all. Just what exactly did I do to the beer I gave Shirley?"

Brooks looked like he'd been shoved into a witness box against his will. His eyes went back and forth between Prince and the others, tennis match eyes. "You told me you were going to taint the beer with the essence of the Dark Lord. That when someone drank it, he or she would become. . .a demon?"

Prince shrugged—a rude, almost cruel gesture. "You're telling the story, Mr. Brooks."

"I don't remember the exact term you used."

Addressing Don, Prince said, "This is the person you're relying on for your facts? His recollection appears patchy at best."

"Fuck you!" Brooks burst out. "You know what happened. You know what you did. Why are you lying?"

"I ask you again: what did I do?"

"You turned an entire town into demons!"

"How do you know I had anything to do with it? Maybe the town's water supply was contaminated."

"Don't try to obfuscate," Brooks said.

"On the contrary, Mr. Brooks, I'm trying to clarify. You told everyone in this room I did something to the beer. What exactly?"

Brooks closed his eyes, sighed. With his eyes still shut he said, "I don't know."

"Marvelous!" Prince said, lifting his hands into a *xiè xie* gesture. "Now we're getting to the nub of the matter. You asked a master of the occult to invoke a batch of beer with the essence of the Dark Lord. Then you walked away and left him to do it in secret because he told you to. You and the simpletons you call superiors were so desperate to have the next weapon of mass destruction you didn't even stop and consider what you were approving. Did they use the word 'greenlight'? I bet they said greenlight."

Without opening his eyes, Brooks rubbed a hand across his forehead. Then nodded.

"Of course they did," Prince said. He could have been Sherlock Holmes explaining to the hapless Watson how he solved the case. "Dullards are Lucifer's closest allies. He loves them as God loves the meek."

Brooks opened his now-limpid eyes. As he stared at Prince, a single tear sprang out and sparkled on his cheek. "So can you reverse the effects or not?"

"Certainly, I can," Prince said, his tone suffixing the sentence with an unspoken *silly billy*. "But what on earth makes you think I would?"

Quick as light Maurice launched forward, grabbed a handful of Prince's hair and slammed a fist into his midsection. Prince groaned and tried to double over, but Maurice wrenched his head up and screamed into his face, "Do it or you're fucking dead! You understand? You stole my Truman and you need to give him back."

He tossed Prince's head away. Prince took a moment to compose himself, then licked his lips and smiled at Maurice. "*Your* Truman? Very well, then. But only because you asked so nicely."

Prince leaned back in his chair and raised his hands above his head, then closed his eyes and brought his hands down so his thumbs rested against his forehead. In a theatrical tenor he began to recite, "*A meretricis magnæ, et ad actus homosexuales deambulatio hominis infirmi, in deversorium.*" Then he lowered his hands and beamed at the room, as though seeking approval or applause.

"Does anyone know what he said?" Don asked.

Patrick put down the scotch bottle. "It was something in Latin," he said. "I don't know what though. It's been too many years."

Brooks sighed exhaustedly and said, "A whore, a faggot and a cripple walk into a bar. . ."

"Ah," Patrick said, slapping his thigh and snapping his fingers, "that's it."

Quietly, as if passing through a library, Don went over to the bar and picked up the carving knife. He came back exhibiting the same calmness, then stabbed the blade at Prince's throat. The tip stopped a fingernail's width from his Adam's apple. Prince's eyes widened and his throat bobbed, but otherwise, he remained motionless. After a time, the patient smile reappeared.

"We both know you don't intend to kill me, so perhaps we can forego any further displays of machismo?"

Don swiped the knife sideways and Prince hissed air through his teeth. A red line appeared on his neck, weeping out a liquid ruby. "I don't know why you did this," Don said, "but you're going to fix it. Maurice's partner, Shirley's daughter, the people of Black Wattle, none of them deserved this. If I can't save them from damnation, then you can be damned sure I'm going to take vengeance on their behalf."

"My, my, such melodrama," Prince said. "Really tugs at the heartstrings, doesn't it, Mark?"

Mark nodded and grunted in assent.

"Fine, then. Let's see what I can do."

Once again, the eyes to the ceiling, the thumbs to the forehead, the evangelical voice.

"Ubi prius fuerunt daemones daemonibus et non erunt ultra."

He placed his hands in his lap again, prim as a 1950s wifey. "There you go," Prince said. "The spell is lifted."

All eyes went to Brooks. He shrugged his shoulders. "It's no incantation I'm familiar with. But with no rites. . .no pentagram. . .it's hard to say with any certainty—"

"Balderdash," Prince spat. "Primitive props and symbolism designed to impress superstitious dolts. Words and intent are what matter."

"Well. . .the words were. . .I suppose they were appropriate."

"Of course they were appropriate you waffling imbecile. I assure you, all of you, the spell is lifted."

"Really?" Don said. "Then, I'm sure you won't mind if we put that claim to the test." He patted Mark on the shoulder. "Old Marky-Mark here has been getting on our nerves. If we put him outside, do you reckon that might attract some interest? Worm on a hook?"

Prince shrugged. "Fine by me."

But Mark began to make mumming sounds around his rope gag, stamped his feet, shook his head as though a bee were crawling in his hair.

"No need to cause a scene, Mark," Prince said. "It's perfectly safe now, you have my word."

Don looked at the others, pulled on an earlobe. "There's only one way to find out if he's telling the truth."

He and Shirley moved the barricading table away from the door, while Brooks and Maurice carried Mark, chair and all, as if he were some small-time pharaoh. He tried to buck himself out, but they tipped the chair back so gravity held him in place. He wriggled and fought and before they could get to the open door he flipped his legs over his head and performed a backward roll, evacuating from the chair and crash-landing on his knees and elbows. He growled his pain and then tried to get away in a series of shuffling caterpillar arches. Brooks caught him beneath the armpits and Maurice grabbed his legs.

"If you'd rather stand, you could have just said so," Brooks said.

They tossed him onto the pavement, then retreated inside and locked the door. Don and Shirley put the table-barricade back in place. All the while Prince watched them—a curious scientist watching ants go about their business, Patrick thought. The whisky sang to him in a high and sustained soprano note and he put his hands over his ears to drown it out.

The rest stood at the door; zoo visitors watching feeding time at the tiger enclosure. Not game to leave Prince unattended, Patrick shifted a few paces closer and craned his neck to peer around Shirley's shoulders. Mark now sat on the footpath, legs out, an L-shape. His face turned this way and that, trying to see everywhere at once. *Bet he wishes he had a fly's peepers,* Patrick thought. He made eye contact with his observers and yelled something, although the gag and the glass doors filtered out its meaning.

After a time he scooted backwards to put some space between him and his deceased workmate and then just sat hugging his knees. This display of fatalism turned up the volume on Patrick's inner soprano. His hand gripped the scotch bottle tighter. He looked back at the second bottle, in front of the chair where he had left it. Two was surplus, really. They had Prince now, they weren't going anywhere. Even if he drank the rest of this one, the other one was near enough to full. Plenty in reserve.

"Anyone see anything?" Don said.

Maurice shook his head. "Nothing. What did you say the demons looked like?"

"Don't worry, you'll know one when you see it."

Shirley rested a hand on Don's shoulder and stood on her toes to whisper in his ear. From where he stood, Patrick could scarcely detect her voice, but in concert with her moving lips the message reached him: "Is it possible he's telling the truth?"

Don's eyes dwelled on her hand, just for a tick, then he said, "I suppose it is. But I don't believe so." He leaned across and murmured to Brooks, "What do you think?"

"No way to be sure."

"What did he actually say?"

"Something along the lines of, 'Where there were demons, let there be demons no more'."

"So is that a spell or not?"

"I don't know."

"How can you not know? You're supposed to be an expert in all this shit, aren't you?"

"I'm an expert in the occult," Brooks said, bristling. "I don't practice satanic rites. Anyway, I never pretended I had all the answers."

"A little disagreement over there?" Prince enquired.

"Shut your trap," Don said. "No one's asking you."

"Dear me. That's gratitude for you. One minute it's, 'Please lift the spell' and in the next breath, you're telling me to be quiet. Do try to be consistent."

Don stalked towards to Prince, finger pointed. "I've had just about enough of you. I'm starting to think luring you here was a mistake."

"Probably," Prince said, as if he had already wearied of the conversation. "I certainly can't understand what you're trying to achieve."

"We want our town back, goddamn it!"

Don backhanded him across the face, hard enough to rock Prince sideways and upset the chair. It stood on two legs, gravity and momentum tussling, before gravity won out and the chair righted itself with a wooden *clack*. Redness stamped Prince's cheek in a rough heart shape.

He shook some hair out of his eyes and regarded Don with disdain. "Violence is the language of the ignorant," he said, "and hitting a man when he can't lift a finger in his own defense is just gutless. But then that's the only way you can hope to win a fight these days, isn't it? Go ahead, hit me again if it will make you feel better."

Don looked at his hand as though it were as useless as his other one. Patrick watched him deflate, authority escaping via slow leak. Prince had punctured him. Eventually, he turned to Prince and said, "Why are you doing this?"

Prince only smiled.

"There!" Maurice cried. "There, I see—Jesus! Fuck!"

He stutter-stepped away from the door and tumbled over backwards. The others, who had drawn in around Don, now rushed to Maurice's aid while staring through the glass. A demon latched onto Mark's shoulders, wasp-like, and sank its teeth into his skull. Blood spilled down his face in octopus tentacles as he squealed and tried to bat it off with an awkward chopping motion. It didn't even blink in response to this puny assault, crushing its jaws closed, digging its dagger-like teeth deeper. Then it threw itself back and tore off Mark's scalp in a single violent motion, exposing the glistening red skull beneath. A ragged wig hung from its teeth, dripping blood, then the demon tossed it aside and jumped off, leaving behind rows of weeping scarlet holes across Mark's back and shoulders. Eyes scrubbed blank with shock stared out beneath the ruins of his head.

Then Patrick noticed something else. Even though the attack had sagged Mark's posture, the demon stood no taller than he.

A child. Until a few hours ago, the wasp-demon had been someone's child.

Contemplating this, Patrick's mind began to teeter. The child-demon swiped its claws across Mark's exposed neck, opening three horizontal wounds. More blood gushed, the high-vis yellow of Mark's vest now all but saturated in scarlet. He fainted forward, only his bound hands preventing him from folding in two completely. The demon performed a skittering little jig, as if it still had murderous energy to burn, then sprang onto the window and dug its claws into the wooden frame.

The whole band cried out in unison, tried to scramble backwards, fell over one another like puppies in a playpen. The demon pressed its face against the windowpane, yellow eyes blazing, seeking, ravening. Patrick chose that moment to glance down at Prince and found a gluttonous smile slathered across his chops, as if on the brink of salivating at the situation he had orchestrated.

Hands trembling and slick with sweat, Patrick unscrewed the bottle cap and cast it aside. "In the name of God!" he proclaimed, before lunging forward and splashing the holy scotch into Prince's face.

CHAPTER TWENTY

ONCE *SOMETHING STIMULATED* a man's ardor it never shut off until flat-out rejection cut the power. At best it went into standby mode, the little red light of passion waiting until a signal triggered it back into full glowing intensity. It was a binary system, ready or go, and just like a machine it never considered social niceties.

Such were Don's thoughts as Shirley flinched away from the doors and bumped into him, their legs tangling and sending them both to the floor. She sort of fell in his lap and his nose nuzzled into her hair, an intimate embrace that thrilled and mortified him in equal measure. How could his mind turn to such matters when only a pane of glass stood between Shirley and a hell-child that had just savaged a grown man?

The momentary flash of desire passed as fast as it arrived, Shirley rolling off him and onto her hands and knees. Don had propped himself on an elbow when he heard Patrick's voice raised to its fullest preaching boom. He strained his neck in time to see him douse Prince's face in scotch.

Prince squeezed his eyes shut and turned away. Don's heart hammered against his ribs and Patrick stood there agape, as though he had just bet his life savings on black and the roulette wheel had started to spin.

For a long time Prince remained motionless, head lowered, scotch dripping from the long strands of his fringe. Then his face came up with a deliberate slowness that reminded Don of the famous scene in *Nosferatu*, and a chill tinkled along his spine. Prince smiled at Patrick and licked his lips.

"You have a fine taste in vintages," he said. "Thank you for sharing it with me."

"You. . ." Patrick said, extending a shaking finger at him, ". . .you should have. . ."

Prince showed the room a cheery face. "Anyone know what our friend is rambling about?"

"He hoped you'd burn up like one of those abominations outside," Don said.

"Burn up?" Prince said, arching an eyebrow. "I see. You've been casting a spell or two of your own, have you, Father?"

Patrick backpedaled a few steps, shaking his head. The open bottle hung from his hand, limp, as if at the end of a noose.

"Perhaps you thought you'd torture the spell out of me, was that it?"

Patrick fell onto his backside, scotch shooting out the top of the bottle like a volcanic eruption.

"Be my guest, do your worst."

"Oh, don't worry," Don said, advancing on him. "We intend to."

"What do you intend to do, big man? Punch me? Pull out my fingernails? You don't understand what you've blundered into. Not even Mr. Brooks has the faintest inkling. Every person in this town is now a foot soldier for the Dark Lord. At sunset, from your precious hilltop, an army of fire-spawn will charge forth and consume the earth. I am the floodgate. Should you kill me, you will only hasten the inevitable, bring it forward from sundown to now."

"Look," Patrick said, the fold of his robes falling away to expose his bony arm. His finger tremored.

Every panel in the pub's concertina door framed a demonic body, a mosaic of cauterized flesh pressed up against the glass, smearing it in cloudy streaks or sloughing off in chunks that stuck to it like fish bait. The serried masses had darkened the room, blotting out late afternoon light that should have streamed through the western windows. They seethed against and on top of one another, like sawfly larvae swarming on a tree trunk. The herds that assaulted Brooks' men near the roadblock had showed remnant human characteristics in the way they moved.

These had evolved, if evolved was the right word—perhaps *devolved*, because the crawling motion of their bodies spoke more of voracious caterpillars ready to consume everything in their path than the delicate architecture of butterfly wings. Doom overtook Don, drove a shaft deep into his soul.

"Why don't they break in?" Shirley said, her voice laced with sick awe. She had addressed the question to no one in particular, but it was Prince who responded.

"I am under the Dark Lord's protection," he said. "They will not risk injuring me in an attack. And why would they? The hour of their ascendency draws near. . ."

Prince continued to ramble on about the apocalypse and their futile resistance but Don's mind zoned out. He had plucked a single phrase from Prince's windy monologue and now cupped it in his metaphorical hands, examining it.

The hour of their ascendency.

Something in that combination of words twanged his copper's instincts, blunted though they were. But the vibrations wouldn't cohere to form a complete note; they remained maddeningly indistinct. Don pushed one ear on his shoulder and pressed the flat of his hand against the other so he could muffle out Prince's declarations, contemplate the words in silence.

A second later, he had it.

A man less accustomed to interrogations might have blurted something out, but Don relaxed into a poker face. Then, from that neutral baseline, he broke out in a smile and put a hand on Shirley's shoulder.

"Well, I don't know about the rest of you," he said, interrupting Prince, "but I've heard about enough of this blathering. Prince reckons there's nothing we can do to avert his apocalypse, and his word is good enough for me. I move we repair the cellar, lock the door and get good and shit-faced on all the top-shelf stuff Shirley has hidden away down there. How about it, Shirl?"

Maurice and Brooks gawped, as if Don had grown daisies out of his ears. Shirley studied him thoughtfully. Patrick rose to his feet, grinning, and said, "That's the best suggestion I've heard all day."

After a while, Shirley nodded. "What the hell. There are worse ways to go. And if there is an apocalypse at sunset, the liquor will just go to waste anyway. Come on, then. Drinks are on me."

As they began to move off, Brooks said, "I. . .uh, I don't drink."

Jesus fucking Christ, Brooks. Read between the lines.

Keenly aware Prince was watching this exchange with those beady, all-seeing eyes, Don said, "What, not even a beer on a hot day?"

"I don't like alcohol."

"Okay, great, you stay here and keep an eye on Prince. Make sure he doesn't disturb us. This is your mess, anyway, you don't deserve a drink."

Initially, Brooks looked put-out. But after a while he nodded, a child who had decided to take his medicine. "He's not going anywhere."

"Why should I wish to go anywhere on the eve of my success?" Prince said, but Don roundly ignored him and the others did the same. Shirley led the way along the corridor and down the cellar stairs, Patrick tailgating her the whole way. Don walked through last and shut the door behind him.

"Where shall we start?" Patrick said, rubbing his hands together. "I thought—"

"Stow it, Patrick," Don said as he joined the group, "I didn't get you down here so you could drink your woes away. I wanted to talk to you all in private, without that snooty devil-worshipping dipshit trying to mess with our heads."

Disappointment rippled across Patrick's face.

"What is it, Don?" Shirley said. "I don't think we should leave Brooks alone up there any longer than we have to."

"Agreed, so here it is. During his mad-Mussolini victory speech, Prince mentioned 'the hour of their ascendency', and that got me thinking. He's a normal man, we know that, otherwise he would have snapped the cable ties and brought hellfire down on our heads or something. But if he's a normal man, even one that worships the devil, why the hell would he want hell on earth? Unless. . ."

A smile dawned on Shirley's face. "Unless the devil is going to give him his due."

"And that means he has something to lose," Maurice said, snapping his fingers.

"Right. We don't know what that thing is and Prince would never tell us because it's his soft underbelly. But this is a wedge, something we can use against him. We need to make it count. I have an idea how we can force his hand, but we'll need to hook up one of those Red Horn kegs without him knowing."

"As I recall, there's one near the bottom of the stairs and the other one is almost right in front of him," Maurice said. "We'll never get a keg down here without Prince noticing."

"Unless we distract him somehow," Shirley said.

She let them know what she had in mind. Don didn't much care for it, but sunset drew down around six o'clock in September. They were out of time and options.

"All right. Maurice, you're a fit-looking rooster. Reckon you can handle the keg?"

"Of course."

"Good. Because if you can't do it, that leaves Patrick or me. Can't see either of those options turning out too well."

"Speak for yourself," Patrick said. "I'm as fit as a Mallee bull."

"You're as fit as that cow you ran down with your car. Come on let's get on with it. Break a leg, you two."

Shirley and Maurice climbed the stairs together. Don leaned against the wall and wished he could cross his arms. Spiders of jealousy crawled all over him, even if Maurice was gay. That should be him up there with Shirley, doing the heavy lifting while she plied her feminine wiles. But the nerveless dangling appendage he called an arm couldn't even scratch his nose.

"Fancy a tipple?" Patrick asked.

Don looked at Patrick's dry complexion, carved up with wrinkles and dusted in yellowing whiskers that belonged to a man twenty years older, and shook his head.

"This town's full of bloody wowsers," Patrick said. He sat on the second step from the bottom and planted his chin in his hands.

Not in part, Don knew, because prior to that they had been shaking.

CHAPTER TWENTY-ONE

"**A** WOMAN'S WORK is never done."

So went the old saying, and it felt truer than ever to Shirley as she strode up the corridor to match wits with Prince for the second time that day. Don's insight had given them a method to tighten the screws on Prince, but putting that method into practice had fallen to her. That she had volunteered seemed immaterial—somehow everything in life became her responsibility or it failed. This was Richard and the Ironstone Hotel all over again, history repeating itself. The man rode the uprush of inspiration and then watched on from above while the woman slaved away in the engine room to keep the cogs greased and turning.

You're selling Don short. He's not like Richard. If today has proved anything, it's that.

True enough, but trying to be fair and objective in the face of what lay ahead took more mental resolve than Shirley could muster. Maurice hung back, rolling heel-to-toe to mask his steps, and two-thirds of the way up the corridor he pressed himself to the wall so he could watch on unobserved and try to pick the right moment to zip out and grab the keg.

When she rounded the corner she discovered Brooks with his head inclined towards Prince's moving lips. Her entrance startled him and he snapped himself upright. His eyes showed white, almost cow-like, and Shirley spent half a second wondering what the two men could have had to discuss in confidence, then gave it away. Paranoia used up creative energy and her supply was already dwindling.

"Hello, my dear," Prince said. "I didn't expect to see you back up here. As a matter of fact, I didn't expect to see you ever again."

"No such luck, I'm afraid," she replied, smiling sweetly. She circled around him in slow and deliberate steps, until her back was to the main door and its moving horror mural. "I've come to make you a proposal."

"Have you, indeed?" said Prince. "This should prove amusing. Brooks, be a good fellow and lift up the cuff of my jacket, would you?"

Brooks shot a half-querying and half-apologetic look Shirley's way, then darted forward and pulled the cuff up onto Prince's forearm. It unveiled a glistering Omega wristwatch, the sort of thing Richard coveted his entire life but could never afford.

"Let's see now, five past four. That gives you exactly one hour and fifty minutes before this hotel implodes with demons and the end of the world begins. Plenty of time to hear your proposal, whatever it might be. Dazzle me."

What she wanted to do was knock that smug self-assuredness off his face, but baser emotions would have to wait. It was showtime and this would need to be the performance of her life. Of two lives. Perhaps billions, if Prince's claims were true.

"Well. . .is there anything I can do to make you reconsider? You know, call off the demon apocalypse?"

Shirley dropped to her knees in a single fluid motion, then took hold of the chair on which Prince sat and dragged it around to face her. She put her hands on Prince's lower thighs and began to slide them up the smooth fabric of his trousers. "I'd be immensely grateful if you spared our lives. In fact, if you lifted the spell and freed my daughter, I'd be willing to do just about anything." Her hands continued to climb until they reached the stiffer material around the zipper.

"Nothing you have to offer could possibly tempt me," Prince said, although Shirley knew that wasn't entirely true—she could feel him taking shape beneath her fingers. Fighting against bodily revulsion, she began to massage his repulsive slug. In her peripheral vision, she saw Maurice dart out on his tiptoes and squat beside the keg.

"Nothing at all?" Shirley said. Her fingers found the zipper's tab and tugged it down.

Maurice hugged the keg, lifted with his legs. Brooks, fixated on the show, had no idea Maurice was only three running steps behind him.

The open zipper could have been a little mouth with brass-colored teeth, a vermillion tongue inside. When Shirley's fingers touched the soft cotton of his underpants, Prince suddenly batted her hand away and curled up his knees in a protective gesture.

"I already have a deal, you brazen harlot," Prince said, glowering at her. "Get out of my sight! Ava Satanas! Ava Satanas!"

Maurice waddled into the corridor and out of sight. Shirley rolled back onto her haunches, stood up, and tried to appear distraught. "Why?" she said. "Why do you want to do this? Why are you so hellbent on destroying the world?"

"I'm not destroying it," Prince said, relaxing his legs and tugging the zipper on his pants closed again. "I'm passing it on to its rightful heir. God stole this realm from the archangel Lucifer. Because he was a scared, weak little lamb, just like his followers. But tonight, that injustice will be corrected. This town is an egg sac. Presently, it will crack open and spill the Dark Lord's legions across the earth."

Shirley screwed up her face and tried to make herself cry. She had Elle's harrowing transformation to use as motivation and the tears flowed. She lowered her head and shambled away towards the corridor, a picture of despair. The last person on earth (she hoped) Prince would suspect of plotting his downfall. She added a parting sob, one of a woman who had debased herself to no purpose.

In the corridor's gloom, she could just make out Maurice shouldering the door aside as he lugged his prize into the light. Together, they had pulled it off. An amphetamine euphoria tingled from the back of her head all the way down to her toes. A nice feeling, but also disturbing in its borderline mania.

Patrick took the keg off Maurice's hands as he reached the bottom of the stairs and Don gave him a pat on the back. "Nice work, mate."

Maurice glanced up the stairs. "Thanks. But Shirley deserves the credit. She had the hard job." He put a hand on her shoulder as she stepped onto the cellar floor. "Are you okay?"

"I used to work in marketing," she said. "I've whored myself out for less."

This drew the tension-relieving laugh she'd hoped for, and hearing it made her feel less antsy, less on the edge. "Let's get this devil's brew connected up."

She reattached the coupler to the keg and connected the line that ran to the carbon dioxide tanks. The pressure gauge showed

12psi, about right for a lager. She wondered if cursed lager needed more or less pressure and a nutty laugh tried to jump out of her mouth. She squeezed in her lips to prevent its escape.

"That should do it," she said. "Red Horn lager is officially on tap again."

"Nice drop, but it gives you one hell of a hangover," Patrick said.

"Righto," Don said, "let's get back up top. I believe it's happy hour, isn't it, Shirl?"

"Two dollars a schooner," she said. "But for a distinguished guest like Damon Prince, the beer is on the house."

Shirley led them upstairs, feeling like a gunslinger at the head of a posse. Was this a lynching, in a sense? She supposed it was, and she felt not the least qualm or compunction.

When she emerged into the pub this time she found Brooks more than an arm's length from Prince. What had Prince said that now compelled Brooks to stand away from him? Not that it mattered. Prince still wore that self-satisfied leer.

"Well now, what have we here?" he said. "Back with the whole team, I see."

"It's cold and miserable down there," Shirley said. "We decided we'd rather be warm and miserable up here. There's still plenty of beer on tap, although I smashed most of the spirits—sorry Patrick."

The blessed scotch bottles were in his hands again. He lifted them in a sort of shrugging gesture. "Not to worry. Might as well drink these now. Who knows, the whisky could afford me some protection once it's in my bloodstream."

Prince laughed. "It'll be an eye-dropper of water in the Great Sandy Desert, I assure you. Remind me, what was Black Wattle's population?"

That Prince used the word 'was' rather than 'is' wasn't lost on Shirley. She made her way behind the bar and picked another schooner glass from the ornate pile she had created.

"About a thousand, give or take," Don said. "It's been more take than give since the drought and the bushfires."

"Every one of those residents is now in the Dark Lord's service," Prince said. "You're outnumbered by one hundred to one." He turned his gaze on Patrick. "Fancy those odds, my dear fellow?"

Patrick's jaundiced eyes evaluated him through the half-open shutters of his booze-burnished eyelids. Shirley braced herself for a remark of such dry and withering wit that it would shrivel Prince to a peach stone. That had become a Patrick Burnham hallmark in his latter days, after the demon drink had stolen his tact and decorum and left only his sardonic intellect. But instead, he looked sadly at one of the bottles and tipped it to his lips.

Prince consulted his watch. "Looks like last drinks for the evening," he said grinning all around. "Our good friend here has just called time."

"Interesting you should say that." Shirley emerged from behind the bar holding a beer with a deep golden hue and a perfect half-inch of head. "I've poured a drink just for you, Mr. Prince. Can you guess what it is?"

Prince's grin faltered. He looked over his shoulder and discovered a bare floor where earlier a keg had stood. Shirley stopped in front of him, a leg's length away. "What's the matter, Mr. Prince? Cat got your tongue? All out of witty rejoinders?"

"Not at all," he said, settling again. The self-satisfied smile returned. "You don't honestly believe I would have cursed the beer without making myself impervious to its effects, do you?"

His words dug into her, verbal chisels. His plan had been so exacting, so detailed, so devious to that point. Would he really have overlooked something so vital?

The entire afternoon had been one long poker game and she refused to offer a tell for this mental pair of twos. Instead, she presented her sweetest smile and said, "Probably not. But it would be silly to assume, wouldn't it? What's that old joke? 'Assume makes an 'ass' out of 'u' and 'me'. Maurice, would you mind holding his arms?"

"You're wasting your time, you silly girl," Prince said.

"Maybe so. But it's not as if we need to be somewhere, is it?"

Maurice came up behind Prince's chair and wrapped his arms around him, locking his hands just below Prince's sternum.

"This is how you wish to spend your final minutes before you are enslaved for eternity?"

"Well, I don't have Netflix and I'm not much of a reader. Don, can you keep his legs still for me?"

Don nodded and got to one knee, curling his good arm around Prince's ankles.

"I thought you were smarter than this," Prince said. The

patronizing smile had guttered away to a thin line. Had his pupils dilated? Shirley suspected they had. "You're only putting yourself in danger carrying that beer around. If some of it should spill or get splashed on—"

"My goodness, are you mansplaining the situation to me, Mr. Prince? Patrick, be a dear and clamp your hands around his head."

"I'm not 'mansplaining' anything you stupid—"

"Last chance. Reverse the spell now or I force-feed you some of your devil's brew."

"I can't reverse the spell," Prince blustered, "if you would just—"

"Bottoms up," Shirley said, putting the glass under his nose. Prince struggled and tried to turn his head but Patrick wrestled it still. She pressed the rim of the glass against his bottom lip and began to tilt it.

"Nnnnuurrr!" Prince cried, straining backwards again Patrick's hands and curling his lips inwards. "Okay, okay, okay! I relent, just get it away from me."

Shirley withdrew the glass slowly, careful not to slop any on her wrist.

Don released his ankles and got to his feet. "So you are just a regular person," he said, shaking his head. "I don't get it. Why would you want to do this? What's in it for you?"

"I don't have to explain anything," Prince said sulkily.

"Unless you want me to quench your thirst," Shirley said, raising the beer glass, "I suggest you humor him."

Prince ruminated on this, eyes glittering with fury. Then all at once they cleared. "Are you certain you wish to know the full story? You might come to regret it."

"Spare us the mind games," Don said. "You tried that and you lost. We've got the upper hand and we're not buying your line of bullshit. Just talk."

"Very well, if you insist. When the sun sets, the fire-spawn will flood the earth and claim it as the Dark Lord's dominion—"

"Yes, yes," Don said, "you already told us that part."

If looks could lacerate, Don would have been ribbons. Prince cleared his throat delicately. "But this town will be spared. It will become an oasis of virgins and I will be its sole master, indulging an eternity of pleasures."

"Oh, Jesus," Shirley groaned, "not that hackneyed old crap again. What is it with religious whackos and virgins?"

Don and Maurice snickered. Patrick said, "I prefer a woman with some experience, myself," and the entire pub burst out laughing, even Brooks.

Everyone, that was, except Prince.

Shirley first interpreted his expression as sourness, the face of a schoolyard nerd subjected to derisive laughter. But the energy about him had changed. His wasn't a sour face but a serious one, the face of a man about to propose a billion-dollar business deal.

"Did any of you stop to wonder why the Dark Lord's domination of this realm will not take place until sunset?"

The chortling dried up. Don and Shirley stared at one another. His face reflected the sudden fear she felt.

"Shall I presume from your silence that the answer is no?"

Nobody deigned to reply.

"Call it a little insurance on my part," Prince said languidly. In an old movie, he might have lit a pipe before proceeding. "Satan is generous but he is also deceitful. They don't call it a 'deal with the devil' for nothing. The fire-spawn will be contained until the Dark Lord has fulfilled his part of the bargain. Should you force me to drink that beer, become one of the fire-spawn, not even Black Wattle will be spared. The entire earth will seethe with his minions. I cannot undo what has been done. The deal must be honored. But perhaps, if you agree to it, we can alter the bargain."

The pub hung heavy with his words, as if they had humidified the air. Terrified to ask—but also terrified not to ask—she let the pertinent question fall from her mouth. "Alter the bargain how?"

"Don't," Brooks said.

"Oh, shut your fucking mouth!" Shirley screamed at him. "You're the reason Elle is one of *them!*"

Cringing back, Brooks said, "Don't you think I know that? I know better than anyone—"

"Careful, Mr. Brooks," Prince said. "A man who runs his mouth is apt to say something he shouldn't."

"What the hell does that mean?" Don said.

Prince lifted his cable-tied hands and pointed a finger at his watch. "Time's ticking away. Are you sure you wish to waste valuable minutes arguing with one another?"

A discomfiting silence. No one knew where to look. That drove Shirley's anger to an all-new altitude. "I want to hear what he has to say."

"So do I," said Maurice.

After a deliberate pause, Prince said: "Any further objections? I have all the time in the world. Perhaps you'd like to put it to a vote?"

"Just lay your cards on the table," Don said. "Stop tormenting us."

"Tormenting you? Goodness me, now you're simply casting aspersions. As I recall, I offered—"

"All right, all right, forget I said anything. Get on with it. Tell us why Shirley shouldn't just pour that demon grog straight down your throat."

Prince inclined his head, a magnanimous gesture. "As I said, at sunset the Dark Lord will reign supreme. That is incontrovertible and irreversible. But I believe he might permit me to alter the finer details of our bargain. Give you back some of the things you have lost. He has waited millennia to right the wrongs against him. Granting the desires of a few insignificant mortals will be grains of sand in an hourglass."

"What desires?" Shirley said.

Prince arched his eyebrows. "Let's not get ahead of ourselves, my dear. Before we discuss specifics, we must ensure all interested parties are present..."

He lifted his chin, closed his eyes, brought his bound hands to his forehead in a gesture of prayer. Or perhaps, Shirley thought, a gesture of supplication.

"Not this malarkey again," Don said under his breath.

"*Diabolum acturum qui accedunt ad mensam.*"

The room blacked out.

CHAPTER TWENTY-TWO

THE SUN IS a blinding jewel resting on blue velvet as Don rolls his classic Ford V8 sedan out of the gravel carpark and onto the highway. It's been one of the hottest summers he can remember and he tugs on the Ford's air conditioning lever. A hopeful gesture; even though he re-gassed it a month ago it's temperamental and prone to curmudgeonly behavior. Not unlike him, he supposes, and to be expected since they're only a few months apart in age. Today, though, it blows chilled air at his face and knuckles and Nettie turns her palms up to the vents. "Oh, that's better," she says.

A bittersweet flavor lingers on Don's tongue, appropriate since it has been a bittersweet week. Dinner at the pub was the final stop in a week-long sojourn to Sydney to spend time with their son, Blair, who is now in the air and on his way to Canada where a university position awaits. Neither Nettie nor Don had an academic predisposition and Don only muddled through his final year at high school because he needed the qualification to join the coppers. So Blair's achievement is exciting and saddening and bewildering all at the same time. Once they were through the security checkpoint Don bought drinks at the airport bar and, when they were consumed, he bought more. Then a third round. "It's a long way to Canada," Don said as if he knew, even though he'd flown no further than New Zealand. And that had been in the early nineties. "A few beers will help you sleep."

Oftentimes Nettie would be the sober voice in their marriage—Don sometimes called her his handbrake and meant it with genuine affection and gratitude—but the imminent departure of her son to a country 15,000km away had worn her down and her third wine disappeared before Don and Blair were halfway through their beers. No mother had ever been prouder of her son, but Blair living in Sydney had already been too distant for Nettie's liking. During the final countdown to boarding, she gazed upon him with increasing fervor, as though compressing memories into her mind. Don, derived from more stoic stock, tried to savor his final moments with Blair and ignore the gnawing at his heart.

When the desk attendant invited business-class guests to board, Blair hugged his parents tight, showed his boarding pass and disappeared into the airbridge tunnel. Don and Nettie went to the windows beside the gate and stood watching with avid and tearful eyes as the airbridge pulled back, the forward door sealed shut and the plane taxied out and trundled off to the runway. Neither one of them moved until the landing gear parted ways with the airstrip. Then they turned away and Nettie burst into a fresh round of tears—the quiet and constrained tears unique to bereft parents at busy airports. Don wanted to join in, but the stoicism that lined his character wouldn't permit it.

"I could use another drink," he said.

Nettie nodded and they seated themselves at the airport bar again.

With a fourth drink under their belts, some good humor returned and they discussed their newfound empty-nester status in a more philosophical light. They walked back to the short-term carpark heedless of the blazing sun, sealed in their own little bubble. Reduced down to its dry elements, that had been their marriage—two peas in a pod, two caterpillars in a cocoon, two nuts sharing a nutshell. They would move through this and on to the next stage of their lives together, just as they always had.

It had been Don's notion to stop in the Southern Highlands for an early dinner rather than press on and cook at home. While working his way through a chicken parmigiana dressed up with fancy garnish, he had polished off beer number five for the day, some full-bodied craft thing that numbed his tastebuds. Only when the bottle was empty did he examine the label and find *5.8% alc. vol. Approximately 1.6 standard drinks.* His drive out of Sydney had been a roll of the dice, but he knew well enough the random breath-testing strategies and hotspots, and some of the older coppers would still wave him on untested if he produced his badge. Between the Highlands and Black Wattle, he more or less *was* the law, so knowing he was almost certainly over the limit again didn't much perturb him. Besides, he had driven this road back and forth so many times he reckoned he could do it shitfaced drunk or even blindfolded.

Now he and Nettie are cruising along the highway, one plus one, the bubble as it used to be in their early twenties. Blair was a treasure they cherished until it was time for him to leave their bubble and find his own, but Don can see the upside to his departure. The future stretches out in much the same way as the road they are on, deserted yet full of promise. Nettie reclines her seat. The heavy pub meal and wine intake soon close her eyes.

Encroaching dusk lengthens the shadows such that they stripe and dapple the road. The Ford surmounts a crest and Don lets it freewheel to the gully below. A van approaches from the opposite direction, nondescript white with faded lettering on the side, perhaps a cityside courier returning from a parts delivery to Black Wattle or beyond. The kangaroo springs from the trees on the van driver's side and straight into his path. A country motorist would firm his hands around the wheel and brace for impact, but the van driver acts on instinct and swerves to avoid the animal.

Don anticipates what's coming and tries to jerk the Ford onto the shoulder, but its ocean liner steering and his beer-dulled reflexes cost him a vital half-second. The van's blunt nose ploughs into the driver's side headlight. The world spins and turns white, like a color wheel, and amid this weird confluence of shock and disorientation he is vaguely aware of a stabbing pain that commutes into numb throbbing. The Ford's squealing tires fall silent as it runs out of centrifugal motion and comes to rest, wobbling on its springs. Something ticks, perhaps the air conditioner breathing its last.

When Don dares open his eyes he finds the steering wheel six inches closer than before and an intricate scarring of cracks across the windscreen. Through a crazed section of glass, he watches a distorted kangaroo hop by, tail high, as casual as you please. When it disappears into the bush he looks down at his right arm, which now hangs beside him like an old curtain. It disobeys his mental command to rise up and that's the moment Don realizes he might be in trouble, far worse than anything he encountered on Sydney's streets. He tries to turn his head and the tendons between his right ear and his shoulder blade burn.

But the burning diminishes to mere irritation when he claps eyes on Nettie. She would be facing him if not for her lolling head;

instead, she appears to be intensely interested in her right thigh. Her hair, which she hasn't quite summoned up the courage to cut short, hangs in a shroud over her face. Something liquid depends from a stringer of hair and plips into the crevice between the seat and the center console. With an awakening horror, Don raises his eyes to the B-pillar on the passenger's side and sees a single red splotch on its green frame.

Don reaches out his left hand and cups it beneath Nettie's chin. He is about to lift her head and witness her cratered skull and her beautiful blue eye extruded from its socket, but before he can relive the moment a hand presses down on his right shoulder.

He turns in that direction, teeth bared. The hand belongs to Damon Prince. Beyond it, his face exhibits sympathy.

"In pain?" he asks.

An almost imperceptible nod.

"It never stopped hurting, did it? Not even when the pain went away."

A tear escapes Don's eye.

"The Dark Lord can end your suffering. If you do not oppose his will, he will share with you the oasis he creates for his mortal allies. Within its bounds, earth will become heaven. An end to sorrow. An end to regrets. The salvation of all that was lost to human folly and frailty." Prince points a finger. "Observe."

Don turns his head back again, wincing in anticipation, but the whiplash pain is no more. In the passenger's seat, where he remembers Nettie with one side of her head bashed in and blood running in rivulets down her ash-blonde hair, he finds her upright and whole, her face effervescent. "We could pick up where we left off, Donny," she says. No one else called him Donny. No one would have dared. "Be together again. Share the years that van driver stole from us."

Don turns back to Prince. "This isn't real," he says.

Prince gives him a beatific smile. "Not yet. But it could be. Do not try to deny my destiny and you and your Nettie will be reunited in paradise. Sound good?"

Don nods.

Prince offers his hand. "Shake on it?"

Don lifts his left hand, as he has ever since the accident. Prince shakes his head and smiles. It takes Don a moment to understand Prince is not spurning his cack-handshake, but implying something else. Don's right hand comes up under its own power for the first time in close on two years. It seems to levitate, float in the air under some magical power. Then it moves forward and the dead fingers come to life and clasp Prince's hand.

Back behind the concrete curtain. It's been more than a year, but not enough. No matter how hard he tries, Patrick can't seem to break ties with Sydney. Every time he thinks he's freed himself from the umbilical cord, something pulls it taut and drags him back to this overpopulated hellhole.

In the past it has been for work or family gatherings or some sort of financial or civic business he can't conduct online or over the phone. Today, however, it is none of those things.

Today, Patrick would walk a mile over broken glass to trade his present situation for Christmas dinner with his tedious father-in-law or a conference room full of priests vying to see who can mortgage their faith the fastest to impress political trendies.

Sydney has reeled him back to its festering teat because it has the state's top oncologists and his wife, Rebecca, is undergoing chemotherapy to treat an aggressive form of leukemia. The first round put her into partial remission and the doctor permitted her to go home for a week and recover, but she has been on a downward trajectory ever since. Most days, Patrick remains by her bedside, reading while she sleeps, joking and trying to lift her spirits when she wakes, ensuring she eats when her meals arrive (or sneaking in some food if her chemo nausea is acute). Of an evening, just before visiting hours close, he sits at her bedside and they pray together. If Becky is to have any hope of a permanent cure, she needs a compatible bone marrow transplant. It's a long waiting list and matches are few.

Each night, at eight o'clock, he kisses his wife's forehead then makes his way through the rabbit warren of corridors that lead past the nurses' station and terminate at the lift. From the ground floor he crosses a busy road, walks across a park populated with old figs and dry grass that are hanging onto life thanks to recycled irrigation water, and continues along the street until he arrives at the motel. It's cheap and old—a cinderblock relic from a time when travelers were happy so long as a motel had a kettle and tea bags— but it's clean and has an attached restaurant and bar.

Between eight-thirty and ten, he sits alone at a table and drinks to decompress. The restaurant opens to the public; but most nights, save for Friday and Saturday, it's Patrick and the bored-looking bartender (Monday to Wednesday it's a guy, Thursday and Sunday a girl, both on the busy nights). Chivas Regal is as premium as the bar's top-shelf spirits get, but there's no bottle shop nearby and Patrick drinks for its numbing effect rather than its flavor.

His brain is assailed all day with questions and fears and emotional combinations he hadn't imagined before Becky's hand swelled up and their GP rushed her for a blood test to confirm the grave diagnosis he obviously suspected but wouldn't name until the pathology results came back. The whisky provides a buffer between Patrick and these worries and helps him sleep when he retires to bed at closing time. Most mornings, he wakes with a mild hangover and sits outside his door on a plastic seat drinking instant coffee. Watching the motel's colorful patrons come and go—sex workers, criminals, and sleazy businessmen make up the bulk so far as he can tell—helps him feel better about his own situation. But as his wristwatch counts down the minutes to 9:45 a.m., the sun intensifies his hangover and his second cup of coffee sends him jittery and manic. During the walk across the park every morning he curses himself, making promises not to drink again that night. At the end of another day spent watching his wife's body disintegrate from the inside out, however, all his good resolutions are dissolved. He orders a scotch and makes light-hearted chit-chat with the bartender to prove he isn't ashamed.

Then, one morning, a glow softens his dark daily routine. Becky's oncologist, Dr Chi, says they have turned up a matching bone marrow donor. Extracting bone marrow hurts like hell, he explains, so bone marrow donors are even scarcer than blood donors. This anonymous angel lives somewhere in North America, apparently, but patient confidentiality prevents more specific identification. Patrick sends a silent prayer of thanks to him or her. For the first night in more than two weeks, he bypasses the bar and spends the night in his motel room watching the tiny LCD television.

It's a fine Monday morning and Patrick is strolling across the park on his way to the hospital when the phone in his pocket vibrates. It is Dr Chi.

"Can you please come to my office at midday," he says. "We

need to discuss Rebecca's treatment. Tell my PA who you are and she'll show you through."

Lunch arrives just as Patrick is leaving Becky's ward. Breakfast did not go well. Even with the anti-nausea drugs, she consumed only two spoonfuls of porridge and gagged on each before it went down. Patrick is grateful he has an excuse not to bear witness as Becky attempts to choke down a cheese sandwich. This in turn incites a dust-storm of self-loathing. He is supposed to be her carer, but it's getting to the point where seeing her struggle makes him feel like he is coming down with something himself. Emotional flu. His feet carry him quickly to the elevator, which whisks him up to Dr Chi's room where he makes himself known. Dr Chi's personal assistant shows him through. Dr Chi finishes typing something on his computer as his PA closes the door. Total silence prevails. It's the first time in weeks Patrick's head hasn't been filled with urban cacophony or an array of interminable beeping. Everything Becky is hooked up to—chemo drip, heart-rate monitor—beeps and bongs, demanding attention from an overworked nurse. The soundproof office provides welcome respite. Patrick could almost be back in his beloved St Luke's waiting for the Sunday morning congregation to arrive.

"Hello Patrick, please have a seat."

Patrick does. The office no longer feels like a hushed church. More like a headmaster's office.

"I've been to see Rebecca this morning and reviewed her most recent blood test. It's not good news. The last round of chemotherapy was ineffective. It made almost no difference to her white cell count. I'm afraid the prognosis isn't hopeful."

"But. . .you said at the outset we were working towards a cure. Last week you were talking about a bone marrow transplant. What happened to that?"

"Her condition has deteriorated," Dr Chi says. "She's increasingly weak and not responding to treatment. If we try to give her the transplant now it will likely kill her."

"Likely? How likely?"

"A bone marrow transplant effectively destroys the patient's immune system and rebuilds a new one. It takes an enormous toll on the body and even a relatively healthy patient runs a serious risk."

"I know the risks. Tell me what you think her chances are."

Dr Chi consults his knuckles before replying. "Perhaps one or two percent. The treatment will put Rebecca through a great deal of pain with almost no chance of survival. It might be time to consider palliative care."

Palliative. The word pulls the shade closed on Patrick's lantern of hope.

"What would that involve?"

"We make her as comfortable as possible for the remainder of her life. No more chemotherapy and she can have as much pain relief as she needs."

Patrick can't process this turn of events. "What do you think I should do?"

"I can't answer that for you," Dr Chi says. "And Rebecca is no longer in any state to make decisions about her own welfare. As her carer, you must decide on her behalf."

Someone presses a comforting hand on Patrick's shoulder.

"You wish you'd tried the transplant, don't you?" Prince says.

Patrick nods. His neck feels weak, so he drops his head and closes his eyes. "Dr Chi didn't want her death on his conscience," he says. "So instead it ended up on mine."

"The Dark Lord can ease your burden, if you choose not to oppose my will. He can return to you what was lost, what was taken from you. Observe."

Patrick raises his head and discovers he is now standing at the pulpit in St Luke's. Light streams through the stained-glass windows, painting the congregation in vibrant watercolors. Every pew is packed tight with the faithful who have come to listen to him preach. Their faces are expectant, almost euphoric, as if illumined by heaven itself. In the front row sits Becky.

The buzz cut, the sunken eyes, the sallow flesh, the cracked and peeling lips might never have been as she tucks a lock of hair behind her ear and beams at him.

"She was always so proud of me," Patrick says.

"And she can be again," Prince replies. "Do not try to deny the Dark Lord's chosen destiny and you will be reunited in paradise. Where there are no addictions, only pleasures."

He hands Patrick a glass of scotch and then raises his own in *salut.* "Do we have a deal?"

"Cheers," Patrick says.

They clink their glasses together.

One drizzly evening in the earliest days of his success, when art dealers and critics first evinced interest in his colorful interpretations of the world, a publicist had invited Truman to a house party at a swanky residence on Sydney Harbour's southern shores. Truman barely knew him beyond a couple of professional gatherings and everyone else at the party was a stranger. Not wishing to say something out of turn, Truman had nursed a glass of red for half an hour and then switched to soda water. While visiting the bathroom he left his glass unattended and unbeknownst to him someone dropped a square of acid laced with mescaline into his drink. The host's standard practical joke on "party poopers" the publicist would later explain without remorse.

The drug kicked in while Truman leaned against a wall trying to maintain small talk with a writer who had come out of the gate a little too hard and now couldn't get her tongue around sibilant sounds, turning every fifth word to mush. Deciphering this flow of noises became more and more troublesome and then the wall seemed to bend in behind him, as though it were tofu rather than plasterboard. Truman sprang forward and turned around, expecting to see a crack, but found the wall bare and unblemished. Every light in the room developed a comet trail.

When his eyes focused on his companion, her face wouldn't maintain its symmetry. Her cheeks and chin moved around like amoebas and her eyelids stuttered open and shut, as though every second frame of Truman's perception had been spliced out. His heart fluttered and tried to find a way out of its ribcage. His limbs became disembodied from the rest of him. The writer's unintelligible words attacked his ears. His mouth tasted of aluminum foil. Every sense seemed to be at war with reality.

He fled the house, passing a gauntlet of mad-clown faces, and ran into the street. Wet bitumen reflected the overhead streetlight, the silver glare dazzling his eyes until he feared it had burned his retinas. He sat in the gutter, tucked his face into his knees and wondered how humdrum existence had metamorphosed into a hallucinatory nightmare. No one came to find him. Terrified, he blundered through a suburban hellscape of unfamiliar streets, each hour stretching on towards infinity. Dawn would lighten the night before Truman's faculties could once again cope with ordinary input.

Today, that acid nightmare has resumed, only multiplied to the nth power. Cold fire burns him from the inside out. Serpentine trees writhe and reach for him with gnarled branch fingers, grass stabs its yellow spikes into his bloated skin. Relentless rage drives his every thought, infuses him with a sick energy to seek out those in God's image and slash them, tear them, until they relent to the service of the Dark Lord. He drags himself through the ochre dirt, the raw stumps of his legs now caked with mud and leaves. His feet are forgotten, at least in the sandstorm that now passes for the top level of his mind. In the lightless depths of the narrow well below, however, the old Truman raises pleading arms towards a pinpoint of light and cries out. He knows this is the song of the doomed, and in the Dark Lord's realm, a billion-strong chorus howls it in eternal despair.

A hand reaches down and clutches his own in a monkey grip, filling him with a strange mix of euphoria and terror. The hand draws him into the light and puts Truman on his own two feet, which are reattached to his body. He stares at this marvel before noticing another, more momentous, change: the raging sandstorm has abated, the unrelenting agony of being is no more. He looks up into his savior's face.

"Who are you?"

"Damon Prince, at your service."

"Prince? You're. . .him?"

"Your friends have been busy in your absence, Mr. Smythe. Devious and troublesome. They spent the afternoon attempting to dismantle my careful plans and, finding myself at the mercy of their desperation, I yielded. We are in the midst of some. . .negotiations. The Dark Lord and I have granted you a reprieve from eternal damnation because you are crucial to the success of those negotiations."

"Me?"

Something doesn't feel right. Truman squints mole-like at his surroundings. They offend every mote of his aesthetic senses.

"This isn't real," he says.

"Not in the physical sense, perhaps. But what happens on this sub-plane will have a bearing on the physical world, I assure you."

"What is it you want from me, Prince?"

"After you left us to join the Dark Lord's army, we had an unexpected arrival. Should he try to oppose me, it could disrupt the bargain I have made with the Dark Lord. I need you to persuade this person not to oppose his will."

"What person? What on earth are you—"

Prince brings up his hand in a game show wave, as if drawing the audience's attention to a prize. Materializing beneath it in a spray of orange sparks is not a new car, but a bewildered Maurice.

"Truman!" he says, reaching for him and pulling him close. After the limitless loneliness and despair, this contact—virtual or artificial as it may be—fills him with a skydiving elation. Maurice's touch, his smell, his just *being* bring Truman greater happiness than anything ever has in his adult life. Maurice leans back and gazes into Truman's eyes, as though drinking him in.

"Do not deny my destiny, Maurice, and you and your lover will be reunited in paradise. A peaceful place, free from persecution or judgment. All mistakes unwritten, all grievances quashed. Eternal happiness. On the other hand, should you choose to oppose my will. . .well. Perhaps you might fill him in on the alternative, Mr. Smythe? The more thorough your explanation, the longer you will be spared a return to the depths."

Dread chokes him, a sea urchin lodged in his throat. Truman takes Maurice's hand, looks into his eyes, and begins to talk.

Stars twinkle in such numbers they look like powdered sugar sprinkled across the sky. Shirley sits on her cottage's front porch in an old garden chair she found dumped on the roadside. A cup of tea rests in her lap, cooling. She almost wishes it were a beer, but Shirley has never been a drinker, not in the good times or the bad. This is a bad time. The country firmament, so breathtaking compared to the city's wan and washed-out black, tonight makes her feel small and alone.

Her first night without Elle. Her first night without her baby in fifteen years. It's only a weekend this time, two nights, but she is such a distance away it adds up to forever.

She sips the tea, grimaces, tosses the teacup over the porch rail. It lands in the uncut grass with a soft *whish*, unharmed. While sneering at it, she becomes aware someone is sitting next to her.

How this can be is quite the riddle, since the salvaged garden chair was singular, not a two-piece set. She turns and is not in the least alarmed to see Prince. He peers through a gap between the porch rail's slats, taking considered interest in the teacup. It rests at a crooked angle, as though baking its porcelain skin under the moon's cool light.

"Everything is taken from you, Shirley. Have you noticed that?"

She opens her mouth to protest, to say her life has not been that way at all, but then she closes it again as her mind tots it up. A military father whose work took him away from her for months at a time. Any semblance of a stable family life uprooted whenever the army redeployed him, usually at a moment's notice. Then Shirley and her mother got him back for good, only it wasn't him anymore. It was the broken and tangled PTSD version that only lasted two months before they discovered him in bed with his mouth agape and an empty bottle of sleeping pills on the bedside table. Shirley then, for all intents and purposes, lost her reeling mother, who could scarcely function beyond working and sleeping. By the time her mother was restored to some former version of herself, Shirley was old enough to drive. They had maybe three good years before her mother's "out of sync periods", which was how the uterine cancer first made itself known. Shirley would be an orphan before she had paid off the loan on her first car.

That triggered the binge drinking. Getting annihilated in the name of fun, but really to forget. To anesthetize the sorrow, if only for a few hours. Then one Saturday night, a few weeks after starting university, she attended a party at a riverside park. Hit the pre-mixers pretty hard and then shared a vodka bottle with a cute guy from her three o'clock tutorial. One for you, one for me. She has an idea she consented to what happened a short while later, but only as well as someone in her state could be said to give consent. Whatever the case, her virginity was taken away that night and her one clear recollection of the event is her back scraping against a slab of bush rock in the underbrush. In the morning, the bathroom mirror showed her the grazes from her probably-less-than-consensual dalliance and she vowed off alcohol for good. Her next drink would be a sip of champagne at her wedding ten years later.

She plunged herself into work, the one thing that promised stability and reward in exchange for effort, and eighteen months into her first job she met Richard at the work Christmas party. A company lawyer, well-dressed, witty, handsome in a bookish way. Kind-hearted and generous, Shirley had thought, until the going got tough at the Ironstone and her accomplished lawyer husband crumbled like some half-witted hoodlum under cross-examination. Whereupon he had run off and left her holding two babies, one of which, she had been lukewarm about in the first place. The one Shirley had wanted and loved from first sight he took from her every month or so.

A baby that had now transformed into a demon.

Shirley found herself staring at the teacup, just as Prince had. She turned to face him again and found him nodding.

"Everything that was yours shall be returned to you, Shirley," he said. "Provided you do not dishonor my pact with the Dark Lord."

"Returned to me?"

Climbing the stairs is her Ellie-Bellie, whole and human again, wearing the tight jeans and sneakers she often favors in her country home. Her blonde hair glimmers, and when she smiles her teeth are pearlescent in the darkness.

"I miss you, Mum," she says.

Shirley rises from the garden chair, its bowed plastic legs jumping back to attention. Elle stands at the top of the porch stairs, happiness radiating off her like a corona. She goes to her and Elle opens her arms. The embrace is all Shirley dreamed it would be: relief, fulfillment, pleasure, a soothing poultice for her scarred and inflamed soul.

CHAPTER TWENTY-THREE

THE BLACKNESS LIFTED and Elle became smoke in her arms. Shirley tried to hold onto her daughter and her fingers snatched at nothing but air.

"No! Please, give her back!"

She and the others were still in the pub. Almost no time had elapsed if the late afternoon light was any guide. Every face she saw wore the same thunderstruck look. Every face except Prince's. He looked like the cat that got the cream.

"The deal is struck," he said, holding up his bound hands in jubilance. Demons pressed against the hotel windows, maggots boiling over a decaying corpse. Every eye in the place fell on the beer in Shirley's hand. Hers included. "Perhaps now would be an appropriate time to divest yourself of that glass. We wouldn't wish anything unfortunate to happen, would we? Not when we are so close."

Shirley looked to the others for guidance. Apparently, no one was disposed to talk. Eyes dipped away, sought distant objects, became interested in shoelaces. Only Brooks held her gaze, a strange expression enlivening his face. He licked his lips and shook his head.

"Don't believe him," Brooks said.

"Oh dear," said Prince, rolling his eyes. "Are you coming over all altruistic, Mr. Brooks? Well, better late than never, I suppose."

"Don't listen to him, Shirley. None of you should."

"Ah, but they should listen to you, I suppose, Mr. Brooks? The man almost single-handedly responsible for the mess in which they now find themselves?"

"I didn't mean for this to—"

"Perhaps not, but here we are," Prince said. "Fifteen minutes to sunset, by my reckoning, and all you have to offer them is death and damnation. Under my auspices, we have negotiated a deal with the Dark Lord. Each man and woman's individual paradise. Nobody loses."

"Except the billions who will be condemned."

Prince spread his hands as best he could, an appeal to reason. "They will be condemned whether you force me to join their ranks or not. The only losers will be these brave and self-reliant people who stood tall and won the Dark Lord's respect. Should they listen to your boneheaded counsel, they will lose their one chance at happiness."

Brooks' eyelid twitched. "Only assuming you're telling the truth."

Prince sighed, looked away, then returned his gaze to Brooks' face with renewed vigor. "You speak as though you are impartial or uninvolved, Mr. Brooks. But you and I both know that is false. Don't we?"

The words appeared to gut-shoot Brooks. That weird cousin-to-paranoia expression wrought his face again. Shirley's mind went to the moment she had stepped from the corridor to find Prince and Brooks concluding some sort of whispered congress.

"I thought the situation was hopeless," Brooks said, appealing to the room as a whole. "Prince offered me—"

"I offered to share paradise with him," Prince said, "and he was willing to betray you all to get it. Could not agree with my terms fast enough, as a matter of fact."

"Don't listen to him," Brooks said. "He makes empty promises, I know that better than most. Nothing's real."

"Real? What is 'real'? Reality is perception. Everything you experienced on the sub-plane will be real in the Dark Lord's refuge. An opportunity to live your lives as they could have been before your greatest regrets corrupted them. All you need do is spare me, withhold your interference until sunset, and paradise lost will be yours again."

Closing her eyes, Shirley could once again feel her daughter's warmth pressing against her, the tightness of her arms, her hands on her back. Gooey caramel. Such a stark contrast to the day's suffering. She opened her eyes.

"Would I be in charge of my reality?" she said, hating the simpering tone in her voice but powerless to degrade it. "Would I be able to. . .shape it?"

"To your every whim, my dear. Your heart's content would be the architect of your domain."

If that were so, perhaps she could rewind the tape of her marriage to an earlier point. To the moment when she capitulated to Richard's harebrained pie-in-the-sky tree-change idea, which had become a concrete block that dragged their marriage to the bottom of a river. She could intercept it, divert it, explore the opposing fork in the road. After all, Prince was right; what was the alternative? Death, misery, horror. Why jump in the volcano with the rest of humanity when Prince offered a map back down the mountain and into an oasis?

Don, Maurice and Patrick were all looking at her, eyes deep with empathy and understanding, as if tasting the same thing she was tasting. What had Prince promised them, she wondered idly? Would they share Shirley's oasis or be partitioned off, exist in separate dimensions, as it had been during the blackout? Shirley found it no longer mattered. Nothing did except reuniting with Elle and pursuing the life she had lost, the life denied to her.

"Put down the beer, Shirley," Prince wheedled. "It is time to embrace our destiny. The Dark Lord has promised us a labyrinth of wonders and pleasures beyond anything we could hope to experience in this purgatory we call life. Let this process run its course."

"He's lying to us, Shirley," Brooks said. "He is the Prince of lies."

"A man who resorts to epithets has run out of arguments," Prince said. He bent his wrist to expose his watch. "Sunset draws near. Let us waste no more time. Unbind my hands and feet so we might share our glorious ascension as equals."

"Yes," Shirley said. Sublime smiles surrounded her. Reassuring, comforting. An eternity of bliss lay ahead. All she need do was set aside the beer and allow the clock to run down. So simple. A beatific calm stole over her, like a morphine drip spilling its magic into her veins. She turned towards the bar, a robotic sideways motion.

Before she could set the beer down, Brooks' hand shot out in a cobra-strike and snatched it from her grasp.

CHAPTER TWENTY-FOUR

HAD *SHIRLEY'S VOICE* always been so hypnotic?

Don allowed as a romantic admirer he would be predisposed to appreciate its every cadence, even if she sounded like a tabby cat with a sore throat. But this was something else, each word melodious and mellifluous, the music of angels. His was a physical reaction beyond the usual biochemistry of love. Her voice enchanted him, literally. It muddled his mind in the most delicious way. A waking dream.

Why had they resisted so long? The notion now seemed preposterous. So much easier to listen to Shirley's voice, let its gentle waves carry them towards the pacific afterlife Prince had promised. No man could swim an ocean, Don could see that now, least of all a man with one arm. His mind called up a memory from Prince's blackout, of having two arms again. Of being whole. Sentiment for his lost arm washed over him. No more than ten minutes till sundown. Soon his arm would be restored and the first thing he planned to do was put it around the shoulders of his—

Brooks lunged forward and grabbed the beer glass from Shirley's hand. Some of its contents slopped onto the floor. Shirley tried to snatch it back, but Brooks turned away and her clawing fingers raked across his shoulder instead. Don could see what Brooks meant to do. Not content with sacrificing a thousand Black Wattle residents and then the bulk of humanity to a satanic apocalypse, he now wanted to spoil it for the remaining few whose mettle and initiative had spared them the same fate. A startling rage fired him into action and he made a grab for Brooks' shirt collar.

Still emerging from Prince's waking trance, however, he instinctively reached out with a right hand that in the real world did not respond. Don let out an anguished grunt. He had to turn to grab with his left hand and that split second gave Brooks the buffer he needed. He leapt forward and clenched his fingers around Prince's throat, momentum tipping the chair onto its back. Brooks moved his hand from Prince's neck to his cheeks and squeezed until his lips protruded in a goldfish face. The rim of the beer glass hovered over the hole. Don's fingers slotted into the gap between Brooks' collar and the chafed-pink skin on his neck. Bracing his knees, Don prepared to reef Brooks off the man who had promised him nirvana. But Prince's eyes were locked on the beer flowing down the side of the glass and he had no idea rescue was at hand.

In a girlish squeal far removed from his suave James Bond lilt, he cried out, "*Ave Satanas!* Take mercy upon me, Dark Lord!"

The first drips of beer were about to splash on his lips when a column of energy burst up through the floor, evaporating the beer as it went and sending a shockwave through the pub. The force blasted Don off his feet and threw him into the side of the bar. Brooks slammed into him an instant later and Don felt the telltale pop of ribs breaking. The world greyed out for a spell. When it cleared, what he saw made him wonder if he had succumbed to some injured-brain hallucination.

Where Prince had been seated most of the afternoon there now stood a towering being, the knobbles on its skull almost brushing the pub's rafters. Its gleaming skin had the crimson hue of a waratah flower and the whole body heaved, a living bellows. Its breath came at them like a hot desert wind, black-mirror eyes inscrutable and piercing. The others had been flung in all directions. Maurice now lay sprawled across the stairs, out cold with a gash across his forehead. Shirley and Patrick, no longer under Prince's spell, apparently unharmed, had assumed identical crouching postures, hands on the floor, like chimpanzees preparing to flee a predator.

Brooks leaned forward, causing Don to growl in agony, and got to his feet. Prince—or whatever the hell he had become—turned to face him, thews rippling beneath its gleaming hide. Fumes twisted from its flared nostrils and accumulated into a faint cloud. Never taking his eyes off that infernal face, Brooks stooped to collect something next to his feet. A guttural rumbling fluttered Don's eardrums and he understood with some alarm it was emerging from the Prince Demon's billowing chest. Brooks now wielded

Truman's meat axe. He straightened his legs and put his shoulders back.

"I reject your offer, Prince," he said. "I reject you and I reject everything you and your Dark Lord stand for. You might take my life, but you will never have my soul."

The demon's upper lip fluttered, revealing rows of spear-like teeth. The bass-rumbling in its chest developed a crunching edge, sandstone in a cement mixer. Its huge musculature swelled and strained and there was a sharp crack as its head snapped one of the rafters. Its black hole eyes seemed to draw in everything around them while emitting a fiery hate at Brooks.

Bellowing, Brooks charged the demon, arm cocked back and knuckles bulging around the meat cleaver's handle. The demon, motionless, watched him come; Don could see a tiny Brooks reflected in its huge insectile orbs. The real Brooks launched himself into the air and brought the cleaver down in a wild overhand swing. The blade hit the top of the demon's thigh with a rubbery thud and the impact juddered the cleaver from Brooks' grip. It flew off, end over end, like a runaway rotor. Brooks cried out, cradling his injured wrist in his other hand.

The demon looked down at him, sniffed something sulfurous from its nostrils, and pulled back its lips into a bristling grin. Then one of its huge arms shot out and swatted Brooks across the room. He crashed headlong into the stairway's timber banister, shattering it to matchsticks, then tumbled down into a shapeless heap beside Maurice. The demon admired its handiwork for a moment before turning its deep-space eyes back to the room.

Don braced himself against the bar and tried to get to his feet. Anything more than a shallow inhalation lanced a burning pain through his chest. He tried to keep his torso immobile, let his thighs do the work, but his core muscles came into play nonetheless and tightened around his cracked ribs. His face twisted up and he groaned. When at last he got himself upright he leaned his elbow on the bar top and mopped sweat from his eyes with his shoulder. Unsure what else to do, Don said, "What now, Prince?"

The demon, whose gaze had been trained on Patrick (although with no pupils for reference it was hard to be certain) now turned its head to Don. For a few seconds it said nothing and Don wondered if it could understand English or even speak. Then it took a single step forward, shuddering the floorboards beneath its tread, and bent at the hips until Don could have reached out and touched its protuberant chin. A rotten egg smell filtered into his nose and it was all he could do not to gag.

"There is no more Prince," the demon said in its quarry-truck bass note.

"What have you done to him?"

"Only what he asked. I have spared him an eternity among the fire-spawn. In exchange, he surrendered his mortal existence to me."

"But we had a bargain."

The demon smiled, assuming something so cruel and savage might be deemed a smile. "There is no more Prince. There is no more bargain."

While Don held the demon's attention, Shirley collected up the carving knife and circled around in cautious but continual steps. Don kept her in the corner of his eye so as not to alert the demon.

"Who am I speaking to, then?"

The demon chuckled. Smoke puffed from its nostrils. It stood up to its full height again and flexed its muscles. It seemed to fill the whole room with its straining, sinewy mass. It took a deep breath and all the oxygen in Don's lungs vanished. Then the demon opened its cavernous mouth and roared, "I am mighty! I am LEGION!"

In unison, as if part of a single circuit, every demon outside the hotel burst into flames. They continued to press up against the windows, and peer in with scarlet-teardrop eyes. Seconds later Don felt their heat permeate the room. The window glass fogged up at their touch until each pane resembled a cataract. The timbers in the frame began to ignite. If they weren't broiled alive inside, Don thought, the pub would lose structural integrity soon enough and crush them to death. He tried in vain not to cower under the force of the demon's abhorrent desert-air breath. But once his ears had stopped ringing, he stood tall again and forced himself to stare into the endless fathoms of its eyes.

"You couldn't even reclaim the earth without that weirdo's help," Don said, not sure at all why he was goading the devil but pushing ahead anyway. "I'd say you're about as mighty as an earthworm."

Its shoulders heaved, heat radiated off its skin. Those black eyes never changed, yet Don fancied he could feel them expelling hate. Then the demon lunged forward and brought down its fist in a hammerstrike.

Don pushed off with his one good hand and rolled away, his broken ribs grinding together and setting off a pain supernova. Air buffeted across his head and neck and then a section of the bar beside him exploded under the demon's fist, wood chips spraying out and stinging Don's cheek. Patrick scuttled away, mouse-like, and disappeared behind the bar. Don—unable to get up, struggling to even breathe—slumped to his knees and watched the demon rise again and lift its war-hammer hand for a second and final strike.

Shirley seized the moment, running full tilt, leaping into the air and plunging the carving knife into the demon's spine. Or such had been her intent; the blade simply snapped off and tinkled harmlessly to the floor. Shirley wailed in pain and dropped the handle, backing up with her now-bleeding hand tucked into her opposite armpit. The demon glanced over its shoulder, as if irritated at this interruption, and shot out its foot in a donkey kick. It hit Shirley square across the chest, her crossed arms the only cushion against the impact. It propelled her across the room and she came down back-first onto one of the tables, snapping the top off the frame. It tipped her onto the floor and her limbs lolled about in ragdoll fashion before she finished up on her side. Don could just make out her face amid the lambent shadows. Blood dribbled from her nose and lips. Between the fire-spawn's flaming bodies and the opaque windows, he could no longer tell whether it was dawn, day or dusk. He rolled his eyes towards his wristwatch.

"Sunset is imminent, pitiful mortal," the Prince Demon said. "This is my domain now. You will serve me or you will be destroyed."

Don gathered up all his available saliva and spat it in the Prince Demon's direction. The gobbet landed on his foot, sizzling. Black-glass eyes observed this with ostensible detachment, but when they found Don again they discharged blast-furnace outrage.

"You stink like shit, did you know that?" Don wheezed.

The Prince Demon flexed its tree-trunk legs and hurled itself at him.

CHAPTER TWENTY-FIVE

SO MANY YEARS wasted on God.

Inside Patrick's head scotch bottles marched back and forth in a colorful parade of labels and amber fluid. Becky sat beside him in a deck chair, her warm hand clasped about his, her flesh firm and pink, sapphire eyes sparkling. A daydream, yes, memory leftovers jumbled into a small fantasy, but one that would be real when the day drew to a close. Where God asked mortals to rail against their desires and accept the outrageous slights that infested His faulted universe, Lucifer bent the universe to accommodate what those in his favor desired. What had Prince said? No addictions, only pleasures. No more endurance, no more temperance, no more denial. No need to tolerate suffering in the belief that it served God's will.

More than any of the others Patrick was running down the clock to the Dark Lord's embrace. He barely registered the transition between Prince's blackout sub-plane and the increasingly shadowy pub, such was the ambrosia of idyllic imaginings that filled his head. He heard Brooks' voice, acquired the words, but didn't compile them into a gist. It might as well have been the burr of a lawnmower on a Saturday morning. Extant, familiar, but in the end meaningless.

So when Prince invoked the Dark Lord, when the infernal force blasted through the pub and tossed Patrick off his feet, it came as a perfect surprise. One moment he was indulging in a cornucopia of anticipation and the next he found himself flat on his back with an eyeful of old ceiling timbers webbed in fairy lights. Before he could prop himself up on his elbows, a wild lust for alcohol besieged him, a trillion cells crying out in unison for their fix. It manifested as a physiological pain and Patrick understood that whatever spell Prince had cast upon him—upon them all?—had been damping his addiction. With that plug pulled, it now came back in a double-force rush and it was all he could do to stagger to his feet as he beheld the impossible reality of the Prince Demon overshadowing Brooks like a brimstone tower.

Yet even in this absurd and apocalyptic milieu, his thirst yearned to be slaked. Where had he left his whisky? One remained near the bar where he'd earlier fallen onto his backside, too dangerous to now acquire, but the other stood behind the bar where he had secreted himself and tripped Prince as he tried to make his escape. God and the Devil had both tested him and both had found him wanting. That only made Patrick want to drink more. There would be a certain self-destructive satisfaction in guzzling down those plentiful draughts of holy scotch.

Prince, or what passed for him now, slapped Brooks aside with a frightening and indifferent power. Patrick checked to see if Shirley remained beside him and found her crouched in a similar fight-or-flight position, except her eyes were steel. He wished he possessed half her courage. His gaze shifted to Don, then to Brooks and Maurice who lay draped across the stairs like rugs. His mind lifted up and away to poor old Truman, perhaps the gutsiest of them all, who had taken on the demons single-handedly and survived only to become one through unfortunate blood-to-blood contact.

Patrick's eyelids flew open, exposing the whites around his ice-blue irises.

In his wide-ranging ramblings through theological academia, he had come across the word 'teleology'. He remembered it because it was the best single-world summation he had found for 'it's all part of God's plan'. Everything happens for a reason. Each man and woman present had been spared infection from Prince's satanic brew and the resulting fallout, beating odds of two hundred to one to do so. This convocation of souls in the Ironstone Hotel was no coincidence.

The Prince Demon tried to smash Don into oblivion, his gigantic crimson fist shattering a section of the hardwood bar to kindling. Patrick seized this distracted moment and darted through the gap in the bar, the original one the pub's builders had fashioned and not the Prince Demon's destructive carpentry. He tried to block out his earlier humiliation, when scotch dripped down Prince's smug and knowing face. God had given him strength to abstain from drinking the scotch long enough to reach this moment. This time would be different, it had to be. Teleology.

Shirley threw herself at the Prince Demon, tried to stick him like a pig, and was sent hurtling across the pub to crash-land on a table and roll to the floor. Patrick's sense of destiny heightened. As the Prince Demon wound up for another blow, aiming to make Don a smear of blood and bone fragments, Patrick stepped outside the bar and turned to face him. The whisky bottle dangled from his fingers, like a gunslinger's shooting iron. Biblical quotations rushed through his head, fulsome, grandiose, not so different from Prince's earlier ranting. In the end, he dismissed them all.

"This is the Ironstone Hotel," he said. "The licensee is Shirley Goodsall."

At the sound of Patrick's voice the Prince Demon paused, colossal arm crooked and ready to strike. Outside, the fire-spawn burned brighter and the pub's windows began to crack.

"She practices the responsible service of alcohol."

Turning side on, Patrick lobbed the scotch bottle as though it were a cold Molotov cocktail. It caught the Prince Demon across the bridge of his raptor nose and shattered into a dozen pieces. Before the first bottle made impact Patrick sprang forward and dashed for the second bottle, picking it up on the fly and side-arming it, a cricketer taking a shy at the stumps. It also obliterated on impact, this time against the Prince Demon's leg. Patrick stumbled to his knees and fell sidelong, rolled over, got his feet beneath him again. The blessed whisky had darkened the Prince Demon's hide in a vermillion cruciform splotch. A sign God was with him, it had to be. Patrick looked up.

The Prince Demon's arm remained poised and ready to annihilate, but the entire crushing weight of those black eyes, heavy as dark matter, now pressed down upon Patrick instead of Don. Every muscle in the colossal red body tensed and pulled taut. Patrick flinched and turned his head away, prepared to be smashed to a pulp for his mindless superstition and unceasing foolishness.

When nothing happened for a time, Patrick dared raise his head again. The Prince Demon's lidless eyes had fogged over grey, black plastic left to oxidize in the sun. The muscles continued to tremble, the tremors escalating until the entire body seemed to vibrate. Patrick wondered if another shockwave, like the one that had accompanied the Devil's possession of Prince's body, was about to rip through the hotel. Rip through *them*, scorch them to ashes. But rather than a blast, the Prince Demon emitted a high-pitched whistling. It reminded Patrick of his grandmother's old tea kettle. Smoke rose from the legs and face in plumes and when it reached Patrick's lungs it seemed to clog them with acrid soot. He coughed so hard he was close to vomiting. Between each paroxysm, he noticed Don doing the same, face wrinkled in abject agony. The whistling grew louder, more extreme, until Patrick thought his ears might bleed. It was like standing right next to a house alarm. It had reached an unbearable crescendo when the hotel's windows imploded, creating a glass-storm within. Patrick covered up, but shards still nicked his hands and ears and neck.

When the stinging wind had abated he lowered his hands and found them seeping blood from a dozen cuts. He could feel more blood trickling into his ears and soaking his shirt collar.

Even though the windowpanes were now bare of glass the pub's interior was sauna-hot. Any passage of air, it seemed, would cook Patrick's skin and he half expected to burst into flames.

But through tear-blurred eyes he noticed something: although the fire-spawn had easy access to the hotel's interior, they remained at the threshold. Did they appear hesitant? Did Patrick see something uncertain, even fearful, in their candle-flame eyes?

The first piece fell off the Prince Demon. His falcon nose dropped to the floor and exploded in a puff of red dust. Next came his left cheek and half his chin with it. He reached up with a long-nailed hand to touch the afflicted area and two fingers dropped off, clattering to the floor between his taloned toes. A moan sounded in his chest and progressed into a full-throated roar that thrummed the floorboards. Then it stopped abruptly as the Prince Demon's throat blasted outward, showering Patrick in dry viscera that smelled of rotten-egg gas. The damp crucifix shape on his thigh caved inward, the knee joint cracked, the calf folded up and bent at right angles to the rest of the leg.

Like an ancient turpentine tree that had succumbed to a woodchopper's axe, the Prince Demon fell sideways and crashed onto the floor. He disintegrated into a hundred pieces that sprayed outward like earth around a meteor strike. Between the rising dust and the smoke the air became nigh-on unbreathable, but as Patrick struggled to his feet amid the miasma he saw the fire-spawn winking out, one by one. When their flames snuffed they dropped to the ground, as if a connection had been cut. The fires that had sprung up at their touch also extinguished spontaneously, charred wood the only thing left to attest that they had existed.

Lungs burning, almost gagging on the thin air, Patrick crawled infant-like towards Don, who now lay on his back with one hand clutching his side. Patrick came in close and touched his shoulder. Don's head lolled towards him and he said in a breathless voice, "Just busted ribs. I'll be okay. Make sure Shirley's all right."

Pulling his collar up over his nose and mouth, Patrick kept low and made his way across the pub to where Shirley lay. A pond of blood had formed below her lips and as Patrick inched closer he noticed her normally light-tan complexion had gone the color of the smoke palling in the pub's rafters. He moved forward faster, spluttering as he inhaled more smoggy air, and pressed his fingers to her neck. He waited, moved his fingers, waited again.

No pulse.

CHAPTER TWENTY-SIX

AS DON SLUMPED against the bar his chest cavity no longer seemed large enough to contain his lungs. Every breath pushed against his ribs and elicited a dull throb. The pain and oxygen deprivation caused a brownout in his brain; he could see and think but everything seemed to be operating at half amperage. With detached elation he watched the Demon Prince crumble in on himself and the fire-spawn flame out.

Then he watched as Patrick went on hands and knees to Shirley's side. They might have been two sea creatures in murky water. Through smoke and dust Don could just make out Patrick putting his fingers to Shirley's neck. He moved them around a few times and, when he looked back over his shoulder and shook his head, the lights in Don's head came back at full wattage.

"I can't find a pulse," Patrick said. "I don't think she's breathing."

"Fuck," Don said hoarsely. He straightened his back, gritting his teeth against fresh protests from his ribs. "Do you know CPR?"

Patrick shook his head.

With one arm, and ribs snapped like breadsticks, Don had no hope of administering it properly. "You'll have to do it." Expelling each word was an effort. And although the power was back on in his brain, it felt as though rats had chewed the wiring. "Do you think you can drag her outside first? We need fresh air."

Patrick nodded and then looked around, assessing the situation. He began to clear a path through the maze of tables and chairs. Don tried not to count the priceless seconds this would cost Shirley, particularly since neither man knew when her heart had stopped. How long until brain damage occurred? Five minutes was the figure that popped into Don's head. He wasn't sure if he had learned that as part of his first aid course, picked it up as a random factoid, or simply made it up altogether. Whatever the case, Patrick's progress was agonizing to watch.

Unable to stand it any longer, Don worked himself onto his knees and with great care brought one foot forward. When this motion didn't upset his ribs he put his weight on that foot and propped his hand on his thigh. With a final controlled flex, he got himself upright. The motion jogged his injury a touch, but once standing his ribs actually seemed happier than they had sitting. He pulled his shirt up over his nose, knowing even a light cough would result in an outburst of pain. He walked across to join Patrick and tried to drag a chair out of his path, but even this simple action brought a warning twinge from his ribs.

Infuriated at his own impotence, Don swore again and put a hand across his eyes, wishing he could somehow plug up the ducts from which tears threatened to run. Christ, they had managed to vanquish an embodiment of Satan himself, and now they were about to lose Shirley because he couldn't perform the simple act of cardiopulmonary resuscitation.

While still obscured in this dark despair, he felt a hand press gently against his shoulder. He opened his eyes and found Maurice standing beside him, blood drying in his eyelashes. "I know CPR," he said, then as he dropped to his knees he said to Patrick, "Finishing clearing the way."

He covered Shirley's lips with his own and blew air into her lungs, commenced compressions, delivered more air. Once an unobstructed path had been created, he forked his hands beneath Shirley's knees and armpits and carried her through the pub. He placed her gently among the fallen demons and restarted CPR. Don stood at a prudent distance, aware of how annoying space invaders could be in an emergency situation, and watched Maurice work.

He let his tears fall and didn't try to pretend they were a reaction to the smoke and dust, not even when Patrick stood alongside him. He loathed the way Shirley's chest bowed beneath the heel of Maurice's palm, even though he understood it was necessary to keep the blood pumping around her body. The sun's final glow faded from the sky as they watched on and Don prayed Shirley's ashen complexion and blue-lined lips were a trick of the departing light. After a while, he couldn't bear to watch anymore and let his eyes wander.

He and Patrick could have been side-by-side in an alien

graveyard. Bodies littered the ground three and four deep, arms snarled into astringent shapes, faces frozen in grimaces and silent screams. He scanned the scene to make a quick estimate. It seemed the entire town had been congregated around the pub at the end. Their lumpy and translucent demon skin had burned until it encrusted them in what looked like overcooked fish batter. It even had a smell, Don noted dully, a faint aroma of pork crackling. Most likely Truman numbered among those forms. Elle, too.

Maybe it's better if you don't come back, Shirley, he thought.

But women were nothing if not contrary and she chose that instant to cough into Maurice's mouth and buck her hips and drag in a whistling breath. It quickly dissipated into another string of wracking coughs that shuddered her entire body. Don tried not to think about the complications that could arise from lung damage, fun little things such as pneumonia. Between coughs and chest heaves Shirley spat something onto the asphalt, something dark, and a gong of terror clanged in Don's heart. But once her coughing died down Shirley improved rapidly and, now able to think clearly, Don figured she had spat a mixture of soot and dust and dried blood.

"You gave us a scare there, Shirl," he said.

"Prince," she said, eyes widening, as if remembering an important appointment. "What happened—"

"Don't worry, Patrick took care of him," Don said.

Patrick nodded and smiled ruefully. "Terrible waste of good scotch, though."

"But here's the real hero of the hour," Don said, stepping forward and offering Maurice his hand. Maurice shook it firmly but his eyes had a faraway look, as though his mind were elsewhere fighting other battles.

"Yes, thank you, Maurice," Shirley said, as he helped her to her feet. Her forearms were a paisley pattern of mottled purple bruising. Ugly but superficial injuries that had apparently deflected anything more serious. She drew Maurice into a hug, one that persisted a long time. When they parted, Shirley's eyes had that same distracted look as Maurice's. It wasn't hard to guess why.

"I don't know about you lot, but I'm as dry as a nun's nasty," Patrick said. "How about a drink, Shirl?"

She looked at him askance.

"Water, I mean," he said.

She gave him a wan smile and nodded. "Free water is part of RSA regulations."

They stepped around bodies piled outside the doorway. Since Shirley had missed the final round of festivities Don thought she would be curious to know what had happened to the fire-spawn, but she only spared them the attention necessary that she didn't trip over an arm or leg. Threads of shock were the only things holding together the fabric of her sanity, Don realized.

Wisps of breeze passed through the pub's now-permanently open windows and the cross ventilation had thinned out the smoke. Shirley snapped on the lights. Most illuminated, but one row remained dark. Don traced the exposed wiring from the dead lights and saw it had been severed where the Prince Demon fractured the rafters. The pub didn't appear in danger of immediate collapse, but nor was it structurally sound. Shirley would need to get it repaired, which would require supports and some sort of scissor lift to reach the damaged timbers. An expensive job, in other words. With her few regulars now resembling the citizens of Pompeii after Mount Vesuvius incinerated their city, Don doubted she could afford to glaze a window.

Pebbled glass crunched beneath their feet as they walked in. "You have a seat, Shirl, rest up," Don said. "I'll get the water."

His chest still felt tight, as though an invisible rope were cinched around his diaphragm, but provided he didn't reach up or bend down, he found his ribs didn't bother him too much. He lined up four schooner glasses and filled them with water from the post-mix hose, garnished them with some ice. Patrick distributed the glasses and everyone drank in silence. Don relished the soothing chill on his tongue and throat, cold rain falling on a desert. A simple pleasure amongst so much pain. His mind went again to the scores of Black Wattle residents lying outside in twisted regiments, their demon skins broiled to a crust. Though he could not be held culpable for their deaths, they would be on his conscience all the same. A country copper looked after his own and, while he might be retired and armless, they had remained his people.

He placed his schooner glass on the bar top and stared into its clear emptiness. That was Black Wattle now, an empty vessel. The thought almost moved him to tears again and he realized he had been holding his acknowledgment of this truth at arm's length.

Everything he knew, everyone he loved, wiped out in a single hot minute.—

No. Not everything.

He watched as Shirley sipped her water, a middle-distance stare giving her face an odd alien quality. Black Wattle had become her home, too, its people her people. Yet she had lost more than Don. He knew loss, was on intimate terms with it, and it hurt his heart to imagine what it must be like to outlive a child, especially one so young and vital as Elle.

Maurice, too. What must he be feeling? Not just grief for a lost love, but resentment and hostility towards the town that had stolen Truman and cost Maurice any chance at reconciliation. Guilt, too. Self-loathing that he had pushed him away to a hillbilly backwater like Black Wattle in the first place.

Christ, Don thought. *What did we do? We might have saved the rest of humanity, but what did we do to ourselves?* Prince's promised oasis had a sudden retrospective attractiveness, even if it was hewn from emotional manipulation and laid out on a blanket of lies. They had prevented the earth from becoming hell on earth, but sentenced themselves to their own private hell.

An eerie quiet infused the pub. With the roadblocks still in place, they were the only living beings for five kilometers in any direction. Night had fallen in earnest, blacking out the pub windows, yet not even the whirr of a cricket or a rodent scuttling through the grass broke the flawless silence. Don became aware of his own breath whooshing through his sinuses. He knew this sound well enough. It was the sound of loneliness. A shared enemy had bonded their ragtag circle, had been the updraught that floated their common purpose. Now they had descended back to a desolate plain.

As though hoping to counteract this mood, Patrick clapped down his glass and said, "What do we do now?"

Introspective eyes cleared and focused on him. The atmosphere in the pub changed; Don sensed it the way a Geiger counter sensed radioactivity. Shirley placed her glass by her feet and winced as she rested her elbows on her knees. She looked like a hardened criminal sitting on a prison bunk. "What do we do?" she said. "Haven't we done enough?"

Patrick's eyes darted away. In a small voice he said, "I didn't mean we—"

"No, you never *mean* anything, do you, Patrick? You don't mean to get blind drunk and stumble around insulting people, you don't mean to put me in an awkward situation when you come begging for booze, you don't mean—"

"I never begged!" Patrick said, riling. "I paid for every drop and without my money, you would have been filing for bankruptcy six months ago."

"You wish," Shirley said.

Patrick grinned, got to his feet. "You think it's a big secret? The whole town knew you were going under. Fuck me dead, if you hadn't been trying to flog this dead horse you call a hotel, we wouldn't be in this mess."

"Now hang on a minute," Don interrupted.

"No, let him talk," Shirley said, also rising to her feet. "Go on, Patrick. I can't wait to hear how this is all my fault."

"If you hadn't been so desperate, you never would have taken Prince's beer, would you?"

"That's rich," Shirley said. "Like you're the grand champion of good decisions. Driving so drunk you don't notice half a ton of cow wandering out onto the road."

"I wasn't drunk! I'd had a few wines at lunch, I'll admit, but I would never knowingly put anyone in jeopardy. Anyway, if it weren't for me, we'd all be dead and your precious pub would be matchsticks."

"Oh, please," Shirley said, rolling her eyes. "Don't come over all holier-than-thou. I saw the way you looked at the scotch in the cellar. You would have happily drunk yourself into oblivion and let events run their course, to hell with everyone else."

"That's not true!"

"Just give it a rest, both of you!" Don roared. "Prince is dead but he's still manipulating us, can't you see that? We're still playing his game, blaming ourselves for something he did."

"Shh!" Maurice said.

"What?" Don said, rounding on him.

"I said shush! Listen."

They fell silent. At first, Don heard nothing. Then, just as he was about to speak, he heard it too. A ceramic scraping, as though someone was sifting through a pile of bricks or moving a terracotta pot across a tiled patio. Their eyes met, understood, agreed. Maurice led the way with a kind of cautious crab-walk towards the

Prince Demon's body, which looked like a fallen idol amidst the ruins of an ancient civilization.

Moving closer, Don heard that terracotta sound again. The mound of petrified torso piled in the middle of the floor heaved, sending down a small avalanche of pebbles that rattled across the floor. Don's eyes went to his gun, still unloaded and innocuous near the stairs, then to the broken carving knife, then hunted for the meat cleaver. Where had that gone? Without it, they were unarmed. Not that Truman's kitchenware had proved much use against the Prince Demon.

While Don dithered, Maurice reached for the top of the mound and dug his fingers beneath a slab of stone that had once been part of the Prince Demon's pectoral muscle. He flipped it off and it landed on the floor with a rocky crash, breaking into half a dozen pieces. Although light at this end of the pub was chancy owing to the snapped wiring, there was no mistaking Prince's business-like attire, now ochre with dust from the Devil's crumbled body.

"Well, I'll be goddamned," Don said.

Maurice pushed more rubble away. Prince's neck and shoulders were also a dusty red. He turned his face up but his eyes remained shut. He might have been a mole emerging from the earth.

Don moved forward and kicked the broken slabs off his back and legs, then collared him and yanked him to his feet. He brought up a dust cloud that made Don's lungs itch, but he refused to give Prince the satisfaction of hearing him cough. Instead he barked, "Move!" and trundled him through the pub before shoving him into a seat. Once there, Prince lifted his face again and, millimeter by millimeter, opened his squinting eyes. Wherever he had been prior to that moment, his eyes had grown accustomed to darkness.

"How did I get here?" he asked Don.

"You tell me and we'll both know. One thing's for sure, though, you're going to pay for what you did to Black Wattle."

Prince blinked at him a few times. "What's Black Wattle?"

Don sneered at him. "Don't come the raw prawn with me, Prince. You think I'm some sort of soft-headed country bumpkin? We've got your measure now. The mind games are over."

For a long while Prince only stared at him, as if processing the words, trying to translate what he'd heard into something he understood. Then he said, "I'm a prince?"

"Holy shit," Don said, turning his eyes to the ceiling and turning away. Then he turned back and pointed a finger towards the door. "There are a thousand bodies out there," he said. "I'd be more than happy to add one more to the pile. No one's going to ask questions."

Prince looked bewildered and scared. He followed the direction of Don's finger and then looked back at him. "I don't know what's going on."

Patrick said cautiously, "I think he might be telling the truth, Don."

"How on earth did he get back here?" Maurice said. "Wasn't he. . .?"

"How did you come back, Prince?" Don demanded.

"I don't know," he said in a fretful voice. "I don't even know who I am."

"This is bullshit," Don said. "Has to be."

But no one spoke up to agree and, even though Don had spoken the words, he didn't think much of them either. There was no artfulness in Prince's eyes now, no sense he was engaging in mental chess. Just a small, scared man looking out on a world that was as foreign to him as it would be to a newborn baby. A command of English appeared to be the only thing the Devil's possession had not stripped from his consciousness.

"Shirl, can you go and grab us some more cable-ties? Maybe it is how he says it is, but I'm not taking any chances."

"Okay," she said. She sounded abstracted, but she disappeared into the cellar and re-emerged with a fistful of cable-ties. Maurice stood beside Prince and said, "We're going to cable-tie your wrists and feet. It's for your own protection."

Prince didn't look happy about the prospect, but he nodded and let Maurice hold his arms while Shirley put a tie around his wrists and zipped it shut. They did the same with his ankles. When they were finished they stood back and fell into a thoughtful silence.

Because Don's mind was on a different wavelength—he was still trying to ascertain to his satisfaction that Prince wasn't fooling them again—he didn't notice the heaviness of that shared silence. Maurice looked at Shirley and said, "Are you thinking what I'm thinking?"

She raised her eyes to him slowly and nodded. "If Prince survived possession, then maybe. . ."

Don gawped at them, the import of their words sluicing into his brain like an ice floe. He snapped his head around and glared at Patrick. "Find that meat cleaver and keep an eye on this piece of shit. We need to check something out. Shirl, do you have a flashlight?"

She found one in her office. Once she had flicked it on and off to be sure it worked, the three of them scuttled out of the pub and into the darkness.

CHAPTER TWENTY-SEVEN

ONLY WHEN THEY were outside, with the flashlight cutting a thin beam through the inky blackness, did Shirley twig to her overweening optimism. Assuming anyone *had* survived the transformation from human to fire-spawn and back again (ostensibly a different process to Prince's invocation of the Devil), nearly the entire town lay in drifts around their feet. The crusted casing made each body almost identical anyway, and with nothing but the flashlight and the feeble glow from the pub lights, identifying Elle and Truman among the multitudes would be impossible. Nor had she forgotten her daughter's transformation, the way she vomited and shat out her organs. Assuming her body did exist within one of these shells, it might be a lifeless husk itself.

She drew a deep breath, exhaled and said, "Well, first things first, I guess."

She squatted, rested one knee on the pavement and directed her light on a fire-spawn's face. The skin looked mummified, as if the body had been at rest in a tomb for five-thousand years, but as Shirley shined the flashlight into the eye sockets she felt hope jackrabbit in her chest. The sockets were no such thing, but rather hollows, at the bottom of which she could see the smooth baby-skin of closed eyelids. The raddled demon flesh was not a death mask, not necessarily. It could be a life mask.

"What do you see?" Maurice asked.

"I'm not certain yet," she said, unwilling to raise his hopes in vain. She transferred the flashlight from her right hand to her left and then eased a finger into one of the mask's eye hollows. It felt dry and bumpy, like overcooked chicken skin, and the sensation put her teeth on edge. Ignoring this, she hooked her finger and slid it between the demon skin and the soft eyelid. She tugged on the skin and it pulled outward with a slobbery tearing sound.

"Christ," Don said weakly.

Shirley applied a little more force and the wet ripping sound got louder. She could feel the demon skin peeling away from the substrate below, not much different from peeling a sticker from its backing. . .but what was happening to that substrate? Could she be skinning someone alive?

The demon shell began to stretch, so she moved her finger to a spot where the tear duct would have been, and drew towards the nose. The hole widened, and when it had reached the size of a plum she stopped to bring the flashlight closer. The sub-layer of skin appeared to be flensed and bloodied, but when she dabbed at it with a clean finger the blood wiped away, leaving only pink beneath. Maurice and Don were now hunched forward and peering over her shoulders, one on each side.

"That has to be a good sign, doesn't it?" Maurice said. He sounded like he was trying to convince himself as much as ask a question.

Now Shirley knew she wasn't damaging whichever unfortunate person lay beneath the demon skin, she felt emboldened to pull harder. The skin came away easily enough, but it was almost like a thin sheet of rubber or leather and difficult to tear.

"There's a pair of scissors in the desk drawer of my office," she said to whomever happened to be listening. "Can you go and grab them for me?"

"Right," Don said, stepping over a demon body and trotting inside.

Shirley handed Maurice the flashlight. "This will be quicker if I use two hands."

She continued to tear off the demon skin. Even with two hands to draw it apart, the work was slow and laborious and Shirley was glad when Don returned and placed the scissors in her hand. They were near-new and a robust size, and the blades cut through the knobbly skin without much fuss. Pull, snip, pull, snip. Soon she had removed an entire caul, exposing the blood-splotched head beneath. Bald and somewhat familiar, from what few details she could make out in the flashlight's beam. She leaned forward and used the lower section of her tee-shirt to wipe the face clean. She sat back on her haunches and the wisp of a smile touched her lips. He had been difficult to recognize without his ever-present glasses.

"Dr. Sneddon," she said.

"Is he alive?" Maurice asked.

"Good question."

She leaned forward again and this time to put her ear to his lips. She heard nothing, felt no touch of breath. She was about to pronounce him dead when she thought she noticed something else. She pressed her ear more firmly against his mouth and there could be no question about it.

Warmth.

It might be some residual heat from his stint as a fire-spawn, she supposed, but the demon carcass had not been at all hot to the touch. It was as if, when Patrick had extinguished the Prince Demon, every trace of devil's fire had been extinguished with him.

While pondering this, she felt it. A small exhalation, not much bigger than an infant's. It made next to no sound, less than a whisper, but the sensitive skin and hairs inside her ear knew it.

"He's breathing," she said. Her heart restarted its little jackrabbit kicks. "Let's get the rest of this skin off him."

She and Maurice began to work in tandem, one pulling the lips of the skin apart and the other running the scissors down the middle. Don stood by, keeping the flashlight beam directed at the cutting site. It reminded Shirley of open-heart surgery as they separated the skin all the way down to Dr Sneddon's pelvis and then started in on the left leg. Dr Sneddon was naked underneath, the demon skin bonded to his skin across every inch of his body. Shirley took special care not to snip anything she shouldn't. Dr Sneddon wouldn't appreciate an impromptu vasectomy.

Shirley bit down on a lunatic laugh, lest she feel obliged to explain it to Don and Maurice. The élan rippling through her as she freed Dr Sneddon from his demonic straitjacket felt perilously close to mania, but she went with it, rode it the way a big-wave surfer skims across a wall of water that could crush him in an instant.

As she cut along the balls of his feet, Dr Sneddon stirred and started to cough, a dry, hacking that lifted his body off the ground. Once his lungs cleared, though, he lay flat again and his eyes stared straight upwards. From what Shirley could make out in the dim light they appeared both blank and overwhelmed, as if seeing into the center of the galaxy. The skin around his hands and fingers did not seem to be bonded in the same way as the rest of his body and the final demon derma came off like a pair of washing-up gloves.

Maurice helped him sit up and the action appeared to clear his sight. He looked around with growing puzzlement.

"How are you feeling, doc?" Don asked.

"I appear to be all right," he said, wiping a hand down each arm. This created small blood-slicks. He shook them away.

Shirley said, "What do you remember?"

"What do I remember?" Dr Sneddon said. "All of it, I'm afraid. Nearly every person in the pub started going into seizures all at once, or so I thought. I ran to Molly Cameron's aid and while I was trying to examine her she grew enormous claws and stabbed them into the side of my neck. There was an awful lot of blood and I was worried she might have hit my carotid artery, but next thing I knew my veins were on fire and I began to change as well. Beyond that. . .it's fuzzy. I was there and not there, like someone with delirium. Then the footage in my memory just stopped. The next thing I knew, I was staring at a night sky."

This recount silenced them for a time. After a while, Shirley said, "So you remember who you are?"

"Oh, who I am isn't in doubt," he said, "but I am curious to know how it happened and why I'm outside. In the dark. Wearing no clothes."

"Chilly night, too," Patrick interjected from where he stood at the pub door, "although that doesn't seem to be much of a problem for you, doc." Noticing Don's hard stare he added, "Don't worry, Prince isn't going anywhere. He doesn't remember a thing and he's scared shitless. We're the closest thing to family he's got." Returning his gaze to Dr Sneddon's nude form he said, "Wish mine looked like that on a cold morning."

"Rather than discussing my anatomy, perhaps you could obtain some clothes for me?"

"Y' don't want these grubby old duds," Patrick said, lifting his shirt sleeve to demonstrate.

"You're probably better off heading home to get cleaned up anyway, doc," Don said. "That demon blood stinks to high heaven."

"Demon blood?"

"Long story. We'll fill you in later."

"I have an overcoat in the office," Shirley said. "It's on a coat hanger on the back of the door. Would you mind grabbing it for him, Patrick?"

"You bet."

The country night was already turning frosty and by the time Patrick returned with Shirley's coat the doctor's limbs were shuddering and his teeth chattering. Shirley and Patrick helped him to his feet and Patrick put the coat around his shoulders. Dr Sneddon did up the top and bottom buttons, but his protruding pink belly prevented him from fastening the others. "Well, at least it preserves my modesty," he said wryly, arching an eyebrow in Patrick's direction. "Thank you, Shirley. I'll wash it and bring it back to you."

"After you've had your love spuds all over it?" Patrick said. "I'd burn it with fire, Shirl."

"Shut up, you," said Dr Sneddon, grinning.

"Do you want me to run you home, doc?" Don said.

The doctor took in all the bodies surrounding his bare feet, littering the footpath, spilling out onto the street. "Is it safe to walk?"

Don considered this. "Should be."

"Then I think I'll walk," Dr Sneddon said. "It's not far and for some reason, I don't like the thought of being cooped up in a car." He looked around him again. "I'll come back once I've showered and dressed. I imagine my wife is inside one of these exoskeletons or whatever they are."

"Most likely," Don agreed.

"Very well. Good evening for now."

Dr Sneddon picked his way around the bodies and then commenced to walk west along Goldfields Road, the hem of Shirley's overcoat flapping against his thighs. The coat was black and, as the doctor faded into the distance, he became two disembodied legs. A contemplative silence had stolen over those who remained. Shirley was unsure what the others had on their minds, but in hers was a single thought, clear and distinct. Its presence discomfited her, so she decided to speak it out loud just to be rid of it.

"Would anyone think badly of me if I suggested we try to find Elle before we free everyone else?"

Don smiled and patted her shoulder. "You won't get any grief from me, Shirl. If Dr. Sneddon's any indication, they seem to be in some sort of stasis or hibernation, anyway."

She turned to Maurice, awaiting the judgment she felt she deserved. But he just blew a raspberry and said, "As if I wasn't thinking the same thing about Truman."

"That settles it then," Don said. "Do you have another pair of scissors, Shirl? Many hands make light work, even if I've only got one to offer. Patrick can pull back the demon skin and I'll cut."

"I've probably got another pair somewhere."

After some rummaging around she located a second pair of scissors down in the cellar. A full moon had risen above the pub's pitched roof, bathing the scene in cold light and allowing Don and Patrick to cut open demon cases without the aid of a flashlight. It proved to be like breaking open soft-centered chocolates and finding out what flavor lurked inside. A few faces were unfamiliar, but not many. Between them, she and Maurice found Al Bragg (who ran the farm supplies store), Jason Cuneen (who had taken over his father's sheep farm after he retired the year before), Dolly Watkins (proprietor of a craft shop that somehow stayed open even though she never seemed to sell a single item) and Venera Katsopoulis (whose chocolate and candy shop was the only business that seemed largely immune to the town's economic misfortunes). The job involved a lot of crouching and Shirley's thighs were soon aching. The temperature continued to drop, too, careless that they were all still dressed for a sunny Black Wattle spring day. The increasing chill cut to Shirley's core even as sweat broke out on her forehead, an odd and irritating combination. When she and Maurice cut open their twentieth demon skin and it revealed Robert Sharp's red-bearded butcher's face, she whined like a dog.

"We're going to be here all night," she said.

"Keep at it," Maurice said, moving on to the next body. "Elle and Truman have to be here somewhere. We'll find them."

Shirley's hand grew sore from working the scissors and in the off-cast glow from the flashlight, she could see beads of perspiration had sprung up on Maurice's brow. She relented and gave away the crouching, but soon her knees began to graze from continual shifting around on the concrete and asphalt.

"Let's try over on the bush side of the pub next," Shirley said, tossing her hair out of her eyes and massaging her hand. "My knees are killing—"

"I think we've got her!" Don shouted.

Shirley and Maurice's heads snapped up and they glanced at one another for half a second before leaping to their feet. Don and Patrick were on the wide dusty strip that separated the pub from the nearest residence on the town side. In her hurry, Shirley caught the toe of her shoe on an out-thrown arm and went into a running stumble; she might well have lost her balance and tumbled into the dirt, if Maurice hadn't caught her by the shoulders. She mumbled a word of thanks and motored ahead to where Don stood, just below a pub window.

"It's her, isn't it?" he said.

The flashlight beam shone on the person's face. Patrick knelt beside her, his shirtsleeve painted red where he had wiped away the blood. Elle lay at rest in her demon-skin sarcophagus (which was only opened to the breastbone), her face as peaceful as a sleeping infant's.

While Shirley watched on, Dr Sneddon's words entered her head—"What do I remember? All of it, I'm afraid"—and she burst into tears. Her legs wobbled and she dropped to her knees, heedless of the acidic sting it wrought. She snatched the scissors from Patrick's hands and he stepped away respectfully as she went into a cutting frenzy. Maurice got to work, too, pulling back the skin while Don hovered above directing the flashlight.

When they had the skin opened to the waist, Elle began to cough. Don pointed the flashlight at the hollow of her neck so as to illuminate her face but not dazzle her. In time she opened her eyes and they were the flawless green marbles Shirley had always treasured, the rotten bloodshot eggs now relegated to the dark and mildewed corner where Shirley's mind kept its most disturbing memories. Like Dr Sneddon, she at first appeared to see nothing, or to be seeing past everything, but in time her eyes refocused on the world.

Shirley put a hand against her cheek, almost fainting at its softness and warmth.

"Hello, Ellie-Bellie."

Elle's eyelashes fluttered a few times, butterfly air-kisses, then her eyes found her mother's face.

"Hello, Shirley-Whirly," she said.

CHAPTER TWENTY-EIGHT

S*TARS.*
They seemed to emerge from the blackness, like a sparkling armada emerging from heavy fog on the open sea, until they filled his vision's entire vista. Truman thought he must be in Prince's promised oasis, that Maurice had heeded the tale of the infernal nightmare that awaited should the Devil claim his soul. But then the same finely honed sensibilities that had let him detect Prince's artificial world assured him this was solid reality. He blinked a few times and the vista widened, revealing Maurice on one side and Don on the other. Again he questioned whether this could be real, whether the unceasing torment could be over without Prince's simulated paradise. But the concerned faces, the night air on his brow, the coarse sensation of whatever enclosed his arms and legs, the pungent smoky smell ablating his nostrils. . .these were not the broad strokes of manufactured happiness, but the mundane details inherent in true human experience.

When Maurice saw him wake, his eyes lit up and he began to yank at the crusty outer skin with greater verve. It pulled on Truman's own skin and the sensation was not unlike having an old bandage removed; it tugged on his chest hairs but didn't rip them out. Every time Maurice exposed some more skin to the night chill it tingled, as though the nerves below were relearning how to process a cool sensation.

"Don't worry," Maurice said, snipping the scissors along the inside of his thigh and down to his knee. "We'll have you out of this horrible thing in no time."

Such a sunburst of love filled Truman's chest, it almost made him giddy. His man had not only forgiven his unconscionable infidelity, he had pursued him into the boonies to bring him back from his childish self-imposed exile and was now liberating him from the shroud that represented the final link to a burning horror beyond mortal understanding. The urge to pull him close, to kiss him, to be as one and share the warmth of existence was almost irresistible and he reached out to do just that. . .but then realized his hand remained in the gloved confines of the demon skin. He drew it back again, not only because he wanted to feel Maurice's skin against his own, but because nothing on earth would force him to touch Maurice with that awful deep-fried obscenity. Instead, he lay back and waited, the sight of his lover caring for him—almost nursing him—was pleasure enough for the time being.

Maurice worked the scissors along Truman's shin and the flashlight followed his progress, a helicopter searchlight in miniature. The snipping stopped and Maurice pulled at the skin, Truman admiring the play of muscles in his shoulders. He remained still for a long moment, head down, then said, "What happened to his foot?"

Maurice addressed Don with this query and Truman felt like a child sitting in a hospital bed as his father spoke to a surgeon about matters beyond his understanding. Also, Maurice's tone unsettled him; it was that of a man in a restaurant who had been served the wrong dish.

"What do you mean?" Don said.

"Look for yourself." Maurice pulled back hard on the demon skin. "There's just a stump. Where the hell is his fucking foot?"

The nova of happiness around Truman's heart turned frigid and collapsed in on itself, a dead star. It was as if he had woken from a nightmare only to find the wakeful state was, in fact, a vivid dream within a dream into which remnants of the nightmare had begun to infiltrate. But his hyper-sensitive mind knew this was no subconscious state. The sight of a stump resting in a bed of seared demon flesh was blunt-force-trauma reality. What hurt more than that, however, was the pain in Maurice's eyes.

"Please don't be angry," Truman said, a tear trickling onto his cheek and glinting moonlight. "I chopped my feet off just before I. . .before I became one of those things. I didn't want to harm anyone. I'm sorry, Maurice. I'm so sorry."

Don stared at the stump, eyes like golf balls. The flashlight left Truman's foot and shone off into the never-never as Don put his hand to his mouth; he might have been stifling an indigestive burp. Maurice raised the scissors above his head, forearm straining with effort, as if fighting to hold them. Truman thought for one awful moment he meant to stab himself or perhaps plunge the scissors into Truman's chest. But then he dashed them into the dirt instead and burst into tears.

Still somewhat hampered by the demon skin, Truman pushed himself up into a straight-legged sitting position. He began to rip at the skin on his shoulders, which stuck to him like a leather shawl. Truman needed the horrid stuff off him, to pull Maurice into a hug and tell him everything would be all right, even if he didn't believe it himself. The skin didn't want to budge though; it peeled away with agonizing slowness, as if glued on. He growled at it through gnashed teeth, pulled at it until he thought his shoulder tendons would snap.

But then a hand slid between the demon skin and the tender skin of his real neck. A long-fingered and muscular hand whose touch he knew as well as his own. Maurice drew him close until their temples touched, then they sat together and cried. Overwrought, broken, down in the dirt and leaves, but together again at last.

When the emotional storm had blown by and left only lingering clouds, Maurice set to work cutting away the remainder of the demon skin. Never had Truman felt so clean before; it was like emerging from a hot shower after being caked in shit. The word 'reborn' seemed apt. Once he and the skin were entirely parted, Maurice picked him up and carried him into the pub. Truman's arms were wrapped around his shoulders and he leaned forward to plant a kiss on Maurice's lips.

"I could get used to this," he said.

Maurice rolled his eyes and placed him in one of the pub seats. Someone handed Truman a blanket to cover his nakedness. That was when he spotted Prince, also seated but with his hands bound, looking frightened and sorry for himself. "I guess this didn't turn out the way you expected, did it Mr. Prince?" he said.

Prince glanced at him with haunted eyes, then looked away again.

"He doesn't remember anything," Maurice said.

"Really? How convenient."

"No, I mean he doesn't remember *anything*. He doesn't even know who he is or how he got here, let alone what he did to everyone. Can I get you some water?"

"Please," Truman said vaguely. Although he was thirsty, he barely noticed it. He stared at Prince a while, then lifted his legs to stare at the stumps which now jutted out just below the blanket's hem. If what Maurice said was accurate, Prince had been reborn in a sense, too. But his cerebral whiteboard was now almost blank. Truman couldn't decide if that was hopeful or one of the most terrifying things he had ever heard.

Maurice returned with the water, which Truman drank down in three gulps. Passing the glass back to Maurice, he wondered if his gluttony would come back to bite him. He didn't fancy dragging himself across the tiled floor in the men's. How did a person with no feet take a piss? Truman found he had only the faintest notion. The social justice types in his circle of friends and acquaintances probably knew the intimate details, but Truman had spent most of his adult life with his head either in a creative cloud or a tempest of booze.

"I need to go back out and help now," Maurice said. "Are you comfortable, honey? Can I get you anything else?"

Any other time in the past five years Truman would have asked for a scotch; his lips even parted to form the words. But the thought of it made him feel dirty, it would be like climbing back into the demon skin. He had spent the past two days feeling as awful as it was possible to feel. The thought of self-inflicting more harm, even if it was only a cheap scotch hangover, was anathema. Being clean was his new high. How long it would last was anyone's guess, but he intended to ride the high as long as he could.

"I'm okay for now," he said. He patted Maurice on the backside. "You go be my hero."

Maurice groaned theatrically and said, "I prefer corn for dinner." But he smiled before he went outside.

Truman leaned back in his seat, examined his stumps again for a few seconds, then dropped them out of sight and turned to Prince.

"So you really don't remember anything?"

Prince shook his head. He looked like an abused dog in a cage at an animal shelter. Hate trammeled through Truman's heart but he recognized immediately it was now hate with no terminus, an incomplete circuit. He might as well hate a baby because it had thrown up on his shoulder. Prince had a stump, too. . .his mind.

After a while, he leaned across and outstretched his arm.

"My name's Truman," he said.

CHAPTER TWENTY-NINE

AS *PROMISED,* Dr. Sneddon returned within the hour to help remove the Black Wattle residents from their burnt-skin cocoons. He brought with him a pair of surgical-grade shears that cut through the leathery hide as though it were silk. He also sported a pair of jeans, something Don had never seen him wear before and, if pressed to guess, would have assumed he didn't own. But then it had been a queer forty-eight hours, so what better time to learn the town's GP sometimes dressed down far enough to wear denim?

Around eight o'clock, clouds came in from the west and assembled in the sky above Black Wattle, blocking out the moon and starlight and making Don more sought after than before. Many of the liberated townsfolk got cleaned up and dressed and came back to lend a hand.

Soon there were a dozen teams, armed with flashlights and scissors or box cutters or tin-snips, making their way through the masses of prostrate forms. The way they crouched and moved around reminded Don of market gardeners. As they worked, a curious community spirit rose up, like mist from low-lying grass. Everyone knew everyone in Black Wattle and soon the area around the pub sounded much like the interior had a couple of years earlier, with voices raised in chatter and laughter and good-humored remarks about nudity.

Off to Don's left, there came a sharp sheepdog-style whistle. "Hey, Don!" Patrick called. "Guess who I've found?"

Don made his way over and added his own flashlight to the scene. A demon-skin caul had been split apart like a clamshell and the face inside, though sleeping and ruddy with smeared blood, was unmistakable.

"What do you reckon we should do with him?"

Don's mind did a quick spin. "Get someone to help carry him to my car."

While Patrick enlisted assistance, Don opened his station wagon's tailgate and laid the second-row seats flat. He sat cross-legged and waited until Patrick and another man slid their quarry into the cargo space.

"Thanks, gents," Don said. "Patrick, can you finish cutting him open and then close the tailgate, please?"

Patrick worked his scissors along the demon skin torso and stretched it wide, then shut the tailgate and left. With all doors and windows closed it blocked out the convivial community noise enough that Don could hear his fellow occupant's breath. After a few moments, the blood-caked eyelids drew open. Don cocked the hammer on his pistol. The dry *click* broke the catatonia and Mark sat up.

"Welcome back," Don said. "Bet this isn't what you were expecting to see."

Mark's eyes took in the pistol, Don's face, the station wagon's interior, the demon skin still covering his arms and legs. "Is. . .did the. . .what happened?"

"That's what you're going to tell me," Don said.

Mark's eyes dipped.

"I know what you went through, Mark. I've heard from the others. You can't tell me you're still loyal to Prince after what he did to you."

"It's not that." He licked his lips.

"I wouldn't worry about Prince. His mind's been wiped clean. He doesn't know who he is, let alone who you are."

Mark stared at him. "Wiped clean? What did you do to him?"

"We didn't do anything. He did it to himself. Or the Devil did it to him. I don't know, it's been a confusing evening."

"The Devil?" Mark said, now saucer-eyed. "He wasn't part of the plan. What the hell happened while I was. . ."

He gesticulated in a vague way, as though implying a small whirlwind.

Don filled him in and he listened, eyes avid. Occasionally he studied the demon skin on his hands and forearms, like a prisoner wondering if the bars on his cell were rusty enough to break, or the barrel of the pistol.

"There's one thing I don't get, though," Don said when he'd got

Mark up to speed. "If hell on earth was Prince's objective, why didn't he just taint Sydney's water supply or something? Why go to all the bother of brewing up beer and giving it to a country pub?"

"I don't know," Mark said. "I wasn't much more than a grunt. Prince only told me what I needed to know."

Don replayed these sentences through his cop's mind filter, evaluating their veracity. He decided they were plausible, or at least held fast to what few facts he knew, but Prince's world was one of mistrust. And Mark had been a denizen of that world.

Before Don could reach any satisfactory conclusion, Mark surprised him by asking timidly, "Can I see him?"

"See who? Prince?"

Mark nodded.

"Like hell. You were his accomplice in this nasty shitstorm."

"What am I going to do? You said his memory's been wiped."

"I don't know what you're going to do, that's the point. Actually, you know what? On second thoughts, let's go. You can see what mucking around with all this occult malarkey did for Prince."

Mark lifted his arms. The demon skin creaked, like old, cracked leather. "Can you get me out of this first?"

Don lowered his pistol for the first time and sighed contemplatively. "Fine. I'll find someone to cut you out. But if I free you, you're confined to the hotel, understand? Go walkabout and I'll have a hundred cops on your tail within the hour."

"Understood. I'll be a good boy."

Don flagged a volunteer and within a few minutes Mark was wiping himself down with an old towel Don kept in the boot of his car. They crossed the road and went into the pub. Together, hunched in quiet conversation, were Truman and Prince. Don hung back to watch as Mark approached them in small, indefinite steps. Prince paused in whatever he was saying and looked up at his former lackey. A quizzical smile brushed his lips but he showed no recognition whatsoever. It reminded Don of his maternal grandmother, who in the early stages of her dementia would sometimes look at Don the same way.

"Hello, Prince," Mark said.

Prince flinched with alarm that this stranger should know his name. Then closed his eyes for a brief second before extending his hand. "I take it we were once acquainted. I'm afraid I don't know your name. . .?"

"Mark."

The two men shook hands. Mark sat beside him, in the manner of somebody visiting a loved one in hospital. "You really don't remember anything?"

Prince shook his head. "I'm afraid not."

"I'm going outside to help free the rest," Don said. "Remember our agreement."

"Don't worry, I'm not going anywhere."

This Don believed without reservation, yet he couldn't shake a lingering disquiet. Perhaps Mark planned to exact some sort of surreptitious retribution on Prince. If that were so, Don thought he could turn a blind eye without aching his conscience too much. After another moment's consideration, he reclaimed his flashlight and headed back outside.

Two minutes before the illuminated clock on the old community progress hall ticked over to midnight the final person was cut from a demon skin and welcomed back (Gerald Reid, the town vet who had retired five years ago but never quite stopped working). With the job done, most took their flashlights and scissors and went home to sleep. A few stood in clusters, despite the icy night, and discussed their experiences. Those conversations reminded Don of the decompression sessions he and his fellow officers often had at the pub after a long shift on Sydney's streets. Dr. Sneddon's words came back to haunt him, just as they had Shirley a few hours earlier: *How much do I remember? All of it.* In some ways, the entire town of Black Wattle would now have an ex-serviceman's psyche, post-traumatic stress to a greater or lesser degree.

Ruminating on this, he went back inside the Ironstone. Shirley had stoked up a roaring blaze in the fireplace, but with the pub's exposure to the elements, it could do little to combat the cold more than a meter or two beyond the hearth. She, Elle, Truman, Maurice, Patrick, Mark and Prince were all huddled around it. Most had a glass in hand or at their feet, but not one, Don noticed, contained alcohol. Not even Patrick's.

When Truman saw him, he passed his glass to Maurice and shifted around in his seat. "Don, could I have a word with you, please?"

"Sure."

"Uh. . .in private, if that's all right."

"In private?" Don shrugged. "If you like."

"Maurice, would you mind taking me to a quieter corner of the pub, please?"

Without comment, Maurice got to his feet and hefted Truman into his arms. He carried his partner across the hotel and up the stairs to the first bedroom, then sat him on the edge of it. "Call out when you're done," he said to Don, "and I'll bring him back down."

He left, closing the door behind him.

"What did you want to talk about?"

"Maybe I'm being stupid, but. . .I didn't think Maurice would understand. He went through this in his own way, but not like you and I did. I was hoping you could check on something for me."

"Tonight?"

Truman gave him an apologetic smile. "If you could. It's sort of important."

Don pinched the bridge of his nose and rubbed his eyes. "It won't wait until I've had a few hours' sleep?"

"I'm afraid not. By morning it will be too late."

"Okay. Name it."

"I need you to check on Sadie for me."

"Sadie? The barista at the Old Rose?"

Truman nodded.

"Why would I need to check on her? She's Marla's concern now."

"Because. . .she was the demon I cut into pieces. I hacked her head off her body."

"Well, that's a shame, but we all did things we. . .wait." Don's eyes darted up and away as Truman's insinuation hit home. "You're worried she could still be alive?"

Truman nodded again. "Under any other circumstances I'd say it was ridiculous, but considering recent events. . .well, who's to say what's ridiculous?"

"I hear you," Don said. He rubbed his hand across his mouth. "Where will I find her?"

"She should be in the Old Rose kitchen. That's where I left her. No telling what happened if she transformed into fire-spawn like the rest of them."

"Righto," Don said. "Leave it with me."

His hand was on the doorknob when Truman said, "There's one more thing."

Don turned back. Truman looked like a teenager trying to work up the courage to ask out a girl (or boy) for the first time. "What's that?"

"Can you please try to find my feet? I know it sounds stupid, but I'd feel better if you did it rather than Maurice. Because. . .well, because you understand, I suppose."

"I've still got my arm," Don said, lifting the flesh-colored tassel that passed for a limb. "It's just been on strike for a few years. But I take your point. Where will I find them?"

"They should be near a tree, somewhere in this direction," he said, pointing. "I don't remember exactly how far. Things were pretty hazy by that stage."

"Okay. Got it."

Don turned to the door, tarried a moment, turned back. "For what it's worth, I'm sorry this happened to you," he said motioning toward Truman's legs.

Truman tried to smile, but his expression looked more indicative of wind pains. "So am I. Although, truth be told, I wasn't using them much. Drinking yourself to death doesn't require a lot of athleticism."

Don sniffed a half-laugh and nodded his head. There seemed nothing else to add, so he opened the door and left.

When he got to the bottom of the stairs, he hunted around in the shadows until he located his revolver. He slipped it into his waistband. Then he went around to the fireplace, the muted conversation ceasing altogether when he joined their circle again.

"Truman's ready for you," Don said.

He expected Maurice to ask questions—even a simple "What did he want?"—but Maurice only nodded and got up. With his height, calm demeanor and his predisposition to speaking only when necessary, he might have made a good cop, Don thought. The bullies and blabbermouths were the ones you didn't want on your unit. Those who had *been* bullied weren't much better, sad to say. In Don's experience, someone who had been bullied at school often wanted to join the police force to enact revenge. Sooner or later, that sort of person would put the police in the newspapers for the wrong reasons. A dark-skinned gay man like Maurice had almost certainly been bullied as a teenager, but Don doubted he was the type to exorcise his grudges.

When Maurice had topped the stairs Don said to the others, "I have a couple of errands to run for Truman. I suggest you all go home and get some sleep. I expect tomorrow will be a busy day."

"What about him?" Patrick said, jerking a thumb in Prince's direction.

Don ruminated on this. Prince was now *persona non grata*, even to himself. The closest thing he had to next of kin was Mark, who also had nowhere to stay. The pub was a crime scene, probably the most important real estate in Black Wattle as far as the authorities were concerned. But which authorities would that be? Don's head began to pulse, as if it were overfull, and all at once he resented Truman's little errand.

"Can he and Mark stay here, Shirl? The upstairs windows are still intact."

She nodded. "Easily done."

Prince smiled at her gratefully. It was weird to see. As rehabilitation went, being possessed and then dispossessed by the Devil appeared far more effective than handicrafts and adult coloring books.

"I also need you to grab as many photos of this mess as you can. On your phone will do. We might not need them for evidence, but you never know. Then Mark and Prince can help you move the bodies down into the cellar. It's good and cool in there and you don't want them stinking up the place."

The color drained out of Shirley's face. "Would the police. . .is there any way I could be implicated? As an accomplice or something?"

"I doubt it'll get that far, Shirl. My guess is Black Wattle will shortly receive a visit from someone in charge, and I don't mean the sergeant from Goulburn Police. We'll be telling the same story, corroborating one another. But it can't hurt to have some photographic evidence that it all went down the way we say it did, just in case."

"Okay," she said. She didn't sound okay about it.

"The roadblocks are still in place. The state coppers won't start sticking their noses into federal business for another day or so at least. Don't sweat it. We beat the Devil, for Christ's sake, we'll be fine."

Maurice returned with Truman in his arms and put him in front of the fire.

"Right, I have that errand to run. Look after yourselves. I'll see you in the morning."

Don left the pub with his mind buzzing, a hive of questions and thoughts and contradictory ideas. He got in his car and switched on the radio in a bid to quiet the internal humming. The Old Rose was only half a kilometer down Goldfields Road, but he made a detour to his house and took some bullets from the ammo box in the safe. Six, in fact, one for each chamber in the gun, which rested on the passenger's seat as he made the quick drive back and parked outside the café.

Don grabbed the gun, got out and butted the door closed with his backside. The earlier chill had evolved into a bitter cold and Don cursed himself for failing to grab a jacket off the rack while he was collecting his ammunition. He went up the small step onto the Old Rose's porch and pressed his forehead to the glass door. With the starlight still cloud-shrouded, he could make out nothing but dark shapes. He counted to ten, eyes roving. But from the door, it looked like any other café closed up for the night.

He shouldered his way inside and bent his elbow so his firearm pointed towards the ceiling. When the door closed, it brought down silence so perfect the café could have been a solid stone crypt. Don tried to remember where the light switches were and couldn't, not for sure. Somewhere behind the counter, perhaps? He didn't want to go blundering in and fall over a box of paper cups or something. A sudden impact like that could drive his broken ribs into his lungs, and the last thing he wanted after vanquishing Satan was to die in mundane fashion, such as drowning in his own blood. If he kept a straight course he knew it would be more or less clear and take him to the Old Rose's kitchen door.

His hard-soled shoes made clopping sounds on the tiled floor no matter how quietly he tried to tread. Any attempt to sneak up on whatever was on the other side of the kitchen door was futile, unless said thing happened to be deaf. So he walked the length of the café in his regular gait and then slowed again as he reached the vague outline of the swinging door. He nudged it ajar with his shoulder and sent his gun in first.

The kitchen was even more lightless than the café's seating area. And, while he had spent almost as much time in the Old Rose as he had in his own home over the years, Don knew nothing of the kitchen's floor plan other than the occasional glimpse he had caught as the wait staff were coming and going with food. So he let his ears explore first, seeking out sounds of scuffling or wet and ragged breathing or the click of nails on a hard surface. But the silence remained unspoiled save for the pneumatic wheeze of his own breath.

He tucked the pistol into the couch of his right armpit—he had discovered the weight of his arm would hold certain objects—and patting the wall on his left he found three switches. He clicked them all on at once and rows of fluorescent lights blinked into life.

To begin with he saw nothing untoward except a general untidiness. But as his pupils adjusted to the sudden brightness and he took a few steps to his left he spotted the first indications something unpleasant had indeed gone down in the Old Rose. The white-tiled floor was brown with the demon's smoky blood. So much had spilled that, even after exposure to air for better than ten hours, it remained tacky under his shoes as he crept through it. When he rounded the large island bench, gun sighted and finger on the trigger, he came upon Truman's promised grisly scene. Finger tracks in the blood and the whorled pattern around the legs lent unpleasant hints to what had transpired. Blood boiled down to carbon showed Sadie had burst into flame like all the others, in spite of her remote location and disassembly. Demon in six parts. Not a bad title for an opera or an arthouse film. But this evidence notwithstanding, the demon skin he now observed was whole, no different from any others around the Ironstone. Could it be a different demon? It seemed improbable. Don stared into the hollows of the demon-skin mask, so creepy, like the indentations in a coconut shell.

The demon skin was whole. . .but what if the human inside wasn't? What if the eyes at the end of those narrow pits could still see? What if the brain could still function? And what if, when the face was cut free from the demon skin, Sadie's eyes flew open in abject horror and her mouth opened in a silent scream? What if her hands began to slap the floor, creating fresh prints in the blood, and her legs should resume their fitful cycling? What would retired Sergeant Donald Winslow of Black Wattle do then?

Swallowing, he bent down and prodded Sadie's head with his gun's muzzle. No noise, but then none of them had stirred until the demon skin was incised and their bodies exposed. Sadie might still be in that dreamless hibernation the others had described. Would it be better if he left her that way, in eternal stasis, somewhere between existing and not?

No, he had to be sure one way or another. There could be others like Sadie scattered through the bush or hidden in Black Wattle's shops and homes, like ugly family secrets. When someone from the government came calling—and Don felt surer than ever now someone would—he wanted to know everything. No surprises, no unanswerable questions.

But how to remove Sadie's skin mask?

Another ill-wind of resentment passed through Don. Volunteering a one-armed man for this task had a whiff of thoughtlessness about it, even if it did originate from a recent amputee. Don sighed and shook his head, then looked around for something he could use. Knives were useless, he would finish up slashing Sadie's face to ribbons. He supposed he could hold her head still with his foot and try to rip the skin upwards, as if it were old linoleum, but that risked bruising her or fracturing her skull. Until he could be certain whether she was alive or dead, he needed to be gentle.

He put his revolver on the island bench and commenced opening drawers. Some rooting around produced a pair of shears, the sort a chef used to separate fowl into breasts and drumsticks. A disproportionate sense of achievement infused him and a big grin broke out on his face.

Christ, I'm losing my mind, he thought. Policemen were no strangers to overtime and double shifts, but it had been decades since Don had pulled an all-nighter and his match fitness was long gone. Also, he was fifty-two, and burning the midnight oil was better left to eager twenty-somethings.

He got on one knee and eased the curved blade of the poultry shears into the skin mask's eye socket. Then he snipped up, across the brow, down to the chin, and up to the eye again, in effect creating a window into Sadie's true face. It was slow and fussy work, but with some persistence, he finished the square and put her head between his feet so he could peel the skin away.

The eyes inside remained closed. He used his fingers to wipe some blood from the eyelids, which were warm to his touch. Just to be one hundred percent certain, he prized open one of Sadie's eyelids and the pupil constricted in response. As quickly as he could he cut downward past her chin and to the hollow of her throat.

Which was attached to her torso.

Don let out a stuttery breath and relaxed his bunched shoulders. He slumped back against the island bench, a motion which outraged his ribs. He stayed that way a while, eyes shut against the light, against input, against the world. In that moment, he understood he was no longer a perky young copper or even the seasoned sergeant presiding over his town. He was a greying man with a gimpy arm and a pot belly who had been awake nearly twenty-four hours and now just wanted a shower and his bed. Truman would have to wait a little longer to be reunited with his feet. It wasn't like he'd be needing them.

Don took his time getting up (broken ribs were very particular about how a man moved), then he collected his firearm and snapped off the lights in the Old Rose kitchen. Sadie would also keep until morning; the demon skin seemed to act like a cocoon or a stasis chamber. He supposed he should tell Marla about her café's gruesome contents before she discovered them for herself, but it was pushing on towards one a.m. and she would likely be asleep. That was how he rationalized it to himself as he closed the café door and got back in his car, anyway. It was harder to apply when he saw the white plastic shopping bag, which he had brought along to contain Truman's feet, in the passenger's side footwell. But justifiable or not, Don started his car and drove home.

Inside, he unloaded his pistol and put it back in the safe, then went and stood under a hot shower for fifteen minutes before easing himself into bed. He thought his ribs or his conscience or recounting the day's uncountable horrors might keep him awake, but a minute after he pulled the duvet up to his chin, he drifted into a deep sleep and barely moved for the next six hours.

CHAPTER THIRTY

ATTUNED TO EARLY STARTS, Don's body clock woke him just before seven. Despite the sleep's brevity, it put back together his mind's fragmented pieces, and a bowl of cereal and a cup of tea sealed up the cracks. When he left the house at seven-thirty, he had the morning planned out in his head like a street map. First order of business was to drive to the Ironstone. Once there, he hopped out, plastic bag in hand, and started searching the area he thought best aligned with Truman's description. Last night's clouds were still hanging around like wet washing, refusing to give up any moisture but keeping the light to an even grey caste. This meant no shadows or dappled light and Don's treasure hunt lasted less than a minute.

The flesh had turned a similar color to the sky, while the toenails stood out in bright white contrast, looking more like teeth. The earth around the severed stumps now had a dark crust.

A circle of bone winked from each foot. A few flies had already begun to take an interest; in high summer Truman's trotters would have been a crawling mass of winged bodies. Don waved them away, then took each foot by the big toe and plopped it into his shopping bag. It rustled as he carried it up the gentle slope to the footpath. Whether the pub was open or not was now immaterial, since anyone could pass through the concertinaed doors as they pleased, but he could see Shirley already inside scrubbing a mop across the floor. A vacuum cleaner stood in one corner, as if sent there for naughty behavior. Unfair punishment, since it had sucked up all the Prince Demon's dust; only the larger segments of his stone-like body remained in a neat pile. Wrinkles cut deeply across Shirley's forehead, and it looked as though she had accidentally applied eye shadow below her eyes.

"Morning, Shirl."

"Morning yourself," she said, leaning on the mop.

"Get much sleep?"

"Not a lot. I left Elle at home with a note to call me when she wakes up. She can sleep till midday at the best of times."

Don nodded. "Has Truman surfaced yet?"

"Nope. When I went upstairs and checked, the door to room one was closed."

"I have some shopping for him," Don said, lifting the bag. Its sheer plastic skin tightened around the contents, revealing them. Shirley wrinkled her nose.

"He wanted me to collect them for some reason. Can I put them downstairs with Brooks?"

"Sure, what the hell," Shirley said, throwing her hand up in mock exasperation. "A girl can't have too many body parts in her cellar, can she?"

Don grinned and she grinned back. Mad humor was better than no humor at all. "Don't worry, I'm going to get this sorted out and get everyone back to their normal lives. Freezer unlocked?"

"Yep."

Don ventured down and slid back the coolroom's heavy door. Brooks's body lay straight and neat, like a cadaver in its casket. Only an unnatural kink in his torso gave hint to the savagery that led to his demise. The man had been a first-prize jerk, no question, but he had redeemed himself in the end. Don placed Truman's feet beside him, almost as if they were a wreath to acknowledge his sacrifice. Then he departed, closed the freezer door behind him, and ascended the stairs.

"Where are Mark and Prince?" he asked Shirley.

"Asleep in room three."

"Can you wake Prince up and give him some breakfast? I'm going to need him later this morning."

"Sure. But what use will he be with no memory?"

"I don't know yet. One thing's for certain, though, we can't let the government get its hands on him or we'll end up with another disaster. Beyond that. . .well, I'm sort of working this out as I go along."

"Aren't we all."

She went back to her mopping and Don went back to his car, which he drove to the eastern roadblock. As he stepped out, a small, refrigerated truck approached the line of vehicles impeding its progress. From a distance, Don could just make out the driver's disbelieving expression. The truck idled a while, then the driver smacked the steering wheel and his lips formed a profanity. The transmission clunked and the truck reversed before making a three-point turn and disappearing back the way it had come. Don wondered how many truck drivers had done the same thing overnight and that morning, and the probable effect on Black Wattle in the coming weeks. The sooner whomever was responsible for the trucks came and took them away, the better.

In Don's back seat were some of his clothes—pants, shirt, shoes—and a pair of heavy-duty sewing scissors Nettie had inherited from her grandmother. Don picked up the scissors, shut the door and trudged into the field, grass crackling beneath his feet.

The last soldiers to fall would have been protecting the border, or so went his reasoning. He traipsed around the field a while and turned up nothing—no bodies, no demon cocoons, nothing save for grass darkened with yesterday's blood. Perhaps every demon had congregated around the Ironstone in those final moments before they transformed into the fire-spawn. Growing frustrated, Don returned to the roadway with a plan to scour the forest before returning to town if his second search proved fruitless. But as he stepped onto the crumbling shoulder, a shape caught his eye.

Just outside the door of the operations van from which Brooks had first emerged there now lay a single cocoon. Don hustled over to it, a hopeful grin on his face. He prayed it wouldn't be Bob Mellor the diesel mechanic or some old widow. He dropped to his knees hard enough to graze them through his trousers and slotted the scissors' mean metal point into an eye socket.

Designed to cut through leather, the scissors made easy work of the demon skin and a few minutes later he had exposed an Asian face, youngish, perhaps late twenties. No one Don recognized, which lifted his hopes to another level. The man's peaceful lost-to-hibernation look persisted a few moments and then the eyes opened, absorbing the grey skies. They widened abruptly and the man tried to sit bolt upright, but the stiff demon skin enclosing his body prevented it.

"The demons!" he screamed.

"It's okay, soldier," Don said. "Rest easy. The threat's been neutralized. Along with your boss, I'm afraid."

"You mean Brooks?"

Don nodded.

"Not my boss," he said. "Well, not really."

Don laughed. "Yeah, I got that impression. What's your name, kid?"

"Andrew. Corporal Andrew Chang. I was in charge of field operations. You. . .you're the guy Brooks was arguing with."

"I prefer 'Don'."

Chang smiled. "Okay, Don. Mind telling me how I ended up in this flak jacket and why you're the one cutting me out of it?"

While he continued to free Chang from the demon skin, Don gave him the blurb of what went down in the Ironstone. Once the cut had reached Chang's navel he was able to assist by holding the flaps aside and pulling, which sped up the process. By the time Chang had his legs out, he looked like he'd been clopped across the face with a gumboot.

"It all sounds so crazy," he said. "I mean I saw the demons for myself, I *was* one, but. . .well I guess I never really believed they were demons in the biblical sense."

"We were seconds from the end of times," Don said. "If Patrick had hesitated even a few seconds, or missed with that first bottle. . ."

Chang shook his head, pulled his right foot from the demon's skin's adhesive 'shoe'. "Brooks told us it was foolproof, that we were only there as a failsafe in case one of the locals escaped the test site or the beer didn't work exactly as Prince had promised."

"The whole thing was built on lies," Don said. "Which brings us to the crux of the matter, actually. I imagine Brooks had a boss who would be missing him by now?"

Chang thought this over, then nodded. "Brooks was supposed to report in once the test had been conducted."

"Report in to who?"

"Some special assistant to the Defense Minister was what I heard. Ex-military. But I'm pretty sure no one other than Brooks and Prince knew who he was."

Don ran this information through his mind. "So it's fair to assume our mystery man expected Brooks to report in sometime last night. When he couldn't raise Brooks, he would have worked his way down the chain of command and become very alarmed when no one answered their phone or radio. Which means he's probably on his way here from the capital as we speak."

Don closed his eyes for a second, then opened them again and looked Chang square in the face. "I intend to make sure this insane project never gets off the ground again and to do that I need your team's help. But I used to be a copper myself and I understand the chain of command. Loyalty to a commanding officer dies hard. If your sense of duty conflicts with what I'm proposing—"

Chang shook his head vehemently. "I joined the Green Machine to defend my country. What I went through as that demon. . .I wouldn't wish that on a terrorist. Even if they could control it, there's no honor in supernatural warfare. It's just germ warfare under a different guise. The sort of thing politicians who've never served a day in their lives think is a good idea. I can't speak for the men under my command, but if they suffered the same way I did. . ." He grimaced. "They'll do whatever it takes to stop this project, too."

Don searched Chang's face for signs of guile and found none.

"Thank you," he said. "Let's finish getting you out. We have a lot of work to do before our government friend arrives."

The upside to a pisspot little town like Black Wattle, where everyone (especially Marla) minded everyone else's business, was that volunteers were never far away. Anyone living the rural life long enough knew lending a hand was important, because one day you could be the one who needed a hand up. In a place where mobile phone signals could still be patchy, the nearest emergency services were an hour away and the shops shut dead on five (sometimes three on a weekend), accepting charity was inevitable.

Which was why Don's phone call to Shirley instigated a domino effect of communication that saw a dozen volunteers back at the Ironstone before eight o'clock ensuring the demon skins couldn't be seen from the road. They were out of sight entirely, in fact, unless someone made the unlikely decision to break the lock on Darren Busby's garage across the road and roll up the shutters. In the main part of town, Black Wattle residents set themselves to sweeping up glass, mopping away blood, removing damaged vehicles from sight, disguising scuffed doors and broken windows any way they could. When he returned to town himself, Don caught the final stages and was put in mind of the way bees worked in droning harmony. Perhaps it was merely the regular empathy that came with a country community. . .but the phrase that bubbled up in his head was *hive mind*. Everyone he had spoken to appeared normal, themselves, yet he couldn't shake the feeling that their shared experience as demons had somehow linked them.

Even crotchety old Doherty at the Goldmine Motel did his bit, calling Shirley to let her know a large black sedan had just passed his place. She then rang Don, explaining the car had slowed as it passed the pub but hadn't stopped. The car's windows were tinted almost to mirrors, so she had no other information to offer.

Moments after she hung up, a besuited man pushed through the door to Don's museum. Not that it looked much like a museum, with Don's exhibits still shunted to the wings so it could moonlight as a central war room for Brooks and his band of soldiers. The man, around Don's own age, had the shaved-to-a-shine look older bald men seemed to favor but which, in Don's opinion, made them look like tortoises. While he entered alone, two other men (both much younger, taller and in uniform) posted themselves outside the door.

Corporal Chang sat on a stool at the reception desk—the only thing that continued to resemble the museum as Don had left it—tapping away on a laptop. Upon the man's entry, Chang rose to his feet and offered him a crisp salute. The man ignored it and peered into the war room, eyes searching and skeptical. Finding nothing he said, "Who the hell are you?"

"Corporal Chang, sir, field operations commander."

"Tremendous, your mother must be proud. Where's Chris Brooks?"

"Dead, sir."

A look of surprise crossed the man's face, then creased into annoyance. "Dead?"

"Damon Prince murdered him, sir."

"Prince. . .why?"

"The beer was a total failure. He and Brooks got into a heated argument and then next thing—well, I'm writing up the report now. I'm recommending we withdraw from Black Wattle, cut our losses and pursue other opportunities. The town's residents don't seem any the wiser. Prince is a charlatan and his 'supernatural warfare' was a farce from start to finish."

The man stared at Chang for a while, leaned his elbows on the reception desk and studied what was on the laptop's screen, then stepped back and stared at Chang again.

"Where is Brooks now?"

"The town has no morgue or mortuary, so his body has been stored in an industrial refrigerator until it can be transported to a more appropriate facility."

"And what about Prince?"

"Still at large, sir. He fled the scene and two of my men pursued him, but it was dark and he disappeared into the bush. We opted not to alert the police given the situation's sensitivity."

"Hmm. And why aren't you in uniform?"

"It got beer spilt on it when the scuffle broke out between Prince and Brooks."

The man nodded, frowning. His eyes scanned the war room again, lighting from corner to corner, object to object. After a while he said, "If you're in charge of field operations, what are you doing in here?"

Up to that point, Chang had done a perfect job, stuck to the script, but this question caught him off-guard. Fear lassoed Don's heart. Chang was a soldier, not a performer. His mouth worked as he tried to ad-lib, but he was flummoxed. As the delay stretched from one second into two, his interrogator's brow creased. Don gave it one more beat, just in case Chang came up with some last-minute off-the-cuff corker, but when he did nothing except clear his throat Don knew Plan A was shot. He stepped from behind the antique privacy screen and in a cheerful voice said, "Good morning!"

"Who are you?"

"Don Winslow's the name."

"What the hell are you doing in here?"

"I might ask you the same question."

"This is a restricted area," the government man said, "you can't—"

"Oh, don't start in with that authoritarian jibber-jabber," Don said, waving a dismissive hand, "I've heard about a year's worth of it in the past two days. Most of it from Chris Brooks, who's now chilling out in a hotel cellar."

At the mention of Brooks, a sudden calmness overcame the government man. His steel-blue eyes seemed ready to pop from his small tortoise head. "What did you do to Mr. Brooks?"

"I didn't do anything to him. He did."

Don cocked a thumb at the privacy screen. This time, Prince emerged. The government man examined him a while, then said, "And who might he be?"

Don turned his eyes upwards and chuckled. "Sweet Jesus. This project must have been scribbled on the back of a coaster after Friday night drinks. Does the name Damon Prince mean anything to you?"

"Oh," the government man said. "I never met him. He insisted on dealing only with Brooks."

"So I heard. If it's any consolation, Mr. Prince doesn't know who Mr. Prince is, either."

"What?"

"Never mind. Long story. Now, Corporal Chang is who he says he is. I cut him out of a demon skin this morning and, unlike Mr. Prince, he remembers everything, so he'll be able to fill you in on the details. But I can give you the short version. Your little experiment almost unleashed hell on earth, literally. Turns out trusting a Satanist to create your next weapon of mass destruction isn't the cleverest idea. Funny that."

Upon hearing this synopsis, the government man turned a shade of grey not a lot healthier than Truman's dismembered feet. "That was supposed to be classified. Top secret."

"Yeah, well, the residents of Black Wattle lost a good ten hours of their lives to your big secret and it's no secret anymore. Brooks was killed trying to put the cork back in the volcano. Another man is permanently disabled. To say nothing of the ongoing psychological damage. A few of your own men are still scattered around the town in demon cocoons, too. So you'll pardon me if I don't give a fuck about you or your top-secret project."

The government man's tongue crowned from his mouth, made a dry run around his lips, went back in its hole. His skin had gone so pallid he now resembled a cue ball instead of a tortoise. When he swallowed, Don heard his throat click. But then he gathered himself and tried to walk it back. "You have interfered with an official federal police operation. That carries a prison sentence of up to—"

Don raised his hand, like some *mafioso*, and to his great surprise and satisfaction the government man's words evanesced. "My friends and I sent the Devil back to hell last night, Mr. . . .?"

A sullen sneer. Then: "General Dryden."

"Mr. Dryden. When you've gone to-to-toe with the Dark Lord, as Mr. Prince here liked to call him, some government weed's attempts at intimidation are about as fearsome as fairy floss."

"I could have you arrested, right now," Dryden said. "There are two federal officers standing right outside the door."

"Sure, I guess," Don said. "But then again the people's trust in governments isn't at an all-time high, is it? And I'd have roughly a thousand Black Wattle residents ready to corroborate my version of events if I happened to go missing or decided to 'commit suicide' while in custody."

"You don't understand," Dryden said, trying on an ingratiating smile that almost made Don vomit, "this project is vital to national security."

"You're not very good at this Mr. Dryden," Don said, looking over the man's shoulder towards the door, as if he had lost interest in the conversation. "Brooks filled me in on everything, the whole grubby shebang. You were willing to sacrifice Black Wattle so you could run to the US president and show him your new toy."

"You don't know what you're talking about," Dryden said, voice quavering. "Brooks told us he could handle it. You don't understand the ramifications if word of this project gets out!"

"The ramifications for *you*, you mean. Look, Mr. Dryden, be smart. Let this thing go. Brooks can be the fall guy. Prince doesn't remember a thing so he couldn't blab even if he wanted to, and the Black Wattle townsfolk just want to get on with their lives. Even if someone did talk, who would believe their story? They'd sound like every other toothless hick ranting on about Bigfoot and UFOs and conspiracy theories."

Dryden sniffed. "I've heard enough. I'll be lucky if I still have a job after this. We burned up millions on this project and we need to get something out of it. I can't let you or anyone else jeopardize that. Keene, Goldman! Place this man under arrest."

"Sir," said Chang, "with all due respect you weren't out there—"

"Keep your mouth shut, Chang, or you'll end up in handcuffs, too. If we act now, we might be able to salvage *something* from Brooks' godawful mess."

Don barely heard their exchange. A text message had come through on his phone, from Shirley. He didn't need to open it because the home-screen excerpt told the whole story: *Mark not in his room. Gone.*

Before Don could hope to process this information the federal coppers, Keene and Goldman, strode in and stood beside Dryden. They were huge specimens. Don, Chang and Prince might have prevailed against one of them, but as a double act Keene and Goldman would eat them alive and use their bones as toothpicks.

So instead Don lifted his dead arm and let it flop back to his side. He smiled.

"Probably no need for handcuffs," he said.

"Cuff him," Dryden said.

"This isn't in your best interests, Dryden," Don said as Keene snapped the cuffs around his left wrist. "I'll soon have the services of a lawyer."

"Oh, there'll be no lawyers," Dryden said blandly, as if *he* had now lost interest in the conversation. "Aside from some financial records kept under a false file name, this project doesn't exist. Which means I was never here today and there will be no record of Keene and Goldman arresting you. In a few minutes, I'm going to call in reinforcements who will re-establish the perimeter around Black Wattle and a short while after that, the town itself will cease to appear on Google Maps, no matter how close you zoom in."

The cuffs snapped around Don's dead wrist. "What are you going to do?"

"That's none of your concern," Dryden said. "Global interests are at play here, Mr. Winslow, and your town is a speck of fly dirt on Australia's backside. Prince, Chang, you're with us. You can either come under your own steam or in cuffs, too. Choice is yours."

The two men glanced at one another reluctantly.

"No sense making a fuss," Don said to them. "Pick your battles."

"Good advice," Dryden said. "Goldman, you stay here and secure the site. The last thing I need right now is more nosy locals interfering with our operations. Let's go."

Goldman opened the front door while Keene prodded Don in the back to get him moving. Prince and Chang moved off after them. Dryden brought up the rear, his expensive shoes clip-clopping on the floorboards. He must have been lost in thought and planning what to do next, Don reckoned later, because he was outside and in full daylight before he looked up and found himself at the blasty-end of three pistols and a shotgun.

"What is this?" he said.

"You have something that belongs to us," Mark said, motioning the shotgun barrel towards Prince. "We're here to take it back."

"You can't be serious," Don said. "After everything you went through, why would you want to—"

"I don't want anything," Mark replied with an impatient scowl. "My mate Alexi here, well, that's another story."

One of the men holding a smaller gun stared at him with a brown snake's beady-eyed intensity. Understanding dawned in Don's mind. "He's. . .what? Paying you for this?"

"Let's just say there's more than one way to achieve paradise." Mark pumped the shotgun. "I recommend you put your weapons on the ground."

The federal police gave Dryden an uneasy glance but stood firm with pistols raised. Dryden appeared to be boiling from the inside out, his jaw clenched and his lips turned in. "He's not yours," he said after a while. The schoolyard tone in his voice turned Don's stomach. "Prince is mine and you can't have him."

"Four against three," Mark said. "Odds aren't in your favor."

"Perhaps not," Dryden said, "but I'm prepared to die to keep Prince out of the wrong hands. Can you say the same?"

"You wouldn't believe what I've been through to get here, Dryden. Don't test me."

"Test you? I wouldn't dream of it. I'm simply going to count to three, and if you don't lower your weapons before three, Keene and Goldman will open fire. Ready? One. . .Two. . ."

Mark's eyes bunched into fleshy slits. His mouth opened, as though he were about to speak, and then his entire face, from brow to chin, exploded outwards like a corpse flower bursting into bloom. Blood, brains and skull splattered across his forearms and an instant later they went limp, the shotgun clattering to the pavement. As if in sympathy, the men on either side of Alexi buckled at the knees and tumbled forward, wide entry wounds now flourishing red and staining the fabric of their shirts. Dryden and Alexi wore identical expressions of shocked disbelief for a second before Alexi, perhaps having recalculated the odds, let his pistol fall from his trigger finger and raised his hands in surrender. Although their guns didn't waver, Keene and Goldman expelled relieved breaths in stereo.

Like lions emerging from spinifex grass Chang's soldiers

emerged from their positions across the street. One behind a gable, another from the fender of a car, a third from behind the post office mailbox. Before long an even dozen were closing in on the standoff, automatic rifles raised.

"Well done, men," Dryden said. "Take them all into custody. Corporal Chang has. . ."

Dryden trailed off as he registered that all twelve automatic rifles were now either trained on him, Goldman or Keene. Prince blinked in owlish disbelief at this latest development, something Don could well understand.

"Your odds just got a lot worse, Dryden," Chang said. "Uncuff Don now."

"This isn't going to end well for you, Corporal Chang. Or your men."

"On the contrary," Don said, "we know exactly how this is going to end. We tried to give you the easy way out but you were too full of yourself. So now we're giving you a simple choice. One, you collect Chris Brooks from the Ironstone Hotel and go back and tell your political masters the supernatural warfare experiment was a dismal failure. Like I said earlier, Brooks will make the ideal scapegoat. Alternatively, you fail to return from your visit to Black Wattle and when someone comes looking for you, not a single person in town has seen you or even heard your name before. Time to decide."

"You wouldn't dare," Dryden said.

"You know, forty-eight hours ago, I would have agreed. But trauma rewires the brain."

"An entire town can't keep a secret, Mr. Winslow. Tongues wag, consciences become restless. One way or another, you will get caught out."

More and more Black Wattle residents were congregating outside the museum. It would be easy to chalk that up to coincidence, to believe they were milling past and stopped to rubberneck at an interesting scene, but Don thought he knew better.

"Again, two days ago, I would have agreed with you. Black Wattle does love to gossip. But somehow I think this secret will be safe. And even if it does get out, even if everyone involved ends up doing time, that's a small price to pay to make sure your ungodly project stays in mothballs forever."

A vein pulsed in Dryden's forehead and his nostrils flared. Even though the morning remained cool, perspiration beaded his top lip. "I'll make you a deal," he said. "We leave your town and leave you alone, but we take Prince with us. You say his memory has been wiped, but what if it comes back? We can't risk him falling into enemy hands."

Don laughed, a mirthless bleating sound. "I'm getting pretty tired of everyone assuming I'm some gullible country bumpkin. Five minutes after you get Prince to your little government hidey-hole, you'll have him in a lab trying to extract the ritual or incantation or whatever it is from his head. Time's up, Dryden. No more chit-chat. There are bodies in the street. Make your choice."

Dryden's eyes grew harder and more avid, blue-diamond drill bits. They moved from face to face, probing, then enumerated the ever-burgeoning crowd of Black Wattlers.

"Uncuff him, Keene," Dryden said at last.

"I'll have your firearms, too," said Chang.

The handcuffs' steel bite relaxed and Don rolled his good wrist to get the blood flowing again. Chang collected Keene and Goldman's pistols, passed one to his men and kept the other for himself.

"This isn't over, Mr. Winslow. You have to know that."

"The minute you set foot in this town," Chang said, "my men and I will know."

Once again Dryden's gaze bored into Chang's face, then lifted to the gathering of Black Wattle locals, eyeing them the way a deer eyes a pride of lions. Perhaps it was Don's imagination, but he thought Dryden sensed something about them, too. It hadn't occurred to him until that moment that waves of gestalt might also be emanating from Chang and his men. But on reflection, it was logical. They had been demons, too, just like the rest of Black Wattle. A unified town with an elite squad of soldiers on call to defend it would be a hard target and Dryden (much to his chagrin) had figured that out.

"I'll have your job," Dryden said.

The threat was pretty limp, and Chang shrugged. "I have an engineering degree. I'll get by. Now go and get Brooks' body and get the hell out of Black Wattle."

"Not over," Dryden said. He stalked away to his car, Keene and Goldman at his heels like farm dogs. Goldman scuttled ahead and opened the door for him, as though Dryden were some sort of visiting dignitary.

"I'll make sure he does as he's told," Chang said. He and one of his men jumped in a federal police car and tailed Dryden's quasi-limo out of town and up the hill towards the Ironstone. Don called Shirley's number on his mobile phone.

"It was a bit hairy there for a minute, Shirl, but our government man is ready to take delivery of the package in your cellar. Chang is tailing him to make sure he behaves."

The remaining soldiers took possession of Alexi and zipped Mark and his two dead men into body bags. The Black Wattle residents dispersed long before the job was done, that undercurrent of *gestalt* now silent, as though its generator had been switched off. Don watched Marla Smith return to the Old Rose in her fast little bird-like strides. Pam Daley disappeared into her office, Oscar Wainwright got into his old truck and rolled away in a cloud of diesel smoke. A minute or two later, a passing tourist would never guess anything much had been amiss in Black Wattle.

In a way, nothing had changed, and yet everything had. Don stood alone outside the door to his museum, trying to fit a garage of thoughts into a matchbox. He gave up and went inside to see if he couldn't take the first steps towards reverting the war room back into his museum.

THE FINAL CHAPTER

TWO NIGHTS AFTER Elle had been cut from the demon skin, a blood-curdling scream started Shirley awake. She kicked off the covers as though they were on fire, dashed to Elle's bedroom and snapped on the light.

Elle lay on her side, bedsheets twisted into a rope between her thighs. Perspiration matted her hair and pasted it to her forehead and cheeks. Shirley sat on the edge of the bed and pressed a hand to Elle's brow to feel for an elevated temperature, something she hadn't done in five years or more.

"Are you okay, sweetheart?"

Elle's eyelids fluttered and half-opened but her eyes didn't see. It was so reminiscent of her regaining consciousness under the flashlight that a chill fizzed across Shirley's shoulders and down her spine. "Darkness doesn't like the light," Elle murmured, then her eyes closed again and she snuggled her face into the pillow. Shirley remained a long while, running those cryptic words through her head, then kissed her daughter, turned off the light and left her to sleep.

It was well past the witching hour before sleep comforted Shirley with its embrace.

Over a late breakfast the next morning she quizzed Elle about the incident and she professed not to remember it at all. Shirley kept a close eye on her throughout the day, watching for signs of distress or moodiness or depression, but she appeared to be the same outdoors-loving-yet-tech-obsessed teenager she had been prior to a demon misappropriating her soul. By day's end, Shirley's mind had cast off its worries, like a ship's captain dumping rotten cargo. She slept soundly until Elle's scream cut through the night. Shirley hurried to her room and switched on the light to find the bedclothes once again thrashed into disarray, but Elle's careworn expression had already started to relax into a sleeping teenager's unlined face. This time, when Shirley sat beside her, Elle uttered no half-waking riddle-words.

The next day Elle again insisted she remembered nothing—neither the thrashing and screaming, nor the nightmare that presumably instigated restless sleep. Whatever she had experienced as the Devil's slave did not trouble her waking thoughts but had apparently polluted the underground stream of her subconscious. Shirley wondered how much the situation contributed to this, whether the daily reminders from life in Black Wattle were helping dredge up the worst unconscious muck.

Nightmares notwithstanding, within a few days their lives had resumed a course pretty close to normal. It persisted until the time came for Elle to spend the weekend with her father.

While Maurice and Truman were bidding farewell to Don and Shirley and promising to keep in touch, Patrick made a point of slipping away to the men's room. He knew from a short but intense dalliance with reality TV in his younger years that when you put a group of strangers in a confined space they formed almost instant bonds that had all the conviction of lifelong friendships. . .but when removed from that unusual or artificial environment and integrated back into normal life, such 'friendships' dissolved like sugar in water. He remained in a cubicle, musing on this, until the faint din of voices wound down to near silence, at which time he emerged, washed his hands, and came out to tell Don and Shirley he would see them around. To the soldiers, he felt no more obligation than a hand lifted in farewell.

It was not that he disliked Truman or Maurice, Patrick thought, as he let himself into the rectory. He had avoided them for the same reason he was now avoiding the Black Wattle townsfolk and the same reason he had spent the past year trying to drown himself in a scotch bottle.

While it need not be the end, grief ate a hole in a person's heart, and that hole had to be filled. . .or it would swallow up its host.

Patrick's hole consisted of his late wife and his congregation (a combination that felt more like a canyon than a hole) and each morning he woke up to St Luke's, it excavated the hole deeper.

Patrick had tried to fill that hole with whisky, but sooner or later liquid in a hole became stagnant and dried up. He'd tried to blame the booze for his troubles, but the real reason he'd lost his flock and his few remaining friends was that he'd turned into a rolled-gold arsehole. Everyone had been reaching in, trying to lift him out of the grief-pit, and he had slapped their hands aside with criticism and slurs and drunken sermons until one day all the hands were gone and he had nothing left but whisky.

A man of the cloth dealt in symbols and the symbolism of throwing away his blessed scotch to serve a higher purpose was not lost on him. Between furtive visits to town where he deflected too-polite enquiries about his health while trying to buy a newspaper or a measly cup of coffee, he often thought about the renewed sense of purpose he had felt fighting Prince and his demons.

A man needed purpose. Not so long ago—had it only been a year? It didn't seem possible—Becky and St Luke's had been that purpose. But cancer had stolen one and he had tossed away the other during a six-month rage at a betrayer God from whom he had withdrawn belief in as an act of vengeance. Neither could ever be his again. Becky because death was a final and unbreakable contract without clauses, and St Luke's because, in a small town like Black Wattle, memories seemed hereditary and grudges could be passed down from generation to generation. In a city, he could hope for redemption. Big populations worked like the sea, eroding away all but the most stubborn and ground-in history. In Black Wattle, the stain of his indiscretions would always be upon him.

Patrick loved his town and he loved St Luke's. But a man with no purpose and no hope would soon look to dull his existential pain. Whisky would be there waiting to enfold him in its numbing embrace.

Three days into his new-found sobriety, Patrick understood it would be his new-lost sobriety if he didn't take drastic action, and fast. A phone call was his first order of business. He had just lifted the handset on the rectory's old landline when knuckles rapped at the door. He considered ignoring the knock, then dumped the phone back in its cradle and went to see who the hell it could be. Two faces greeted him, one much darker in complexion than the other, both with a somber expression.

"Hello, Patrick," Truman said. He sat in a wheelchair, which Dr Sneddon must have rustled up from who knew where. Occupying his lap was a plastic shopping bag. "I know we didn't get off on. . .well, things between us have been fractious. But I hoped I might ask you a special favor."

Truman lifted the bag. "We got these out of Shirley's freezer. It would mean a lot to me if we could bury them in your little cemetery."

Patrick stared at the bag and then looked towards the churchyard with its rotted cast-iron fence and headstones that poked out at all angles thanks to subsidence and erosion. To his knowledge, no one had been buried there in more than fifty years.

He shrugged. "I suppose so. Why do you want to bury your feet there?"

"I don't know," Truman said. "It just feels right for some reason."

"Did you want me to. . .erm. . .conduct a ceremony or something?"

"No, no need for that. I guess I just want them to have a proper burial."

"Fine by me."

"I'll go and get the shovel," Maurice said. He smiled at Patrick. "Don loaned it to us, but I didn't want to be presumptuous."

Patrick watched on from the rectory doorway as Maurice pushed Truman over to the churchyard, shovel resting across the wheelchair's handles. Flakes of rust pattered at his feet as he wrenched the gate open and then he and Truman scouted around for a plot. Headstones crowded the small graveyard and Maurice was on the high side before he stopped and commenced digging. Drought had left the ground iron-hard and the shallowest grave required ten minutes of toil. When at last Maurice cast the shovel to one side his bald dome glistened silver with sweat. Truman emptied the bag into the waiting hole and the two of them stood there a short while, heads bowed, before Maurice filled in the hole and tamped down the soil.

They offered Patrick simple but heartfelt thanks and went on their way. Once they had departed, Patrick stood alone in the rectory and found it hard to believe the whole episode had not been a symptom of *delirium tremens*.

He picked up the phone again and this time he completed the call.

The morning after Dryden's departure, Don strolled past the Old Rose and peered casually through its front window. Prince sat in a booth nibbling something which might have been carrot cake. All around him soldiers chatted and slurped at cups of coffee, yet Prince looked as alone as he could be, a dog dumped at a shelter. Though Don could scarcely believe it, he felt sorry for the man. What lay ahead for Prince? Isolation and loneliness of one form or another. Watching his back.

Don continued on, but his mind stayed with Prince. When he arrived at his cluttered museum he rooted through his belongings and turned up an old address book, which he'd kept even after the NSW Police moved to digital comms. He was glad he had. Under C, in his neat pre-accident script, he found what he was looking for: *Colin Cathcart*. The number beside it was an old-fashioned landline, but then Colin was nearly a decade into retirement and pretty old-fashioned himself. Don dialed the number, half-expecting a recorded voice would tell him it had been disconnected. Instead, he heard the satisfying burr of a phone ringing at the other end.

"G'day, Colin. Don Winslow here, mate."

"Don! How the hell are you?"

"Oh, no sense complaining, no bastard listens anyway."

"It's been a while."

"Yeah, must be four or five years, eh? Look, I'm afraid this isn't a social call. I'm ringing to see if you can help me out with something."

"Of course, Don. Name it."

"I need to arrange a new identity for a witness and it has to be on the down-low. No official paperwork, no questions asked. That something you could arrange?"

Colin allowed that he could and asked Don for some particulars. Ten minutes later, Don hung up with a satisfied smile. He sauntered back down to the Old Rose and slid into the booth so he and Prince were facing one another.

Prince gave him a guarded look. "Good morning."

Don returned what he hoped was a reassuring smile. "Can I buy you another coffee?"

"No, thank you. If I have another one, I'll get the jitters. Jitters are something I can do without at the moment."

Don folded his arms, then leaned forward and put his elbows on the table. "Dryden and his men won't rest until they've got you back in their clutches. You know that, don't you?"

Prince nodded, a resigned gesture.

"You don't appear to have any documented history—not in this country, anyway. Damon Prince was probably an assumed name. I don't think anyone's missing you, if you know what I mean."

Prince shook his head. "It doesn't sound like I was a very nice person."

"How would you like to be someone else? Make a fresh start."

When Don explained what he had in mind, Prince looked pleased for the first time since they'd dug him out of the rubble. "Is Tasmania a nice place?"

"Beautiful. Weather's a bit like England's, too, which I gather is where you're from originally. My mate's going to line you up a job, too. Nothing flash, but it'll be enough to live off until you figure out. . .well, what's next, I guess. I'll ask Corporal Chang if he can spare a couple of men to escort you there."

"Thank you, Don."

Before Chang and his team collected up their equipment and demountables and returned to face the music—if indeed there proved to be any music to face—they staged a working bee to put Don's museum back to its original state. Grateful beyond words, Don bought them all lunch packs to take on the road. While they were distributed, Don and Chang stood outside the museum and Don explained his plan for Prince.

Chang looked relieved. "Relocation's a good idea. Better than protective custody, which was what I had in mind. Although to be honest, I hadn't given it much thought. Been too busy with the interrogation."

"How did it go? Any luck?"

"More than we'd hoped. Once we spelled out the situation for Alexi—jail if he refused to talk, or deportation for co-operation—he sang like a bird. Prince and Mark filled him in on everything. Turns out Prince never had any intention of unleashing hell on earth. All that talk about sunset. . .that was bogus. He was just trying to get you to play along so he could fulfill the deal."

"What deal?"

"Our friend Alexi is a representative for a foreign arms dealer. Nasty dude and cashed up like you wouldn't believe. He was willing to pay Prince half a billion dollars if he could deliver a containable and repeatable weapon of supernatural warfare."

"Which is why the demons couldn't spread beyond the Black Wattle town limits."

"Right. It was all part of the pact. I suspect the Devil agreed because he knew once Prince's recipe landed in nefarious hands it would wind up abused or spread accidentally. Prince figured he couldn't lose no matter what happened. The government paid him to set it up, then either he could buy paradise or the Devil would provide it for him. But he did lose, thanks to you, Don. You saved your town."

"Hardly. This was a team effort."

Chang smiled and the two men shook hands before Chang joined his men and Prince in the troop carrier chugging at idle outside the museum. As Don watched it depart and leave behind the familiar spring drowse, a sense of peace stole over him—not dissimilar to post-exercise euphoria.

But during the days that followed he found himself feeling like the museum's mustiest exhibit. The small windows admitted almost no light (Black Wattle's overcast weather persisted) which, combined with the dark wood paneling and overstuffed hoarder's-house feeling Don had cultivated to make his smallish collection seem more substantial, gave the museum an oppressive atmosphere. Everything was back the way it was supposed to be but somehow nothing seemed right. Don still took his morning walks and kept a cursory eye out for trinkets or artefacts, yet the prospect of new historical finds had lost its luster.

One morning, when his sense of disenfranchisement had reached a fresh peak, Don got up and switched the sign on the museum's glass door to SORRY WE'RE CLOSED, then went to his car and hopped in. Until he had his hand on the wheel he had no idea what he was doing or where he was going but contact with it seemed to electrify his mind. He backed out onto Goldfields Road and headed east.

Spring's touch had warmed the foothills and valleys around Black Wattle, which was just as well because the Ironstone still had no window glass. Inside, a few lunchtime regulars enjoyed an alfresco beer and pie. Shirley signed something for a delivery man in a high-vis vest and Don hung back until he was gone. Then he ambled up and leaned on the bar.

"How's trade?" he said.

"Could be better."

Don nodded in commiseration. "Did you dispose of the Red Horn beer?"

"Corporal Chang's men buried it for me."

"Where?"

"Only they and I know the location."

"Good thinking," Don said. He gestured towards one of the windows. "Pub's still well ventilated, I see."

Shirley smiled. "I've been in touch with the insurance company and they're going to cover the replacement as an act of vandalism, but it could be a few more days until they can get a tradesman out here. I'm just glad I scraped together the money to pay this year's premium. The local SES guy, Cameron? He secured the roof beam and offered to put up plastic sheeting in the interim, but I don't really see the point. There's no rain forecast and it will only make the hotel look ugly from the street. You'd be surprised how important curb appeal is for a country pub."

"Well, that's good news, I guess," Don said. "I heard on the grapevine that the state government has approved an increase in funding for the shire's marketing budget. It should come through just in time to catch the tail end of the high season. Got any bright ideas for drumming up trade? I could sure use some."

Shirley averted her eyes and let out a slow breath. "To be honest with you, I'm thinking about selling the pub."

"You are?" Don blurted out. The regulars glanced over at him, then returned to their beers and pies and form guides. Don lowered his voice. "Why?"

"No one thing in particular. I mean, it's barely turning a profit, but if that was the only consideration I would have offloaded it twelve months ago. Part of the reason is Elle. She's a good sport about living out in the sticks and flying up to Richard's place one weekend a month, but it's not fair on her. A fifteen-year-old shouldn't have to do all that travel and have so much instability in her life. She starts senior high school next year and I can't imagine state-hopping twelve times a year would be conducive to good study habits. Also. . ."

For a moment, Shirley seemed to regret allowing that

conjunction between sentences to emerge from her mouth. But she bit her lip and ploughed on.

"Also, she's been having nightmares, Don. Awful ones, by the sounds of it, although she reckons she doesn't remember them the next morning. I can't help wondering if keeping her trapped in Black Wattle is somehow contributing to that."

Don's mind had drifted off to contemplate a life in which Shirley Goodsall played no part and it took considerable effort to bring it back to the present conversation. "If it's any consolation, I don't think she's the only one. I was in the Old Rose yesterday and Marla was telling everyone how her husband keeps waking her in the middle of the night. 'Then he has the hide to say I was the one waking him!'" Don said, falling into his best Marla impersonation. It gladdened him to see a smile warm Shirley's lips. "Maybe it's some sort of. . .I don't know. . .post-traumatic stress reaction?"

"Could be," Shirley agreed. "I thought something similar myself. But if I'm honest, it's not just the money and it's not just Elle and the nightmares and the relentless back-and-forth travel. My heart's just not in it anymore, Don. I don't care about the Ironstone."

Don opened his mouth to say, *You know what, it's the strangest thing, I feel the same way about the museum,* but then some other part of his brain—perhaps the one that had impelled him to get in his car and drive down to the pub in the first place—butted in and said, "Have dinner with me one night, Shirl."

As non-sequiturs went it was a doozy, Don could appreciate that from an objective standpoint, but to that maverick part of his brain, it seemed as natural as adding "You're welcome" to a thank you. Shirley appeared to reside more in the former camp, because she gave him a nonplussed look and said, "Why?"

The self-loathing side of Don's personality—the one that had by and large run the show since the accident—brought him to the brink of muttering an apology and slinking out with his tail between his legs. But the old Don, the one whose self-image still included two functioning arms and the respect of his fellow citizens, had been burnished in the Devil's hellfire forge. Just enough, anyway, to keep Don's shoes rooted to the spot and let him speak his heart.

"Because you're a wonderful woman and I want to make you part of my life."

This seemed to be a revelation to Shirley. Her eyes dropped to the bar top and she ran a hand through her hair before looking up at Don again. "You mean like a date?"

No sense turning to jelly now. "That's what I mean."

"You want to date a divorcee with no money, a boot-load of emotional baggage and a teenaged daughter in tow?"

Don smiled, pleasant disbelief sluicing through him. "Well, it's not like a middle-aged widower on a disability pension who spends his time hoarding junk and pretending it's treasure is such a prize catch."

Shirley laughed out loud at this. Don realized he hadn't seen her laugh unabashedly in months and another rivulet of pleasurable emotions flowed through him.

"I'm game if you are," she said.

"Oh, I'm game. Let's make it breakfast instead. Eight o'clock tomorrow at my place. Leave Elle a note and let her sleep in. I'll help you open up the pub afterwards. It's not like the museum ever has customers."

"See you tomorrow, then."

As Don turned to go, he caught a glimpse of the regulars. They'd removed their noses from their form guides and were grinning across the room like fools.

On the morning he and Maurice made their goodbyes to Don, Shirley and the others, Truman misled himself into believing he had come to terms with the amputation and could now view it philosophically. Plenty had it worse. The homeless, the terminally ill, the profoundly disabled, just to name a few. Not even the confronting reality that he and Maurice would need a tow truck to take his old hatchback to Sydney could douse his high spirits.

"We could always ask someone in Black Wattle to drive it to us and then pay their way back home," he had suggested to Maurice with a child's bright-eyed enthusiasm. "Or maybe Don could sell it for us and transfer the money, less a seller's fee!"

Perfectly reasonable, since Maurice drove most of the time. And fouling the air with fossil fuel emissions wasn't something Truman would mourn anyway.

On the run back east from Black Wattle he had plugged in his smartphone—Maurice's car was no relic like his—and put on his favorite song. The sun emerged through the dispersing clouds, as if it had heard the upbeat tune and decided to smile down on him. The euphoria continued right up to the point where Maurice pulled into the slip lane for a roadside rest area and parked outside the long-drop toilet.

"Shouldn't have had that last coffee," he said, shaking his head. "I never learn. Do you need to go?"

Truman's answer was a flood of tears and the sort of chest-wracking sobs he had grown out of in primary school. The thought that he couldn't even take a piss unassisted unless he crawled through the dirt, up a splintery ramp and across a concrete floor soiled with the effluvia of a hundred careless travelers cut through in a way more urbane and academic considerations hadn't. Not only had he lost his feet, the loss was self-inflicted. And not only had he condemned himself to a life of misery, he had done it for *no fucking reason.* He bawled until his eyes and throat ached. He slumped onto the armrest with his face buried in his crossed arms and would have been pleased to die on the spot had Maurice's hand not reached across and clasped his neck, the warm and strong fingers soothing and dissolving the sudden onrush of despair.

Almost five minutes passed before the final sob drained out. Without comment, Maurice came around to his side of the car and carried him up the ramp (as an old couple that occupied the rest area's lone picnic table watched with shameless, almost prurient, interest). The way he placed him on the toilet seat somehow allowed Truman to retain his dignity. Then Maurice withdrew, a courtier leaving the king's court, and said so only Truman could hear, "Clear your throat when you're done."

The one true upside to sacrificing his feet was that it had rendered moot the question of whether he and Maurice should remain in their townhouse with its tainted memories. While they sought out a single-level rental property, Maurice had to carry him upstairs at bedtime or whenever Truman wanted to have a bath (in a small mercy, the townhouse did have a downstairs toilet). Being waited on hand and. . .well, other hand, got old faster than Truman would have imagined and, although Maurice never complained, Truman was pretty sure he was getting sick of it, too.

He had been measured up for prosthetic feet, but they were high-quality customized items and wouldn't be ready for nearly a fortnight—and it would take weeks of training and practice before he dared tackle the townhouse's narrow staircase.

One morning after breakfast, Truman sat on the sofa searching real estate websites on his phone while Maurice did the same on his laptop in the downstairs study nook. Except Truman had stopped searching a good five minutes earlier and spent most of that time trying to work up the courage to say something.

"Mad idea," he said when he'd amassed sufficient gumption. "Why don't we see out the lease on that house in Black Wattle?"

Maurice had been tapping in some sort of search string and now the tapping ceased. He spun around on his office chair to face Truman. "You want to go back there?"

"I know I told Pam we'd let the lease lapse, but we still have to go back at some point and pick up all the art stuff I left there. We need a new place and that house only has the three steps up onto the porch. Easy, even with prosthetic feet. I already have a studio set up there and I was painting again, Maurice. Not just trying, actually doing it. *Wanting* to do it.

"The other thing is, I'm too close to my old life here. It'll be too easy to slip into the old habits. Danielle called me yesterday and invited me out for a drink. I didn't want to mention it because I thought you'd worry. I told her no, of course, said I was feeling under the weather, but it was really my legs that kept me honest. And once I get used to my prosthetic feet, I'll have no. . . Wait."

Truman shook his head, hung it in shame. "That didn't take long, did it? Back home less than a week and it's already all about Truman. I'm sorry, Maurice. What do you think? Could we make it work?"

Maurice left his office chair and joined Truman on the sofa. "Honey, I want you well more than anyone, and I'd do anything to make you happy, you know that. But there are other considerations. My job at the agency, for one."

"You're right, you're right," Truman said, leaning back into the sofa and sighing. "'Old pie-in-the-sky Trevor,' that's what Dad used to call me. How right he was."

"I'm not saying no."

Truman turned to face him. He tried not to grin and couldn't help it.

"I'm not saying yes, either," Maurice added. "Let me talk to my partners and see if I can arrange something. It might be pie in the sky, but it's worth a try."

"You're a poet and you don't know it," Truman said, pulling him in for a kiss.

Shirley opened the pub at ten on the dot and a minute later Patrick sauntered in wearing only jeans, a collared shirt and some old sneakers. Even from behind the bar she clocked the other differences—clean-shaven, eyes whiter and clearer, skin smoother. Nevertheless, as he came closer she could see the strain behind his smile. Something oily dropped into her belly. She hadn't seen Patrick for the best part of a week and she assumed he had been making a good fist of his sobriety. But now she wondered if the improvements to his complexion were mainly in her imagination and he had been stocking up at the general store to avoid the shame of purchasing it from her.

But before she could finish these thoughts Patrick said to her, "Don't worry, I'm still on the wagon. I've just come to say goodbye."

He stuck his hand across the bar and she shook it, but her arm felt wooden and distant. "Goodbye?" she said. "You love this town more than anyone."

"Perhaps," Patrick said. "The trouble is, it doesn't love me. Not anymore."

"Oh, Patrick," she said. "That's not true. Maybe you—"

"It is, though." It wasn't a rude interruption, just firm and resigned. "You know better than most what a small town is like. You've been here, what, two years? And yet you're still an interloper in some ways and probably will be until every person older than you is dead. I could try to redeem myself. Patrick Burnham might earn forgiveness eventually, but *Father* Patrick Burnham never would. Religious leaders are held to a higher standard, and fair enough, otherwise they're just bombastic men in fancy dress. Anyway, I spoke to the head of the dioceses in this region and tendered my resignation from St Luke's. To his credit, he tried to sound disappointed. Greg has always been a gracious man."

"Black Wattle might not miss you," Shirley said, walking around the bar, "but *I* will." She put her arms around him and he squeezed her back. She rubbed his shoulders affectionately. "When are you leaving?"

"This afternoon. I'm getting the red-eye to Perth."

"Perth!"

He smiled. "When I make a clean break, I don't do it by halves. My mother grew up there, so I know it a bit. And it was the only parishioner's job available at such short notice. But more importantly, no one over there knows who I am. There might be some second cousins or something, but we'd be strangers to each other."

"Well, send me an email and let me know how you get on."

"It's Perth. It'll probably have to be a postcard."

"Your kind and gentle humor's sure to be a winner over there, too."

Patrick laughed then, a cackle that sounded both nervous and carefree. "Take care, Shirl," he said.

Before she could do much to process Patrick's news, Shirley's mobile phone rang. She trotted back behind the bar and when she saw the caller ID her heart blipped.

"Elle, is everything okay?"

"Of course it is," she said, in that insouciant way only teenagers and young adults were naïve enough to muster. "Dad didn't forget to pick me up this time and I didn't have to meet his lady friend, so it was a pretty awesome weekend. I'm just ringing to let you know he dropped me off at the airport. I thought you'd freak out if I only sent you a text."

"Thank you," Shirley said. She couldn't bring herself to hang up just yet; she wanted to savor Elle's voice a little longer. "How have you been, sweetheart?"

"Fine."

"You didn't tell your dad about. . .anything that went on?"

"Of course not. We *agreed* we wouldn't."

"I know, I know, I just thought that if you had one of your nightmares and he came running into your bedroom. . ."

"I didn't have any nightmares."

"How do you know? You never remember them the next day."

"Dad's a light sleeper and it's only a small apartment. If I'd screamed out or whatever it is you reckon I do, he would have heard it."

Shirley couldn't dispute this.

"All right, Mum, I'm at the security checkpoint. I'll call you when I'm half an hour out."

"Okay, sweetheart. Bye."

Shirley hung up and leaned against the bar with the phone clutched to her chest, thought lines pinching her eyebrows.

No nightmares. Her first time outside Black Wattle since the demons and no nightmares. It could just be a coincidence.

Or not.

The removalist truck rumbled at idle outside the Black Wattle real estate agency. Truman sat in the passenger's seat, reveling in the swelling springtime sunshine that bathed his face through the window. Maurice had gone inside to reclaim the keys from Pam and the sense of promise that lay ahead was intoxicating. Truman didn't want to make too much of it, in case Maurice didn't share his enthusiasm, but returning to Black Wattle felt like returning home. The door to the estate agent opened out and fresh excitement tickled him. To his surprise, it wasn't Maurice who exited, but Don.

He quickly rolled down the window and leaned out. "Don!"

Poor Don must have been lost in thought because he startled like a stray cat. He shaded his eyes, searching for the voice's source. "Truman? What are you doing back here?"

"You didn't see Maurice in there? He and I are moving into the cottage on Panorama Avenue. Strictly on a trial basis until we see whether it agrees with him."

"Huh," Don said, scratching his ear. "I thought you'd never want to see Black Wattle again. Demons aren't a town's most endearing trait."

"Well, there are demons and there are demons," Truman said. "I decided I preferred the demons in Black Wattle to the ones that were waiting for me back in Sydney. What are you doing in a real estate office?"

"I'm closing my museum."

"You are? Why?"

This question appeared to cause Don a great deal of consternation. "I don't think I have a satisfactory answer to that," he said after a while. "A lot of vague little reasons that added up to one big one is probably as close as I can get."

"I'll be the town's only remaining arts and humanities representative," Truman said.

"Dolly Watkins does crocheting."

"I'm not sure that comes under the fine arts."

"Heh, bitchy. You'll fit right in here."

"Hey, Maurice!" Truman said. "Don just called me bitchy. Are you going to defend my honor?"

"It's only slander if it's untrue," Maurice said, winking at Don.

"Truman tells me you're moving into Panorama Avenue?"

"That's right." He jingled the keys. "Will it cause a scandal?"

"A few weeks ago it might have caused a lot of gossiping behind your back. But. . .somehow, I don't think that's going to be a problem now."

At Don's words, Truman reflected on that curious sense of returning home. He thought about mentioning it, but once again opted not to.

Don welcomed them to town and shook their hands, then ventured off down the road. Maurice climbed into the truck and handed Truman the house keys.

"Let's go and set up our new home," he said.

Truman smiled and put a hand on Maurice's knee. Country sunshine flooded the cabin as Maurice brought the truck around and they coasted down the hill towards the cottage.

On a map, the town hadn't looked far from Perth at all, just beyond the outskirts, really, but in its own way, the tyranny of distance between the city and Swan Crossing was more severe than that between Sydney and Black Wattle. In addition to its church, Swan Crossing was home to a small cluster of shops with green corrugated iron roofs that tried to look bucolic (and failed spectacularly), about a thousand scattered homes ranging in vintage from the nineteen-thirties to last week, a school, a couple of parks, and rest area popular among road trippers taking the scenic route west and north into the more remote towns.

The church boasted none of St Luke's historical charm. Built from the same red brickwork as most of the older homes in the area, a white-painted timber cross above its door was the only accoutrement to distinguish it. The lazy luxury of an attached rectory was a fond memory, Patrick now neighbors with a number of his flock.

But he did have a flock again. A small congregation, to be sure, a long way from the heady days at Black Wattle, but eight pews from empty, too. Following his first sermons, a number of the faithful had pulled him aside to have a quiet word about how much more entertaining he was than his predecessor, an elderly reverend who, when he wasn't reciting psalms with his bespectacled face buried in his Bible, had droned on in a monotone. "I've had to drag my son to church every Sunday for the past two years," one woman told Patrick with an under-the-breath confidentiality. "Today was the first time he wanted to go!"

But rather than give him the yips or make him anxious, this praise fueled him to do even better. The equivalent of cheers for a footballer returning from injury or a stand-up comedian scoring his first room-wide belly laugh after a decade away from the circuit.

"I'm sure you've heard an awful lot about God's love," he told his congregation once they'd settled and he'd welcomed them to his Sunday sermon. "But I doubt anyone has ever tried to explain what it is. That's probably because love is a bit of a slippery word. The things we love are the most important things. . .but only when they love us in return. Unrequited love, faithless love, impure love, love of material possessions. . .they are the poisons we administer to ourselves. Sometimes the things we *do* love are not the things we *should* love. Sometimes the things we hold onto are the things we should let go. . ."

Even with its new windows and recent renovations, the Ironstone Hotel sat on the market a good while. Pam and her spreadsheet of contacts did their best to market it, but Sydney was still emerging from the comet-tail of an economic downturn and entrepreneurs and investors weren't trampling one another for the chance to own a rural pub with underwhelming weekly turnover. It proved to be early November before they got a serious nibble and nearly Christmas before all the contracts were signed and exchanged to every solicitor's satisfaction. But it worked out well in the end, permitting Elle to finish year ten before they uprooted for the Gold Coast.

Shirley secretly longed to move back to Sydney, but the price she got for the pub—factoring in all the renovations and overheads during her two-and-a-bit years as owner and hotelier, plus fees and taxes—meant she more or less broke even. It galled her to be moving up to the Gold Coast (it was almost as though Richard had been proven right or rewarded for being a chickenshit), but her meagre budget went much further up there, she knew she could score a job in marketing pretty quickly (or pulling beers if it came to that), and it would mean much-needed stability for Elle and an end to her ridiculous monthly commute.

She and Don had talked around what her move meant for their sapling relationship without arriving at any firm conclusion. Shirley wanted to get herself and Elle settled in on the Gold Coast and find some sort of rhythm with Richard and their custody arrangements before she contemplated Don. And while he had closed his museum, Don appeared to have misgivings about moving so far from the town he had called home his entire life (not least of which was what to do with his collection of historical artefacts, presently residing in a farmer's disused outbuilding for a fifty-dollar-a-month gratuity). But Don was a capable and self-possessed man and she knew he would be upfront in whatever he decided to do.

On the morning Shirley and Elle were set to depart, clouds glowered in the west and then moved in across the Black Wattle sky. They were nothing like the thick but benign cloud cover that had blanketed the town on the night that now seemed as much fairytale as reality. These ones meant business. Elle sat on the bonnet of the car, phone in hand, flicking through something on social media. The nightmares had started up again on her first night back in Black Wattle. That, as much as anything else, had decided Shirley on leaving town. Yet she suspected it was a selfish motive, because the bad dreams or night terrors or whatever they were didn't seem to bother Elle in the slightest. It was Shirley's sleep they disturbed. Each night she lay half-awake, like a soldier camped near a battlefield, and could never find true rest until Elle's screams railed down the hallway and chilled her bones. After the third week, she hadn't bothered going into her daughter's room anymore, but it made hearing those screams no easier to cope with.

"You ready to go, Ellie-Bellie?"

Elle glanced up from her phone. "When you are, Shirley-Whirley."

The first raindrop fell as Shirley stepped off the porch, a big cold splat on top of her head. A serpent's tongue of lightning tasted the earth somewhere west of Cowra. Distant thunder grumbled in discontent. The fat raindrops proliferated as Shirley and Elle hustled into the car. By the time they had the doors shut and the engine running it was coming down so hard, it sounded like hands drumming on the roof. She backed the car down the drive, de-mister blowing and windscreen wipers flip-flopping. Fissures in the cracked earth were already filling, forming miniature creeks in the front yard. As she put the car in drive and set off, Shirley looked up the hill towards Oscar Wainwright's property.

The old farmer stood motionless and alone, a scarecrow in a barren field, and watched the rain come down.

The barn probably hadn't housed livestock in a decade or more, yet their scents lingered on, seasoning the old timbers and the compacted dirt floors. The inventory from Don's museum was now in an organized pile in the back corner, where he had adjudged roof leaks would be least likely. Sun slanted in from the opposite window, as if to highlight the barn's contents for anyone who entered.

Almost nothing held intrinsic value; he would be lucky to get fifty dollars in scrap value. Its historical worth, although greater than its monetary value, would not set many hearts aquiver. A lot of men had gone panning and prospecting during Australia's nineteenth-century gold rush and pans and picks weren't given to rapid disintegration. And Don intended to hang onto the police memorabilia. So although it hurt like hell to admit it, the primary value of his collection could be measured in sentiment.

He leaned against an old post and tucked his hand under his armpit. In the end, the decision was pretty stark, pretty cut and dried. He could remain in Black Wattle with his junk and his memories, or he could try to make a new life and new memories up on the Gold Coast. Freighting all his trinkets and treasures up there would cost more than they were worth and would also be sort of pathetic. A thousand kilometers from the town in which he had salvaged them, not only would they be worthless they would be pointless. Who in the Gold Coast, with its canal-fronted estates and sun-bathed suburbs, would give one toss about old tools and coins from an extinct mining town?

It belonged in Black Wattle and someone in Black Wattle should have it. If no one took it immediately, fifty bucks a month wouldn't bust his budget. It could remain in the barn until the right person—someone who shared his mad-amateur enthusiasm—found it and put it back on display. Because, strange to say, Don knew he was no longer the heart and the spine of Black Wattle. Something had shifted. He thought about the strange hive mind the rest of the Black Wattle locals all seemed to have now. Although Shirley insisted it was for Elle's benefit that they leave, Don had an idea Elle might move back to Black Wattle one day. Under some pretext, like wanting a tree change, but in truth drawn through unconscious yearning to be near her fellow survivors. He also had a sneaking suspicion Corporal Chang and his men might move nearer to Black Wattle or retire there once discharged.

Don took one last look at his accumulated history, then shut the barn doors, shot the bolt and fastened the padlock. Jim Sherman had left to go and pick up a spare part somewhere out of town, so Don dropped the padlock key in his letterbox and sent him a text message asking for his online banking details so he could continue to transfer the fifty bucks each month. He doubted Jim would go crook about money for (almost) nothing.

Recent rains had brought about what the farmers called a 'green drought'; grass now carpeted the hillsides and had sent tendrils into the bare patches. It would elate the men running sheep and cattle, but it would take more consistent rain before crop farmers could hope for a successful sow and harvest. Nevertheless, the verdant hue almost hurt Don's eyes—as though they had forgotten how to process colors other than yellow and brown.

With nothing else to moor him there, Don got into his battered station wagon and reversed it up Jim's long driveway. Then he took the short access track up to Goldfields Road and turned left, bearing east. The car was packed to the gunwales with every portable part of Don's current life. He intended to whittle it back when he knew what he would need for his new one. The thought made him nervous, but not in a negative way.

As he passed through the town he noted all the familiar faces going about their business. Again he mused that nothing had changed and yet everything had. It seemed to happen that way in country communities, whether the catalyst was a demonic apocalypse or something more pedestrian. Sometimes a community survived and sometimes it faded until it was no more than a ramshackle pub on a barren highway.

Right at that instant, Don passed the Ironstone Hotel and noticed the SOLD sign had been taken down. A youngish man in jeans and a white shirt swept a push broom along the pavement outside. One of the local farmer's sons, if he wasn't mistaken, perhaps hoping to cut the agriculture apron strings or bring in a secondary source of family income. Don smiled.

Black Wattle wasn't his town anymore, but he thought it would get along without him just fine.

THE END?

Not if you want to dive into more of Crystal Lake Publishing's Tales from the Darkest Depths!

Check out our amazing website and online store
or download our latest catalog here.
https://geni.us/CLPCatalog

Looking for award–winning Dark Fiction?
Download our latest catalog.

Includes our anthologies, novels, novellas, collections,
poetry, non–fiction, and specialty projects.

Where Stories Come Alive!

We always have great new projects and content on the website to
dive into, as well as a newsletter, behind the scenes options,
social media platforms, our own dark fiction shared-world series
and our very own webstore. Our webstore even has categories
specifically for KU books, non-fiction, anthologies, and of course
more novels and novellas.

ABOUT THE AUTHOR

Award-winning writer and editor Kris Ashton has published several novels and nearly fifty short stories. He is best known for his tales of horror and dark speculative fiction and is also a noted essayist, taking out the Australian Shadows Award for non-fiction in 2023.

Kris graduated from Western Sydney University in 1997 with a Bachelor of Arts, majoring in creative writing and literature. He has had a 25-year career as a journalist and is currently editor of *Open Road*, one of the most widely-read magazines in Australia.

He lives in the wilds of south-western Sydney with his wife, two children and a crippling mortgage.

Readers . . .

Thank you for reading *Demon Drink*. We hope you enjoyed this novel.

If you have a moment, please review *Demon Drink* at the store where you bought it.

Help other readers by telling them why you enjoyed this book. No need to write an in-depth discussion. Even a single sentence will be greatly appreciated. Reviews go a long way to helping a book sell, and is great for an author's career. It'll also help us to continue publishing quality books.

Thank you again for taking the time to journey with Crystal Lake Publishing.

Visit our Linktree page for a list of our social media platforms. https://linktr.ee/CrystalLakePublishing

Follow us on Amazon:

MISSION STATEMENT:

Since its founding in August 2012, Crystal Lake has quickly become one of the world's leading publishers of Dark Fiction and Horror books. In 2023, Crystal Lake officially transitioned into an entertainment company, joining several other divisions, genres, and imprints, including Torrid Waters, Crystal Lake Comics, Crystal Lake Games, Crystal Lake Kids, and many more.

While we strive to present only the highest quality fiction and entertainment, we also endeavour to support authors along their writing journey. We offer our time and experience in non-fiction projects, as well as author mentoring and services, at competitive prices.

With several Bram Stoker Award wins and many other wins and nominations (including the HWA's Specialty Press Award), Crystal Lake Publishing puts integrity, honor, and respect at the forefront of our publishing operations.

We strive for each book and outreach program we spearhead to not only entertain and touch or comment on issues that affect our readers, but also to strengthen and support the Dark Fiction field and its authors.

Not only do we find and publish authors we believe are destined for greatness, but we strive to work with men and women who endeavour to be decent human beings who care more for others than themselves, while still being hard working, driven, and passionate artists and storytellers.

Crystal Lake Publishing is and will always be a beacon of what passion and dedication, combined with overwhelming teamwork and respect, can accomplish. We endeavour to know each and every one of our readers, while building personal relationships with our authors, reviewers, bloggers, podcasters, bookstores, and libraries.

We will be as trustworthy, forthright, and transparent as any business can be, while also keeping most of the headaches away from our authors, since it's our job to solve the problems so they can stay in a creative mind. Which of course also means paying our authors.

We do not just publish books, we present to you worlds within your world, doors within your mind, from talented authors who sacrifice so much for a moment of your time.

There are some amazing small presses out there, and through collaboration and open forums we will continue to support other presses in the goal of helping authors and showing the world what quality small presses are capable of accomplishing. No one wins when a small press goes down, so we will always be there to support hardworking, legitimate presses and their authors. We don't see Crystal Lake as the best press out there, but we will always strive to be the best, strive to be the most interactive and grateful, and even blessed press around. No matter what happens over time, we will also take our mission very seriously while appreciating where we are and enjoying the journey.

What do we offer our authors that they can't do for themselves through self-publishing?

We are big supporters of self-publishing (especially hybrid publishing), if done with care, patience, and planning. However, not every author has the time or inclination to do market research, advertise, and set up book launch strategies. Although a lot of authors are successful in doing it all, strong small presses will always be there for the authors who just want to do what they do best: write.

What we offer is experience, industry knowledge, contacts and trust built up over years. And due to our strong brand and trusting fanbase, every Crystal Lake Publishing book comes with weight of respect. In time our fans begin to trust our judgment and will try a new author purely based on our support of said author.

With each launch we strive to fine-tune our approach, learn from our mistakes, and increase our reach. We continue to assure our authors that we're here for them and that we'll carry the weight of the launch and dealing with third parties while they focus on their strengths—be it writing, interviews, blogs, signings, etc.

We also offer several mentoring packages to authors that include knowledge and skills they can use in both traditional and self-publishing endeavours.

We look forward to launching many new careers.

This is what we believe in. What we stand for. This will be our legacy.

Welcome to Crystal Lake Publishing—
Where stories come alive!